Short Stories Old and New

and New

Edited by
C. Alphonso Smith

Short Stories Old and New

Contact:
BibliotechPress@gmail.com

The present edition is a reproduction of 1916 publication of this work. Minor typographical errors may have been corrected without note, however, for an authentic reading experience the spelling, punctuation, and capitalization have been retained from the original text.

ISBN: 978-1-61895-106-9

INTRODUCTION

Every short story has three parts, which may be called Setting or Background, Plot or Plan, and Characters or Character. If you are going to write a short story, as I hope you are, you will find it necessary to think through these three parts so as to relate them interestingly and naturally one to the other; and if you want to assimilate the best that is in the following stories, you will do well to approach them by the same three routes.

The Setting or Background gives us the time and the place of the story with such details of custom, scenery, and dialect as time and place imply. It answers the questions When? Where? The Plot tells us what happened. It gives us the incidents and events, the haps or mishaps, that are interwoven to make up the warp and woof of the story. Sometimes there is hardly any interweaving; just a plain plan or simple outline is followed, as in "The Christmas Carol" or "The Great Stone Face." We may still call the core of these two stories the Plot, if we want to, but Plan would be the more accurate. This part of the story answers the question What? Under the heading Characters or Character we study the personalities of the men and women who move through the story and give it unity and coherence. Sometimes, as in "The Christmas Carol" or "Markheim," one character so dominates the others that they are mere spokes in his hub or incidents in his career. But in "The Gift of the Magi," though more space is given to Della, she and Jim act from the same motive and contribute equally to the development of the story. In one of our stories the main character is a dog, but he is so human that we may still say that the chief question to be answered under this heading is Who?

Many books have been written about these three parts of a short story, but the great lesson to be learned is that the excellence of a story, long or short, consists not in the separate excellence of the Setting or of the Plot or of the Characters but in the perfect blending of the three to produce a single effect or to impress a single truth. If the Setting does not fit the Plot, if the Plot does not rise gracefully from the Setting, if the Characters do not move naturally and self-revealingly through both, the story is a failure. Emerson might well have had our three parts of the short story in mind when he wrote,

> All are needed by each one;
> Nothing is fair or good alone.

CONTENTS

ESTHER [1]
AUTHOR UNKNOWN

[Setting. The events take place in Susa, the capital of Persia, in the reign of Ahasuerus, or Xerxes (485-465 B.C.). This foreign locale intensifies the splendid Jewish patriotism that breathes through the story from beginning to end. If the setting had been in Jerusalem, Esther could not have preached the noble doctrine, "When in Rome, don't do as Rome does, but be true to the old ideals of home and race."

Plot. "Esther" seems to me the best-told story in the Bible. Observe how the note of empty Persian bigness versus simple Jewish faith is struck at the very beginning and is echoed to the end. Thus, Ahasuerus ruled over one hundred and twenty-seven provinces, the opening banquet lasted one hundred and eighty-seven days, the king's bulletins were as unalterable as the tides, the gallows erected was eighty-three feet high, the beds were of gold and silver upon a pavement of red and blue and white and black marble, the money wrested from the Jews was to be eighteen million dollars, etc. The word "banquet" occurs twenty times in this short story and only twenty times in all the remaining thirty-eight books of the Old Testament. In other words, Ahasuerus and his trencher-mates ate and drank as much in five days as had been eaten and drunk by all the other Old Testament characters from "Genesis" to "Malachi."

Note also the contrast between the two queens, the two prime ministers, the two edicts, and the two later banquets. The most masterly part of the plot is the handling of events between these banquets. Read again from chapter v, beginning at verse 9, through chapter vi, and note how skillfully the pen is held. In motivation as well as in symmetry and naturalness the story is without a peer. There is humor, too, in the solemn deliberations over Vashti's "No" (chapter i, verses 12-22) and in the strange procession led by pedestrian Haman (chapter vi, verses 6-11).

The purpose of the story was to encourage the feast of Purim (chapter ix, verses 20-32) and to promote national solidarity. It may be compared to "A Christmas Carol," which was written to restore the waning celebration of Christmas, and to our Declaration of Independence, which is re-read on every Fourth of July to quicken our sense of national fellowship. But "Esther" is more than an institution. It is the old story of two conflicting civilizations, one representing bigness, the other greatness; one standing for materialism, the other for idealism; one enthroning the body, the other the spirit.

Characters. These are finely individualized, though each seems to me a type. Ahasuerus is a tank that runs blood or wine according to the

---

[1] From the Old Testament, Authorized Version.

1

hand that turns the spigot. He was used for good but deserves and receives no credit for it. No man ever missed a greater opportunity. He was brought face to face with the two greatest world-civilizations of history; but, understanding neither, he remains only a muddy place in the road along which Greek and Hebrew passed to world-conquest. Haman, a blend of vanity and cruelty and cowardice but not without some power of initiative, was a fit minister for his king. He lives in history as one who, better than in Hamlet's illustration, was "hoist with his own petard," the petard in his case being a gallows. He typifies also the just fate of the man who, spurred by the hate of one, includes in his scheme of extermination a whole people. Collective vengeance never received a better illustration nor a more exemplary punishment. Mordecai is altogether admirable in refusing to kowtow to Haman and in his unselfish devotion to his fair cousin, Esther. The noblest sentiment in the book—"Who knoweth whether thou art come to the kingdom for such a time as this?"—comes from Mordecai.

But the leading character is Esther, not because she was "fair and beautiful" but because she was hospitable to the great thought suggested by Mordecai. None but a Jew could have asked, "Who knoweth whether thou art come to the kingdom for such a time as this?" and none but a Jew could have answered as Esther answered. The question implied a sense of personal responsibility and of divine guidance far beyond the reach of Persian or Mede or Greek of that time. It calls up many a quiet hour when Esther and Mordecai talked together of their strange lot in this heathen land and wondered if the time would ever come when they could interpret their trials in terms of national service rather than of meaningless fate. Imagine the blank and bovine expression that Ahasuerus or Haman would have turned upon you if you had put such a question to either of them. But in the case of Esther, Mordecai's appeal unlocked an unused reservoir of power that has made her one of the world's heroines. She had her faults, or rather her limitations, but since her time men have gone to the stake, have built up and torn down principalities and powers, on the dynamic conviction that they had been sent to the kingdom "for such a time as this."]

CHAPTER I
THE STORY OF VASHTI

1. Now it came to pass in the days of Ahasuerus, (this is Ahasuerus which reigned from India even unto Ethiopia, over a hundred and seven and twenty provinces,)

2. That in those days, when the king Ahasuerus sat on the throne of his kingdom, which was in Shushan the palace,

3. In the third year of his reign, he made a feast unto all his princes and his servants; the power of Persia and Media, the nobles and princes of the provinces, being before him:

4. When he shewed the riches of his glorious kingdom and the honour of his excellent majesty many days, even a hundred and fourscore days.

5. And when these days were expired, the king made a feast unto all the people that were present in Shushan the palace, both unto great and small, seven days, in the court of the garden of the king's palace.

6. Where were white, green, and blue hangings, fastened with cords of fine linen and purple to silver rings and pillars of marble: the beds were of gold and silver, upon a pavement of red, and blue, and white, and black marble.

7. And they gave them drink in vessels of gold, (the vessels being diverse one from another,) and royal wine in abundance, according to the state of the king.

8. And the drinking was according to the law; none did compel: for so the king had appointed to all the officers of his house, that they should do according to every man's pleasure.

9. Also Vashti the queen made a feast for the women in the royal house which belonged to king Ahasuerus.

10. On the seventh day, when the heart of the king was merry with wine, he commanded Mehuman, Biztha, Harbona, Bigtha, and Abagtha, Zethar, and Carcas, the seven chamberlains that served in the presence of Ahasuerus the king,

11. To bring Vashti the queen before the king with the crown royal, to shew the people and the princes her beauty: for she was fair to look on.

12. But the queen Vashti refused to come at the king's commandment by his chamberlains: therefore was the king very wroth, and his anger burned in him.

13. Then the king said to the wise men, which knew the times, (for so was the king's manner toward all that knew law and judgment:

14. And the next unto him was Carshena, Shethar, Admatha, Tarshish, Meres, Marsena, and Memucan, the seven princes of Persia and Media, which saw the king's face, and which sat the first in the kingdom,)

15. What shall we do unto the queen Vashti according to law, because she hath not performed the commandment of the king Ahasuerus by the chamberlains?

16. And Memucan answered before the king and the princes, Vashti the queen hath not done wrong to the king only, but also to all the princes, and to all the people that are in all the provinces of the king Ahasuerus.

17. For this deed of the queen shall come abroad unto all women, so that they shall despise their husbands in their eyes, when it shall be reported, The king Ahasuerus commanded Vashti the queen to be brought in before him, but she came not.

18. Likewise shall the ladies of Persia and Media say this day unto all the king's princes, which have heard of the deed of the queen. Thus shall there arise too much contempt and wrath.

19. If it please the king, let there go a royal commandment from him, and let it be written among the laws of the Persians and the Medes, that it

be not altered, That Vashti come no more before king Ahasuerus; and let the king give her royal estate unto another that is better than she.

20. And when the king's decree, which he shall make, shall be published throughout all his empire, (for it is great,) all the wives shall give to their husbands honour, both to great and small.

21. And the saying pleased the king and the princes; and the king did according to the word of Memucan:

22. For he sent letters into all the king's provinces, into every province according to the writing thereof, and to every people after their language, that every man should bear rule in his own house, and that it should be published according to the language of every people.

CHAPTER II
ESTHER MADE QUEEN

1. After these things, when the wrath of king Ahasuerus was appeased, he remembered Vashti, and what she had done, and what was decreed against her.

2. Then said the king's servants that ministered unto him, Let there be fair young virgins sought for the king:

3. And let the king appoint officers in all the provinces of his kingdom, that they may gather together all the fair young virgins unto Shushan the palace, to the house of the women, unto the custody of Hegai the king's chamberlain, keeper of the women; and let their things for purification be given them:

4. And let the maiden which pleaseth the king be queen instead of Vashti. And the thing pleased the king; and he did so.

5. Now in Shushan the palace there was a certain Jew, whose name was Mordecai, the son of Jair, the son of Shimei, the son of Kish, a Benjamite;

6. Who had been carried away from Jerusalem with the captivity which had been carried away with Jeconiah king of Judah, whom Nebuchadnezzar the king of Babylon had carried away.

7. And he brought up Hadassah, that is, Esther, his uncle's daughter: for she had neither father nor mother, and the maid was fair and beautiful; whom Mordecai, when her father and mother were dead, took for his own daughter.

8. So it came to pass, when the king's commandment and his decree was heard, and when many maidens were gathered together unto Shushan the palace, to the custody of Hegai, that Esther was brought also unto the king's house, to the custody of Hegai, keeper of the women.

9. And the maiden pleased him, and she obtained kindness of him; and he speedily gave her her things for purification, with such things as belonged to her, and seven maidens, which were meet to be given her, out

of the king's house: and he preferred her and her maids unto the best place of the house of the women.

10. Esther had not shewed her people nor her kindred: for Mordecai had charged her that she should not shew it.

11. And Mordecai walked every day before the court of the women's house, to know how Esther did, and what should become of her.

12. Now when every maid's turn was come to go in to king Ahasuerus, after that she had been twelve months, according to the manner of the women, (for so were the days of their purifications accomplished, to wit, six months with oil of myrrh, and six months with sweet odours, and with other things for the purifying of the women,)

13. Then thus came every maiden unto the king; whatsoever she desired was given her to go with her out of the house of the women unto the king's house.

14. In the evening she went, and on the morrow she returned into the second house of the women, to the custody of Shaashgaz, the king's chamberlain, which kept the concubines: she came in unto the king no more, except the king delighted in her, and that she were called by name.

15. Now when the turn of Esther, the daughter of Abihail the uncle of Mordecai, who had taken her for his daughter, was come to go in unto the king, she required nothing but what Hegai the king's chamberlain, the keeper of the women, appointed. And Esther obtained favour in the sight of all them that looked upon her.

16. So Esther was taken unto king Ahasuerus into his house royal in the tenth month, which is the month Tebeth, in the seventh year of his reign.

17. And the king loved Esther above all the women, and she obtained grace and favour in his sight more than all the virgins; so that he set the royal crown upon her head, and made her queen instead of Vashti.

18. Then the king made a great feast unto all his princes and his servants, even Esther's feast; and he made a release to the provinces, and gave gifts, according to the state of the king.

19. And when the virgins were gathered together the second time, then Mordecai sat in the king's gate.

20. Esther had not yet shewed her kindred nor her people, as Mordecai had charged her: for Esther did the commandment of Mordecai, like as when she was brought up with him.

MORDECAI SAVES THE KING'S LIFE

21. In those days, while Mordecai sat in the king's gate, two of the king's chamberlains, Bigthan and Teresh, of those which kept the door, were wroth, and sought to lay hand on the king Ahasuerus.

22. And the thing was known to Mordecai, who told it unto Esther the queen; and Esther certified the king thereof in Mordecai's name.

23. And when inquisition was made of the matter, it was found out;

therefore they were both hanged on a tree: and it was written in the book of the chronicles before the king.

CHAPTER III
THE CONSPIRACY OF HAMAN

1. After these things did king Ahasuerus promote Haman the son of Hammedatha the Agagite, and advanced him, and set his seat above all the princes that were with him.

2. And all the king's servants, that were in the king's gate, bowed, and reverenced Haman: for the king had so commanded concerning him. But Mordecai bowed not, nor did him reverence.

3. Then the king's servants, which were in the king's gate, said unto Mordecai, Why transgressest thou the king's commandment?

4. Now it came to pass, when they spake daily unto him, and he hearkened not unto them, that they told Haman, to see whether Mordecai's matters would stand: for he had told them that he was a Jew.

5. And when Haman saw that Mordecai bowed not, nor did him reverence, then was Haman full of wrath.

6. And he thought scorn to lay hands on Mordecai alone; for they had shewed him the people of Mordecai: wherefore Haman sought to destroy all the Jews that were throughout the whole kingdom of Ahasuerus, even the people of Mordecai.

7. In the first month, that is, the month Nisan, in the twelfth year of king Ahasuerus, they cast Pur, that is, the lot, before Haman from day to day, and from month to month, to the twelfth month, that is, the month Adar.

8. And Haman said unto king Ahasuerus, There is a certain people scattered abroad and dispersed among the people in all the provinces of thy kingdom; and their laws are diverse from all people; neither keep they the king's laws: therefore it is not for the king's profit to suffer them.

9. If it please the king, let it be written that they may be destroyed: and I will pay ten thousand talents of silver to the hands of those that have the charge of the business, to bring it into the king's treasuries.

10. And the king took his ring from his hand, and gave it unto Haman the son of Hammedatha the Agagite, the Jews' enemy.

11. And the king said unto Haman, The silver is given to thee, the people also, to do with them as it seemeth good to thee.

12. Then were the king's scribes called on the thirteenth day of the first month, and there was written according to all that Haman had commanded unto the king's lieutenants, and to the governors that were over every province, and to the rulers of every people of every province according to the writing thereof, and to every people after their language; in the name of king Ahasuerus was it written, and sealed with the king's ring.

6

13. And the letters were sent by posts into all the king's provinces, to destroy, to kill, and to cause to perish, all Jews, both young and old, little children and women, in one day, even upon the thirteenth day of the twelfth month, which is the month Adar, and to take the spoil of them for a prey.

14. The copy of the writing for a commandment to be given in every province was published unto all people, that they should be ready against that day.

15. The posts went out, being hastened by the king's commandment, and the decree was given in Shushan the palace. And the king and Haman sat down to drink; but the city Shushan was perplexed.

CHAPTER IV

FASTING AMONG THE JEWS

1. When Mordecai perceived all that was done, Mordecai rent his clothes, and put on sackcloth with ashes, and went out into the midst of the city, and cried with a loud and a bitter cry;

2. And came even before the king's gate: for none might enter into the king's gate clothed with sackcloth.

3. And in every province, whithersoever the king's commandment and his decree came, there was great mourning among the Jews, and fasting, and weeping, and wailing; and many lay in sackcloth and ashes.

4. So Esther's maids and her chamberlains came and told it her. Then was the queen exceedingly grieved; and she sent raiment to clothe Mordecai, and to take away his sackcloth from him: but he received it not.

5. Then called Esther for Hatach, one of the king's chamberlains, whom he had appointed to attend upon her, and gave him a commandment to Mordecai, to know what it was, and why it was.

6. So Hatach went forth to Mordecai unto the street of the city, which was before the king's gate.

7. And Mordecai told him of all that had happened unto him, and of the sum of the money that Haman had promised to pay to the king's treasuries for the Jews, to destroy them.

8. Also he gave him the copy of the writing of the decree that was given at Shushan to destroy them, to shew it unto Esther, and to declare it unto her, and to charge her that she should go in unto the king, to make supplication unto him, and to make request before him for her people.

9. And Hatach came and told Esther the words of Mordecai.

10. Again Esther spake unto Hatach, and gave him commandment unto Mordecai;

11. All the king's servants, and the people of the king's provinces, do know, that whosoever, whether man or woman, shall come unto the king

into the inner court, who is not called, there is one law of his to put him to death, except such to whom the king shall hold out the golden sceptre, that he may live: but I have not been called to come in unto the king these thirty days.

12. And they told to Mordecai Esther's words.

THE GREAT APPEAL

13. Then Mordecai commanded to answer Esther, Think not with thyself that thou shalt escape in the king's house, more than all the Jews.

14. For if thou altogether holdest thy peace at this time, then shall there enlargement and deliverance arise to the Jews from another place; but thou and thy father's house shall be destroyed: and who knoweth whether thou art come to the kingdom for such a time as this?

15. Then Esther bade them return Mordecai this answer,

16. Go, gather together all the Jews that are present in Shushan, and fast ye for me, and neither eat nor drink three days, night or day: I also and my maidens will fast likewise; and so will I go in unto the king, which is not according to the law: and if I perish, I perish.

17. So Mordecai went his way, and did according to all that Esther had commanded him.

CHAPTER V

THE COURAGE OF ESTHER

1. Now it came to pass on the third day, that Esther put on her royal apparel, and stood in the inner court of the king's house, over against the king's house: and the king sat upon his royal throne in the royal house, over against the gate of the house.

2. And it was so, when the king saw Esther the queen standing in the court, that she obtained favour in his sight: and the king held out to Esther the golden sceptre that was in his hand. So Esther drew near, and touched the top of the sceptre.

3. Then said the king unto her, What wilt thou, queen Esther? and what is thy request? it shall be even given thee to the half of the kingdom.

4. And Esther answered, If it seem good unto the king, let the king and Haman come this day unto the banquet that I have prepared for him.

5. Then the king said, Cause Haman to make haste, that he may do as Esther hath said. So the king and Haman came to the banquet that Esther had prepared.

6. And the king said unto Esther at the banquet of wine, What is thy petition? and it shall be granted thee: and what is thy request? even to the half of the kingdom it shall be performed.

7. Then answered Esther, and said, My petition and my request is;

8. If I have found favour in the sight of the king, and if it please the king to grant my petition, and to perform my request, let the king and Haman come to the banquet that I shall prepare for them, and I will do to-morrow as the king hath said.

BETWEEN BANQUETS

9. Then went Haman forth that day joyful and with a glad heart: but when Haman saw Mordecai in the king's gate, that he stood not up, nor moved for him, he was full of indignation against Mordecai.

10. Nevertheless Haman refrained himself: and when he came home, he sent and called for his friends, and Zeresh his wife.

11. And Haman told them of the glory of his riches, and the multitude of his children, and all the things wherein the king had promoted him, and how he had advanced him above the princes and servants of the king.

12. Haman said moreover, Yea, Esther the queen did let no man come in with the king unto the banquet that she had prepared but myself; and to-morrow am I invited unto her also with the king.

13. Yet all this availeth me nothing, so long as I see Mordecai the Jew sitting at the king's gate.

14. Then said Zeresh his wife and all his friends unto him, Let a gallows be made of fifty cubits high, and to-morrow speak thou unto the king that Mordecai may be hanged thereon: then go thou in merrily with the king unto the banquet. And the thing pleased Haman; and he caused the gallows to be made.

CHAPTER VI

BETWEEN BANQUETS (CONTINUED)

1. On that night could not the king sleep, and he commanded to bring the book of records of the chronicles; and they were read before the king.

2. And it was found written, that Mordecai had told of Bigthana and Teresh, two of the king's chamberlains, the keepers of the door, who sought to lay hand on the king Ahasuerus.

3. And the king said, What honour and dignity hath been done to Mordecai for this? Then said the king's servants that ministered unto him, There is nothing done for him.

4. And the king said, Who is in the court? Now Haman was come into the outward court of the king's house, to speak unto the king to hang Mordecai on the gallows that he had prepared for him.

5. And the king's servants said unto him, Behold, Haman standeth in the court. And the king said, Let him come in.

6. So Haman came in. And the king said unto him, What shall be done unto the man whom the king delighteth to honour? Now Haman thought in his heart, To whom would the king delight to do honour more than to myself?

7. And Haman answered the king, For the man whom the king delighteth to honour,

8. Let the royal apparel be brought which the king useth to wear, and the horse that the king rideth upon, and the crown royal which is set upon his head:

9. And let this apparel and horse be delivered to the hand of one of the king's most noble princes, that they may array the man withal whom the king delighteth to honour, and bring him on horseback through the street of the city, and proclaim before him, Thus shall it be done to the man whom the king delighteth to honour.

10. Then the king said to Haman, Make haste, and take the apparel and the horse, as thou hast said, and do even so to Mordecai the Jew, that sitteth at the king's gate: let nothing fail of all that thou hast spoken.

11. Then took Haman the apparel and the horse, and arrayed Mordecai, and brought him on horseback through the street of the city, and proclaimed before him, Thus shall it be done unto the man whom the king delighteth to honour.

12. And Mordecai came again to the king's gate. But Haman hasted to his house mourning, and having his head covered.

13. And Haman told Zeresh his wife and all his friends every thing that had befallen him. Then said his wise men and Zeresh his wife unto him, If Mordecai be of the seed of the Jews, before whom thou hast begun to fall, thou shalt not prevail against him, but shalt surely fall before him.

14. And while they were yet talking with him, came the king's chamberlains, and hasted to bring Haman unto the banquet that Esther had prepared.

CHAPTER VII

ESTHER'S BANQUET: HAMAN HANGED

1. So the king and Haman came to banquet with Esther the queen.

2. And the king said again unto Esther on the second day at the banquet of wine, What is thy petition, queen Esther? and it shall be granted thee: and what is thy request? and it shall be performed, even to the half of the kingdom.

3. Then Esther the queen answered and said, If I have found favour in thy sight, O king, and if it please the king, let my life be given me at my petition, and my people at my request:

4. For we are sold, I and my people, to be destroyed, to be slain, and to perish. But if we had been sold for bondmen and bondwomen, I had held my tongue, although the enemy could not countervail the king's damage.

5. Then the king Ahasuerus answered and said unto Esther the queen, Who is he, and where is he, that durst presume in his heart to do so?

6. And Esther said, The adversary and enemy is this wicked Haman. Then Haman was afraid before the king and the queen.

7. And the king arising from the banquet of wine in his wrath went into the palace garden: and Haman stood up to make request for his life to Esther the queen; for he saw that there was evil determined against him by the king.

8. Then the king returned out of the palace garden into the place of the banquet of wine; and Haman was fallen upon the bed whereon Esther was. Then said the king, Will he force the queen also before me in the house? As the word went out of the king's mouth, they covered Haman's face.

9. And Harbona, one of the chamberlains, said before the king, Behold also the gallows fifty cubits high, which Haman had made for Mordecai, who had spoken good for the king, standeth in the house of Haman. Then the king said, Hang him thereon.

10. So they hanged Haman on the gallows that he had prepared for Mordecai. Then was the king's wrath pacified.

CHAPTER VIII

THE JEWS PERMITTED TO
DEFEND THEMSELVES

1. On that day did the king Ahasuerus give the house of Haman the Jews' enemy unto Esther the queen. And Mordecai came before the king; for Esther had told what he was unto her.

2. And the king took off his ring, which he had taken from Haman, and gave it unto Mordecai. And Esther set Mordecai over the house of Haman.

3. And Esther spake yet again before the king, and fell down at his feet, and besought him with tears to put away the mischief of Haman the Agagite, and his device that he had devised against the Jews,

4. Then the king held out the golden sceptre toward Esther. So Esther arose, and stood before the king,

5. And said, If it please the king, and if I have found favour in his sight, and the thing seem right before the king, and I be pleasing in his eyes, let it be written to reverse the letters devised by Haman the son of

Hammedatha the Agagite, which he wrote to destroy the Jews which are in all the king's provinces:

6. For how can I endure to see the evil that shall come unto my people? or how can I endure to see the destruction of my kindred?

7. Then the king Ahasuerus said unto Esther the queen and to Mordecai the Jew, Behold, I have given Esther the house of Haman, and him they have hanged upon the gallows, because he laid his hand upon the Jews.

8. Write ye also for the Jews, as it liketh you, in the king's name, and seal it with the king's ring: for the writing which is written in the king's name, and sealed with the king's ring, may no man reverse.

9. Then were the king's scribes called at that time in the third month, that is, the month Sivan, on the three and twentieth day thereof; and it was written according to all that Mordecai commanded unto the Jews, and to the lieutenants, and the deputies and rulers of the provinces which are from India unto Ethiopia, a hundred twenty and seven provinces, unto every province according to the writing thereof, and unto every people after their language, and to the Jews according to their writing, and according to their language.

10. And he wrote in the king Ahasuerus' name, and sealed it with the king's ring, and sent letters by posts on horseback, and riders on mules, camels, and young dromedaries:

11. Wherein the king granted the Jews which were in every city to gather themselves together, and to stand for their life, to destroy, to slay, and to cause to perish, all the power of the people and province that would assault them, both little ones and women, and to take the spoil of them for a prey,

12. Upon one day in all the provinces of king Ahasuerus, namely, upon the thirteenth day of the twelfth month, which is the month Adar.

13. The copy of the writing for a commandment to be given in every province was published unto all people, and that the Jews should be ready against that day to avenge themselves on their enemies.

14. So the posts that rode upon mules and camels went out, being hastened and pressed on by the king's commandment. And the decree was given at Shushan the palace.

15. And Mordecai went out from the presence of the king in royal apparel of blue and white, and with a great crown of gold, and with a garment of fine linen and purple: and the city of Shushan rejoiced and was glad.

16. The Jews had light, and gladness, and joy, and honour.

17. And in every province, and in every city, whithersoever the king's commandment and his decree came, the Jews had joy and gladness, a feast and a good day. And many of the people of the land became Jews; for the fear of the Jews fell upon them.

CHAPTER IX

THE JEWS DEFEND THEMSELVES

1. Now in the twelfth month, that is, the month Adar, on the thirteenth day of the same, when the king's commandment and his decree drew near to be put in execution, in the day that the enemies of the Jews hoped to have power over them; (though it was turned to the contrary, that the Jews had rule over them that hated them,)

2. The Jews gathered themselves together in their cities throughout all the provinces of the king Ahasuerus, to lay hand on such as sought their hurt: and no man could withstand them; for the fear of them fell upon all people.

3. And all the rulers of the provinces, and the lieutenants, and the deputies, and officers of the king, helped the Jews; because the fear of Mordecai fell upon them.

4. For Mordecai was great in the king's house, and his fame went out throughout all the provinces: for this man Mordecai waxed greater and greater.

5. Thus the Jews smote all their enemies with the stroke of the sword, and slaughter, and destruction, and did what they would unto those that hated them.

6. And in Shushan the palace the Jews slew and destroyed five hundred men.

7. And Parshandatha, and Dalphon, and Aspatha,

8. And Poratha, and Adalia, and Aridatha,

9. And Parmashta, and Arisai, and Aridai, and Vajezatha,

10. The ten sons of Haman the son of Hammedatha, the enemy of the Jews, slew they; but on the spoil laid they not their hand.

11. On that day the number of those that were slain in Shushan the palace was brought before the king.

12. And the king said unto Esther the queen, The Jews have slain and destroyed five hundred men in Shushan the palace, and the ten sons of Haman; what have they done in the rest of the king's provinces? now what is thy petition? and it shall be granted thee: or what is thy request further? and it shall be done.

13. Then said Esther, If it please the king, let it be granted to the Jews which are in Shushan to do to-morrow also according unto this day's decree, and let Haman's ten sons be hanged upon the gallows.

14. And the king commanded it so to be done: and the decree was given at Shushan; and they hanged Haman's ten sons.

15. For the Jews that were in Shushan gathered themselves together on the fourteenth day also of the month Adar, and slew three hundred men at Shushan; but on the prey they laid not their hand.

16. But the other Jews that were in the king's provinces gathered themselves together, and stood for their lives, and had rest from their

enemies, and slew of their foes seventy and five thousand, but they laid not their hands on the prey,

17. On the thirteenth day of the month Adar; and on the fourteenth day of the same rested they, and made it a day of feasting and gladness.

18. But the Jews that were at Shushan assembled together on the thirteenth day thereof, and on the fourteenth thereof; and on the fifteenth day of the same they rested, and made it a day of feasting and gladness.

19. Therefore the Jews of the villages, that dwelt in the unwalled towns, made the fourteenth day of the month Adar a day of gladness and feasting, and a good day, and of sending portions one to another.

THE FEAST OF PURIM

20. And Mordecai wrote these things, and sent letters unto all the Jews that were in all the provinces of the king Ahasuerus, both nigh and far,

21. To establish this among them, that they should keep the fourteenth day of the month Adar, and the fifteenth day of the same, yearly,

22. As the days wherein the Jews rested from their enemies, and the month which was turned unto them from sorrow to joy, and from mourning into a good day: that they should make them days of feasting and joy, and of sending portions one to another, and gifts to the poor.

23. And the Jews undertook to do as they had begun, and as Mordecai had written unto them;

24. Because Haman the son of Hammedatha, the Agagite, the enemy of all the Jews, had devised against the Jews to destroy them, and had cast Pur, that is, the lot, to consume them, and to destroy them;

25. But when Esther came before the king, he commanded by letters that his wicked device, which he devised against the Jews, should return upon his own head, and that he and his sons should be hanged on the gallows.

26. Wherefore they called these days Purim after the name of Pur. Therefore for all the words of this letter, and of that which they had seen concerning this matter, and which had come unto them,

27. The Jews ordained, and took upon them, and upon their seed, and upon all such as joined themselves unto them, so as it should not fail, that they would keep these two days according to their writing, and according to their appointed time every year;

28. And that these days should be remembered and kept throughout every generation, every family, every province, and every city; and that these days of Purim should not fail from among the Jews, nor the memorial of them perish from their seed.

29. Then Esther the queen, the daughter of Abihail, and Mordecai the Jew, wrote with all authority, to confirm this second letter of Purim.

30. And he sent the letters unto all the Jews, to the hundred twenty

and seven provinces of the kingdom of Ahasuerus, with words of peace and truth,

31. To confirm these days of Purim in their times appointed, according as Mordecai the Jew and Esther the queen had enjoined them, and as they had decreed for themselves and for their seed, the matters of the fastings and their cry.

32. And the decree of Esther confirmed these matters of Purim; and it was written in the book.

CHAPTER X

MORDECAI PRIME MINISTER

1. And the king Ahasuerus laid a tribute upon the land, and upon the isles of the sea.

2. And all the acts of his power and of his might, and the declaration of the greatness of Mordecai, whereunto the king advanced him, are they not written in the book of the chronicles of the kings of Media and Persia?

3. For Mordecai the Jew was next unto king Ahasuerus, and great among the Jews, and accepted of the multitude of his brethren, seeking the wealth of his people, and speaking peace to all his seed.

THE HISTORY OF ALI BABA AND THE FORTY ROBBERS [2]

AUTHOR UNKNOWN

[Setting. This story, like "Esther," takes place in Persia. The stories of "The Arabian Nights" as a whole probably originated in India, were modified and augmented by the Persians, and had the finishing touches put upon them by the Arabians. Bagdad on the Tigris is the city that figures most prominently in the stories, and the good caliph Haroun Al-Raschid (or Alraschid), who ruled from 786 to 809, A.D., is the monarch most often mentioned.

> "A goodly place, a goodly time,
> For it was in the golden prime
> Of good Haroun Alraschid."

However old the germs of the stories are, the form in which we have them hardly antedates the year 1450. The absence of all mention of coffee and tobacco precludes, at least, a date much later. They began to be translated into the languages of Europe during the reign of Queen Anne and, with the exception of the Old Testament, have been the chief orientalizing influence in modern literature. The setting of "Ali Baba" shows the four characteristics of all these Perso-Arabian tales: it has to do with town life, not country life; it presupposes one faith, the Mohammedan; it shows a fondness for magic; and it takes for granted an audience interested not in moral or ethical distinctions but in story-telling for story-telling's sake.

Plot. The plot of the short story as a distinct type of literature has been said to show a steady progress from the impossible through the improbable and probable to the inevitable. When we say of a story that the conclusion is inevitable we mean that, with the given background and characters, it could not have ended in any other way, just as, with a given multiplier and multiplicand, one product and only one is possible. This cannot be said of "Ali Baba," because the five parts are not linked together in a logical sequence as are the events in "The Gold-Bug," or by any controlling idea of reform such as we find in "A Christmas Carol," or by any underlying moral purpose like that which gives unity and dignity to "The Great Stone Face." These Perso-Arabian tales, in other words, are stories of random incident, loosely but charmingly told, with always the note of strangeness and unexpectedness. The incidents, however, reflect accurately the manners and customs of time and place. We do not believe

---

[2] From "The Arabian Nights."

that a door ever opened to the magic of mere words, but we do believe and cannot help believing that the author tells the truth when he writes of leather jars full of oil, of bands of mounted robbers, of a poor man who could support himself by hauling wood from the free-for-all forest, of slavery from which one might escape by notable fidelity, of funeral rites performed by the imaum and other ministers of the mosque, and of the unwillingness of an assassin to attempt the life of a man with whom he had just eaten salt. Fancy, it is true, mingles with fact in "The Arabian Nights," but it does not replace fact.

Characters. Morgiana is the leading character. She furnishes all the brains employed in the story. The narrator praises her "courage" twice, but she had more than courage. Fidelity, initiative, and resourcefulness must also be put among her assets. We can hardly imagine her as acting from Esther's high motive, but she lived up to the best standards of conduct that she knew. Whoever serves as a model for his own time may serve as a model for ours. Duties change, but duty remains.]

I

CASSIM, ALI BABA'S BROTHER, DISCOVERED AND KILLED BY THE ROBBERS

There once lived in a town of Persia two brothers, one named Cassim and the other Ali Baba. Their father divided his small property equally between them. Cassim married a very rich wife, and became a wealthy merchant. Ali Baba married a woman as poor as himself, and lived by cutting wood and bringing it upon three asses into the town to sell.

One day, when Ali Baba had cut just enough wood in the forest to load his asses, he noticed far off a great cloud of dust. As it drew nearer, he saw that it was made by a body of horsemen, whom he suspected to be robbers. Leaving the asses, he climbed a large tree which grew on a high rock, and had branches thick enough to hide him completely while he saw what passed beneath. The troop, forty in number, all well mounted and armed, came to the foot of the rock on which the tree stood, and there dismounted. Each man unbridled his horse, tied him to a shrub, and hung about his neck a bag of corn. Then each of them took off his saddle-bag, which from its weight seemed to Ali Baba full of gold and silver. One, whom he took to be their captain, came under the tree in which Ali Baba was concealed; and, making his way through some shrubs, spoke the words: "Open, Sesame." [3] As soon as the captain of the robbers said this, a door opened in the rock, and after he had made all his troop enter before him, he followed them, when the door shut again of itself.

The robbers stayed some time within, and Ali Baba, fearful of being

---

[3] Sesame (pronounced séssamy), a small grain.

caught, remained in the tree. At last the door opened again, and the captain came out first, and stood to see all the troop pass by him. Then Ali Baba heard him make the door close by saying: "Shut, Sesame." Every man at once bridled his horse, fastened his wallet, and mounted again. When the captain saw them all ready, he put himself at their head, and they returned the way they had come.

Ali Baba watched them out of sight, and then waited some time before coming down. Wishing to see whether the captain's words would have the same effect if he should speak them, he found the door hidden in the shrubs, stood before it, and said: "Open, Sesame." Instantly the door flew wide open.

Instead of a dark, dismal cavern, Ali Baba was surprised to see a large chamber, well lighted from the top, and in it all sorts of provisions, rich bales of silk, brocade and carpeting, gold and silver ingots in great heaps, and money in bags.

Ali Baba went boldly into the cave, and collected as much of the gold coin, which was in bags, as he thought his asses could carry. When he had loaded them with the bags, he laid wood over them so that they could not be seen, and, passing out of the door for the last time, stood before it and said: "Shut, Sesame." The door closed of itself, and he made the best of his way to town.

When he reached home, he carefully closed the gate of his little yard, threw off the wood, and carried the bags into the house. They were emptied before his wife, and the great heap of gold dazzled her eyes. Then he told her the whole adventure, and warned her, above all things, to keep it secret.

Ali Baba would not let her take the time to count it out as she wished, but said: "I will dig a hole and bury it."

"But let us know as nearly as may be," she said, "how much we have. I will borrow a small measure, and measure it, while you dig a hole."

Away she ran to the wife of Cassim, who lived near by, and asked for a measure. The sister-in-law, knowing Ali Baba's poverty, was curious to learn what sort of grain his wife wished to measure out, and artfully managed to put some suet in the bottom of the measure before she handed it over. Ali Baba's wife wanted to show how careful she was in small matters, and, after she had measured the gold, hurried back, even while her husband was burying it, with the borrowed measure, never noticing that a coin had stuck to its bottom.

"What," said Cassim's wife, as soon as her sister-in-law had left her, "has Ali Baba gold in such plenty that he measures it? Whence has he all this wealth?" And envy possessed her breast.

When Cassim came home, she said to him: "Cassim, you think yourself rich, but Ali Baba is much richer. He does not count his money; he measures it." Then she explained to him how she had found it out, and they looked together at the piece of money, which was so old that they could not tell in what prince's reign it was coined.

Cassim, since marrying the rich widow, had never treated Ali Baba as a brother, but neglected him. Now, instead of being pleased, he was filled with a base envy. Early in the morning, after a sleepless night, he went to him and said: "Ali Baba, you pretend to be wretchedly poor, and yet you measure gold. My wife found this at the bottom of the measure you borrowed yesterday."

Ali Baba saw that there was no use of trying to conceal his good fortune, and told the whole story, offering his brother part of the treasure to keep the secret.

"I expect as much," replied Cassim haughtily; "but I must know just where this treasure is and how to visit it myself when I choose. Otherwise I will inform against you, and you will lose even what you have now."

Ali Baba told him all he wished to know, even to the words he must speak at the door of the cave.

Cassim rose before the sun the next morning, and set out for the forest with ten mules bearing great chests which he meant to fill. With little trouble he found the rock and the door, and, standing before it, spoke the words: "Open, Sesame." The door opened at once, and when he was within closed upon him. Here indeed were the riches of which his brother had told. He quickly brought as many bags of gold as he could carry to the door of the cavern; but his thoughts were so full of his new wealth, that he could not think of the word that should let him out. Instead of "Sesame," he said "Open, Barley," and was much amazed to find that the door remained fast shut. He named several sorts of grain, but still the door would not open.

Cassim had never expected such a disaster, and was so frightened that the more he tried to recall the word "Sesame," the more confused his mind became. It was as if he had never heard the word at all. He threw down the bags in his hands, and walked wildly up and down, without a thought of the riches lying round about him.

At noon the robbers visited their cave. From afar they saw Cassim's mules straggling about the rock, and galloped full speed to the cave. Driving the mules out of sight, they went at once, with their naked sabres in their hands, to the door, which opened as soon as the captain had spoken the proper words before it.

Cassim had heard the noise of the horses' feet, and guessed that the robbers had come. He resolved to make one effort for his life. As soon as the door opened, he rushed out and threw the leader down, but could not pass the other robbers, who with their scimitars soon put him to death.

The first care of the robbers was to examine the cave. They found all the bags Cassim had brought to the door, but did not miss what Ali Baba had taken. As for Cassim himself, they guessed rightly that, once within, he could not get out again; but how he had managed to learn their secret words that let him in, they could not tell. One thing was certain,—there he was; and to warn all others who might know their secret and follow in Cassim's footsteps, they agreed to cut his body into four quarters—to hang two on one side and two on the other, within the door of the cave. This they did at once, and leaving the place of their hoards well closed, mounted their horses and set out to attack the caravans they might meet.

II
THE MANNER OF CASSIM'S
DEATH CONCEALED

When night came, and Cassim did not return, his wife became very uneasy. She ran to Ali Baba for comfort, and he told her that Cassim would certainly think it unwise to enter the town till night was well advanced. By midnight Cassim's wife was still more alarmed, and wept till morning, cursing her desire to pry into the affairs of her brother and sister-in-law. In the early day she went again, in tears, to Ali Baba.

He did not wait for her to ask him to go and see what had happened to Cassim, but set out at once for the forest with his three asses. Finding some blood at the door of the cave, he took it for an ill omen; but when he had spoken the words, and the door had opened, he was struck with horror at the dismal sight of his brother's body. He could not leave it there, and hastened within to find something to wrap around it. Laying the body on one of his asses, he covered it with wood. The other two asses he loaded with bags of gold, covering them also with wood as before. Then bidding the door shut, he came away, but stopped some time at the edge of the forest, that he might not go into the town before night. When he reached home he left the two asses, laden with gold, in his little yard for his wife to unload, and led the other to his sister-in-law's house.

Ali Baba knocked at the door, which was opened by Morgiana, a clever slave, full of devices to conquer difficulties. When he came into the court and unloaded the ass, he took Morgiana aside, and said to her:—

"You must observe a strict secrecy. Your master's body is contained in these two panniers. We must bury him as if he had died a natural death. Go now and tell your mistress. I leave the matter to your wit and skillful devices."

They placed the body in Cassim's house, and, charging Morgiana to act well her part, Ali Baba returned home with his ass.

Early the next morning, Morgiana went to a druggist, and asked for a sort of lozenge used in the most dangerous illness. When he asked her for whom she wanted it, she answered with a sigh: "My good master Cassim. He can neither eat nor speak." In the evening she went to the same druggist, and with tears in her eyes asked for an essence given to sick persons for whose life there is little hope. "Alas!" said she, "I am afraid even this will not save my good master."

All that day Ali Baba and his wife were seen going sadly between their house and Cassim's, and in the evening nobody was surprised to hear the shrieks and cries of Cassim's wife and Morgiana, who told everybody that her master was dead.

The next morning at daybreak she went to an old cobbler, who was always early at work, and, putting a piece of gold in his hand, said:—

"Baba Mustapha, you must bring your sewing-tackle and come with me; but

I must tell you, I shall blindfold you when we reach a certain place."

"Oh! oh!" replied he, "you would have me do something against my conscience or my honor."

"God forbid!" said Morgiana, putting another piece of gold in his hand; "only come along with me, and fear nothing."

Baba Mustapha went with Morgiana, and at a certain place she bound his eyes with a handkerchief, which she never unloosed till they had entered the room of her master's house, where she had put the corpse together.

"Baba Mustapha," said she, "you must make haste, and sew the parts of this body together, and when you have done, I will give you another piece of gold."

After Baba Mustapha had finished his task, she blindfolded him again, gave him the third piece of gold she had promised, and, charging him with secrecy, took him back to the place where she had first bound his eyes. Taking off the bandage, she watched him till he was out of sight, lest he should return and dog her; then she went home.

At Cassim's house she made all things ready for the funeral, which was duly performed by the imaum 4 and other ministers of the mosque. Morgiana, as a slave of the dead man, walked in the procession, weeping, beating her breast, and tearing her hair. Cassim's wife stayed at home, uttering doleful cries with the women of the neighborhood, who, according to custom, came to mourn with her. The whole quarter was filled with sounds of sorrow.

Thus the manner of Cassim's death was hushed up, and, besides his widow, Ali Baba, and Morgiana, the slave, nobody in the city suspected the cause of it. Three or four days after the funeral, Ali Baba removed his few goods openly to his sister-in-law's house, in which he was to live in the future; but the money he had taken from the robbers was carried thither by night. As for Cassim's warehouse, Ali Baba put it entirely under the charge of his eldest son.

III

THE ROBBERS' PLOT FOILED
BY MORGIANA

While all this was going on, the forty robbers again visited their cave in the forest. Great was their surprise to find Cassim's body taken away, with some of their bags of gold.

---

4 Imaum, a Mohammedan priest.

"We are certainly found out," said the captain; "the body and the money have been taken by some one else who knows our secret. For our own lives' sake, we must try and find him. What say you, my lads?"

The robbers all agreed that this must be done.

"Well," said the captain, "one of you, the boldest and most skillful, must go to the town, disguised as a stranger, and try if he can hear any talk of the man we killed, and find out where he lived. This matter is so important that the man who undertakes it and fails should suffer death. What say you?"

One of the robbers, without waiting to know what the rest might think, started up, and said: "I submit to this condition, and think it an honor to expose my life to serve the troop."

This won great praise from the robber's comrades, and he disguised himself at once so that nobody could take him for what he was. Just at daybreak he entered the town, and walked up and down till he came by chance to Baba Mustapha's stall, which was always open before any of the shops.

The old cobbler was just going to work when the robber bade him good-morrow, and said:—

"Honest man, you begin to work very early; how can one of your age see so well? Even if it were lighter, I question whether you could see to stitch."

"You do not know me," replied Baba Mustapha; "for old as I am I have excellent eyes. You will not doubt me when I tell you that I sewed the body of a dead man together in a place where I had not so much light as I have now."

"A dead body!" exclaimed the robber amazed.

"Yes, yes," answered Baba Mustapha; "I see you want to know more, but you shall not."

The robber felt sure that he was on the right track. He put a piece of gold into Baba Mustapha's hand, and said to him:—

"I do not want to learn your secret, though you could safely trust me with it. The only thing I ask of you is to show me the house where you stitched up the dead body."

"I could not do that," replied Baba Mustapha, "if I would. I was taken to a certain place, whence I was led blindfold to the house, and afterwards brought back again in the same manner."

"Well," replied the robber, "you may remember a little of the way that you were led blindfold. Come, let me blind your eyes at the same place. We will walk together, and perhaps you may recall the way. Here is another piece of gold for you."

This was enough to bring Baba Mustapha to his feet. They soon reached the place where Morgiana had bandaged his eyes, and here he was blindfolded again. Baba Mustapha and the robber walked on till they came to Cassim's house, where Ali Baba now lived. Here the old man stopped, and when the thief pulled off the band, and found that his guide could not tell him whose house it was, he let him go. But before he started back for the forest himself, well pleased with what he had learned, he marked the door with a piece of chalk which he had ready in his hand.

Soon after this Morgiana came out upon some errand, and when she returned she saw the mark the robber had made, and stopped to look at it.

"What can this mean?" she said to herself. "Somebody intends my master harm, and in any case it is best to guard against the worst." Then she fetched a piece of chalk, and marked two or three doors on each side in the same manner, saying nothing to her master or mistress.

When the robber rejoined his troop in the forest, and told of his good fortune in meeting the one man that could have helped him, they were all delighted.

"Comrades," said the captain, "we have no time to lose. Let us set off at once, well armed and disguised, enter the town by twos, and join at the great square. Meanwhile our comrade who has brought us the good news and I will go and find out the house, and decide what had best be done."

Two by two they entered the town. Last of all went the captain and the spy. When they came to the first of the houses which Morgiana had marked, the spy pointed it out. But the captain noticed that the next door was chalked in the same manner, and asked his guide which house it was, that or the first. The guide knew not what answer to make, and was still more puzzled when he and the captain saw five or six houses marked after this same fashion. He assured the captain, with an oath, that he had marked but one, and could not tell who had chalked the rest, nor could he say at which house the cobbler had stopped.

There was nothing to do but to join the other robbers, and tell them to go back to the cave. Here they were told why they had all returned, and the guide was declared by all to be worthy of death. Indeed, he condemned himself, owning that he ought to have been more careful, and prepared to receive the stroke which was to cut off his head.

The safety of the troop still demanded that the second comer to the cave should be found, and another of the gang offered to try it, with the same penalty if he should fail. Like the other robber, he found out Baba Mustapha, and, through him, the house, which he marked, in a place remote from sight, with red chalk.

But nothing could escape Morgiana's eyes, and when she went out, not long after, and saw the red chalk, she argued with herself as before, and marked the other houses near by in the same place and manner.

The robber, when he told his comrades what he had done, prided himself on his carefulness, and the captain and all the troop thought they must succeed this time. Again they entered the town by twos; but when the robber and his captain came to the street, they found the same trouble. The captain was enraged, and the robber as much confused as the former guide had been. Thus the captain and his troop went back again to the cave, and the robber who had failed willingly gave himself up to death.

IV

THE ROBBERS, EXCEPT THE CAPTAIN, DISCOVERED AND KILLED BY MORGIANA

The captain could not afford to lose any more of his brave fellows, and decided to take upon himself the task in which two had failed. Like the others, he went to Baba Mustapha, and was shown the house. Unlike them he put no mark on it, but studied it carefully and passed it so often that he could not possibly mistake it.

When he returned to the troop, who were waiting for him in the cave, he said:—

"Now, comrades, nothing can prevent our full revenge, as I am certain of the house. As I returned I thought of a way to do our work, but if any one thinks of a better, let him speak."

He told them his plan, and, as they thought it good, he ordered them to go into the villages about, and buy nineteen mules, with thirty-eight large leather jars, one full of oil, and the others empty. Within two or three days they returned with the mules and the jars, and as the mouths of the jars were rather too narrow for the captain's purpose, he caused them to be widened. Having put one of his men into each jar, with the weapons which he thought fit, and having a seam wide enough open for each man to breathe, he rubbed the jars on the outside with oil from the full vessel.

Thus prepared they set out for the town, the nineteen mules loaded with the thirty-seven robbers in jars, and the jar of oil, with the captain as their driver. When he reached Ali Baba's door, he found Ali Baba sitting there taking a little fresh air after his supper. The captain stopped his mules, and said:—

"I have brought some oil a great way to sell at to-morrow's market; and it is now so late that I do not know where to lodge. Will you do me the favor to let me pass the night with you?"

Though Ali Baba had seen the captain in the forest, and had heard him speak, he could not know him in the disguise of an oil-merchant, and bade him welcome. He opened his gates for the mules to go into the yard, and ordered a slave to put them in a stable and feed them when they were unloaded, and then called Morgiana to get a good supper for his guest. After supper he charged her afresh to take good care of the stranger, and said to her:—

"To-morrow morning I intend to go to the bath before day; take care to have my bathing linen ready; give it to Abdalla" (which was his slave's name), "and make me some good broth against my return." After this he went to bed.

In the mean time the captain of the robbers went into the yard, and took off the lid of each jar, and told his people what they must do. To each, in turn, he said:—

"As soon as I throw some stones out of the chamber window where I lie, do not fail to come out, and I will join you at once."

Then he went into the house, and Morgiana showed him his chamber, where he soon put out the light, and laid himself down in his clothes.

To carry out Ali Baba's orders, Morgiana got his bathing linen ready, and bade Abdalla to set on the pot for the broth; but soon the lamp went out, and there was no more oil in the house, nor any candles. She knew not what to do, till the slave reminded her of the oil-jars in the yard. She thanked him for the thought, took the oil-pot, and went out. When she came nigh the first jar, the robber within said softly: "Is it time?"

Of course she was surprised to find a man in the jar instead of the oil, but she saw at once that she must keep silence, as Ali Baba, his family, and she herself were in great danger. Therefore she answered, without showing any fear: "Not yet, but presently." In this manner she went to all the jars and gave the same answers, till she came to the jar of oil.

By this means Morgiana found that her master had admitted to his house thirty-eight robbers, of whom the pretended oil-merchant, their captain, was one. She made what haste she could to fill her oil-pot, and returned to her kitchen, lighted her lamp, and taking a great kettle went back to the oil-jar and filled it. Then she set the kettle on a large wood fire, and as soon as it boiled went and poured enough into every jar to stifle and destroy the robber within.

When this deed, worthy of the courage of Morgiana, was done without any noise, as she had planned, she returned to the kitchen with the empty kettle, put out the lamp, and left just enough of the fire to make the broth. Then she sat silent, resolving not to go to rest till she had seen through the window that opened on the yard whatever might happen there.

It was not long before the captain of the robbers got up, and, seeing that all was dark and quiet, gave the appointed signal by throwing little stones, some of which hit the jars, as he doubted not by the sound they gave. As there was no response, he threw stones a second and a third time, and could not imagine why there was no answer to his signal.

Much alarmed, he went softly down into the yard, and, going to the first jar to ask the robber if he was ready, smelt the hot boiled oil, which sent forth a steam out of the jar. From this he suspected that his plot was found out, and, looking into the jars one by one, he found that all his gang were dead. Enraged to despair, he forced the lock of a door that led from the yard to the garden, and made his escape. When Morgiana saw him go, she went to bed, well pleased that she had saved her master. and his family.

Ali Baba rose before day, and went to the baths without knowing of what had happened in the night. When he returned he was very much surprised to see the oil-jars in the yard and the mules in the stable.

"God preserve you and all your family," said Morgiana when she was asked what it meant; "you will know better when you have seen what I have to show you."

25

So saying she led him to the first jar, and asked him to see if there was any oil. When he saw a man instead, he started back in alarm.

"Do not be afraid," said Morgiana; "he can do neither you nor anybody else the least harm. He is dead. Now look into all the other jars."

Ali Baba was more and more amazed as he went on, and saw all the dead men and the sunken oil-jar at the end. He stood looking from the jars to Morgiana, till he found words to ask: "And what is become of the merchant?"

"Merchant!" answered she; "he is as much one as I am."

Then she led him into the house, and told of all that she had done, from the first noticing of the chalk-mark to the death of the robbers and the flight of their captain. On hearing of these brave deeds from Morgiana's own lips, Ali Baba said to her:—

"God, by your means, has delivered me from death. For the first token of what I owe you, I give you your liberty from this moment, till I can fully reward you as I intend."

Near the trees at the end of Ali Baba's long garden, he and Abdalla dug a trench large enough to hold the bodies of the robbers. When they were buried there, Ali Baba hid the jars and weapons; and as the mules were of no use to him, he sent them at different times to be sold in the market by his slave.

V

THE CAPTAIN DISCOVERED AND KILLED BY MORGIANA

The captain of the forty robbers had returned to his cave in the forest, but found himself so lonely there that the place became frightful to him. He resolved at the same time to avenge the fate of his comrades, and to bring about the death of Ali Baba. For this purpose he returned to the town, disguised as a merchant of silks. By degrees he brought from his cavern many sorts of fine stuffs, and to dispose of these he took a warehouse that happened to be opposite Cassim's, which Ali Baba's son had occupied since the death of his uncle.

He took the name of Cogia Houssain, and as a newcomer was very civil to the merchants near him. Ali Baba's son was one of the first to converse with him, and the new merchant was most friendly. Within two or three days Ali Baba came to see his son, and the captain of the robbers knew him at once, and soon learned from his son who he was. From that time forth he was still more polite to Ali Baba's son, who soon felt bound to repay the many kindnesses of his new friend.

As his own house was small, he arranged with his father that on a certain afternoon, when he and the merchant were passing by Ali Baba's house, they should stop, and he should ask them both to sup with him. This plan was carried out, though at first the merchant, with whose own plans it agreed perfectly, made as if to excuse himself. He even gave it as a reason for not remaining that he could eat no salt in his victuals.

"If that is all," said Ali Baba, "it need not deprive me of the honor of your company"; and he went to the kitchen and told Morgiana to put no salt into anything she was cooking that evening.

Thus Cogia Houssain was persuaded to stay, but to Morgiana it seemed very strange that any one should refuse to eat salt. She wished to see what manner of man it might be, and to this end, when she had finished what she had to do in the kitchen, she helped Abdalla carry up the dishes. Looking at Cogia Houssain, she knew him at first sight, in spite of his disguise, to be the captain of the robbers, and, scanning him very closely, saw that he had a dagger under his garment.

"I see now why this greatest enemy of my master would eat no salt with him. He intends to kill him; but I will prevent him."

While they were at supper Morgiana made up her mind to do one of the boldest deeds ever conceived. She dressed herself like a dancer, girded her waist with a silver-gilt girdle, from which hung a poniard, and put a handsome mask on her face. Then, when the supper was ended, she said to Abdalla:—

"Take your tabor, and let us go and divert our master and his son's friend, as we sometimes do when he is alone."

They presented themselves at the door with a low bow, and Morgiana was bidden to enter and show Cogia Houssain how well she danced. This, he knew, would interrupt him in carrying out his wicked purpose, but he had to make the best of it, and to seem pleased with Morgiana's dancing. She was indeed a good dancer, and on this occasion outdid herself in graceful and surprising motions. At the last, she took the tabor from Abdalla's hand, and held it out like those who dance for money.

Ali Baba put a piece of gold into it, and so did his son. When Cogia Houssain saw that she was coming to him, he pulled out his purse from his bosom to make her a present; but while he was putting his hand into it, Morgiana, with courage worthy of herself, plunged the poniard into his heart.

"Unhappy woman!" exclaimed Ali Baba, "what have you done to ruin me and my family?"

"It was to preserve, not to ruin you," answered Morgiana. Then she showed the dagger in Cogia Houssain's garment, and said: "Look well at him, and you will see that he is both the pretended oil-merchant and the captain of the band of forty robbers. As soon as you told me that he would eat no salt with you, I suspected who it was, and when I saw him, I knew."

Ali Baba embraced her, and said: "Morgiana, I gave you your liberty before, and promised you more in time; now I would make you my daughter-in-law. Consider," he said, turning to his son, "that by marrying Morgiana, you marry the preserver of my family and yours."

The son was all the more ready to carry out his father's wishes, because they were the same as his own, and within a few days he and Morgiana were married, but before this, the captain of the robbers was buried with his comrades, and so secretly was it done, that their bones were not found till many years had passed, when no one had any concern in making this strange story known.

For a whole year Ali Baba did not visit the robbers' cave. At the end of that time, as nobody had tried to disturb him, he made another journey to the forest, and, standing before the entrance to the cave, said: "Open, Sesame." The door opened at once, and from the appearance of everything within the cavern, he judged that nobody had been there since the captain had fetched the goods for his shop. From this time forth, he took as much of the treasure as his needs demanded. Some years later he carried his son to the cave, and taught him the secret, which he handed down in his family, who used their good fortune wisely, and lived in great honor and splendor.

RIP VAN WINKLE [5] (1819)

BY WASHINGTON IRVING (1783-1859)

[Setting. The Hudson River and the Kaatskill Mountains were first brought into literature through this story, Irving being the first American master of local color and local tradition. Since 1870 the American short story, following the example of Irving, has been the leading agency by which the South, the West, and New England have made known and thus perpetuated their local scenery, legends, customs, and dialect. Irving, however, seemed afraid of dialect. There were, it is true, many legends about the Hudson before Irving was born, but they had found no expression in literature. Mrs. Josiah Quincy, who made a voyage up the Hudson in 1786, wrote: "Our captain had a legend for every scene, either supernatural or traditional or of actual occurrence during the war, and not a mountain reared its head unconnected with some marvellous story." Irving, therefore, did not have to manufacture local traditions; he only gave them wider currency and fitted them more artistically into their natural settings.

Irving chose for his setting the twenty years that embrace the Revolutionary War because the numerous social and political changes that took place then enabled him to bring Rip back after his sleep into a "world not realized." You will appreciate much better the art of this time-setting if you will try your hand on a somewhat similar story and place it between 1820 and 1840, when railroads, telegraph lines, and transatlantic steamers made a new world out of the old; or, if your story takes place in the South, you might make your background include the interval between 1855 and 1875, when slavery was abolished, when the old plantation system was changed, when the names of new heroes emerged, and when new social and political and industrial problems had to be grappled with.

Plot. The plot is divided into two almost equal parts, which we may call "before and after taking." A recent critic has said: "The actual forward movement of the plot does not begin until the sentence, 'In a long ramble of the kind on a fine autumnal day, Rip had unconsciously scrambled to one of the highest parts of the Kaatskill Mountains.'" The critic has missed, I think, the main structural excellence of the story. Dame Van Winkle, the children who hung around Rip, his own children, his dog, the social club at the inn with the portrait of George the Third, Van Bummel, and Nicholas Vedder, all had to be mentioned before Rip began the ascent of the mountain. Otherwise, when he returned, we should have had no means of measuring the swift passage of time during his sleep. Each is a skillfully set

---

[5] From "The Sketch Book." The elaborate Knickerbocker notes with which Irving, following a passing fashion of the time, sought to mystify the reader, are here omitted. They are hindrances now rather than helps.

timepiece or milepost which, on Rip's return, misleads the poor fellow at every turn and thus produces the exact kind of "totality of effect" that Irving intended. The forward movement of the plot begins with this careful planning of the route that Rip is to take on his return trip, when twenty years shall have done their work. Cut out these points de repère and see how effectively the forward movement of the plot is retarded.

Characters. Rip was the first character in American fiction to be known far beyond our own borders, and he remains one of the best known. In the class with him belong James Fenimore Cooper's Leatherstocking (or Natty Bumppo), Harriet Beecher Stowe's Uncle Tom, Joel Chandler Harris's Uncle Remus, and Mark Twain's Huckleberry Finn and Tom Sawyer. He has been called un-American, and so he is, and so Irving plainly intended him to be. If one insists on finding a bit of distinctive Americanism somewhere in the story, he will find it not in Rip but in the number and rapidity of the changes that American life underwent during the twenty years that serve as background to the story. George William Curtis calls Rip "the constant and unconscious satirist of American life," but surely Irving would have smiled at finding so purposeful a mission laid upon the stooping shoulders of his vagabond ne'er-do-well hero. Rip is no satirist, conscious or unconscious. He is a provincial Dutch type, such as Irving had seen a hundred times; but he is so lovable and is sketched so lovingly that we hardly realize the consummate art, the human sympathy, and the keen powers of observation that have gone into his making. Every other character in the story, including Wolf, is a sidelight on Rip. Of "The Legend of Sleepy Hollow" Irving said: "The story is a mere whimsical band to connect the descriptions of scenery, customs, manners, etc." The emphasis, in other words, was put on the setting. Of "Rip Van Winkle" might he not have said, "The descriptions of scenery, customs, manners, etc. are but so many channels through which the character of Rip finds outlet and expression"?]

Whoever has made a voyage up the Hudson must remember the Kaatskill Mountains. They are a dismembered branch of the great Appalachian family, and are seen away to the west of the river, swelling up to a noble height, and lording it over the surrounding country. Every change of season, every change of weather, indeed, every hour of the day, produces some change in the magical hues and shapes of these mountains, and they are regarded by all the good wives, far and near, as perfect barometers. When the weather is fair and settled, they are clothed in blue and purple, and print their bold outlines on the clear evening sky; but sometimes when the rest of the landscape is cloudless they will gather a hood of gray vapors about their summits, which, in the last rays of the setting sun, will glow and light up like a crown of glory.

At the foot of these fairy mountains, the voyager may have descried the light smoke curling up from a village, whose shingle-roofs gleam among the trees, just where the blue tints of the upland melt away into the fresh green of the nearer landscape. It is a little village of great antiquity, having been founded by some of the Dutch colonists in the early time of the province, just about the beginning of the government of the good Peter Stuyvesant (may he rest in peace!), and there were some of the houses of the original settlers standing within a few years, built of small yellow bricks brought from Holland, having latticed windows and gable fronts, surmounted with weathercocks.

In that same village, and in one of these very houses (which, to tell the precise truth, was sadly time-worn and weather-beaten), there lived many years since, while the country was yet a province of Great Britain, a simple, good-natured fellow, of the name of Rip Van Winkle. He was a descendant of the Van Winkles who figured so gallantly in the chivalrous days of Peter Stuyvesant, and accompanied him to the siege of Fort Christina. He inherited, however, but little of the martial character of his ancestors. I have observed that he was a simple, good-natured man; he was, moreover, a kind neighbor, and an obedient henpecked husband. Indeed, to the latter circumstance might be owing that meekness of spirit which gained him such universal popularity; for those men are most apt to be obsequious and conciliating abroad, who are under the discipline of shrews at home. Their tempers, doubtless, are rendered pliant and malleable in the fiery furnace of domestic tribulation; and a curtain lecture is worth all the sermons in the world for teaching the virtues of patience and long-suffering. A termagant wife may, therefore, in some respects be considered a tolerable blessing, and if so, Rip Van Winkle was thrice blessed.

Certain it is, that he was a great favorite among all the good wives of the village, who, as usual with the amiable sex, took his part in all family squabbles; and never failed, whenever they talked those matters over in their evening gossipings, to lay all the blame on Dame Van Winkle. The children of the village, too, would shout with joy whenever he approached. He assisted at their sports, made their playthings, taught them to fly kites and shoot marbles, and told them long stories of ghosts, witches, and Indians. Whenever he went dodging about the village, he was surrounded by a troop of them hanging on his skirts, clambering on his back, and playing a thousand tricks on him with impunity; and not a dog would bark at him throughout the neighborhood.

The great error in Rip's composition was an insuperable aversion to all kinds of profitable labor. It could not be from the want of assiduity or perseverance; for he would sit on a wet rock, with a rod as long and heavy as a Tartar's lance, and fish all day without a murmur, even though he should not be encouraged by a single nibble. He would carry a fowling-piece on his shoulder for hours together, trudging through woods and swamps, and up hill and down dale, to shoot a few squirrels or wild pigeons. He would never refuse to assist a neighbor, even in the roughest toil, and was a foremost man at all country frolics for husking Indian corn, or building stone-fences; the women of the village, too, used to employ him to run their errands, and to do such little odd jobs as their less obliging husbands would not do for them. In a word, Rip was ready to attend to anybody's business but his own; but as to doing family duty, and keeping his farm in order, he found it impossible.

In fact, he declared it was of no use to work on his farm; it was the most pestilent little piece of ground in the whole country; everything about it went wrong, and would go wrong, in spite of him. His fences were continually falling to pieces; his cow would either go astray or get among the cabbages; weeds were sure to grow quicker in his fields than anywhere else; the rain always made a point of setting in just as he had some outdoor work to do; so that though his patrimonial estate had dwindled away under his management, acre by acre, until there was little more left than a mere patch of Indian corn and potatoes, yet it was the worst-conditioned farm in the neighborhood.

His children, too, were as ragged and wild as if they belonged to nobody. His son Rip, an urchin begotten in his own likeness, promised to inherit the habits, with the old clothes of his father. He was generally seen trooping like a colt at his mother's heels, equipped in a pair of his father's cast-off galligaskins, which he had much ado to hold up with one hand, as a fine lady does her train in bad weather.

Rip Van Winkle, however, was one of those happy mortals, of foolish, well-oiled dispositions, who take the world easy, eat white bread or brown, whichever can be got with least thought or trouble, and would rather starve on a penny than work for a pound. If left to himself, he would have whistled life away in perfect contentment; but his wife kept continually dinning in his ears about his idleness, his carelessness, and the ruin he was bringing on his family. Morning, noon, and night her tongue was incessantly going, and everything he said or did was sure to produce a torrent of household eloquence. Rip had but one way of replying to all lectures of the kind, and that, by frequent use, had grown into a habit. He shrugged his shoulders, shook his head, cast up his eyes, but said nothing. This, however, always provoked a fresh volley from his wife; so that he was fain to draw off his forces, and take to the outside of the house—the only side which, in truth, belongs to a henpecked husband.

Rip's sole domestic adherent was his dog Wolf, who was as much henpecked as his master; for Dame Van Winkle regarded them as companions in idleness, and even looked upon Wolf with an evil eye, as the cause of his master's going so often astray. True it is, in all points of spirit befitting an honorable dog, he was as courageous an animal as ever scoured the woods—but what courage can withstand the ever-during and all-besetting terrors of a woman's tongue? The moment Wolf entered the house his crest fell, his tail drooped to the ground, or curled between his legs, he sneaked about with a gallows air, casting many a sidelong glance at Dame Van Winkle, and at the least flourish of a broomstick or ladle he would fly to the door with yelping precipitation.

Times grew worse and worse with Rip Van Winkle as years of matrimony rolled on; a tart temper never mellows with age, and a sharp tongue is the only edged tool that grows keener with constant use. For a long while he used to console himself, when driven from home, by frequenting a kind of perpetual club of the sages, philosophers, and other idle personages of the village, which held its sessions on a bench before a small inn, designated by a rubicund portrait of His Majesty George the Third. Here they used to sit in the shade through a long lazy summer's day, talking listlessly over village gossip, or telling endless sleepy stories about nothing. But it would have been worth any statesman's money to have heard the profound discussions that sometimes took place, when by chance an old newspaper fell into their hands from some passing traveller. How solemnly they would listen to the contents, as drawled out by Derrick Van Bummel, the schoolmaster, a dapper, learned little man, who was not to be daunted by the most gigantic word in the dictionary; and how sagely they would deliberate upon public events some months after they had taken place.

The opinions of this junto were completely controlled by Nicholas Vedder, a patriarch of the village, and landlord of the inn, at the door of which he took his seat from morning till night, just moving sufficiently to avoid the sun and keep in the shade of a large tree; so that the neighbors could tell the hour by his movements as accurately as by a sun-dial. It is true he was rarely heard to speak, but smoked his pipe incessantly. His adherents, however (for every great man has his adherents), perfectly understood him, and knew how to gather his opinions. When anything that was read or related displeased him, he was observed to smoke his pipe vehemently, and to send forth short, frequent and angry puffs; but when pleased, he would inhale the smoke slowly and tranquilly, and emit it in light and placid clouds; and sometimes, taking the pipe from his mouth, and letting the fragrant vapor curl about his nose, would gravely nod his head in token of perfect approbation.

From even this stronghold the unlucky Rip was at length routed by his termagant wife, who would suddenly break in upon the tranquillity of the assemblage and call the members all to naught; nor was that august personage, Nicholas Vedder himself, sacred from the daring tongue of this terrible virago, who charged him outright with encouraging her husband in habits of idleness.

Poor Rip was at last reduced almost to despair; and his only alternative, to escape from the labor of the farm and clamor of his wife, was to take gun in hand and stroll away into the woods. Here he would sometimes seat himself at the foot of a tree, and share the contents of his wallet with Wolf, with whom he sympathized as a fellow-sufferer in persecution. "Poor Wolf," he would say, "thy mistress leads thee a dog's life of it; but never mind, my lad, whilst I live thou shalt never want a friend to stand by thee!" Wolf would wag his tail, look wistfully in his master's face, and if dogs can feel pity, I verily believe he reciprocated the sentiment with all his heart.

In a long ramble of the kind on a fine autumnal day, Rip had unconsciously scrambled to one of the highest parts of the Kaatskill Mountains. He was after his favorite sport of squirrel shooting, and the still solitudes had echoed and re-echoed with the reports of his gun.

Panting and fatigued, he threw himself, late in the afternoon, on a green knoll, covered with mountain herbage, that crowned the brow of a precipice. From an opening between the trees he could overlook all the lower country for many a mile of rich woodland. He saw at a distance the lordly Hudson, far, far below him, moving on its silent but majestic course, with the reflection of a purple cloud, or the sail of a lagging bark, here and there sleeping on its glassy bosom, and at last losing itself in the blue highlands.

On the other side he looked down into a deep mountain glen, wild, lonely, and shagged, the bottom filled with fragments from the impending cliffs, and scarcely lighted by the reflected rays of the setting sun. For some time Rip lay musing on this scene; evening was gradually advancing, the mountains began to throw their long blue shadows over the valleys; he saw that it would be dark long before he could reach the village, and he heaved a heavy sigh when he thought of encountering the terrors of Dame Van Winkle.

As he was about to descend, he heard a voice from a distance, hallooing, "Rip Van Winkle! Rip Van Winkle!" He looked round, but could see nothing but a crow winging its solitary flight across the mountain. He thought his fancy must have deceived him, and turned again to descend, when he heard the same cry ring through the still evening air: "Rip Van Winkle! Rip Van Winkle!"—at the same time Wolf bristled up his back, and giving a low growl, skulked to his master's side, looking fearfully down into the glen. Rip now felt a vague apprehension stealing over him; he looked anxiously in the same direction, and perceived a strange figure slowly toiling up the rocks, and bending under the weight of something he carried on his back. He was surprised to see any human being in this lonely and unfrequented place; but supposing it to be some one of the neighborhood in need of his assistance, he hastened down to yield it.

On nearer approach he was still more surprised at the singularity of the stranger's appearance. He was a short, square-built old fellow, with thick bushy hair, and a grizzled beard. His dress was of the antique Dutch fashion: a cloth jerkin strapped round the waist, several pairs of breeches, the outer one of ample volume, decorated with rows of buttons down the sides, and bunches at the knees. He bore on his shoulder a stout keg, that seemed full of liquor, and made signs for Rip to approach and assist him with the load. Though rather shy and distrustful of this new acquaintance, Rip complied with his usual alacrity; and mutually relieving one another, they clambered up a narrow gully, apparently the dry bed of a mountain torrent. As they ascended, Rip every now and then heard long rolling peals like distant thunder, that seemed to issue out of a deep ravine, or rather cleft, between lofty rocks, toward which their rugged path conducted. He paused for a moment, but supposing it to be the muttering of one of those transient thunder-showers which often take place in mountain heights, he proceeded. Passing through the ravine, they came to a hollow, like a small amphitheatre, surrounded by perpendicular precipices, over the brinks of which impending trees shot their branches, so that you only caught glimpses of the azure sky and the bright evening cloud. During the whole time Rip and his companion had labored on in silence; for though the former marvelled greatly what could be the object of carrying a keg of liquor up this wild mountain, yet there was something strange and incomprehensible about the unknown, that inspired awe and checked familiarity.

On entering the amphitheatre, new objects of wonder presented themselves. On a level spot in the center was a company of odd-looking personages playing at ninepins. They were dressed in a quaint outlandish fashion; some wore short doublets, others jerkins, with long knives in their belts, and most of them had enormous breeches of similar style with that of the guide's. Their visages, too, were peculiar; one had a large beard, broad face, and small piggish eyes; the face of another seemed to consist entirely of nose, and was surmounted by a white sugar-loaf hat, set off with a little red cock's tail. They all had beards, of various shapes and colors. There was one who seemed to be the commander. He was a stout old gentleman, with a weather-beaten countenance; he wore a laced doublet, broad belt and hanger, high-crowned hat and feather, red stockings, and high-heeled shoes, with roses in them. The whole group reminded Rip of the figures in an old Flemish painting in the parlor of Dominie Van Shaick, the village parson, which had been brought over from Holland at the time of the settlement.

What seemed particularly odd to Rip was, that though these folks were evidently amusing themselves, yet they maintained the gravest faces, the most mysterious silence, and were, withal, the most melancholy party of pleasure he had ever witnessed. Nothing interrupted the stillness of the scene but the noise of the balls, which, whenever they were rolled, echoed along the mountains like rumbling peals of thunder.

As Rip and his companion approached them, they suddenly desisted from their play, and stared at him with such, fixed, statue-like gaze, and such strange, uncouth, lack-lustre countenances, that his heart turned within him, and his knees smote together. His companion now emptied the contents of the keg into large flagons, and made signs to him to wait upon the company. He obeyed with fear and trembling; they quaffed the liquor in profound silence, and then returned to their game.

By degrees Rip's awe and apprehension subsided. He even ventured, when no eye was fixed upon him, to taste the beverage, which he found had much of the flavor of excellent Hollands. He was naturally a thirsty soul, and was soon tempted to repeat the draught. One taste provoked another; and he reiterated his visits to the flagon so often that at length his senses were overpowered, his eyes swam in his head, his head gradually declined, and he fell into a deep sleep.

On waking, he found himself on the green knoll whence he had first seen the old man of the glen. He rubbed his eyes—it was a bright, sunny morning. The birds were hopping and twittering among the bushes, and the eagle was wheeling aloft, and breasting the pure mountain breeze. "Surely," thought Rip, "I have not slept here all night." He recalled the occurrences before he fell asleep. The strange man with a keg of liquor—the mountain ravine—the wild retreat among the rocks—the woe-begone party at ninepins—the flagon—"Oh! that flagon! that wicked flagon!" thought Rip—"what excuse shall I make to Dame Van Winkle?"

He looked round for his gun, but in place of the clean, well-oiled fowling-piece, he found an old firelock lying by him, the barrel incrusted with rust, the lock falling off, and the stock worm-eaten. He now suspected that the grave roisterers of the mountain had put a trick upon him, and, having dosed him with liquor, had robbed him of his gun. Wolf, too, had disappeared, but he might have strayed away after a squirrel or partridge. He whistled after him, and shouted his name, but all in vain; the echoes repeated his whistle and shout, but no dog was to be seen.

He determined to revisit the scene of the last evening's gambol, and if he met with any of the party, to demand his dog and gun. As he rose to walk, he found himself stiff in the joints, and wanting in his usual activity. "These mountain beds do not agree with me," thought Rip, "and if this frolic should lay me up with a fit of the rheumatism, I shall have a blessed time with Dame Van Winkle." With some difficulty he got down into the glen; he found the gully up which he and his companion has ascended the preceding evening; but to his astonishment a mountain stream was now foaming down it, leaping from rock to rock, and filling the glen with babbling murmurs. He, however, made shift to scramble up its sides, working his toilsome way through thickets of birch, sassafras, and witch-hazel, and sometimes tripped up or entangled by the wild grapevines that twisted their coils or tendrils from tree to tree, and spread a kind of network in his path.

At length he reached to where the ravine had opened through the cliffs to the amphitheatre; but no traces of such opening remained. The rocks presented a high, impenetrable wall, over which the torrent came tumbling in a sheet of feathery foam, and fell into a broad, deep basin, black from the shadows of the surrounding forest. Here, then, poor Rip was brought to a stand. He again called and whistled after his dog; he was only answered by the cawing of a flock of idle crows, sporting high in air about a dry tree that overhung a sunny precipice; and who, secure in their elevation, seemed to look down and scoff at the poor man's perplexities. What was to be done? the morning was passing away, and Rip felt famished for want of his breakfast. He grieved to give up his dog and gun; he dreaded to meet his wife; but it would not do to starve among the mountains. He shook his head, shouldered the rusty firelock, and, with a heart full of trouble and anxiety, turned his steps homeward.

As he approached the village he met a number of people, but none whom he knew, which somewhat surprised him, for he had thought himself acquainted with every one in the country round. Their dress, too, was of a different fashion from that to which he was accustomed. They all stared at him with equal marks of surprise, and whenever they cast their eyes upon him, invariably stroked their chins. The constant recurrence of this gesture induced Rip, involuntarily, to do the same, when, to his astonishment, he found his beard had grown a foot long!

He had now entered the skirts of the village. A troop of strange children ran at his heels, hooting after him, and pointing at his gray beard. The dogs, too, not one of which he recognized for an old acquaintance, barked at him as he passed. The very village was altered; it was larger and more populous. There were rows of houses which he had never seen before, and those which had been his familiar haunts had disappeared. Strange names were over the doors—strange faces at the windows— everything was strange. His mind now misgave him; he began to doubt whether both he and the world around him were not bewitched. Surely this was his native village, which he had left but the day before. There stood the Kaatskill Mountains—there ran the silver Hudson at a distance—there was every hill and dale precisely as it had always been—Rip was sorely perplexed—"That flagon last night," thought he, "has addled my poor head sadly!"

It was with some difficulty that he found the way to his own house, which he approached with silent awe, expecting every moment to hear the shrill voice of Dame Van Winkle. He found the house gone to decay—the roof fallen in, the windows shattered, and the doors off the hinges. A half-starved dog that looked like Wolf was skulking about it. Rip called him by name, but the cur snarled, showed his teeth, and passed on. This was an unkind cut indeed—"My very dog," sighed poor Rip, "has forgotten me!"

He entered the house, which, to tell the truth, Dame Van Winkle had always kept in neat order. It was empty, forlorn, and apparently abandoned. This desolateness overcame all his connubial fears—he called loudly for his wife and children—the lonely chambers rang for a moment with his voice, and then again all was silence.

He now hurried forth, and hastened to his old resort, the village inn—but it, too, was gone. A large, rickety wooden building stood in its place, with great gaping windows, some of them broken and mended with old hats and petticoats, and over the door was painted, "The Union Hotel, by Jonathan Doolittle." Instead of the great tree that used to shelter the quiet little Dutch inn of yore, there now was reared a tall naked pole, with something on the top that looked like a red night-cap, and from it was fluttering a flag, on which was a singular assemblage of stars and stripes— all this was strange and incomprehensible. He recognized on the sign, however, the ruby face of King George, under which he had smoked so many a peaceful pipe; but even this was singularly metamorphosed. The red coat was changed for one of blue and buff, a sword was held in the hand instead of a sceptre, the head was decorated with a cocked hat, and underneath was painted in large characters, GENERAL WASHINGTON.

There was, as usual, a crowd of folk about the door, but none that Rip recollected. The very character of the people seemed changed. There was a busy, bustling, disputatious tone about it, instead of the accustomed phlegm and drowsy tranquillity. He looked in vain for the sage Nicholas Vedder, with his broad face, double chin, and fair long pipe, uttering clouds of tobacco-smoke instead of idle speeches; or Van Bummel, the schoolmaster, doling forth the contents of an ancient newspaper. In place of these, a lean, bilious-looking fellow, with his pockets full of hand-bills, was haranguing vehemently about rights of citizens —elections—members of congress—liberty—Bunker's Hill—heroes of seventy-six—and other words, which were a perfect Babylonish jargon to the bewildered Van Winkle.

The appearance of Rip, with his long grizzled beard, his rusty fowling-piece, his uncouth dress, and an army of women and children at his heels, soon attracted the attention of the tavern-politicians. They crowded round him, eying him from head to foot with great curiosity. The orator bustled up to him, and, drawing him partly aside, inquired "on which side he voted?" Rip stared in vacant stupidity. Another short but busy little fellow pulled him by the arm, and, rising on tiptoe, inquired in his ear, "Whether he was Federal or Democrat?" Rip was equally at a loss to comprehend the question; when a knowing, self-important old gentleman, in a sharp cocked hat, made his way through the crowd, putting them to the right and left with his elbows as he passed, and planting himself before Van Winkle, with one arm akimbo, the other resting on his cane, his keen eyes and sharp hat penetrating, as it were, into his very soul, demanded in an austere tone, "what brought him to the election with a gun on his shoulder, and a mob at his heels, and whether he meant to breed a riot in the village?"—"Alas! gentlemen," cried Rip, somewhat dismayed, "I am a poor quiet man, a native of the place, and a loyal subject of the king, God bless him!"

Here a general shout burst from the bystanders—"A tory! a tory! a spy! a refugee! hustle him! away with him!" It was with great difficulty that the self-important man in the cocked hat restored order; and, having assumed a tenfold austerity of brow, demanded again of the unknown culprit what he came there for, and whom he was seeking? The poor man humbly assured him that he meant no harm, but merely came there in search of some of his neighbors, who used to keep about the tavern.

"Well—who are they?—name them."

Rip bethought himself a moment, and inquired, "Where's Nicholas Vedder?"

There was a silence for a little while, when an old man replied, in a thin, piping voice: "Nicholas Vedder! why, he is dead and gone these eighteen years! There was a wooden tombstone in the churchyard that used to tell all about him, but that's rotten and gone too."

"Where's Brom Dutcher?"

"Oh, he went off to the army in the beginning of the war; some say he was killed at the storming of Stony Point—others say he was drowned in a squall at the foot of Antony's Nose. I don't know—he never came back again."

"Where's Van Bummel, the schoolmaster?"

"He went off to the wars too, was a great militia general, and is now in Congress."

Rip's heart died away at hearing of these sad changes in his home and friends, and finding himself thus alone in the world. Every answer puzzled him too, by treating of such enormous lapses of time, and of matters which he could not understand: war—Congress—Stony Point; he had no courage to ask after any more friends, but cried out in despair, "Does nobody here know Rip Van Winkle?"

"Oh, Rip Van Winkle!" exclaimed two or three.

"Oh, to be sure! that's Rip Van Winkle yonder, leaning against the tree."

Rip looked, and beheld a precise counterpart of himself, as he went up the mountain: apparently as lazy, and certainly as ragged. The poor fellow was now completely confounded. He doubted his own identity, and whether he was himself or another man. In the midst of his bewilderment, the man in the cocked hat demanded who he was, and what was his name?

"God knows," exclaimed he, at his wit's end; "I'm not myself—I'm somebody else—that's me yonder—no—that's somebody else got into my shoes—I was myself last night, but I fell asleep on the mountain, and they've changed my gun, and everything's changed, and I'm changed, and I can't tell what's my name, or who I am!"

The bystanders began now to look at each other, nod, wink significantly, and tap their fingers against their foreheads. There was a whisper, also, about securing the gun, and keeping the old fellow from doing mischief, at the very suggestion of which the self-important man in the cocked hat retired with some precipitation. At this critical moment a fresh, comely woman pressed through the throng to get a peep at the gray-bearded man. She had a chubby child in her arms, which, frightened at his looks, began to cry. "Hush, Rip," cried she, "hush, you little fool; the old man won't hurt you." The name of the child, the air of the mother, the tone of her voice, all awakened a train of recollections in his mind. "What is your name, my good woman?" asked he.

"Judith Gardenier."

"And your father's name?"

"Ah, poor man, Rip Van Winkle was his name, but it's twenty years since he went away from home with his gun, and never has been heard of since,—his dog came home without him; but whether he shot himself or was carried away by the Indians, nobody can tell. I was then but a little girl."

Rip had but one question more to ask; and he put it with a faltering voice:—"Where's your mother?"

"Oh, she too had died but a short time since; she broke a blood-vessel in a fit of passion at a New England peddler."

There was a drop of comfort, at least, in this intelligence. The honest man could contain himself no longer. He caught his daughter and her child in his arms. "I am your father!" cried he—"Young Rip Van Winkle once—old Rip Van Winkle now! Does nobody know poor Rip Van Winkle?"

All stood amazed, until an old woman, tottering out from among the crowd, put her hand to her brow, and peering under it in his face for a moment, exclaimed, "Sure enough it is Rip Van Winkle—it is himself! Welcome home again, old neighbor—Why, where have you been these twenty long years?"

Rip's story was soon told, for the whole twenty years had been to him but as one night. The neighbors stared when they heard it; some were seen to wink at each other, and put their tongues in their cheeks; and the self-important man in the cocked hat, who, when the alarm was over, had returned to the field, screwed down the corners of his mouth, and shook his head—upon which there was a general shaking of the head throughout the assemblage.

It was determined, however, to take the opinion of old Peter Vanderdonk, who was seen slowly advancing up the road. He was a descendant of the historian of that name, who wrote one of the earliest accounts of the province. Peter was the most ancient inhabitant of the village, and well versed in all the wonderful events and traditions of the neighborhood. He recollected Rip at once, and corroborated his story in the most satisfactory manner. He assured the company that it was a fact, handed down from his ancestor the historian, that the Kaatskill Mountains had always been haunted by strange beings. That it was affirmed that the great Hendrick Hudson, the first discoverer of the river and country, kept a kind of vigil there every twenty years, with his crew of the Half-moon; being permitted in this way to revisit the scenes of his enterprise, and keep a guardian eye upon the river and the great city called by his name. That his father had once seen them in their old Dutch dresses playing at ninepins in a hollow of the mountain; and that he himself had heard, one summer afternoon, the sound of their balls like distant peals of thunder.

To make a long story short, the company broke up and returned to the more important concerns of the election. Rip's daughter took him home to live with her; she had a snug well-furnished house, and a stout cheery farmer for a husband, whom Rip recollected for one of the urchins that used to climb upon his back. As to Rip's son and heir, who was the ditto of himself, seen leaning against the tree, he was employed to work on the farm; but evinced an hereditary disposition to attend to anything else but his business.

Rip now resumed his old walks and habits; he soon found many of his former cronies, though all rather the worse for the wear and tear of time; and preferred making friends among the rising generation, with whom he soon grew into great favor.

Having nothing to do at home, and being arrived at that happy age when a man can be idle with impunity, he took his place once more on the bench at the inn door, and was reverenced as one of the patriarchs of the village, and a chronicle of the old times "before the war." It was some time before he could get into the regular track of gossip, or could be made to comprehend the strange events that had taken place during his torpor. How that there had been a revolutionary war—that the country had thrown off the yoke of old England—and that, instead of being a subject of his Majesty George the Third, he was now a free citizen of the United States.

Rip, in fact, was no politician; the changes of states and empires made but little impression on him; but there was one species of despotism under which he had long groaned, and that was—petticoat government. Happily that was at an end; he had got his neck out of the yoke of matrimony, and could go in and out whenever he pleased, without dreading the tyranny of Dame Van Winkle. Whenever her name was mentioned, however, he shook his head, shrugged his shoulders, and cast up his eyes, which might pass either for an expression of resignation to his fate, or joy at his deliverance.

He used to tell his story to every stranger that arrived at Mr. Doolittle's hotel. He was observed, at first, to vary on some points every time he told it, which was, doubtless, owing to his having so recently awaked. It at last settled down precisely to the tale I have related, and not a man, woman, or child in the neighborhood but knew it by heart. Some always pretended to doubt the reality of it, and insisted that Rip had been out of his head, and that this was one point on which he always remained flighty. The old Dutch inhabitants, however, almost universally gave it full credit. Even to this day they never hear a thunder-storm of a summer afternoon about the Kaatskill, but they say Hendrick Hudson and his crew are at their game of ninepins; and it is a common wish of all henpecked husbands in the neighborhood, when life hangs heavy on their hands, that they might have a quieting draught out of Rip Van Winkle's flagon.

THE GOLD-BUG (1843)

BY EDGAR ALLAN POE (1809-1849)

[Setting. Sullivan's Island is at the entrance of Charleston harbor, just east of Charleston, South Carolina. It is the site of Fort Moultrie, where Poe served as a private soldier in Battery H of the First Artillery, United States Army, from November, 1827, to November, 1828. The atmosphere of the place in Poe's time is well preserved, but no such beetle as the gold-bug has been discovered. Poe may have found a hint for his story in the wreck of the old brigantine Cid Campeador off the coast of South Carolina in 1745, the affidavits of the burying of the treasure being still preserved in the Probate Court Records of Charleston.

Plot. "The Gold-Bug" is recognized as one of the world's greatest short stories and marks a distinct advance in short-story structure. The plot is divided into two parts, which we may call mystery and solution, or complication and explication, or rise and fall. The second part begins with the short paragraph on page 91, beginning "When, at length, we had concluded our examination," etc. Notice how skillfully the interest is preserved and even heightened as the plot passes from the romantic action of part one to the subtle exposition of part two. These two parts may be said to represent the two sides of Poe's genius, the imaginative or poetical, and the intellectual or scientific. The treasure-trove is the symbol of the first, the cryptogram of the second. Stories had been written about buried treasures and about cryptograms before 1843, but the two interests had never before been combined. Poe's example, however, has borne abundant fruit.

Characters. Poe's strength did not lie in the creation of character. He is so intent on the development of the windings and unwindings of his story that the characters become mere puppets, originated and controlled by the needs of the plot. Jupiter deserves mention as one of the earliest attempts made by an American short-story writer to portray negro character. But Jupiter has been so far surpassed in breadth and reality by Joel Chandler Harris, Thomas Nelson Page, and a score of others as to be almost negligible in the count. In defense of Jupiter's barbarous lingo, which has been often criticized, it should be remembered that Poe intended him as a representative of the Gullah (or Gulla) dialect. "It is the negro dialect," says Joel Chandler Harris, "in its most primitive state—the 'Gullah' talk of some of the negroes on the Sea Islands being merely a confused and untranslatable mixture of English and African words."

William Legrand, though not a great or notable character in any way, is admirably fitted to do what is required of him in the story. Like Poe, he was solitary, proud, quick-tempered, and "subject to perverse moods of alternate enthusiasm and melancholy." He had also Poe's passion for puzzles. Jupiter is hardly more than an awkward tool fashioned to display

Legrand's analytic and directive genius; and the other character in the story, like Dr. Watson in Conan Doyle's Sherlock Holmes stories, is introduced merely to ask such questions as must be answered if the reader is to follow intelligently the unfolding of the plot. They are agents rather than characters.]

What ho! what ho! this fellow is dancing mad!
He hath been bitten by the Tarantula.
   "All in the Wrong"

Many years ago, I contracted an intimacy with a Mr. William Legrand. He was of an ancient Huguenot family, and had once been wealthy; but a series of misfortunes had reduced him to want. To avoid the mortification consequent upon his disasters, he left New Orleans, the city of his forefathers, and took up his residence at Sullivan's Island, near Charleston, South Carolina.

This island is a very singular one. It consists of little else than the sea sand, and is about three miles long. Its breadth at no point exceeds a quarter of a mile. It is separated from the mainland by a scarcely perceptible creek, oozing its way through a wilderness of reeds and slime, a favorite resort of the marsh-hen. The vegetation, as might be supposed, is scant, or at least dwarfish. No trees of any magnitude are to be seen. Near the western extremity, where Fort Moultrie stands, and where are some miserable frame buildings, tenanted during summer by the fugitives from Charleston dust and fever, may be found, indeed, the bristly palmetto; but the whole island, with the exception of this western point, and a line of hard white beach on the seacoast, is covered with a dense undergrowth of the sweet myrtle, so much prized by the horticulturists of England. The shrub here often attains the height of fifteen or twenty feet, and forms an almost impenetrable coppice, burdening the air with its fragrance.

In the utmost recesses of this coppice, not far from the eastern or more remote end of the island, Legrand had built himself a small hut, which he occupied when I first, by mere accident, made his acquaintance. This soon ripened into friendship—for there was much in the recluse to excite interest and esteem. I found him well educated, with unusual powers of mind, but infected with misanthropy, and subject to perverse moods of alternate enthusiasm and melancholy. He had with him many books, but rarely employed them. His chief amusements were gunning and fishing, or sauntering along the beach and through the myrtles in quest of shells or entomological specimens;—his collection of the latter might have been envied by a Swammerdamm. In these excursions he was usually accompanied by an old negro, called Jupiter, who had been manumitted before the reverses of the family, but who could be induced, neither by threats nor by promises, to abandon what he considered his right of attendance upon the footsteps of his young "Massa Will." It is not improbable that the relatives of Legrand, conceiving him to be somewhat unsettled in intellect, had contrived to instil this obstinacy into Jupiter, with a view to the supervision and guardianship of the wanderer.

The winters in the latitude of Sullivan's Island are seldom very severe, and in the fall of the year it is a rare event indeed when a fire is considered necessary. About the middle of October, 18—, there occurred, however, a day of remarkable chilliness. Just before sunset I scrambled my way through the evergreens to the hut of my friend, whom I had not visited for several weeks—my residence being at that time in Charleston, a distance of nine miles from the island, while the facilities of passage and repassage were very far behind those of the present day. Upon reaching the hut I rapped, as was my custom, and, getting no reply, sought for the key where I knew it was secreted, unlocked the door, and went in. A fine fire was blazing upon the hearth. It was a novelty, and by no means an ungrateful one. I threw off an overcoat, took an armchair by the crackling logs, and awaited patiently the arrival of my hosts.

Soon after dark they arrived, and gave me a most cordial welcome. Jupiter, grinning from ear to ear, bustled about to prepare some marsh-hens for supper. Legrand was in one of his fits—how else shall I term them?—of enthusiasm. He had found an unknown bivalve, forming a new genus, and, more than this, he had hunted down and secured, with Jupiter's assistance, a scarabæus which he believed to be totally new, but in respect to which he wished to have my opinion on the morrow.

"And why not to-night?" I asked, rubbing my hands over the blaze, and wishing the whole tribe of scarabæi at the devil.

"Ah, if I had only known you were here!" said Legrand, "but it's so long since I saw you; and how could I foresee that you would pay me a visit this very night of all others? As I was coming home I met Lieutenant G——, from the fort, and, very foolishly, I lent him the bug; so it will be impossible for you to see it until the morning. Stay here to-night, and I will send Jup down for it at sunrise. It is the loveliest thing in creation!"

"What?—sunrise?"

"Nonsense! no!—the bug. It is of a brilliant gold color—about the size of a large hickory-nut—with two jet-black spots near one extremity of the back, and another, somewhat longer, at the other. The antennæ are—"

"Dey aint no tin in him, Massa Will, I keep a tellin on you," here interrupted Jupiter; "de bug is a goole-bug, solid, ebery bit of him, inside and all, sep him wing—neber feel half so hebby a bug in my life."

"Well, suppose it is, Jup," replied Legrand, somewhat more earnestly, it seemed to me, than the case demanded, "is that any reason for your letting the birds burn? The color"—here he turned to me—"is really almost enough to warrant Jupiter's idea. You never saw a more brilliant metallic lustre than the scales emit—but of this you cannot judge till to-morrow. In the meantime I can give you some idea of the shape." Saying this, he seated himself at a small table, on which were a pen and ink, but no paper. He looked for some in a drawer, but found none.

"Never mind," said he at length, "this will answer"; and he drew from his waistcoat pocket a scrap of what I took to be very dirty foolscap, and made upon it a rough drawing with the pen. While he did this, I retained my seat by the fire, for I was still chilly. When the design was complete, he handed it to me without rising. As I received it, a low growl was heard, succeeded by a scratching at the door. Jupiter opened it, and a large Newfoundland, belonging to Legrand, rushed in, leaped upon my shoulders, and loaded me with caresses; for I had shown him much attention during previous visits. When his gambols were over, I looked at the paper, and, to speak the truth, found myself not a little puzzled at what my friend had depicted.

"Well!" I said, after contemplating it for some minutes, "this is a strange scarabæus, I must confess; new to me; never saw anything like it before—unless it was a skull, or a death's-head, which it more nearly resembles than anything else that has come under my observation."

"A death's-head!" echoed Legrand—"oh—yes—well, it has something of that appearance upon paper, no doubt. The two upper black spots look like eyes, eh? and the longer one at the bottom like a mouth—and then the shape of the whole is oval."

"Perhaps so," said I; "but, Legrand, I fear you are no artist. I must wait until I see the beetle itself, if I am to form any idea of its personal appearance."

"Well, I don't know," said he, a little nettled, "I draw tolerably—should do it at least—have had good masters, and flatter myself that I am not quite a blockhead."

"But, my dear fellow, you are joking then," said I; "this is a very passable skull,—indeed, I may say that it is a very excellent skull, according to the vulgar notions about such specimens of physiology—and your scarabæus must be the queerest scarabæus in the world if it resembles it. Why, we may get up a very thrilling bit of superstition upon this hint. I presume you will call the bug scarabæus caput hominis [6] or something of that kind—there are many similar titles in the Natural Histories. But where are the antennæ you spoke of?"

"The antennæ!" said Legrand, who seemed to be getting unaccountably warm upon the subject; "I am sure you must see the antennæ. I made them as distinct as they are in the original insect, and I presume that is sufficient."

"Well, well," I said, "perhaps you have—still I don't see them"; and I handed him the paper without additional remark, not wishing to ruffle his temper; but I was much surprised at the turn affairs had taken; his ill humor puzzled me—and as for the drawing of the beetle, there were positively no antennæ, visible, and the whole did bear a very close resemblance to the ordinary cuts of a death's-head.

He received the paper very peevishly, and was about to crumple it, apparently to throw it in the fire, when a casual glance at the design seemed suddenly to rivet his attention. In an instant his face grew violently red—in another as excessively pale. For some minutes he continued to scrutinize the drawing minutely where he sat. At length he arose, took a candle from the table, and proceeded to seat himself upon a sea-chest in the farthest corner of the room. Here again he made an anxious

---

[6] Scarabæus caput hominis, "death's-head beetle."

examination of the paper; turning it in all directions. He said nothing, however, and his conduct greatly astonished me; yet I thought it prudent not to exacerbate the growing moodiness of his temper by any comment. Presently he took from his coat pocket a wallet, placed the paper carefully in it, and deposited both in a writing-desk, which he locked. He now grew more composed in his demeanor; but his original air of enthusiasm had quite disappeared. Yet he seemed not so much sulky as abstracted. As the evening wore away he became more and more absorbed in revery, from which no sallies of mine could arouse him. It had been my intention to pass the night at the hut, as I had frequently done before, but, seeing my host in this mood, I deemed it proper to take leave. He did not press me to remain, but, as I departed, he shook my hand with even more than his usual cordiality.

It was about a month after this (and during the interval I had seen nothing of Legrand) when I received a visit, at Charleston, from his man, Jupiter. I had never seen the good old negro look so dispirited, and I feared that some serious disaster had befallen my friend.

"Well, Jup," said I, "what is the matter now?—how is your master?"

"Why, to speak de troof, massa, him not so berry well as mought be."

"Not well! I am truly sorry to hear it. What does he complain of?"

"Dar! dat's it!—him neber plain of notin—but him berry sick for all dat."

"Very sick, Jupiter!—why didn't you say so at once? Is he confined to bed?"

"No, dat he aint!—he aint find nowhar—dat's just whar de shoe pinch—my mind is got to be berry hebby bout poor Massa Will."

"Jupiter, I should like to understand what it is you are talking about. You say your master is sick. Hasn't he told you what ails him?"

"Why, massa, taint worf while for to git mad bout de matter—Massa Will say noffin at all aint de matter wid him—but den what make him go bout looking dis here way, wid he head down and he soldiers up, and as white as a gose? And then he keeps a syphon all de time—"

"Keeps a what, Jupiter?"

"Keeps a syphon wid de figgurs on de slate—de queerest figgurs I ebber did see. Ise gittin to be skeered, I tell you. Hab for to keep mighty tight eye pon him noovers. Todder day he gib me slip fore de sun up and was gone de whole ob de blessed day. I had a big stick ready cut for to gib him d——d good beating when he did come—but Ise sich a fool dat I hadn't de heart arter all—he look so berry poorly."

"Eh?—what?—ah, yes!—upon the whole I think you had better not be too severe with the poor fellow—don't flog him, Jupiter—he can't very well stand it—but can you form no idea of what has occasioned this illness, or rather this change of conduct? Has anything unpleasant happened since I saw you?"

"No, massa, dey aint bin noffin onpleasant since den—'t was fore den I'm feared—'t was de berry day you was dare."

"How? what do you mean?"

46

"Why, massa, I mean de bug—dare now."

"The what?"

"De bug—I'm berry sartain dat Massa Will bin bit somewhere bout de head by dat goole-bug."

"And what cause have you, Jupiter, for such a supposition?"

"Claws enuff, massa, and mouff too. I nebber did see sich a d——d bug—he kick and he bite every ting what cum near him. Massa Will cotch him fuss, but had for to let him go gin mighty quick, I tell you—den was de time he must ha got de bite. I didn't like de look ob de bug mouff, myself, no how, so I wouldn't take hold ob him wid my finger, but I cotch him wid a piece ob paper dat I found. I rap him up in de paper and stuff piece ob it in he mouff—dat was de way."

"And you think, then, that your master was really bitten by the beetle, and that the bite made him sick?"

"I don't tink noffin about it—I nose it. What make him dream bout de goole so much, if taint cause he bit by de goole-bug? Ise heerd bout dem goole-bugs fore dis."

"But how do you know he dreams about gold?"

"How I know? why, cause he talk about it in he sleep—dat's how I nose."

"Well, Jup, perhaps you are right; but to what fortunate circumstances am I to attribute the honor of a visit from you to-day?"

"What de matter, massa?"

"Did you bring any message from Mr. Legrand?"

"No, massa, I bring dis here pissel"; and here Jupiter handed me a note which ran thus:

MY DEAR——: Why have I not seen you for so long a time? I hope you have not been so foolish as to take offense at any little brusquerie of mine; but no, that is improbable.

Since I saw you I have had great cause for anxiety. I have something to tell you, yet scarcely know how to tell it, or whether I should tell it at all.

I have not been quite well for some days past, and poor old Jup annoys me, almost beyond endurance, by his well-meant attentions. Would you believe it?—he had prepared a huge stick, the other day, with which to chastise me for giving him the slip, and spending the day, solus, among the hills on the mainland. I verily believe that my ill looks alone saved me a flogging.

I have made no addition to my cabinet since we met.

If you can, in any way, make it convenient, come over with Jupiter. Do come. I wish to see you tonight, upon business of importance. I assure you that it is of the highest importance.

Ever yours,
WILLIAM LEGRAND

There was something in the tone of this note which gave me great uneasiness. Its whole style differed materially from that of Legrand. What could he be dreaming of? What new crotchet possessed his excitable brain? What "business of the highest importance" could he possibly have to transact? Jupiter's account of him boded no good. I dreaded lest the continued pressure of misfortune had, at length, fairly unsettled the reason of my friend. Without a moment's hesitation, therefore, I prepared to accompany the negro.

Upon reaching the wharf, I noticed a scythe and three spades, all apparently new, lying in the bottom of the boat in which we were to embark.

"What is the meaning of all this, Jup?" I inquired.

"Him syfe, massa, and spade."

"Very true; but what are they doing here?"

"Him de syfe and de spade what Massa Will sis pon my buying for him in de town, and de debbil's own lot of money I had to gib for em."

"But what, in the name of all that is mysterious, is your 'Massa Will' going to do with scythes and spades?"

"Dat's more dan I know, and debbil take me if I don't believe 'tis more dan he know, too. But it's all cum ob de bug."

Finding that no satisfaction was to be obtained of Jupiter, whose whole intellect seemed to be absorbed by "de bug," I now stepped into the boat and made sail. With a fair and strong breeze we soon ran into the little cove to the northward of Fort Moultrie, and a walk of some two miles brought us to the hut. It was about three in the afternoon when we arrived. Legrand had been awaiting us in eager expectation. He grasped my hand with a nervous empressement, which alarmed me and strengthened the suspicions already entertained. His countenance was pale even to ghastliness, and his deep-set eyes glared with unnatural lustre. After some inquiries respecting his health, I asked him, not knowing what better to say, if he had yet obtained the scarabæus from Lieutenant G——.

"Oh, yes," he replied, coloring violently, "I got it from him the next morning. Nothing should tempt me to part with that scarabæus. Do you know that Jupiter is quite right about it?"

"In what way?" I asked, with a sad foreboding at heart.

"In supposing it to be a bug of real gold." He said this with an air of profound seriousness, and I felt inexpressibly shocked.

"This bug is to make my fortune," he continued, with a triumphant smile, "to reinstate me in my family possessions. Is it any wonder, then, that I prize it? Since Fortune has thought fit to bestow it upon me, I have only to use it properly and I shall arrive at the gold of which it is the index. Jupiter, bring me that scarabæus!"

"What! de bug, massa? I'd rudder not go fer trubble dat bug—you mus git him for your own self." Hereupon Legrand arose, with a grave and stately air, and brought me the beetle from a glass case in which it was enclosed. It was a beautiful scarabæus, and, at that time, unknown to naturalists—of course a great prize in a scientific point of view. There were two round, black spots near one extremity of the back, and a long one near the other. The scales were exceedingly hard and glossy, with all the appearance of burnished gold. The weight of the insect was very remarkable, and, taking all things into consideration, I could hardly blame Jupiter for his opinion respecting it; but what to make of Legrand's agreement with that opinion, I could not, for the life of me, tell.

"I sent for you," said he, in a grandiloquent tone, when I had completed my examination of the beetle, "I sent for you that I might have your counsel and assistance in furthering the views of Fate and of the bug—"

"My dear Legrand," I cried, interrupting him, "you are certainly unwell, and had better use some little precautions. You shall go to bed, and I will remain with you a few days, until you get over this. You are feverish and—"

"Feel my pulse," said he.

I felt it, and, to say the truth, found not the slightest indication of fever.

"But you may be ill, and yet have no fever. Allow me this once to prescribe for you. In the first place, go to bed. In the next—"

"You are mistaken," he interposed, "I am as well as I can expect to be under the excitement which I suffer. If you really wish me well, you will relieve this excitement."

"And how is this to be done?"

"Very easily. Jupiter and myself are going upon an expedition into the hills, upon the mainland, and, in this expedition, we shall need the aid of some person in whom we can confide. You are the only one we can trust. Whether we succeed or fail, the excitement which you now perceive in me will be equally allayed."

"I am anxious to oblige you in any way," I replied; "but do you mean to say that this infernal beetle has any connection with your expedition into the hills."

"It has."

"Then, Legrand, I can become a party to no such absurd proceeding."

"I am sorry—very sorry—for we shall have to try it by ourselves."

"Try it by yourselves! The man is surely mad!—but stay—how long do you propose to be absent?"

"Probably all night. We shall start immediately, and be back, at all events, by sunrise."

"And will you promise me, upon your honor, that when this freak of yours is over and the bug business (good God!) settled to your satisfaction, you will then return home and follow my advice implicitly, as that of your physician?"

"Yes; I promise; and now let us be off, for we have no time to lose."

With a heavy heart I accompanied my friend. We started about four o'clock—Legrand, Jupiter, the dog, and myself. Jupiter had with him the scythe and spades—the whole of which he insisted upon carrying, more through fear, it seemed to me, of trusting either of the implements within reach of his master, than from any excess of industry or complaisance. His demeanor was dogged in the extreme, and "dat d——d bug" were the sole words which escaped his lips during the journey. For my own part, I had charge of a couple of dark lanterns, while Legrand contented himself with the scarabæus, which he carried attached to the end of a bit of whip-cord; twirling it to and fro, with the air of a conjuror, as he went. When I observed this last, plain evidence of my friend's aberration of mind, I could scarcely refrain from tears. I thought it best, however, to humor his fancy, at least for the present, or until I could adopt some more energetic measures with a chance of success. In the meantime I endeavored, but all in vain, to sound him in regard to the object of the expedition. Having succeeded in inducing me to accompany him, he seemed unwilling to hold conversation upon any topic of minor importance, and to all my questions vouchsafed no other reply than "We shall see!"

We crossed the creek at the head of the island by means of a skiff, and, ascending the high grounds on the shore of the mainland, proceeded in a northwesterly direction, through a tract of country excessively wild and desolate, where no trace of a human footstep was to be seen. Legrand led the way with decision; pausing only for an instant, here and there, to consult what appeared to be certain landmarks of his own contrivance upon a former occasion.

In this manner we journeyed for about two hours, and the sun was just setting when we entered a region infinitely more dreary than any yet seen. It was a species of table-land, near the summit of an almost inaccessible hill, densely wooded from base to pinnacle, and interspersed with huge crags that appeared to lie loosely upon the soil, and in many cases were prevented from precipitating themselves into the valleys below merely by the support of the trees against which they reclined. Deep ravines, in various directions, gave an air of still sterner solemnity to the scene.

The natural platform to which we had clambered was thickly overgrown with brambles, through which we soon discovered that it would have been impossible to force our way but for the scythe; and Jupiter, by direction of his master, proceeded to clear for us a path to the foot of an immensely large tulip-tree, which stood, with some eight or ten oaks, upon the level, and far surpassed them all, and all other trees which I had then ever seen, in the beauty of its foliage and form, in the wide spread of its branches, and in the general majesty of its appearance. When we reached this tree, Legrand turned to Jupiter, and asked him if he thought he could climb it. The old man seemed a little staggered by the question, and for some moments made no reply. At length he approached the huge trunk, walked slowly around it, and examined it with minute attention. When he had completed his scrutiny, he merely said:

"Yes, massa, Jup climb any tree he ebber see in he life."

"Then up with you as soon as possible, for it will soon be too dark to see what we are about."

"How far mus go up, massa?" inquired Jupiter.

50

"Get up the main trunk first, and then I will tell you which way to go—and here—stop! take this beetle with you."

"De bug, Massa Will!—de goole-bug!" cried the negro, drawing back in dismay—"what for mus tote de bug way up detree?—d——n if I do!"

"If you are afraid, Jup, a great big negro like you, to take hold of a harmless little dead beetle, why, you can carry it up by this string—but, if you do not take it up with you in some way, I shall be under the necessity of breaking your head with this shovel."

"What de matter now, massa?" said Jup, evidently shamed into compliance; "always want fur to raise fuss wid old nigger. Was only funnin anyhow. Me feered de bug! what I keer for de bug?" Here he took cautiously hold of the extreme end of the string, and, maintaining the insect as far from his person as circumstances would permit, prepared to ascend the tree.

In youth, the tulip-tree, or Liriodendron Tulipifera, the most magnificent of American foresters, has a trunk peculiarly smooth, and often rises to a great height without lateral branches; but, in its riper age the bark becomes gnarled and uneven while many short limbs make their appearance on the stem. Thus the difficulty of ascension, in the present case, lay more in semblance than in reality. Embracing the huge cylinder, as closely as possible, with his arms and knees, seizing with his hands some projections, and resting his naked toes upon others, Jupiter, after one or two narrow escapes from falling, at length wriggled himself into the first great fork, and seemed to consider the whole business as virtually accomplished. The risk of the achievement was, in fact, now over, although the climber was some sixty or seventy feet from the ground.

"Which way mus go now, Massa Will?" he asked.

"Keep up the largest branch,—the one on this side," said Legrand. The negro obeyed him promptly, and apparently with but little trouble, ascending higher and higher, until no glimpse of his squat figure could be obtained through the dense foliage which enveloped it. Presently his voice was heard in a sort of halloo.

"How much fudder is got for go?"

"How high up are you?" asked Legrand.

"Ebber so fur," replied the negro; "can see de sky fru de top ob de tree."

"Never mind the sky, but attend to what I say. Look down the trunk and count the limbs below you on this side. How many limbs have you passed?"

"One, two, tree, four, fibe—I done pass fibe big limb, massa, pon dis side."

"Then go one limb higher."

In a few minutes the voice was heard again, announcing that the seventh limb was attained.

"Now, Jup," cried Legrand, evidently much excited, "I want you to work your way out upon that limb as far as you can. If you see anything strange, let me know."

By this time what little doubt I might have entertained of my poor friend's insanity was put finally at rest. I had no alternative but to conclude him stricken with lunacy, and I became seriously anxious about getting him home. While I was pondering upon what was best to be done, Jupiter's voice was again heard.

"Mos feerd for to ventur pon dis limb berry far—'t is dead limb putty much all de way."

"Did you say it was a dead limb, Jupiter?" cried Legrand in a quavering voice.

"Yes, massa, him dead as de door-nail—done up for sartain—done departed dis here life."

"What in the name of heaven shall I do?" asked Legrand, seemingly in the greatest distress.

"Do!" said I, glad of an opportunity to interpose a word, "why come home and go to bed. Come now!—that's a fine fellow. It's getting late, and, besides, you remember your promise."

"Jupiter," cried he, without heeding me in the least, "do you hear me?"

"Yes, Massa Will, hear you ebber so plain."

"Try the wood well, then, with your knife, and see if you think it very rotten."

"Him rotten, massa, sure nuff," replied the negro in a few moments, "but not so berry rotten as mought be. Mought ventur out leetle way pon de limb by myself, dat's true."

"By yourself!—what do you mean?"

"Why, I mean de bug. 'Tis berry hebby bug. Spose I drop him down fuss, and den de limb won't break wid just de weight ob one nigger."

"You infernal scoundrel!" cried Legrand, apparently much relieved, "what do you mean by telling me such nonsense as that? As sure as you let that beetle fall, I'll break your neck. Look here, Jupiter! do you hear me?"

"Yes, massa, needn't hollo at poor nigger dat style."

"Well! now listen!—if you will venture out on the limb as far as you think safe, and not let go the beetle, I'll make you a present of a silver dollar as soon as you get down."

"I'm gwine, Massa Will—deed I is," replied the negro very promptly—"most out to the eend now."

"Out to the end!" here fairly screamed Legrand, "do you say you are out to the end of that limb?"

"Soon be to de eend, massa,—o-o-o-o-oh! Lorgol-a-marcy! what is dis here pon de tree?"

"Well!" cried Legrand, highly delighted, "what is it?"

"Why, taint nuffin but a skull—somebody bin lef him head up de tree, and de crows done gobble ebery bit ob de meat off."

"A skull, you say!—very well!—how is it fastened to the limb?—what holds it on?"

"Sure nuff, massa; mus look. Why, dis berry curous sarcumstance, pon my word—dare's a great big nail in de skull, what fastens ob it on to de tree."

"Well now, Jupiter, do exactly as I tell you—do you hear?"

"Yes, massa."

"Pay attention, then!—find the left eye of the skull."

"Hum! hoo! dat's good! why, dar aint no eye lef at all."

"Curse your stupidity! do you know your right hand from your left?"

"Yes, I nose dat—nose all bout dat—'tis my lef hand what I chops de wood wid."

"To be sure! you are left-handed; and your left eye is on the same side as your left hand. Now, I suppose you can find the left eye of the skull, or the place where the left eye has been. Have you found it?"

Here was a long pause. At length the negro asked, "Is de lef eye of de skull pon de same side as de lef hand of de skull, too?—cause de skull aint got not a bit ob a hand at all—nebber mind! I got de lef eye now—here de lef eye! what must do wid it?"

"Let the beetle drop through it, as far as the string will reach—but be careful and not let go your hold of the string."

"All dat done, Massa Will; mighty easy ting for to put de bug fru de hole—look out for him dar below!"

During this colloquy no portion of Jupiter's person could be seen; but the beetle, which he had suffered to descend, was now visible at the end of the string, and glistened like a globe of burnished gold in the last rays of the setting sun, some of which still faintly illumined the eminence upon which we stood. The scarabæus hung quite clear of any branches, and, if allowed to fall, would have fallen at our feet. Legrand immediately took the scythe, and cleared with it a circular space, three or four yards in diameter, just beneath the insect, and, having accomplished this, ordered Jupiter to let go the string and come down from the tree.

Driving a peg, with great nicety, into the ground at the precise spot where the beetle fell, my friend now produced from his pocket a tape-measure. Fastening one end of this at that point of the trunk of the tree which was nearest the peg, he unrolled it till it reached the peg, and thence farther unrolled it, in the direction already established by the two points of the tree and the peg, for the distance of fifty feet—Jupiter clearing away the brambles with the scythe. At the spot thus attained a second peg was driven, and about this, as a centre, a rude circle, about four feet in diameter, described. Taking now a spade himself, and giving one to Jupiter and one to me, Legrand begged us to set about digging as quickly as possible.

To speak the truth, I had no especial relish for such amusement at any time, and, at that particular moment, would most willingly have declined it; for the night was coming on, and I felt much fatigued with the exercise already taken; but I saw no mode of escape, and was fearful of disturbing my poor friend's equanimity by a refusal. Could I have depended, indeed, upon Jupiter's aid, I would have had no hesitation in attempting to get the lunatic home by force; but I was too well assured of the old negro's disposition to hope that he would assist me, under any circumstances, in a personal contest with his master. I made no doubt that the latter had been infected with some of the innumerable Southern superstitions about money buried, and that his fantasy had received confirmation by the finding of the scarabæus, or, perhaps, by Jupiter's obstinacy in maintaining it to be "a bug of real gold." A mind disposed to lunacy would readily be led away by such suggestions, especially if chiming in with favorite preconceived ideas; and then I called to mind the poor fellow's speech about the beetle's being the "index of his fortune." Upon the whole, I was sadly vexed and puzzled, but at length I concluded to make a virtue of necessity—to dig with a good will, and thus the sooner to convince the visionary, by ocular demonstration, of the fallacy of the opinions he entertained.

The lanterns having been lit, we all fell to work with a zeal worthy a more rational cause; and, as the glare fell upon our persons and implements, I could not help thinking how picturesque a group we composed, and how strange and suspicious our labors must have appeared to any interloper who, by chance, might have stumbled upon our whereabouts.

We dug very steadily for two hours. Little was said; and our chief embarrassment lay in the yelpings of the dog, who took exceeding interest in our proceedings. He, at length, became so obstreperous that we grew fearful of his giving the alarm to some stragglers in the vicinity; or, rather, this was the apprehension of Legrand; for myself, I should have rejoiced at any interruption which might have enabled me to get the wanderer home. The noise was, at length, very effectually silenced by Jupiter, who, getting out of the hole with a dogged air of deliberation, tied the brute's mouth up with one of his suspenders, and then returned, with a grave chuckle, to his task.

When the time mentioned had expired, we had reached a depth of five feet, and yet no signs of any treasure became manifest. A general pause ensued, and I began to hope that the farce was at an end. Legrand, however, although evidently much disconcerted, wiped his brow thoughtfully and recommenced. We had excavated the entire circle of four feet diameter, and now we slightly enlarged the limit, and went to the farther depth of two feet. Still nothing appeared. The gold-seeker, whom I sincerely pitied, at length clambered from the pit, with the bitterest disappointment imprinted upon every feature, and proceeded slowly and reluctantly to put on his coat, which he had thrown off at the beginning of his labor. In the meantime I made no remark. Jupiter, at a signal from his master, began to gather up his tools. This done, and the dog having been unmuzzled, we turned in profound silence towards home.

We had taken, perhaps, a dozen steps in this direction, when, with a loud oath, Legrand strode up to Jupiter, and seized him by the collar. The astonished negro opened his eyes and mouth to the fullest extent, let fall the spades, and fell upon his knees.

"You scoundrel," said Legrand, hissing out the syllables from between his clenched teeth—"you infernal black villain!—speak, I tell you!—answer me this instant, without prevarication!—which—which is your left eye?"

"Oh, my golly, Massa Will! aint dis here my lef eye for sartain?" roared the terrified Jupiter, placing his hand upon his right organ of vision, and holding it there with a desperate pertinacity, as if in immediate dread of his master's attempt at a gouge.

"I thought so! I knew it! Hurrah!" vociferated Legrand, letting the negro go, and executing a series of curvets and caracoles, much to the astonishment of his valet, who, arising from his knees, looked mutely from his master to myself, and then from myself to his master.

"Come! we must go back," said the latter, "the game's not up yet;" and he again led the way to the tulip-tree.

"Jupiter," said he, when we reached its foot, "come here! Was the skull nailed to the limb with the face outward, or with the face to the limb?"

"De face was out, massa, so dat de crows could get at de eyes good, widout any trouble."

"Well, then, was it this eye or that through which you dropped the beetle?" here Legrand touched each of Jupiter's eyes.

""T was dis eye, Massa—de lef eye—jis as you tell me," and here it was his right eye that the negro indicated.

"That will do—we must try it again."

Here, my friend, about whose madness I now saw, or fancied that I saw, certain indications of method, removed the peg which marked the spot where the beetle fell, to a spot about three inches to the westward of its former position. Taking, now, the tape-measure from the nearest point of the trunk to the peg, as before, and continuing the extension in a straight line to the distance of fifty feet, a spot was indicated, removed, by several yards, from the point at which we had been digging.

Around the new position a circle, somewhat larger than in the former instance, was now described, and we again set to work with the spades. I was dreadfully weary, but, scarcely understanding what had occasioned the change in my thoughts, I felt no longer any great aversion from the labor imposed. I had become most unaccountably interested— nay, even excited. Perhaps there was something, amid all the extravagant demeanor of Legrand—some air of forethought, or of deliberation—which impressed me. I dug eagerly, and now and then caught myself actually looking, with something that very much resembled expectation, for the fancied treasure, the vision of which had demented my unfortunate companion. At a period when such vagaries of thought most fully possessed me, and when we had been at work perhaps an hour and a half, we were again interrupted by the violent howlings of the dog. His uneasiness, in the first instance, had been evidently but the result of playfulness or caprice, but he now assumed a bitter and serious tone. Upon Jupiter's again attempting to muzzle him, he made furious resistance, and, leaping into the hole, tore up the mould frantically with his claws. In a few seconds he had uncovered a mass of human bones, forming two complete skeletons, intermingled with several buttons of metal, and what appeared to be the dust of decayed woollen. One or two strokes of a spade upturned the blade of a large Spanish knife, and, as we dug farther, three or four loose pieces of gold and silver coin came to light.

At sight of these the joy of Jupiter could scarcely be restrained, but the countenance of his master wore an air of extreme disappointment. He urged us, however, to continue our exertions, and the words were hardly uttered when I stumbled and fell forward, having caught the toe of my boot in a large ring of iron that lay half buried in the loose earth.

We now worked in earnest, and never did I pass ten minutes of more intense excitement. During this interval we had fairly unearthed an oblong chest of wood, which, from its perfect preservation and wonderful hardness, had plainly been subjected to some mineralizing process—perhaps that of the bichloride of mercury. This box was three feet and a half long, three feet broad, and two and a half feet deep. It was firmly secured by bands of wrought iron, riveted, and forming a kind of trellis-work over the whole. On each side of the chest, near the top, were three rings of iron—six in all—by means of which a firm hold could be obtained by six persons. Our utmost united endeavors served only to disturb the coffer very slightly in its bed. We at once saw the impossibility of removing so great a weight. Luckily, the sole fastenings of the lid consisted of two sliding bolts. These we drew back—trembling and panting with anxiety. In an instant, a treasure of incalculable value lay gleaming before us. As the rays of the lanterns fell within the pit, there flashed upwards, from a confused heap of gold and of jewels, a glow and a glare that absolutely dazzled our eyes.

I shall not pretend to describe the feelings with which I gazed. Amazement was, of course, predominant. Legrand appeared exhausted with excitement, and spoke very few words. Jupiter's countenance wore, for some minutes, as deadly a pallor as it is possible, in the nature of things, for any negro's visage to assume. He seemed stupefied —thunder-stricken. Presently he fell upon his knees in the pit, and, burying his naked arms up to the elbows in gold, let them there remain, as if enjoying the luxury of a bath. At length, with a deep sigh, he exclaimed, as if in a soliloquy:

"And dis all cum ob de goole-bug! de putty goole-bug! de poor little goole-bug, what I boosed in dat sabage kind ob style! Aint you shamed ob yourself, nigger?—answer me dat!"

It became necessary, at last, that I should arouse both master and valet to the expediency of removing the treasure. It was growing late, and it behooved us to make exertion, that we might get everything housed before daylight. It was difficult to say what should be done, and much time was spent in deliberation—so confused were the ideas of all. We finally lightened the box by removing two-thirds of its contents, when we were enabled, with some trouble, to raise it from the hole. The articles taken out were deposited among the brambles, and the dog left to guard them, with strict orders from Jupiter neither, upon any pretence, to stir from the spot, nor to open his mouth until our return. We then hurriedly made for home with the chest; reaching the hut in safety, but after excessive toil, at one o'clock in the morning. Worn out as we were, it was not in human nature to do more just now. We rested until two, and had supper; starting for the hills immediately afterwards, armed with three stout sacks, which by good luck were upon the premises. A little before four we arrived at the pit, divided the remainder of the booty, as equally as might be, among us, and, leaving the holes unfilled, again set out for the hut, at which, for the second time, we deposited our golden burdens, just as the first streaks of the dawn gleamed from over the tree-tops in the east.

We were now thoroughly broken down; but the intense excitement of the time denied us repose. After an unquiet slumber of some three or four hours' duration, we arose, as if by preconcert, to make examination of our treasure.

The chest had been full to the brim, and we spent the whole day, and the greater part of the next night, in a scrutiny of its contents. There had been nothing like order or arrangement. Everything had been heaped in promiscuously. Having assorted all with care, we found ourselves possessed of even vaster wealth than we had at first supposed. In coin there was rather more than four hundred and fifty thousand dollars— estimating the value of the pieces, as accurately as we could, by the tables of the period. There was not a particle of silver. All was gold of antique date and of great variety: French, Spanish, and German money, with a few English guineas, and some counters of which we had never seen specimens before. There were several very large and heavy coins, so worn that we could make nothing of their inscriptions. There was no American money. The value of the jewels we found more difficulty in estimating. There were diamonds—some of them exceedingly large and fine—a hundred and ten in all, and not one of them small; eighteen rubies of remarkable brilliancy; three hundred and ten emeralds, all very beautiful; and twenty-one sapphires, with an opal. These stones had all been broken from their settings and thrown loose in the chest. The settings themselves, which we picked out from among the other gold, appeared to have been beaten up with hammers, as if to prevent identification. Besides all this, there was a vast quantity of solid gold ornaments: nearly two hundred massive finger and ear-rings; rich chains—thirty of these, if I remember; eighty-three very large and heavy crucifixes; five gold censers of great value; a prodigious golden punch-bowl, ornamented with richly chased vine-leaves and Bacchanalian figures; with two sword-handles exquisitely embossed, and many other smaller articles which I cannot recollect. The weight of these valuables exceeded three hundred and fifty pounds avoirdupois; and in this estimate I have not included one hundred and ninety-seven superb gold watches; three of the number being worth each five hundred dollars, if one. Many of them were very old, and as time-keepers valueless, the works having suffered more or less from corrosion; but all were richly jewelled and in cases of great worth. We estimated the entire contents of the chest, that night, at a million and a half of dollars; and, upon the subsequent disposal of the trinkets and jewels (a few being retained for our own use), it was found that we had greatly undervalued the treasure.

When, at length, we had concluded our examination, and the intense excitement of the time had in some measure subsided, Legrand, who saw that I was dying with impatience for a solution of this most extraordinary riddle, entered into a full detail of all the circumstances connected with it.

"You remember," said he, "the night when I handed you the rough sketch I had made of the scarabæus. You recollect, also, that I became quite vexed at you for insisting that my drawing resembled a death's-head. When you first made this assertion I thought you were jesting; but afterwards I called to mind the peculiar spots on the back of the insect, and admitted to myself that your remark had some little foundation in fact. Still, the sneer at my graphic powers irritated me—for I am considered a good artist—and, therefore, when you handed me the scrap of parchment, I was about to crumple it up and throw it angrily into the fire."

"The scrap of paper, you mean," said I.

"No: it had much of the appearance of paper, and at first I supposed it to be such, but when I came to draw upon it, I discovered it, at once, to be a piece of very thin parchment. It was quite dirty, you remember. Well, as I was in the very act of crumpling it up, my glance fell upon the sketch at which you had been looking, and you may imagine my astonishment when I perceived, in fact, the figure of a death's-head just where, it seemed to me, I had made the drawing of the beetle. For a moment I was too much amazed to think with accuracy. I knew that my design was very different in detail from this—although there was a certain similarity in general outline. Presently I took a candle, and, seating myself at the other end of the room, proceeded to scrutinize the parchment more closely. Upon turning it over, I saw my own sketch upon the reverse, just as I had made it. My first idea, now, was mere surprise at the really remarkable similarity of outline—at the singular coincidence involved in the fact that, unknown to me, there should have been a skull upon the other side of the parchment, immediately beneath my figure of the scarabæus, and that this skull, not only in outline, but in size, should so closely resemble my drawing. I say the singularity of this coincidence absolutely stupefied me for a time. This is the usual effect of such coincidences. The mind struggles to establish a connection—a sequence of cause and effect—and, being unable to do so, suffers a species of temporary paralysis. But, when I recovered from this stupor, there dawned upon me gradually a conviction which startled me even far more than the coincidence. I began distinctly, positively, to remember that there had been no drawing on the parchment when I made my sketch of the scarabæus. I became perfectly certain of this; for I recollected turning up first one side and then the other, in search of the cleanest spot. Had the skull been then there, of course I could not have failed to notice it. Here was indeed a mystery which I felt it impossible to explain; but, even at that early moment, there seemed to glimmer, faintly, within the most remote and secret chambers of my intellect, a glow-wormlike conception of that truth which last night's adventure brought to so magnificent a demonstration. I arose at once, and, putting the parchment securely away, dismissed all farther reflection until I should be alone.

"When you had gone, and when Jupiter was fast asleep, I betook myself to a more methodical investigation of the affair. In the first place I considered the manner in which the parchment had come into my possession. The spot where we discovered the scarabæus was on the coast of the mainland, about a mile eastward of the island, and but a short distance above high-water mark. Upon my taking hold of it, it gave me a sharp bite, which caused me to let it drop. Jupiter, with his accustomed caution, before seizing the insect, which had flown towards him, looked about him for a leaf, or something of that nature, by which to take hold of it. It was at this moment that his eyes, and mine also, fell upon the scrap of parchment, which I then supposed to be paper. It was lying half-buried in the sand, a corner sticking up. Near the spot where we found it, I observed the remnants of the hull of what appeared to have been a ship's long boat. The wreck seemed to have been there for a very great while; for the resemblance to boat timbers could scarcely be traced.

"Well, Jupiter picked up the parchment, wrapped the beetle in it, and gave it to me. Soon afterwards we turned to go home, and on the way met Lieutenant G——. I showed him the insect, and he begged me to let him take it to the fort. On my consenting, he thrust it forthwith into his waistcoat pocket, without the parchment in which it had been wrapped, and which I had continued to hold in my hand during his inspection. Perhaps he dreaded my changing my mind, and thought it best to make sure of the prize at once—you know how enthusiastic he is on all subjects connected with Natural History. At the same time, without being conscious of it, I must have deposited the parchment in my own pocket.

"You remember that when I went to the table, for the purpose of making a sketch of the beetle, I found no paper where it was usually kept. I looked in the drawer, and found none there. I searched my pockets, hoping to find an old letter, and then my hand fell upon the parchment. I thus detail the precise mode in which it came into my possession; for the circumstances impressed me with peculiar force.

"No doubt you will think me fanciful—but I had already established a kind of connection. I had put together two links of a great chain. There was a boat lying on a seacoast, and not far from the boat was a parchment—not a paper—with a skull depicted on it. You will, of course, ask 'where is the connection?' I reply that the skull, or death's-head, is the well-known emblem of the pirate. The flag of the death's-head is hoisted in all engagements.

"I have said that the scrap was parchment, and not paper. Parchment is durable—almost imperishable. Matters of little moment are rarely consigned to parchment; since, for the mere ordinary purposes of drawing or writing, it is not nearly so well adapted as paper. This reflection suggested some meaning—some relevancy—in the death's-head. I did not fail to observe, also, the form of the parchment. Although one of its corners had been, by some accident, destroyed, it could be seen that the original form was oblong. It was just such a slip, indeed, as might have been chosen for a memorandum—for a record of something to be long remembered and carefully preserved."

"But," I interposed, "you say that the skull was not upon the parchment when you made the drawing of the beetle. How then do you trace any connection between the boat and the skull—since this latter, according to your own admission, must have been designed (God only knows how or by whom) at some period subsequent to your sketching the scarabæus?"

"Ah, hereupon turns the whole mystery; although the secret, at this point, I had comparatively little difficulty in solving. My steps were sure, and could afford but a single result. I reasoned, for example, thus: When I drew the scarabæus, there was no skull apparent on the parchment. When I had completed the drawing I gave it to you, and observed you narrowly until you returned it. You, therefore, did not design the skull, and no one else was present to do it. Then it was not done by human agency. And nevertheless it was done.

"At this stage of my reflections I endeavored to remember, and did remember, with entire distinctness, every incident which occurred about the period in question. The weather was chilly (O rare and happy accident!), and a fire was blazing on the hearth. I was heated with exercise and sat near the table. You, however, had drawn a chair close to the chimney. Just as I placed the parchment in your hand, and as you were in the act of inspecting it, Wolf, the Newfoundland, entered, and leaped upon your shoulders. With your left hand you caressed him and kept him off, while your right, holding the parchment, was permitted to fall listlessly between your knees, and in close proximity to the fire. At one moment I thought the blaze had caught it, and was about to caution you, but, before I could speak, you had withdrawn it, and were engaged in its examination. When I considered all these particulars, I doubted not for a moment that heat had been the agent in bringing to light, on the parchment, the skull which I saw designed on it. You are well aware that chemical preparations exist, and have existed time out of mind, by means of which it is possible to write on either paper or vellum, so that the characters shall become visible only when subjected to the action of fire. Zaffre digested in aqua regia, and diluted with four times its weight of water, is sometimes employed; a green tint results. The regulus of cobalt, dissolved in spirit of nitre, gives a red. These colors disappear at longer or shorter intervals after the material written upon cools, but again become apparent upon the reapplication of heat.

"I now scrutinized the death's-head with care. Its outer edges—the edges of the drawing nearest the edge of the vellum—were far more distinct than the others. It was clear that the action of the caloric had been imperfect or unequal. I immediately kindled a fire, and subjected every portion of the parchment to a glowing heat. At first, the only effect was the strengthening of the faint lines in the skull; but, on persevering in the experiment, there became visible at the corner of the slip, diagonally opposite to the spot in which the death's-head was delineated, the figure of what I at first supposed to be a goat. A closer scrutiny, however, satisfied me that it was intended for a kid."

"Ha! ha!" said I, "to be sure I have no right to laugh at you—a million and a half of money is too serious a matter for mirth—but you are not about to establish a third link in your chain: you will not find any especial connection between your pirates and a goat; pirates, you know, have nothing to do with goats; they appertain to the farming interest."

"But I have just said that the figure was not that of a goat."

"Well, a kid, then—pretty much the same thing."

"Pretty much, but not altogether," said Legrand. "You may have heard of one Captain Kidd. I at once looked on the figure of the animal as a kind of punning or hieroglyphical signature. I say signature, because its position on the vellum suggested this idea. The death's-head at the corner diagonally opposite had, in the same manner, the air of a stamp, or seal. But I was sorely put out by the absence of all else—of the body to my imagined instrument—of the text for my context."

"I presume you expected to find a letter between the stamp and the signature."

"Something of that kind. The fact is, I felt irresistibly impressed with a presentiment of some vast good fortune impending. I can scarcely say why. Perhaps, after all, it was rather a desire than an actual belief;—but do you know that Jupiter's silly words, about the bug being of solid gold, had a remarkable effect on my fancy? And then the series of accidents and coincidences—these were so very extraordinary. Do you observe how mere an accident it was that these events should have occurred on the sole day of all the year in which it has been, or may be, sufficiently cool for fire, and that without the fire, or without the intervention of the dog at the precise moment in which he appeared, I should never have become aware of the death's-head, and so never the possessor of the treasure?"

"But proceed—I am all impatience."

"Well; you have heard, of course, the many stories current—the thousand vague rumors afloat about money buried, somewhere on the Atlantic coast, by Kidd and his associates. These rumors must have had some foundation in fact. And that the rumors have existed so long and so continuously, could have resulted, it appeared to me, only from the circumstance of the buried treasure still remaining entombed. Had Kidd concealed his plunder for a time, and afterwards reclaimed it, the rumors would scarcely have reached us in their present unvarying form. You will observe that the stories told are all about money-seekers, not about money-finders. Had the pirate recovered his money, there the affair would have dropped. It seemed to me that some accident—say the loss of a memorandum indicating its locality—had deprived him of the means of recovering it, and that this accident had become known to his followers, who otherwise might never have heard that treasure had been concealed at all, and who, busying themselves in vain, because unguided, attempts to regain it, had given first birth, and then universal currency, to the reports which are now so common. Have you ever heard of any important treasure being unearthed along the coast?"

"Never."

"But that Kidd's accumulations were immense is well known. I took it for granted, therefore, that the earth still held them; and you will scarcely be surprised when I tell you that I felt a hope, nearly amounting to certainty, that the parchment so strangely found involved a lost record of the place of deposit."

"But how did you proceed?"

"I held the vellum again to the fire, after increasing the heat, but nothing appeared. I now thought it possible that the coating of dirt might have something to do with the failure; so I carefully rinsed the parchment by pouring warm water over it, and, having done this, I placed it in a tin pan, with the skull downwards, and put the pan upon a furnace of lighted charcoal. In a few minutes, the pan having become thoroughly heated, I removed the slip, and, to my inexpressible joy, found it spotted, in several places, with what appeared to be figures arranged in lines. Again I placed it in the pan, and suffered it to remain another minute. Upon taking it off, the whole was just as you see it now."

Here, Legrand, having reheated the parchment, submitted it to my inspection. The following characters were rudely traced, in a red tint, between the death's-head and the goat:—

53$$+305))6*;4826)4$.)4$);806*;48+8¶60))85;;]8*;:$*8+83(88)5 *+;46(;88*96*?;8)*$(:485);5*+2:*$(;4956*2(5* 4)8¶8*;4069285);)6+8)4 $$;1($9;48081;8:8$1;48+85;4)485+528806*81($9;48;(88;4($?34;48)4$;161;:188;$?;

"But," said I, returning him the slip, "I am as much in the dark as ever. Were all the jewels of Golconda awaiting me on my solution of this enigma, I am quite sure that I should be unable to earn them."

"And yet," said Legrand, "the solution is by no means so difficult as you might be led to imagine from the first hasty inspection of the characters. These characters, as any one might readily guess, form a cipher—that is to say, they convey a meaning; but then, from what is known of Kidd, I could not suppose him capable of constructing any of the more abstruse cryptographs. I made up my mind, at once, that this was of a simple species—such, however, as would appear, to the crude intellect of the sailor, absolutely insoluble without the key."

"And you really solved it?"

"Readily; I have solved others of an abstruseness ten thousand times greater. Circumstances, and a certain bias of mind, have led me to take interest in such riddles, and it may well be doubted whether human ingenuity can construct an enigma of the kind which human ingenuity may not, by proper application, resolve. In fact, having once established connected and legible characters, I scarcely gave a thought to the mere difficulty of developing their import.

"In the present case—indeed in all cases of secret writing—the first question regards the language of the cipher; for the principles of solution, so far, especially, as the more simple ciphers are concerned, depend on, and are varied by, the genius of the particular idiom. In general, there is no alternative but experiment (directed by probabilities) of every tongue known to him who attempts the solution, until the true one be attained. But, with the cipher now before us, all difficulty is removed by the signature. The pun upon the word 'Kidd' is appreciable in no other language than the English. But for this consideration I should have begun my attempts with the Spanish and French, as the tongues in which a secret of this kind would most naturally have been written by a pirate of the Spanish Main. As it was, I assumed the cryptograph to be English.

"You observe there are no divisions between the words. Had there been divisions, the task would have been comparatively easy. In such case I should have commenced with a collation and analysis of the shorter words, and, had a word of a single letter occurred, as is most likely (a or I, for example), I should have considered the solution as assured. But, there being no division, my first step was to ascertain the predominant letters, as well as the least frequent. Counting all, I constructed a table, thus:

Of the character 8 there are 33
         ; " 26
       4 " 19
      $) " 16
       * " 13
       5 " 12
       6 " 11
     +1 " 8
       0 " 6
     92 " 5
     :3 " 4
      ? " 3
      ¶ " 2
    ]—. " 1

"Now, in English, the letter which most frequently occurs is e. Afterwards the succession runs thus: a o i d h n r s t u y c f g l m w b k p q x z. E predominates, however, so remarkably that an individual sentence of any length is rarely seen, in which it is not the prevailing character.

"Here, then, we have, in the very beginning, the groundwork for something more than a mere guess. The general use which may be made of the table is obvious—but, in this particular cipher, we shall only very partially require its aid. As our predominant character is 8, we will commence by assuming it as the e of the natural alphabet. To verify the supposition, let us observe if the 8 be seen often in couples—for e is doubled with great frequency in English—in such words, for example, as 'meet,' 'fleet,' speed,' 'seen,' 'been,' 'agree,' etc. In the present instance we see it doubled no less than five times, although the cryptograph is brief.

"Let us assume 8, then, as e. Now of all words in the language, 'the' is most usual; let us see, therefore, whether there are not repetitions of any three characters, in the same order of collocation, the last of them being 8. If we discover repetitions of such letters, so arranged, they will most probably represent the word 'the.' On inspection, we find no less than seven such arrangements, the characters being ;48. We may, therefore, assume that the semicolon represents t, that 4 represents h, and that 8 represents e—the last being now well confirmed. Thus a great step has been taken.

"But, having established a single word, we are enabled to establish a vastly important point; that is to say, several commencements and terminations of other words. Let us refer, for example, to the last instance but one, in which the combination ;48 occurs—not far from the end of the cipher. We know that the semicolon immediately ensuing is the commencement of a word, and, of the six characters succeeding this 'the,' we are cognizant of no less than five. Let us set these characters down, thus, by the letters we know them to represent, leaving a space for the unknown—

t eeth.

"Here we are enabled, at once, to discard the 'th,' as forming no portion of the word commencing with the first t; since, by experiment of the entire alphabet for a letter adapted to the vacancy, we perceive that no word can be formed of which this th can be a part. We are thus narrowed into

t ee,

and, going through the alphabet, if necessary, as before, we arrive at the word 'tree' as the sole possible reading. We thus gain another letter, r, represented by (, with the words 'the tree' in juxtaposition.

"Looking beyond these words, for a short distance, we again see the combination ;48, and employ it by way of termination to what immediately precedes. We have thus this arrangement:

the tree;4($?34 the,

or, substituting the natural letters, where known, it reads thus:

the tree thr$?3h the.

"Now, if, in place of the unknown characters, we leave blank spaces, or substitute dots, we read thus:

the tree thr...h the,

when the word 'through' makes itself evident at once. But this discovery gives us three new letters, o, u, and g, represented by $, ? and 3.

"Looking now, narrowly, through the cipher for combinations of known characters, we find, not very far from the beginning, this arrangement:

83(88, or egree,

which, plainly, is the conclusion of the word 'degree,' and gives us another letter, d, represented by +.

"Four letters beyond the word 'degree,' we perceive the combination,
;46(;88*.

"Translating the known characters, and representing the unknown by dots, as before, we read thus:

th.rtee.

an arrangement immediately suggestive of the word 'thirteen,' and again furnishing us with two new characters, i and _n_, represented by 6 and *.

"Referring, now, to the beginning of the cryptograph, we find the combination,

53$$+.

"Translating as before, we obtain

good,

which assures us that the first letter is A, and that the first two words are 'A good.'

"To avoid confusion, it is now time that we arrange our key, as far as discovered, in a tabular form. It will stand thus:

5 represents a + " d 8 " e 3 " g 4 " h 6 " i * " n $ " o (" r ; " t

"We have, therefore, no less than ten of the most important letters represented, and it will be unnecessary to proceed with the details of the solution. I have said enough to convince you that ciphers of this nature are readily soluble, and to give you some insight into the rationale of their development. But be assured that the specimen before us appertains to the very simplest species of cryptograph. It now only remains to give you the full translation of the characters upon the parchment, as unriddled. Here it is:

"'A good glass in the bishop's hostel in the devil's seat twenty one degrees and thirteen minutes northeast and by north main branch seventh limb east side shoot from the left eye of the death's-head a bee line from the tree through the shot fifty feet out.'"

"But," said I, "the enigma seems still in as bad a condition as ever. How is it possible to extort a meaning from all this jargon about 'devil's seats,' 'death's-head,' and 'bishop's hostel'?"

"I confess," replied Legrand, "that the matter still wears a serious aspect, when regarded with a casual glance. My first endeavor was to divide the sentence into the natural division intended by the cryptographist."

"You mean, to punctuate it?"

"Something of that kind."

"But how is it possible to effect this?"

"I reflected that it had been a point with the writer to run his words together without division, so as to increase the difficulty of solution. Now, a not over-acute man, in pursuing such an object, would be nearly certain to overdo the matter. When, in the course of his composition, he arrived at a break in his subject which would naturally require a pause, or a point, he would be exceedingly apt to run his characters, at this place, more than usually close together. If you will observe the MS., in the present instance, you will easily detect five such cases of unusual crowding. Acting on this hint, I made the division thus:

"'A good glass in the Bishop's hostel in the devil's seat—twenty-one degrees and thirteen minutes—northeast and by north—main branch seventh limb east side—shoot from the left eye of the death's-head—a bee-line from the tree through the shot fifty feet out.'"

"Even this division," said I, "leaves me still in the dark."

"It left me also in the dark," replied Legrand, "for a few days; during which I made diligent inquiry, in the neighborhood of Sullivan's Island, for any building which went by the name of the 'Bishop's Hotel'; for, of course, I dropped the obsolete word 'hostel.' Gaining no information on the subject, I was on the point of extending my sphere of search, and proceeding in a more systematic manner, when one morning it entered into my head, quite suddenly, that this 'Bishop's Hostel' might have some reference to an old family, of the name of Bessop, which, time out of mind, had held possession of an ancient manor-house, about four miles to the northward of the island. I accordingly went over to the plantation, and reinstituted my inquiries among the older negroes of the place. At length one of the most aged of the women said that she had heard of such a place as Bessop's Castle, and thought that she could guide me to it, but that it was not a castle, nor a tavern, but a high rock.

"I offered to pay her well for her trouble, and, after some demur, she consented to accompany me to the spot. We found it without much difficulty, when, dismissing her, I proceeded to examine the place. The 'castle' consisted of an irregular assemblage of cliffs and rocks—one of the latter being quite remarkable for its height as well as for its insulated and artificial appearance. I clambered to its apex, and then felt much at a loss as to what should be next done.

"While I was busied in reflection, my eyes fell on a narrow ledge in the eastern face of the rock, perhaps a yard below the summit upon which I stood. This ledge projected about eighteen inches, and was not more than a foot wide, while a niche in the cliff just above it gave it a rude resemblance to one of the hollow-backed chairs used by our ancestors. I made no doubt that here was the 'devil's seat' alluded to in the MS., and now I seemed to grasp the full secret of the riddle.

"The 'good glass,' I knew, could have reference to nothing but a telescope; for the word 'glass' is rarely employed in any other sense by seamen. Now here, I at once saw, was a telescope to be used, and a definite point of view, admitting no variation, from which to use it. Nor did I hesitate to believe that the phrases 'twenty-one degrees and thirteen minutes,' and 'northeast and by north,' were intended as directions for the levelling of the glass. Greatly excited by these discoveries, I hurried home, procured a telescope, and returned to the rock.

"I let myself down to the ledge, and found that it was impossible to retain a seat on it unless in one particular position. This fact confirmed my preconceived idea. I proceeded to use the glass. Of course, the 'twenty-one degrees and thirteen minutes' could allude to nothing but elevation above the visible horizon, since the horizontal direction was clearly indicated by the words, 'northeast and by north.' This latter direction I at once established by means of a pocket-compass; then, pointing the glass as nearly at an angle of twenty-one degrees of elevation as I could do it by guess, I moved it cautiously up or down, until my attention was arrested by a circular rift or opening in the foliage of a large tree that overtopped its fellows in the distance. In the centre of this rift I perceived a white spot, but could not, at first, distinguish what it was. Adjusting the focus of the telescope, I again looked, and now made it out to be a human skull.

"On this discovery I was so sanguine as to consider the enigma solved; for the phrase 'main branch, seventh limb, east side,' could refer only to the position of the skull on the tree, while 'shoot from the left eye of the death's-head' admitted, also, of but one interpretation, in regard to a search for buried treasure. I perceived that the design was to drop a bullet from the left eye of the skull, and that a bee-line, or in other words, a straight line, drawn from the nearest point of the trunk through 'the shot' (or the spot where the bullet fell), and thence extended to a distance of fifty feet, would indicate a definite point—and beneath this point I thought it at least possible that a deposit of value lay concealed."

"All this," I said, "is exceedingly clear, and, although ingenious, still simple and explicit. When you left the Bishop's Hotel, what then?"

"Why, having carefully taken the bearings of the tree, I turned homewards. The instant that I left 'the devil's seat,' however, the circular rift vanished; nor could I get a glimpse of it afterwards, turn as I would. What seems to me the chief ingenuity in this whole business, is the fact (for repeated experiment has convinced me it is a fact) that the circular opening in question is visible from no other attainable point of view than that afforded by the narrow ledge on the face of the rock.

"In this expedition to the 'Bishop's Hotel' I had been attended by Jupiter, who had no doubt observed, for some weeks past, the abstraction of my demeanor, and took especial care not to leave me alone. But on the next day, getting up very early, I contrived to give him the slip, and went into the hills in search of the tree. After much toil I found it. When I came home at night my valet proposed to give me a flogging. With the rest of the adventure I believe you are as well acquainted as myself."

"I suppose," said I, "you missed the spot, in the first attempt at digging, through Jupiter's stupidity in letting the bug fall through the right instead of through the left eye of the skull."

"Precisely. This mistake made a difference of about two inches and a half in the 'shot'—that is to say, in the position of the peg nearest the tree; and had the treasure been beneath the 'shot' the error would have been of little moment; but the 'shot,' together with the nearest point of the tree, were merely two points for the establishment of a line of direction; of course the error, however trivial in the beginning, increased as we proceeded with the line, and, by the time we had gone fifty feet, threw us quite off the scent. But for my deep-seated convictions that treasure was here somewhere actually buried, we might have had all our labor in vain."

"I presume the fancy of the skull—of letting fall a bullet through the skull's eye—was suggested to Kidd by the piratical flag. No doubt he felt a kind of poetical consistency in recovering his money through this ominous insignium."

"Perhaps so; still, I cannot help thinking that common-sense had quite as much to do with the matter as poetical consistency. To be visible from the Devil's seat, it was necessary that the object, if small, should be white; and there is nothing like your human skull for retaining and even increasing its whiteness under exposure to all vicissitudes of weather."

"But your grandiloquence, and your conduct in swinging the beetle—how excessively odd! I was sure you were mad. And why did you insist on letting fall the bug, instead of a bullet, from the skull?"

"Why, to be frank, I felt somewhat annoyed by your evident suspicions touching my sanity, and so resolved to punish you quietly, in my own way, by a little bit of sober mystification. For this reason I swung the beetle, and for this reason I let it fall from the tree. An observation of yours about its great weight suggested the latter idea."

"Yes, I perceive; and now there is only one point which puzzles me. What are we to make of the skeletons found in the hole?"

"That is a question I am no more able to answer than yourself. There seems, however, only one plausible way of accounting for them—and yet it is dreadful to believe in such atrocity as my suggestion would imply. It is clear that Kidd—if Kidd indeed secreted this treasure, which I doubt not—it is clear that he must have had assistance in the labor. But, the worst of this labor concluded, he may have thought it expedient to remove all participants in his secret. Perhaps a couple of blows with a mattock were sufficient, while his coadjutors were busy in the pit; perhaps it required a dozen—who shall tell?"

A CHRISTMAS CAROL (1843)

BY CHARLES DICKENS (1812-1870)

[Setting. In this most famous of Christmas stories Dickens gives us the very atmosphere of the season with all the contrasts that poverty and wealth, miserliness and charity, the past and the future can suggest. Though he had London in mind, any great industrial center would have served as well, for Dickens was thinking primarily of the relations between employer and employee. That Christmas is better kept in England now than when Dickens wrote is a triumph due more to "A Christmas Carol" than to any other one piece of prose or verse.

Plot. The story was planned rather than plotted. By calling it a carol and dividing it into staves, Dickens would have us think of it not as a narrative but as a song, full of the joy and good will that Christmas ought to diffuse. It is a rill from the fountain of the first great Christmas chant, "On earth peace, good will toward men." The theme is not so much the duty of service as the joy of service, the happiness that we feel in making others happy; and the four carols mark the four stages in the conversion of Scrooge from solitary selfishness to social good will. The plan is simple but it is suffused with a love and sympathy that no one but Dickens or O. Henry could have given it. If "The Gold-Bug" is a triumph of the analytic intellect, this story is a triumph of the social impulses that make the world better. "It seems to me," said Thackeray, "a national benefit, and to every man and woman who reads it a personal kindness." While writing it Dickens said: "I wept and laughed and wept again." And yet the psychology of the plot is as soundly intellectual as the style is emotional. Dickens knew that a flint-hearted man like Scrooge could not be changed by forces brought to bear from without. The appeal must come from within. He must himself see his past, his present, and his probable future, but in a new light and from a wider angle of vision. The dream is only a means to this end. A man moves to a higher realm of thought and action not by learning new truths but by seeing the old truths differently related.

Characters. Scrooge is, of course, the central character. He is also a perfect example of the changing character as contrasted with the stationary character. In fact all the other characters remain essentially the same, while Scrooge, who at the beginning is unfriendly and friendless, becomes at the end "as good a friend, as good a master, and as good a man as the good old city knew, or any other good old city, town, or borough in the good old world." It is difficult to create any kind of character, whether stationary or changing, but the latter is the more difficult. Both demand rare powers of observation and interpretation, but the ascending or descending character demands a knowledge of the chemistry of conduct that only the masters have.

The Cratchits must not be overlooked. Tiny Tim's "God bless us every one" has at least become the symbol of Christmas benevolence wherever Christmas is celebrated in English-speaking lands.]

STAVE ONE
MARLEY'S GHOST

Marley was dead, to begin with. There is no doubt whatever about that. The register of his burial was signed by the clergyman, the clerk, the undertaker, and the chief mourner. Scrooge signed it. And Scrooge's name was good upon 'Change for anything he chose to put his hand to.

Old Marley was as dead as a door-nail.

Scrooge knew he was dead? Of course he did. How could it be otherwise? Scrooge and he were partners for I don't know how many years. Scrooge was his sole executor, his sole administrator, his sole assign, his sole residuary legatee, his sole friend, his sole mourner.

Scrooge never painted out old Marley's name, however. There it yet stood, years afterwards, above the warehouse door,—Scrooge and Marley. The firm was known as Scrooge and Marley. Sometimes people new to the business called Scrooge Scrooge, and sometimes Marley. He answered to both names. It was all the same to him.

Oh! But he was a tight-fisted hand at the grindstone, was Scrooge! a squeezing, wrenching, grasping, scraping, clutching, covetous old sinner! External heat and cold had little influence on him. No warmth could warm, no cold could chill him. No wind that blew was bitterer than he, no falling snow was more intent upon its purpose, no pelting rain less open to entreaty. Foul weather didn't know where to have him. The heaviest rain and snow and hail and sleet could boast of the advantage over him in only one respect,—they often "came down" handsomely, and Scrooge never did.

Nobody ever stopped him in the street to say, with gladsome looks, "My dear Scrooge, how are you? When will you come to see me?" No beggars implored him to bestow a trifle, no children asked him what it was o'clock, no man or woman ever once in all his life inquired the way to such and such a place, of Scrooge. Even the blind men's dogs appeared to know him; and when they saw him coming on, would tug their owners into doorways and up courts; and then would wag their tails as though they said: "No eye at all is better than an evil eye, dark master!"

But what did Scrooge care! It was the very thing he liked. To edge his way along the crowded paths of life, warning all human sympathy to keep its distance, was what the knowing ones call "nuts" to Scrooge.

Once upon a time—of all the good days in the year, upon a Christmas eve—old Scrooge sat busy in his counting-house. It was cold, bleak, biting, foggy weather; and the city clocks had only just gone three, but it was quite dark already.

The door of Scrooge's counting-house was open, that he might keep his eye upon his clerk, who, in a dismal little cell beyond, a sort of tank, was copying letters. Scrooge had a very small fire, but the clerk's fire was so very much smaller that it looked like one coal. But he couldn't replenish it, for Scrooge kept the coal-box in his own room; and so surely as the clerk came in with the shovel the master predicted that it would be necessary for them to part. Wherefore the clerk put on his white comforter, and tried to warm himself at the candle; in which effort, not being a man of a strong imagination, he failed.

"A merry Christmas, uncle! God save you!" cried a cheerful voice. It was the voice of Scrooge's nephew, who came upon him so quickly that this was the first intimation Scrooge had of his approach.

"Bah!" said Scrooge; "humbug!"

"Christmas a humbug, uncle! You don't mean that, I am sure?"

"I do. Out upon merry Christmas! What's Christmas time to you but a time for paying bills without money; a time for finding yourself a year older, and not an hour richer; a time for balancing your books and having every item in 'em through a round dozen of months presented dead against you? If I had my will, every idiot who goes about with 'Merry Christmas' on his lips should be boiled with his own pudding, and buried with a stake of holly through his heart! He should!"

"Uncle!"

"Nephew, keep Christmas in your own way, and let me keep it in mine."

"Keep it! But you don't keep it."

"Let me leave it alone, then. Much good may it do you! Much good it has ever done you!"

"There are many things from which I might have derived good, by which I have not profited, I dare say, Christmas among the rest. But I am sure I have always thought of Christmas time, when it has come round,—apart from the veneration due to its sacred origin, if anything belonging to it can be apart from that,—as a good time; a kind, forgiving, charitable, pleasant time; the only time I know of, in the long calendar of the year, when men and women seem by one consent to open their shut-up hearts freely, and to think of people below them as if they really were fellow-travellers to the grave, and not another race of creatures bound on other journeys. And therefore, uncle, though it has never put a scrap of gold or silver in my pocket, I believe that it has done me good, and will do me good; and I say, God bless it!"

The clerk in the tank involuntarily applauded.

"Let me hear another sound from you" said Scrooge, "and you'll keep your Christmas by losing your situation!—You're quite a powerful speaker, sir," he added, turning to his nephew, "I wonder you don't go into Parliament."

"Don't be angry, uncle. Come! Dine with us, to-morrow."

Scrooge said that he would see him—yes, indeed he did. He went the whole length of the expression, and said that he would see him in that extremity first.

"But why?" cried Scrooge's nephew. "Why?"

"Why did you get married?"

"Because I fell in love."

"Because you fell in love!" growled Scrooge, as if that were the only one thing in the world more ridiculous than a merry Christmas. "Good afternoon!"

"Nay, uncle, but you never came to see me before that happened. Why give it as a reason for not coming now?"

"Good afternoon."

"I want nothing from you; I ask nothing of you; why cannot we be friends?"

"Good afternoon."

"I am sorry, with all my heart, to find you so resolute. We have never had any quarrel, to which I have been a party. But I have made the trial in homage to Christmas, and I'll keep my Christmas humor to the last. So, A Merry Christmas, uncle!"

"Good afternoon!"

"And A Happy New Year!"

"Good afternoon!"

His nephew left the room without an angry word, notwithstanding. The clerk, in letting Scrooge's nephew out, had let two other people in. They were portly gentlemen, pleasant to behold, and now stood, with their hats off, in Scrooge's office. They had books and papers in their hands, and bowed to him.

"Scrooge and Marley's, I believe," said one of the gentlemen, referring to his list. "Have I the pleasure of addressing Mr. Scrooge, or Mr. Marley?"

"Mr. Marley has been dead these seven years. He died seven years ago, this very night."

"At this festive season of the year, Mr. Scrooge," said the gentleman, taking up a pen, "it is more than usually desirable that we should make some slight provision for the poor and destitute, who suffer greatly at the present time. Many thousands are in want of common necessaries; hundreds of thousands are in want of common comforts, sir."

"Are there no prisons?"

"Plenty of prisons. But under the impression that they scarcely furnish Christian cheer of mind or body to the unoffending multitude, a few of us are endeavoring to raise a fund to buy the poor some meat and drink, and means of warmth. We choose this time, because it is a time of all others when Want is keenly felt and Abundance rejoices. What shall I put you down for?"

"Nothing!"

"You wish to be anonymous?"

"I wish to be left alone. Since you ask me what I wish, gentlemen, that is my answer. I don't make merry myself at Christmas, and I can't afford to make idle people merry. I help to support the prisons and the workhouses,—they cost enough,—and those who are badly off must go there."

"Many can't go there; and many would rather die."

"If they would rather die, they had better do it, and decrease the surplus population."

At length the hour of shutting up the counting-house arrived. With an ill-will Scrooge, dismounting from his stool, tacitly admitted the fact to the expectant clerk in the Tank, who instantly snuffed his candle out, and put on his hat.

"You'll want all day to-morrow, I suppose?"

"If quite convenient, sir."

"It's not convenient, and it's not fair. If I was to stop half a crown for it, you'd think yourself mightily ill-used, I'll be bound?"

"Yes, sir."

"And yet you don't think me ill-used, when I pay a day's wages for no work."

"It's only once a year, sir."

"A poor excuse for picking a man's pocket every twenty-fifth of December! But I suppose you must have the whole day. Be here all the earlier next morning."

The clerk promised that he would; and Scrooge walked out with a growl. The office was closed in a twinkling, and the clerk, with the long ends of his white comforter dangling below his waist (for he boasted no great-coat), went down a slide, at the end of a lane of boys, twenty times, in honor of its being Christmas eve, and then ran home as hard as he could pelt, to play at blind-man's-buff.

Scrooge took his melancholy dinner in his usual melancholy tavern; and having read all the newspapers, and beguiled the rest of the evening with his banker's book, went home to bed. He lived in chambers which had once belonged to his deceased partner. They were a gloomy suite of rooms, in a lowering pile of building up a yard. The building was old enough now, and dreary enough; for nobody lived in it but Scrooge, the other rooms being all let out as offices.

Now it is a fact, that there was nothing at all particular about the knocker on the door of this house, except that it was very large; also, that Scrooge had seen it, night and morning, during his whole residence in that place; also, that Scrooge had as little of what is called fancy about him as any man in the city of London. And yet Scrooge, having his key in the lock of the door, saw in the knocker, without its undergoing any intermediate process of change, not a knocker, but Marley's face.

Marley's face, with a dismal light about it, like a bad lobster in a dark cellar. It was not angry or ferocious, but it looked at Scrooge as Marley used to look,—with ghostly spectacles turned up upon its ghostly forehead.

As Scrooge looked fixedly at this phenomenon, it was a knocker again. He said, "Pooh, pooh!" and closed the door with a bang.

The sound resounded through the house like thunder. Every room above, and every cask in the wine-merchant's cellars below, appeared to have a separate peal of echoes of its own. Scrooge was not a man to be frightened by echoes. He fastened the door, and walked across the hall, and up the stairs. Slowly, too, trimming his candle as he went.

Up Scrooge went, not caring a button for its being very dark. Darkness is cheap, and Scrooge liked it. But before he shut his heavy door, he walked through his rooms to see that all was right. He had just enough recollection of the face to desire to do that.

Sitting-room, bedroom, lumber-room, all as they should be. Nobody under the table, nobody under the sofa; a small fire in the grate; spoon and basin ready; and the little saucepan of gruel (Scrooge had a cold in his head) upon the hob. Nobody under the bed; nobody in the closet; nobody in his dressing-gown, which was hanging up in a suspicious attitude against the wall. Lumber-room as usual. Old fire-guard, old shoes, two fish-baskets, washing-stand on three legs, and a poker.

Quite satisfied, he closed his door, and locked himself in; double-locked himself in, which was not his custom. Thus secured against surprise, he took off his cravat, put on his dressing-gown and slippers and his night-cap, and sat down before the very low fire to take his gruel.

As he threw his head back in the chair, his glance happened to rest upon a bell, a disused bell, that hung in the room, and communicated, for some purpose now forgotten, with a chamber in the highest story of the building. It was with great astonishment, and with a strange, inexplicable dread, that, as he looked, he saw this bell begin to swing. Soon it rang out loudly, and so did every bell in the house.

This was succeeded by a clanking noise, deep down below, as if some person were dragging a heavy chain over the casks in the wine-merchant's cellar.

Then he heard the noise much louder, on the floors below; then coming up the stairs; then coming straight towards his door.

It came on through the heavy door, and a spectre passed into the room before his eyes. And upon its coming in, the dying flame leaped up, as though it cried, "I know him! Marley's ghost!"

The same face, the very same. Marley in his pigtail, usual waistcoat, tights, and boots. His body was transparent; so that Scrooge, observing him, and looking through his waistcoat, could see the two buttons on his coat behind.

Scrooge had often heard it said that Marley had no bowels, but he had never believed it until now.

No, nor did he believe it even now. Though he looked the phantom through and through, and saw it standing before him,—though he felt the chilling influence of its death-cold eyes, and noticed the very texture of the folded kerchief bound about its head and chin,—he was still incredulous.

"How now!" said Scrooge, caustic and cold as ever. "What do you want with me?"

"Much!"—Marley's voice, no doubt about it.

"Who are you?"

"Ask me who I was."

"Who were you, then?"

"In life I was your partner, Jacob Marley."

"Can you—can you sit down?"

"I can."

"Do it, then."

Scrooge asked the question, because he didn't know whether a ghost so transparent might find himself in a condition to take a chair; and felt that, in the event of its being impossible, it might involve the necessity of an embarrassing explanation. But the ghost sat down on the opposite side of the fireplace, as if he were quite used to it.

"You don't believe in me."

"I don't."

"What evidence would you have of my reality beyond that of your senses?"

"I don't know."

"Why do you doubt your senses?"

"Because a little thing affects them. A slight disorder of the stomach makes them cheats. You may be an undigested bit of beef, a blot of mustard, a crumb of cheese, a fragment of an underdone potato. There's more of gravy than of grave about you, whatever you are!"

Scrooge was not much in the habit of cracking jokes, nor did he feel in his heart by any means waggish then. The truth is, that he tried to be smart, as a means of distracting his own attention, and keeping down his horror.

But how much greater was his horror when, the phantom taking off the bandage round its head, as if it were too warm to wear in-doors, its lower jaw dropped down upon its breast!

"Mercy! Dreadful apparition, why do you trouble me? Why do spirits walk the earth, and why do they come to me?"

"It is required of every man, that the spirit within him should walk abroad among his fellow-men, and travel far and wide; and if that spirit goes not forth in life, it is condemned to do so after death. I cannot tell you all I would. A very little more is permitted to me. I cannot rest, I cannot stay, I cannot linger anywhere. My spirit never walked beyond our counting-house,—mark me!—in life my spirit never roved beyond the narrow limits of our money-changing hole; and weary journeys lie before me!"

"Seven years dead. And travelling all the time? You travel fast?"

"On the wings of the wind."

"You might have got over a great quantity of ground in seven years."

"O blind man, blind man! not to know that ages of incessant labor by immortal creatures for this earth must pass into eternity before the good of which it is susceptible is all developed. Not to know that any Christian spirit working kindly in its little sphere, whatever it may be, will find its mortal life too short for its vast means of usefulness. Not to know that no space of regret can make amends for one life's opportunities misused! Yet I was like this man; I once was like this man!"

"But you were always a good man of business, Jacob," faltered Scrooge, who now began to apply this to himself.

"Business!" cried the ghost, wringing its hands again. "Mankind was my business. The common welfare was my business; charity, mercy, forbearance, benevolence, were all my business. The dealings of my trade were but a drop of water in the comprehensive ocean of my business."

Scrooge was very much dismayed to hear the spectre going on at this rate, and began to quake exceedingly.

"Hear me! My time is nearly gone."

"I will. But don't be hard upon me! Don't be flowery, Jacob! Pray!"

"I am here to-night to warn you that you have yet a chance and hope of escaping my fate. A chance and hope of my procuring, Ebenezer."

"You were always a good friend to me. Thank'ee!"

"You will be haunted by Three Spirits."

"Is that the chance and hope you mentioned, Jacob? I—I think I'd rather not."

"Without their visits, you cannot hope to shun the path I tread. Expect the first to-morrow night, when the bell tolls One. Expect the second on the next night at the same hour. The third, upon the next night, when the last stroke of Twelve has ceased to vibrate. Look to see me no more; and look that, for your own sake, you remember what has passed between us!"

It walked backward from him; and at every step it took, the window raised itself a little, so that, when the apparition reached it, it was wide open.

Scrooge closed the window, and examined the door by which the Ghost had entered. It was double-locked, as he had locked it with his own hands, and the bolts were undisturbed. Scrooge tried to say, "Humbug!" but stopped at the first syllable. And being, from the emotion he had undergone, or the fatigues of the day, or his glimpse of the invisible world, or the dull conversation of the Ghost, or the lateness of the hour, much in need of repose, he went straight to bed, without undressing, and fell asleep on the instant.

STAVE TWO
THE FIRST OF THE THREE SPIRITS

When Scrooge awoke, it was so dark, that, looking out of bed, he could scarcely distinguish the transparent window from the opaque walls of his chamber, until suddenly the church clock tolled a deep, dull, hollow, melancholy ONE.

Light flashed up in the room upon the instant, and the curtains of his bed were drawn aside by a strange figure,—like a child: yet not so like a child as like an old man, viewed through some supernatural medium, which gave him the appearance of having receded from the view, and being diminished to a child's proportions. Its hair, which hung about its neck and down its back, was white as if with age; and yet the face had not a wrinkle in it, and the tenderest bloom was on the skin. It held a branch of fresh green holly in its hand; and, in singular contradiction of that wintry emblem, had its dress trimmed with summer flowers. But the strangest thing about it was, that from the crown of its head there sprung a bright clear jet of light, by which all this was visible; and which was doubtless the occasion of its using, in its duller moments, a great extinguisher for a cap, which it now held under its arm.

"Are you the Spirit, sir, whose coming was foretold to me?"

"I am!"

"Who and what are you?"

"I am the Ghost of Christmas Past."

"Long past?"

"No. Your past. The things that you will see with me are shadows of the things that have been; they will have no consciousness of us."

Scrooge then made bold to inquire what business brought him there.

"Your welfare. Rise, and walk with me!"

It would have been in vain for Scrooge to plead that the weather and the hour were not adapted to pedestrian purposes; that the bed was warm, and the thermometer a long way below freezing; that he was clad but lightly in his slippers, dressing-gown, and night-cap; and that he had a cold upon him at that time. The grasp, though gentle as a woman's hand, was not to be resisted. He rose; but, finding that the Spirit made towards the window, clasped its robe in supplication.

"I am a mortal, and liable to fall."

"Bear but a touch of my hand there," said the Spirit, laying it upon his heart, "and you shall be upheld in more than this!"

As the words were spoken, they passed through the wall, and stood in the busy thoroughfares of a city. It was made plain enough by the dressing of the shops that here, too, it was Christmas time.

The Ghost stopped at a certain warehouse door, and asked Scrooge if he knew it.

"Know it! Was I apprenticed here!"

They went in. At sight of an old gentleman in a Welsh wig, sitting behind such a high desk that, if he had been two inches taller, he must have knocked his head against the ceiling, Scrooge cried in great excitement: "Why, it's old Fezziwig! Bless his heart, it's Fezziwig, alive again!"

Old Fezziwig laid down his pen, and looked up at the clock, which pointed to the hour of seven. He rubbed his hands; adjusted his capacious waistcoat; laughed all over himself, from his shoes to his organ of benevolence; and called out in a comfortable, oily, rich, fat, jovial voice, "Yo ho, there! Ebenezer! Dick!"

A living and moving picture of Scrooge's former self, a young man, came briskly in, accompanied by his fellow-'prentice.

"Dick Wilkins, to be sure!" said Scrooge to the Ghost. "My old fellow-'prentice, bless me, yes. There he is. He was very much attached to me, was Dick. Poor Dick! Dear, dear!"

"Yo ho, my boys!" said Fezziwig. "No more work to-night. Christmas eve, Dick. Christmas, Ebenezer! Let's have the shutters up, before a man can say Jack Robinson! Clear away, my lads, and let's have lots of room here!"

Clear away! There was nothing they wouldn't have cleared away, or couldn't have cleared away, with old Fezziwig looking on. It was done in a minute. Every movable was packed off, as if it were dismissed from public life forevermore; the floor was swept and watered, the lamps were trimmed, fuel was heaped upon the fire; and the warehouse was as snug and warm and dry and bright a ball-room as you would desire to see upon a winter's night.

In came a fiddler with a music-book, and went up to the lofty desk, and made an orchestra of it, and tuned like fifty stomachaches. In came Mrs. Fezziwig, one vast substantial smile. In came the three Miss Fezziwigs, beaming and lovable. In came the six young followers whose hearts they broke. In came all the young men and women employed in the business. In came the housemaid, with her cousin the baker. In came the cook, with her brother's particular friend the milkman. In they all came one after another; some shyly, some boldly, some gracefully, some awkwardly, some pushing, some pulling; in they all came, anyhow and everyhow. Away they all went, twenty couple at once; hands half round and back again the other way; down the middle and up again; round and round in various stages of affectionate grouping; old top couple always turning up in the wrong place; new top couple starting off again, as soon as they got there; all top couples at last, and not a bottom one to help them. When this result was brought about, old Fezziwig, clapping his hands to stop the dance, cried out, "Well done!" and the fiddler plunged his hot face into a pot of porter especially provided for that purpose.

There were more dances, and there were forfeits, and more dances, and there was cake, and there was negus, and there was a great piece of Cold Roast, and there was a great piece of Cold Boiled, and there were mince-pies, and plenty of beer. But the great effect of the evening came after the Roast and Boiled, when the fiddler struck up "Sir Roger de Coverley." Then old Fezziwig stood out to dance with Mrs. Fezziwig. Top couple, too; with a good stiff piece of work cut out for them; three or four and twenty pair of partners; people who were not to be trifled with; people who would dance, and had no notion of walking.

But if they had been twice as many,—four times,—old Fezziwig would have been a match for them, and so would Mrs. Fezziwig. As to her, she was worthy to be his partner in every sense of the term. A positive light appeared to issue from Fezziwig's calves. They shone in every part of the dance. You couldn't have predicted, at any given time, what would become of 'em next. And when old Fezziwig and Mrs. Fezziwig had gone all through the dance,—advance and retire, turn your partner, bow and courtesy, cockscrew, thread the needle, and back again to your place,—Fezziwig "cut,"—cut so deftly, that he appeared to wink with his legs.

When the clock struck eleven this domestic ball broke up. Mr. and Mrs. Fezziwig took their stations, one on either side the door, and, shaking hands with every person individually as he or she went out, wished him or her a Merry Christmas. When everybody had retired but the two 'prentices, they did the same to them; and thus the cheerful voices died away, and the lads were left to their beds, which were under a counter in the back shop.

"A small matter," said the Ghost, "to make these silly folks so full of gratitude. He has spent but a few pounds of your mortal money,—three or four perhaps. Is that so much that he deserves this praise?"

"It isn't that," said Scrooge, heated by the remark, and speaking unconsciously like his former, not his latter self,—"it isn't that, Spirit. He has the power to render us happy or unhappy; to make our service light or burdensome, a pleasure or a toil. Say that his power lies in words and looks; in things so slight and insignificant that it is impossible to add and count 'em up: what then? The happiness he gives is quite as great as if it cost a fortune."

He felt the Spirit's glance, and stopped.

"What is the matter?"

"Nothing particular."

"Something, I think?"

"No, no. I should like to be able to say a word or two to my clerk just now. That's all."

"My time grows short," observed the Spirit. "Quick!"

This was not addressed to Scrooge, or to any one whom he could see, but it produced an immediate effect. For again he saw himself. He was older now; a man in the prime of life.

He was not alone, but sat by the side of a fair young girl in a black dress, in whose eyes there were tears.

"It matters little," she said softly to Scrooge's former self. "To you, very little. Another idol has displaced me; and if it can comfort you in time to come, as I would have tried to do, I have no just cause to grieve."

"What Idol has displaced you?"

"A golden one. You fear the world too much. I have seen your nobler aspirations fall off one by one, until the master-passion, Gain, engrosses you. Have I not?"

"What then? Even if I have grown so much wiser, what then? I am not changed towards you. Have I ever sought release from our engagement?"

"In words, no. Never."

"In what, then?"

"In a changed nature; in an altered spirit; in another atmosphere of life; another Hope as its great end. If you were free to-day, to-morrow, yesterday, can even I believe that you would choose a dowerless girl; or, choosing her, do I not know that your repentance and regret would surely follow? I do; and I release you. With a full heart, for the love of him you once were."

"Spirit! remove me from this place."

"I told you these were shadows of the things that have been," said the

Ghost. "That they are what they are, do not blame me!"

"Remove me!" Scrooge exclaimed. "I cannot bear it! Leave me! Take me back. Haunt me no longer!"

As he struggled with the Spirit he was conscious of being exhausted, and overcome by an irresistible drowsiness; and, further, of being in his own bedroom. He had barely time to reel to bed before he sank into a heavy sleep.

STAVE THREE
THE SECOND OF THE THREE SPIRITS

Scrooge awoke in his own bedroom. There was no doubt about that. But it and his own adjoining sitting-room, into which he shuffled in his slippers, attracted by a great light there, had undergone a surprising transformation. The walls and ceiling were so hung with living green, that it looked a perfect grove. The leaves of holly, mistletoe, and ivy reflected back the light, as if so many little mirrors had been scattered there; and such a mighty blaze went roaring up the chimney, as that petrifaction of a hearth had never known in Scrooge's time, or Marley's, or for many and many a winter season gone. Heaped upon the floor, to form a kind of throne, were turkeys, geese, game, brawn, great joints of meat, sucking pigs, long wreaths of sausages, mince-pies, plum-puddings, barrels of oysters, red-hot chestnuts, cherry-cheeked apples, juicy oranges, luscious pears, immense twelfth-cakes, and great bowls of punch. In easy state upon this couch there sat a Giant glorious to see; who bore a glowing torch, in shape not unlike Plenty's horn, and who raised it high to shed its light on Scrooge, as he came peeping round the door.

"Come in,—come in! and know me better, man! I am the Ghost of Christmas

Present. Look upon me! You have never seen the like of me before!"

"Never."

"Have never walked forth with the younger members of my family; meaning (for I am very young) my elder brothers born in these later years?" pursued the Phantom.

"I don't think I have, I am afraid I have not. Have you had many brothers, Spirit?"

"More than eighteen hundred."

"A tremendous family to provide for! Spirit, conduct me where you will. I went forth last night on compulsion, and I learnt a lesson which is working now. To-night, if you have aught to teach me, let me profit by it."

"Touch my robe!"

Scrooge did as he was told, and held it fast.

The room and its contents all vanished instantly, and they stood in the city streets upon a snowy Christmas morning.

Scrooge and the Ghost passed on, invisible, straight to Scrooge's clerk's; and on the threshold of the door the Spirit smiled, and stopped to bless Bob Cratchit's dwelling with the sprinklings of his torch. Think of that! Bob had but fifteen "Bob" [7] a week himself; he pocketed on Saturdays but fifteen copies of his Christian name; and yet the Ghost of Christmas Present blessed his four-roomed house!

Then up rose Mrs. Cratchit, Cratchit's wife, dressed out but poorly in a twice-turned gown, but brave in ribbons, which are cheap and make a goodly show for sixpence; and she laid the cloth, assisted by Belinda Cratchit, second of her daughters, also brave in ribbons; while Master Peter Cratchit plunged a fork into the saucepan of potatoes, and, getting the corners of his monstrous shirt-collar (Bob's private property, conferred upon his son and heir in honor of the day) into his mouth, rejoiced to find himself so gallantly attired, and yearned to show his linen in the fashionable Parks. And now two smaller Cratchits, boy and girl, came tearing in, screaming that outside the baker's they had smelt the goose, and known it for their own; and, basking in luxurious thoughts of sage and onion, these young Cratchits danced about the table, and exalted Master Peter Cratchit to the skies, while he (not proud, although his collars nearly choked him) blew the fire, until the slow potatoes, bubbling up, knocked loudly at the saucepan-lid to be let out and peeled.

"What has ever got your precious father, then?" said Mrs. Cratchit. "And your brother Tiny Tim! And Martha warn't as late last Christmas day by half an hour!"

"Here's Martha, mother!" said a girl, appearing as she spoke.

"Here's Martha, mother!" cried the two young Cratchits. "Hurrah! There's such a goose, Martha!"

"Why, bless your heart alive, my dear, how late you are?" said Mrs. Cratchit, kissing her a dozen times, and taking off her shawl and bonnet for her.

"We'd a deal of work to finish up last night," replied the girl, "and had to clear away this morning, mother!"

"Well! Never mind so long as you are come," said Mrs. Cratchit. "Sit ye down before the fire, my dear, and have a warm, Lord bless ye!"

"No, no! There's father coming," cried the two young Cratchits, who were everywhere at once. "Hide, Martha, hide!"

So Martha hid herself, and in came little Bob, the father, with at least three feet of comforter, exclusive of the fringe, hanging down before him; and his threadbare clothes darned up and brushed, to look seasonable; and Tiny Tim upon his shoulder. Alas for Tiny Tim, he bore a little crutch, and had his limbs supported by an iron frame!

---

[7] Shillings.

"Why, where's our Martha?" cried Bob Cratchit, looking round.

"Not coming," said Mrs. Cratchit.

"Not coming!" said Bob, with a sudden declension in his high spirits; for he had been Tim's blood-horse all the way from church, and had come home rampant,—"not coming upon Christmas day!"

Martha didn't like to see him disappointed, if it were only in joke; so she came out prematurely from behind the closet door, and ran into his arms, while the two young Cratchits hustled Tiny Tim, and bore him off into the wash-house that he might hear the pudding singing in the copper.

"And how did little Tim behave?" asked Mrs. Cratchit, when she had rallied Bob on his credulity, and Bob had hugged his daughter to his heart's content.

"As good as gold," said Bob, "and better. Somehow he gets thoughtful, sitting by himself so much, and thinks the strangest things you ever heard. He told me, coming home, that he hoped the people saw him in the church, because he was a cripple, and it might be pleasant to them to remember, upon Christmas day, who made lame beggars walk and blind men see."

Bob's voice was tremulous when he told them this, and trembled more when he said that Tiny Tim was growing strong and hearty.

His active little crutch was heard upon the floor, and back came Tiny Tim before another word was spoken, escorted by his brother and sister to his stool beside the fire; and while Bob, turning up his cuffs,—as if, poor fellow, they were capable of being made more shabby, —compounded some hot mixture in a jug with gin and lemons, and stirred it round and round and put it on the hob to simmer, Master Peter and the two ubiquitous young Cratchits went to fetch the goose, with which they soon returned in high procession. **8**

Mrs. Cratchit made the gravy (ready beforehand in a little saucepan) hissing hot; Master Peter mashed the potatoes with incredible vigor; Miss Belinda sweetened up the apple-sauce; Martha dusted the hot plates; Bob took Tiny Tim beside him in a tiny corner at the table; the two young Cratchits set chairs for everybody, not forgetting themselves, and mounting guard upon their posts, crammed spoons into their mouths, lest they should shriek for goose before their turn came to be helped. At last the dishes were set on, and grace was said. It was succeeded by a breathless pause, as Mrs. Cratchit, looking slowly all along the carving-knife, prepared to plunge it in the breast; but when she did, and when the long-expected gush of stuffing issued forth, one murmur of delight arose all round the board, and even Tiny Tim, excited by the two young Cratchits, beat on the table with the handle of his knife, and feebly cried, Hurrah!

There never was such a goose. Bob said he didn't believe there ever was such a goose cooked. Its tenderness and flavor, size and cheapness, were the themes of universal admiration. Eked out by apple-sauce and mashed potatoes, it was a sufficient dinner for the whole family; indeed, as

---

[8] The goose had been cooked in the baker's oven, for economy.

Mrs. Cratchit said with great delight (surveying one small atom of a bone upon the dish), they hadn't ate it all at last! Yet every one had had enough, and the youngest Cratchits in particular were steeped in sage and onion to the eyebrows! But now, the plates being changed by Miss Belinda, Mrs. Cratchit left the room alone,—too nervous to bear witnesses,—to take the pudding up, and bring it in.

Suppose it should not be done enough! Suppose it should break in turning out! Suppose somebody should have got over the wall of the back yard, and stolen it, while they were merry with the goose,—a supposition at which the two young Cratchits became livid! All sorts of horrors were supposed.

Hallo! A great deal of steam! The pudding was out of the copper. A smell like a washing-day! That was the cloth. A smell like an eating-house and a pastry-cook's next door to each other, with a laundress's next door to that! That was the pudding! In half a minute Mrs. Cratchit entered,—flushed but smiling proudly,—with the pudding, like a speckled cannon-ball, so hard and firm, blazing in half of half a quartern of ignited brandy, and bedight with Christmas holly stuck into the top.

O, a wonderful pudding! Bob Cratchit said, and calmly, too, that he regarded it as the greatest success achieved by Mrs. Cratchit since their marriage. Mrs. Cratchit said that now the weight was off her mind, she would confess she had had her doubts about the quantity of flour. Everybody had something to say about it, but nobody said or thought it was at all a small pudding for a large family. Any Cratchit would have blushed to hint at such a thing.

At last the dinner was all done, the cloth was cleared, the hearth swept, and the fire made up. The compound in the jug being tasted and considered perfect, apples and oranges were put upon the table, and a shovelful of chestnuts on the fire.

Then all the Cratchit family drew round the hearth, in what Bob Cratchit called a circle, and at Bob Cratchit's elbow stood the family display of glass,—two tumblers, and a custard-cup without a handle.

These held the hot stuff from the jug, however, as well as golden goblets would have done; and Bob served it out with beaming looks, while the chestnuts on the fire sputtered and crackled noisily. Then Bob proposed:—

"A Merry Christmas to us all, my dears. God bless us!"

Which all the family re-echoed.

"God bless us every one!" said Tiny Tim, the last of all.

He sat very close to his father's side, upon his little stool. Bob held his withered little hand in his, as if he loved the child, and wished to keep him by his side, and dreaded that he might be taken from him.

Scrooge raised his head speedily, on hearing his own name.

"Mr. Scrooge!" said Bob; "I'll give you Mr. Scrooge, the Founder of the Feast!"

"The Founder of the Feast, indeed!" cried Mrs. Cratchit, reddening.

"I wish I had him here. I'd give him a piece of my mind to feast upon, and I hope he'd have a good appetite for it."

"My dear," said Bob, "the children! Christmas day."

"It should be Christmas day, I am sure," said she, "on which one drinks the health of such an odious, stingy, hard, unfeeling man as Mr. Scrooge. You know he is, Robert! Nobody knows it better than you do, poor fellow!"

"My dear," was Bob's mild answer, "Christmas day."

"I'll drink his health for your sake and the day's," said Mrs. Cratchit, "not for his. Long life to him. A merry Christmas and a happy New Year! He'll be very merry and very happy, I have no doubt!"

The children drank the toast after her. It was the first of their proceedings which had no heartiness in it. Tiny Tim drank it last of all, but he didn't care twopence for it. Scrooge was the Ogre of the family. The mention of his name cast a dark shadow on the party, which was not dispelled for full five minutes.

After it had passed away, they were ten times merrier than before, from the mere relief of Scrooge the Baleful being done with. Bob Cratchit told them how he had a situation in his eye for Master Peter, which would bring in, if obtained, full five and sixpence weekly. The two young Cratchits laughed tremendously at the idea of Peter's being a man of business; and Peter himself looked thoughtfully at the fire from between his collars, as if he were deliberating what particular investments he should favor when he came into the receipt of that bewildering income. Martha, who was a poor apprentice at a milliner's, then told them what kind of work she had to do, and how many hours she worked at a stretch, and how she meant to lie abed to-morrow morning for a good long rest; to-morrow being a holiday she passed at home. Also how she had seen a countess and a lord some days before, and how the lord "was much about as tall as Peter"; at which Peter pulled up his collars so high that you couldn't have seen his head if you had been there. All this time the chestnuts and the jug went round and round; and by and by they had a song, about a lost child travelling in the snow, from Tiny Tim, who had a plaintive little voice, and sang it very well indeed.

There was nothing of high mark in this. They were not a handsome family; they were not well dressed; their shoes were far from being water-proof; their clothes were scanty; and Peter might have known, and very likely did, the inside of a pawnbroker's. But they were happy, grateful, pleased with one another, and contented with the time; and when they faded, and looked happier yet in the bright sprinklings of the Spirit's torch at parting, Scrooge had his eye upon them, and especially on Tiny Tim, until the last.

It was a great surprise to Scrooge, as this scene vanished, to hear a hearty laugh. It was a much greater surprise to Scrooge to recognize it as his own nephew's, and to find himself in a bright, dry, gleaming room, with the Spirit standing smiling by his side, and looking at that same nephew.

It is a fair, even-handed, noble adjustment of things, that while there is infection in disease and sorrow, there is nothing in the world so irresistibly contagious as laughter and good-humor. When Scrooge's nephew laughed, Scrooge's niece by marriage laughed as heartily as he. And their assembled friends, being not a bit behindhand, laughed out lustily.

"He said that Christmas was a humbug, as I live!" cried Scrooge's nephew. "He believed it too!"

"More shame for him, Fred!" said Scrooge's niece, indignantly. Bless those women! they never do anything by halves. They are always in earnest.

She was very pretty, exceedingly pretty. With a dimpled, surprised-looking, capital face; a ripe little mouth that seemed made to be kissed,—as no doubt it was; all kinds of good little dots about her chin, that melted into one another when she laughed; and the sunniest pair of eyes you ever saw in any little creature's head. Altogether she was what you would have called provoking, but satisfactory, too. O, perfectly satisfactory!

"He's a comical old fellow," said Scrooge's nephew, "that's the truth; and not so pleasant as he might be. However, his offences carry their own punishment, and I have nothing to say against him. Who suffers by his ill whims? Himself, always. Here he takes it into his head to dislike us, and he won't come and dine with us. What's the consequence? He don't lose much of a dinner."

"Indeed, I think he loses a very good dinner," interrupted Scrooge's niece. Everybody else said the same, and they must be allowed to have been competent judges, because they had just had dinner; and, with the dessert upon the table, were clustered round the fire, by lamplight.

"Well, I am very glad to hear it," said Scrooge's nephew, "because I haven't any great faith in these young housekeepers. What do you say, Topper?"

Topper clearly had his eye on one of Scrooge's niece's sisters, for he answered that a bachelor was a wretched outcast, who had no right to express an opinion on the subject. Whereat Scrooge's niece's sister—the plump one with the lace tucker, not the one with the roses—blushed.

After tea they had some music. For they were a musical family, and knew what they were about, when they sung a Glee or Catch, I can assure you,—especially Topper, who could growl away in the bass like a good one, and never swell the large veins in his forehead, or get red in the face over it.

But they didn't devote the whole evening to music. After a while they played at forfeits; for it is good to be children sometimes, and never better than at Christmas, when its mighty Founder was a child himself. There was first a game at blind-man's-buff, though. And I no more believe Topper was really blinded than I believe he had eyes in his boots. Because the way in which he went after that plump sister in the lace tucker was an outrage on the credulity of human nature. Knocking down the fire-irons, tumbling over the chairs, bumping up against the piano, smothering himself among the curtains, wherever she went there went he! He always knew where the plump sister was. He wouldn't catch anybody else. If you had fallen up against him, as some of them did, and stood there, he would have made a feint of endeavoring to seize you, which would have been an affront to your understanding, and would instantly have sidled off in the direction of the plump sister.

"Here is a new game," said Scrooge. "One half-hour, Spirit, only one!"

It was a Game called Yes and No, where Scrooge's nephew had to think of something, and the rest must find out what; he only answering to their questions yes or no, as the case was. The fire of questioning to which he was exposed elicited from him that he was thinking of an animal, a live animal, rather a disagreeable animal, a savage animal, an animal that growled and grunted sometimes, and talked sometimes, and lived in London, and walked about the streets, and wasn't made a show of, and wasn't led by anybody, and didn't live in a menagerie, and was never killed in a market, and was not a horse, or an ass, or a cow, or a bull, or a tiger, or a dog, or a pig, or a cat, or a bear. At every new question put to him, this nephew burst into a fresh roar of laughter; and was so inexpressibly tickled, that he was obliged to get up off the sofa and stamp. At last the plump sister cried out,—

"I have found it out! I know what it is, Fred! I know what it is!"

"What is it?" cried Fred.

"It's your uncle Scro-o-o-o-oge!"

Which it certainly was. Admiration was the universal sentiment, though some objected that the reply to "Is it a bear?" ought to have been "Yes."

Uncle Scrooge had imperceptibly become so gay and light of heart, that he would have drunk to the unconscious company in an inaudible speech. But the whole scene passed off in the breath of the last word spoken by his nephew; and he and the Spirit were again upon their travels.

Much they saw, and far they went, and many homes they visited, but always with a happy end. The Spirit stood beside sick-beds, and they were cheerful; on foreign lands, and they were close at home; by struggling men, and they were patient in their greater hope; by poverty, and it was rich. In alms-house, hospital, and jail, in misery's every refuge, where vain man in his little brief authority had not made fast the door, and barred the Spirit out, he left his blessing, and taught Scrooge his precepts. Suddenly, as they stood together in an open place, the bell struck twelve.

Scrooge looked about him for the Ghost, and saw it no more. As the last stroke ceased to vibrate, he remembered the prediction of old Jacob Marley, and, lifting up his eyes, beheld a solemn Phantom, draped and hooded, coming like a mist along the ground towards him.

STAVE FOUR
THE LAST OF THE SPIRITS

The Phantom slowly, gravely, silently approached. When it came near him,

Scrooge bent down upon his knee; for in the air through which this Spirit moved it seemed to scatter gloom and mystery.

It was shrouded in a deep black garment, which concealed its head, its face, its form, and left nothing of it visible save one outstretched hand. He knew no more, for the Spirit neither spoke nor moved.

"I am in the presence of the Ghost of Christmas Yet To Come? Ghost of the Future! I fear you more than any spectre I have seen. But as I know your purpose is to do me good, and as I hope to live to be another man from what I was, I am prepared to bear you company, and do it with a thankful heart. Will you not speak to me?"

It gave him no reply. The hand was pointed straight before them.

"Lead on! Lead on! The night is waning fast, and it is precious time to me, I know. Lead on, Spirit!"

They scarcely seemed to enter the city; for the city rather seemed to spring up about them. But there they were in the heart of it; on 'Change, amongst the merchants.

The Spirit stopped beside one little knot of business men. Observing that the hand was pointed to them, Scrooge advanced to listen to their talk.

"No," said a great fat man with a monstrous chin, "I don't know much about it either way. I only know he he's dead."

"When did he die?" inquired another.

"Last night, I believe."

"Why, what was the matter with him? I thought he'd never die."

"God knows," said the first, with a yawn.

"What has he done with his money?" asked a red-faced gentleman.

"I haven't heard," said the man with the large chin. "Company, perhaps.

He hasn't left it to me. That's all I know. By, by!"

Scrooge was at first inclined to be surprised that the Spirit should attach importance to conversation apparently so trivial; but feeling assured that it must have some hidden purpose, he set himself to consider what it was likely to be. It could scarcely be supposed to have any bearing on the death of Jacob, his old partner, for that was Past, and this Ghost's province was the Future.

He looked about in that very place for his own image; but another man stood in his accustomed corner, and though the clock pointed to his usual time of day for being there, he saw no likeness of himself among the multitudes that poured in through the Porch. It gave him little surprise, however; for he had been revolving in his mind a change of life, and he thought and hoped he saw his new-born resolutions carried out in this.

They left this busy scene, and went into an obscure part of the town, to a low shop where iron, old rags, bottles, bones, and greasy offal were bought. A gray-haired rascal, of great age, sat smoking his pipe.

Scrooge and the Phantom came into the presence of this man, just as a woman with a heavy bundle slunk into the shop. But she had scarcely entered, when another woman, similarly laden, came in too; and she was closely followed by a man in faded black. After a short period of blank astonishment, in which the old man with the pipe had joined them, they all three burst into a laugh.

"Let the charwoman alone to be the first!" cried she who had entered first. "Let the laundress alone to be the second; and let the undertaker's man alone to be the third. Look here, old Joe, here's a chance! If we haven't all three met here without meaning it!"

"You couldn't have met in better place. You were made free of it long ago, you know; and the other two ain't strangers. What have you got to sell? What have you got to sell?"

"Half a minute's patience, Joe, and you shall see."

"What odds then! What odds, Mrs. Dilber?" said the woman. "Every person has a right to take care of themselves. He always did! Who's the worse for the loss of a few things like these? Not a dead man, I suppose."

Mrs. Dilber, whose manner was remarkable for general propitiation, said, "No, indeed, ma'am."

"If he wanted to keep 'em after he was dead, a wicked old screw, why wasn't he natural in his lifetime? If he had been, he'd have had somebody to look after him when he was struck with Death, instead of lying gasping out his last there, alone by himself."

"It's the truest word that ever was spoke; it's a judgment on him."

"I wish it was a little heavier judgment, and it should have been, you may depend upon it, if I could have laid my hands on anything else. Open that bundle, old Joe, and let me know the value of it. Speak out plain. I'm not afraid to be the first, nor afraid for them to see it."

Joe went down on his knees for the greater convenience of opening the bundle, and dragged out a large and heavy roll of some dark stuff.

"What do you call this? Bed-curtains!"

"Ah! Bed-curtains! Don't drop that oil upon the blankets, now."

"His blankets?"

"Whose else's, do you think? He isn't likely to take cold without 'em, I dare say. Ah! You may look through that shirt till your eyes ache; but you won't find a hole in it, nor a threadbare place. It is the best he had, and a fine one too. They'd have wasted it by dressing him up in it, if it hadn't been for me."

Scrooge listened to this dialogue in horror.

"Spirit! I see, I see. The case of this unhappy man might be my own. My life tends that way now. Merciful Heaven, what is this?"

The scene had changed, and now he almost touched a bare, uncurtained bed. A pale light, rising in the outer air, fell straight upon this bed; and on it, unwatched, unwept, uncared for, was the body of this plundered unknown man.

"Spirit, let me see some tenderness connected with a death, or this dark chamber, Spirit, will be forever present to me."

The Ghost conducted him to poor Bob Cratchit's house,—the dwelling he had visited before,—and found the mother and the children seated round the fire.

Quiet. Very quiet. The noisy little Cratchits were as still as statues in one corner, and sat looking up at Peter, who had a book before him. The mother and her daughters were engaged in needlework. But surely they were very quiet!

"'And he took a child, and set him in the midst of them.'"

Where had Scrooge heard those words? He had not dreamed them. The boy must have read them out, as he and the Spirit crossed the threshold. Why did he not go on?

The mother laid her work upon the table, and put her hand up to her face.

"The color hurts my eyes," she said.

The color? Ah, poor Tiny Tim!

"They're better now again. It makes them weak by candle-light; and I wouldn't show weak eyes to your father when he comes home, for the world. It must be near his time."

"Past it, rather," Peter answered, shutting up his book. "But I think he has walked a little slower than he used, these few last evenings, mother."

"I have known him walk with—I have known him walk with Tiny Tim upon his shoulder, very fast indeed."

"And so have I," cried Peter. "Often."

"And so have I," exclaimed another. So had all.

"But he was very light to carry, and his father loved him so, that it was no trouble,—no trouble. And there is your father at the door!"

She hurried out to meet him; and little Bob in his comforter—he had need of it, poor fellow—came in. His tea was ready for him on the hob, and they all tried who should help him to it most. Then the two young Cratchits got upon his knees and laid, each child, a little cheek against his face, as if they said, "Don't mind it, father. Don't be grieved!"

Bob was very cheerful with them, and spoke pleasantly to all the family. He looked at the work upon the table, and praised the industry and speed of Mrs. Cratchit and the girls. They would be done long before Sunday, he said.

"Sunday! You went to-day, then, Robert?"

"Yes, my dear," returned Bob. "I wish you could have gone. It would have done you good to see how green a place it is. But you'll see it often. I promised him that I would walk there on a Sunday. My little, little child! My little child!"

He broke down all at once. He couldn't help it. If he could have helped it, he and the child would have been farther apart, perhaps, than they were.

"Spectre," said Scrooge, "something informs me that our parting moment is at hand. I know it, but I know not how. Tell me what man that was, with the covered face, whom we saw lying dead?"

The Ghost of Christmas Yet To Come conveyed him to a dismal, wretched, ruinous churchyard.

The Spirit stood among the graves, and pointed down to One.

"Before I draw nearer to that stone to which you point, answer me one question. Are these the shadows of the things that Will be, or are they shadows of the things that May be only?"

Still the Ghost pointed downward to the grave by which it stood.

"Men's courses will foreshadow certain ends, to which, if persevered in, they must lead. But if the courses be departed from, the ends will change. Say it is thus with what you show me!"

The Spirit was immovable as ever.

Scrooge crept towards it, trembling as he went; and, following the finger, read upon the stone of the neglected grave his own name,— EBENEZER SCROOGE.

"Am I that man who lay upon the bed? No, Spirit! O no, no! Spirit! hear me! I am not the man I was. I will not be the man I must have been but for this intercourse. Why show me this, if I am past all hope? Assure me that I yet may change these shadows you have shown me by an altered life."

For the first time the kind hand faltered.

"I will honor Christmas in my heart, and try to keep it all the year. I will live in the Past, the Present, and the Future. The Spirits of all three shall strive within me. I will not shut out the lessons that they teach. O, tell me I may sponge away the writing on this stone!"

Holding up his hands in one last prayer to have his fate reversed, he saw an alteration in the Phantom's hood and dress. It shrunk, collapsed, and dwindled down into a bedpost.

Yes, and the bedpost was his own. The bed was his own, the room was his own. Best and happiest of all, the Time before him was his own, to make amends in!

He was checked in his transports by the churches ringing out the lustiest peals he had ever heard.

Running to the window, he opened it, and put out his head. No fog, no mist, no night; clear, bright, stirring, golden day!

"What's to-day?" cried Scrooge, calling downward to a boy in Sunday clothes, who perhaps had loitered in to look about him.

"Eh?"

"What's to-day, my fine fellow?"

"To-day! Why, CHRISTMAS DAY."

"It's Christmas day! I haven't missed it. Hallo, my fine fellow!"

"Hallo!"

"Do you know the Poulterer's, in the next street but one, at the corner?"

"I should hope I did."

"An intelligent boy! A remarkable boy! Do you know whether they've sold the prize Turkey that was hanging up there? Not the little prize Turkey,—the big one?"

"What, the one as big as me?"

"What a delightful boy! It's a pleasure to talk to him. Yes, my buck!"

"It's hanging there now."

"Is it? Go and buy it."

"Walk-ER!" [9] exclaimed the boy.

"No, no, I am in earnest. Go and buy it, and tell 'em to bring it here, that I may give them the direction where to take it. Come back with the man, and I'll give you a shilling. Come back with him in less than five minutes, and I'll give you half a crown!"

The boy was off like a shot.

"I'll send it to Bob Cratchit's! He sha'n't know who sends it. It's twice the size of Tiny Tim. Joe Miller never made such a joke as sending it to Bob's will be!"

The hand in which he wrote the address was not a steady one; but write it he did, somehow, and went down stairs to open the street door, ready for the coming of the poulterer's man.

It was a Turkey! He never could have stood upon his legs, that bird. He would have snapped 'em short off in a minute, like sticks of sealing-wax.

Scrooge dressed himself "all in his best," and at last got out into the streets. The people were by this time pouring forth, as he had seen them with the Ghost of Christmas Present; and, walking with his hands behind him, Scrooge regarded every one with a delighted smile. He looked so irresistibly pleasant, in a word, that three or four good-humored fellows said: "Good morning, sir! A merry Christmas to you!" and Scrooge said often afterwards, that, of all the blithe sounds he had ever heard, those were the blithest in his ears.

In the afternoon, he turned his steps towards his nephew's house.

He passed the door a dozen times, before he had the courage to go up and knock. But he made a dash, and did it.

"Is your master at home, my dear?" said Scrooge to the girl. Nice girl!

Very.

"Yes, sir."

"Where is he, my love?"

"He's in the dining-room, sir, along with mistress."

"He knows me," said Scrooge, with his hand already on the dining-room lock. "I'll go in here, my dear."

"Fred!"

---

[9] "Walker!" or "Hookey Walker!" means "What a story!"

"Why, bless my soul!" cried Fred, "who's that?"

"It's I. Your uncle Scrooge. I have come to dinner. Will you let me in, Fred?"

Let him in! It is a mercy he didn't shake his arm off. He was at home in five minutes. Nothing could be heartier. His niece looked just the same. So did Topper when he came. So did the plump sister when she came. So did every one when they came. Wonderful party, wonderful games, wonderful unanimity, won-der-ful happiness!

But he was early at the office next morning. O, he was early there! If he could only be there first, and catch Bob Cratchit coming late! That was the thing he had set his heart upon.

And he did it. The clock struck nine. No Bob. A quarter past. No Bob. Bob was full eighteen minutes and a half behind his time. Scrooge sat with his door wide open, that he might see him come into the Tank.

Bob's hat was off before he opened the door; his comforter too. He was on his stool in a jiffy; driving away with his pen, as if he were trying to overtake nine o'clock.

"Hallo!" growled Scrooge in his accustomed voice, as near as he could feign it. "What do you mean by coming here at this time of day?"

"I am very sorry, sir. I am behind my time."

"You are? Yes. I think you are. Step this way, if you please."

"It's only once a year, sir. It shall not be repeated. I was making rather merry yesterday, sir."

"Now, I'll tell you what, my friend. I am not going to stand this sort of thing any longer. And therefore," Scrooge continued, leaping from his stool, and giving Bob such a dig in the waistcoat that he staggered back into the Tank again,—"and therefore I am about to raise your salary!"

Bob trembled, and got a little nearer to the ruler.

"A merry Christmas, Bob!" said Scrooge, with an earnestness that could not be mistaken, as he clapped him on the back. "A merrier Christmas, Bob, my good fellow, than I have given you for many a year! I'll raise your salary, and endeavor to assist your struggling family, and we will discuss your affairs this very afternoon, over a Christmas bowl of smoking bishop, Bob! Make up the fires, and buy a second coal-scuttle before you dot another i, Bob Cratchit!"

Scrooge was better than his word. He did it all, and infinitely more; and to Tiny Tim, who did NOT die, he was a second father. He became as good a friend, as good a master, and as good a man as the good old city knew, or any other good old city, town, or borough in the good old world. Some people laughed to see the alteration in him; but his own heart laughed, and that was quite enough for him.

He had no further intercourse with spirits, but lived in that respect upon the total-abstinence principle ever afterward; and it was always said of him, that he knew how to keep Christmas well, if any man alive possessed the knowledge. May that be truly said of us, and all of us! And so, as Tiny Tim observed, God bless us every one!

THE GREAT STONE FACE [10] (1850)

BY NATHANIEL HAWTHORNE (1804-1864)

[Setting. The Profile Mountain, a huge "work of Nature in her mood of majestic playfulness," seems to have given the suggestion. The Profile Mountain is a part of Cannon Mountain, which is one of the White Mountains of New Hampshire. But the larger background is to be sought in the interplay of the spiritual and physical forces which Hawthorne has here staged in allegory. The mountain is the symbol of a lofty ideal that blesses those that follow its beckoning and marks the degree of failure of those that slight or ignore it.

Plot. The plan of the story is as simple and beautiful as the teaching is profound and helpful. "Mr. Hawthorne," writes Mrs. Hawthorne, "says he is rather ashamed of the mechanical structure of the story, the moral being so plain and manifest." But what is the "plain and manifest" moral that the structure of the story is designed to bring out? One interpreter says, "That the last shall be first"; another, "That success is not to be measured by human standards." The central thought seems to me to be larger than either of these and to include both. It is rather the assimilative power of a lofty ideal and is best phrased in 2 Corinthians iii, 18: "But we all, with open face beholding as in a glass the glory of the Lord, are changed into the same image from glory to glory." By setting his ideal high and by looking and longing, Ernest grew daily in spiritual stature and was saved from being the victim of the popular and passing allurements of war, money, and politics, allurements to which his neighbors succumbed because they did not live in vital communion with the Great Stone Face. The poet, it is true, felt the appeal of the Great Stone Face but only afar off, for his life did not correspond with his thought. It is one of the finest touches in the story that, though Ernest meets the double requirement of thought and act, he still hoped "that some wiser and better man than himself would by and by appear." If a man once catches up with his ideal, it ceases to be an ideal. Ernest did not think that he had attained.

Characters. Ernest, like Scrooge, is a developing character. He did not have as far to go as Scrooge and his development was differently wrought; but both passed from weakness to strength and from isolation to service, the one through the ministry of a single profound experience, the other through the constant challenge of a high ideal. The other characters fall below Ernest because they did not relate themselves as whole-heartedly to the influence of the Great Stone Face. Mr. Gathergold, type of the merely rich man, Old Blood-and-Thunder, type of the merely military

---

[10] From "The Snow Image, and Other Twice-Told Tales." Used by permission of, and by special arrangement with, Houghton Mifflin Company, publishers of Hawthorne's Works.

93

hero, Old Stony Phiz, type of the merely eloquent statesman, the easily satisfied people, type of the fickle crowd, and at last the gifted poet, type of the discord between words and works, all were natives of the same valley of opportunity. But the Great Stone Face was the measure of their defect rather than the means of their attainment because, unlike Esther and Scrooge and Ernest, they were "disobedient unto the heavenly vision."]

One afternoon, when the sun was going down, a mother and her little boy sat at the door of their cottage, talking about the Great Stone Face. They had but to lift their eyes, and there it was plainly to be seen, though miles away, with the sunshine brightening all its features.

And what was the Great Stone Face?

Embosomed amongst a family of lofty mountains, there was a valley so spacious that it contained many thousand inhabitants. Some of these good people dwelt in log huts, with the black forest all around them, on the steep and difficult hillsides. Others had their homes in comfortable farm-houses, and cultivated the rich soil on the gentle slopes or level surfaces of the valley. Others, again, were congregated into populous villages, where some wild, highland rivulet, tumbling down from its birthplace in the upper mountain region, had been caught and tamed by human cunning, and compelled to turn the machinery of cotton-factories. The inhabitants of this valley, in short, were numerous, and of many modes of life. But all of them, grown people and children, had a kind of familiarity with the Great Stone Face, although some possessed the gift of distinguishing this grand natural phenomenon more perfectly than many of their neighbors.

The Great Stone Face, then, was a work of Nature in her mood of majestic playfulness, formed on the perpendicular side, of the mountain by some immense rocks, which had been thrown together in such a position as, when viewed at a proper distance, precisely to resemble the features of the human countenance. It seemed as if an enormous giant, or a Titan, had sculptured his own likeness on the precipice. There was the broad arch of the forehead, a hundred feet in height; the nose, with its long bridge; and the vast lips, which, if they could have spoken, would have rolled their thunder accents from one end of the valley to the other. True it is, that if the spectator approached too near, he lost the outline of the gigantic visage, and could discern only a heap of ponderous and gigantic rocks, piled in chaotic ruin one upon another. Retracing his steps, however, the wondrous features would again be seen; and the farther he withdrew from them, the more like a human face, with all its original divinity intact, did they appear; until, as it grew dim in the distance, with the clouds and glorified vapor of the mountains clustering about it, the Great Stone Face seemed positively to be alive.

It was a happy lot for children to grow up to manhood or womanhood with the Great Stone Face before their eyes, for all the features were noble, and the expression was at once grand and sweet, as if it were the glow of a vast, warm heart, that embraced all mankind in its affections, and had room for more. It was an education only to look at it. According to the belief of many people, the valley owed much of its fertility to this benign aspect that was continually beaming over it, illuminating the clouds, and infusing its tenderness into the sunshine.

As we began with saying, a mother and her little boy sat at their cottage-door, gazing at the Great Stone Face, and talking about it. The child's name was Ernest.

"Mother," said he, while the Titanic visage smiled on him, "I wish that it could speak, for it looks so very kindly that its voice must needs be pleasant. If I were to see a man with such a face, I should love him dearly."

"If an old prophecy should come to pass," answered his mother, "we may see a man, some time or other, with exactly such a face as that."

"What prophecy do you mean, dear mother?" eagerly inquired Ernest. "Pray tell me all about it!"

So his mother told him a story that her own mother had told to her, when she herself was younger than little Ernest; a story, not of things that were past, but of what was yet to come; a story, nevertheless, so very old that even the Indians, who formerly inhabited this valley, had heard it from their forefathers, to whom, as they affirmed, it had been murmured by the mountain streams, and whispered by the wind among the treetops. The purport was, that, at some future day, a child should be born hereabouts, who was destined to become the greatest and noblest personage of his time, and whose countenance, in manhood, should bear an exact resemblance to the Great Stone Face. Not a few old-fashioned people, and young ones likewise, in the ardor of their hopes, still cherished an enduring faith in this old prophecy. But others, who had seen more of the world, had watched and waited till they were weary, and had beheld no man with such a face, nor any man that proved to be much greater or nobler than his neighbors, concluded it to be nothing but an idle tale. At all events, the great man of the prophecy had not yet appeared.

"O mother, dear mother!" cried Ernest, clapping his hands above his head, "I do hope that I shall live to see him?"

His mother was an affectionate and thoughtful woman, and felt that it was wisest not to discourage the generous hopes of her little boy. So she only said to him, "Perhaps you may."

And Ernest never forgot the story that his mother told him. It was always in his mind, whenever he looked upon the Great Stone Face. He spent his childhood in the log-cottage where he was born, and was dutiful to his mother, and helpful to her in many things, assisting her much with his little hands, and more with his loving heart. In this manner, from a happy yet often pensive child, he grew up to be a mild, quiet, unobtrusive boy, and sunbrowned with labor in the fields, but with more intelligence brightening his aspect than is seen in many lads who have been taught at famous schools. Yet Ernest had had no teacher, save only that the Great Stone Face became one to him. When the toil of the day was over, he would gaze at it for hours, until he began to imagine that those vast features recognized him, and gave him a smile of kindness and encouragement, responsive to his own look of veneration. We must not take upon us to affirm that this was a mistake, although the Face may have looked no more kindly at Ernest than at all the world besides. But the secret was, that the boy's tender and confiding simplicity discerned what other people could not see; and thus the love, which was meant for all, became his peculiar portion.

About this time, there went a rumor throughout the valley, that the great man, foretold from ages long ago, who was to bear a resemblance to the Great Stone Face, had appeared at last. It seems that, many years before, a young man had migrated from the valley and settled at a distant seaport, where, after getting together a little money, he had set up as a shopkeeper. His name—but I could never learn whether it was his real one, or a nickname that had grown out of his habits and success in life—was Gathergold. Being shrewd and active, and endowed by Providence with that inscrutable faculty which develops itself in what the world calls luck, he became an exceedingly rich merchant, and owner of a whole fleet of bulky-bottomed ships. All the countries of the globe appeared to join hands for the mere purpose of adding heap after heap to the mountainous accumulation of this one man's wealth. The cold regions of the north, almost within the gloom and shadow of the Arctic Circle, sent him their tribute in the shape of furs; hot Africa sifted for him the golden sands of her rivers, and gathered up the ivory tusks of her great elephants out of the forests; the East came bringing him the rich shawls, and spices, and teas, and the effulgence of diamonds, and the gleaming purity of large pearls. The ocean, not to be behindhand with the earth, yielded up her mighty whales, that Mr. Gathergold might sell their oil, and make a profit on it. Be the original commodity what it might, it was gold within his grasp. It might be said of him, as of Midas in the fable, that whatever he touched with his finger immediately glistened, and grew yellow, and was changed at once into sterling metal, or, which suited him still better, into piles of coin. And, when Mr. Gathergold had become so very rich that it would have taken him a hundred years only to count his wealth, he bethought himself of his native valley, and resolved to go back thither, and end his days where he was born. With this purpose in view, he sent a skilful architect to build him such a palace as should be fit for a man of his vast wealth to live in.

As I have said above, it had already been rumored in the valley that Mr. Gathergold had turned out to be the prophetic personage so long and vainly looked for, and that his visage was the perfect and undeniable similitude of the Great Stone Face. People were the more ready to believe that this must needs be the fact, when they beheld the splendid edifice that rose, as if by enchantment, on the site of his father's old weather-beaten farm-house. The exterior was of marble, so dazzlingly white that it seemed as though the whole structure might melt away in the sunshine, like those humbler ones which Mr. Gathergold, in his young play-days, before his fingers were gifted with the touch of transmutation, had been accustomed to build of snow. It had a richly ornamented portico, supported by tall pillars, beneath which was a lofty door, studded with silver knobs, and made of a kind of variegated wood that had been brought from beyond the sea. The windows, from the floor to the ceiling of each stately apartment, were composed, respectively, of but one enormous pane of glass, so transparently pure that it was said to be a finer medium than even the vacant atmosphere. Hardly anybody had been permitted to see the interior of this palace; but it was reported, and with good semblance of truth, to be far more gorgeous than the outside, insomuch that whatever was iron or brass in other houses was silver or gold in this; and Mr. Gathergold's bedchamber, especially, made such a glittering appearance that no ordinary man would have been able to close his eyes there. But, on the other hand, Mr. Gathergold was now so inured to wealth, that perhaps he could not have closed his eyes unless where the gleam of it was certain to find its way beneath his eyelids.

In due time, the mansion was finished; next came the upholsterers with magnificent furniture; then, a whole troop of black and white servants, the harbingers of Mr. Gathergold, who, in his own majestic person, was expected to arrive at sunset. Our friend Ernest, meanwhile, had been deeply stirred by the idea that the great man, the noble man, the man of prophecy, after so many ages of delay, was at length to be made manifest to his native valley. He knew, boy as he was, that there were a thousand ways in which Mr. Gathergold, with his vast wealth, might transform himself into an angel of beneficence, and assume a control over human affairs as wide and benignant as the smile of the Great Stone Face. Full of faith and hope, Ernest doubted not that what the people said was true, and that now he was to behold the living likeness of those wondrous features on the mountain-side. While the boy was still gazing up the valley, and fancying, as he always did, that the Great Stone Face returned his gaze and looked kindly at him, the rumbling of wheels was heard, approaching swiftly along the winding road.

"Here he comes!" cried a group of people who were assembled to witness the arrival. "Here comes the great Mr. Gathergold!"

A carriage, drawn by four horses, dashed round the turn of the road. Within it, thrust partly out of the window, appeared the physiognomy of a little old man, with a skin as yellow as if his own Midas-hand had transmuted it. He had a low forehead, small, sharp eyes, puckered about with innumerable wrinkles, and very thin lips, which he made still thinner by pressing them forcibly together.

"The very image of the Great Stone Face!" shouted the people. "Sure enough, the old prophecy is true; and here we have the great man come, at last!"

And, what greatly perplexed Ernest, they seemed actually to believe that here was the likeness which they spoke of. By the roadside there chanced to be an old beggar-woman and two little beggar-children, stragglers from some far-off region, who, as the carriage rolled onward, held out their hands and lifted up their doleful voices, most piteously beseeching charity. A yellow claw—the very same that had clawed together so much wealth—poked itself out of the coach-window, and dropt some copper coins upon the ground; so that, though the great man's name seems to have been Gathergold, he might just as suitably have been nicknamed Scattercopper. Still, nevertheless, with an earnest shout, and evidently with as much good faith as ever, the people bellowed,—

"He is the very image of the Great Stone Face!"

But Ernest turned sadly from the wrinkled shrewdness of that sordid visage, and gazed up the valley, where, amid a gathering mist, gilded by the last sunbeams, he could still distinguish those glorious features which had impressed themselves into his soul. Their aspect cheered him. What did the benign lips seem to say?

"He will come! Fear not, Ernest; the man will come!"

The years went on, and Ernest ceased to be a boy. He had grown to be a young man now. He attracted little notice from the other inhabitants of the valley; for they saw nothing remarkable in his way of life, save that, when the labor of the day was over, he still loved to go apart and gaze and meditate upon the Great Stone Face. According to their idea of the matter, it was a folly, indeed, but pardonable, inasmuch as Ernest was industrious, kind, and neighborly, and neglected no duty for the sake of indulging this idle habit. They knew not that the Great Stone Face had become a teacher to him, and that the sentiment which was expressed in it would enlarge the young man's heart, and fill it with wider and deeper sympathies than other hearts. They knew not that thence would come a better wisdom than could be learned from books, and a better life than could be moulded on the defaced example of other human lives. Neither did Ernest know that the thoughts and affections which came to him so naturally, in the fields and at the fireside, and wherever he communed with himself, were of a higher tone than those which all men shared with him. A simple soul,—simple as when his mother first taught him the old prophecy,—he beheld the marvellous features beaming adown the valley, and still wondered that their human counterpart was so long in making his appearance.

By this time poor Mr. Gathergold was dead and buried; and the oddest part of the matter was, that his wealth, which was the body and spirit of his existence, had disappeared before his death, leaving nothing of him but a living skeleton, covered over with a wrinkled, yellow skin. Since the melting away of his gold, it had been very generally conceded that there was no such striking resemblance, after all, betwixt the ignoble features of the ruined merchant and that majestic face upon the mountain-side. So the people ceased to honor him during his lifetime, and quietly consigned him to forgetfulness after his decease. Once in a while, it is true, his memory was brought up in connection with the magnificent palace which he had built, and which had long ago been turned into a hotel for the accommodation of strangers, multitudes of whom came, every summer, to visit that famous natural curiosity, the Great Stone Face. Thus, Mr. Gathergold being discredited and thrown into the shade, the man of prophecy was yet to come.

It so happened that a native-born son of the valley, many years before, had enlisted as a soldier, and, after a great deal of hard fighting, had now become an illustrious commander. Whatever he may be called in history, he was known in camps and on the battle-field under the nickname of Old Blood-and-Thunder. This war-worn veteran, being now infirm with age and wounds, and weary of the turmoil of a military life, and of the roll of the drum and the clangor of the trumpet, that had so long been ringing in his ears, had lately signified a purpose of returning to his native valley, hoping to find repose where he remembered to have left it. The inhabitants, his old neighbors and their grown-up children, were resolved to welcome the renowned warrior with a salute of cannon and a public dinner; and all the more enthusiastically, it being affirmed that now, at last, the likeness of the Great Stone Face had actually appeared. An aid-de-camp of Old Blood-and-Thunder, travelling through the valley, was said to have been struck with the resemblance. Moreover the schoolmates and early acquaintances of the general were ready to testify, on oath, that, to the best of their recollection, the aforesaid general had been exceedingly like the majestic image, even when a boy, only that the idea had never occurred to them at that period. Great, therefore, was the excitement throughout the valley; and many people, who had never once thought of glancing at the Great Stone Face for years before, now spent their time in gazing at it for the sake of knowing exactly how General Blood-and-Thunder looked.

On the day of the great festival, Ernest, with all the other people of the valley, left their work, and proceeded to the spot where the sylvan banquet was prepared. As he approached, the loud voice of the Rev. Dr. Battleblast was heard, beseeching a blessing on the good things set before them, and on the distinguished friend of peace in whose honor they were assembled. The tables were arranged in a cleared space of the woods, shut in by the surrounding trees, except where a vista opened eastward, and afforded a distant view of the Great Stone Face.

Over the general's chair, which was a relic from the home of Washington, there was an arch of verdant boughs, with the laurel profusely intermixed, and surmounted by his country's banner, beneath which he had won his victories. Our friend Ernest raised himself on his tiptoes, in hopes to get a glimpse of the celebrated guest; but there was a mighty crowd about the tables anxious to hear the toasts and speeches, and to catch any word that might fall from the general in reply; and a volunteer company, doing duty as a guard, pricked ruthlessly with their bayonets at any particularly quiet person among the throng. So Ernest, being of an unobtrusive character, was thrust quite into the background, where he could see no more of Old Blood-and-Thunder's physiognomy than if it had been still blazing on the battle-field. To console himself, he turned towards the Great Stone Face, which, like a faithful and long-remembered friend, looked back and smiled upon him through the vista of the forest. Meantime, however, he could overhear the remarks of various individuals, who were comparing the features of the hero with the face on the distant mountain-side.

"Tis the same face, to a hair!" cried one man, cutting a caper for joy.

"Wonderfully like, that's a fact!" responded another.

"Like! why, I call it Old Blood-and-Thunder himself, in a monstrous looking-glass!" cried a third. "And why not? He's the greatest man of this or any other age, beyond a doubt."

And then all three of the speakers gave a great shout, which communicated electricity to the crowd, and called forth a roar from a thousand voices, that went reverberating for miles among the mountains, until you might have supposed that the Great Stone Face had poured its thunder-breath into the cry. All these comments, and this vast enthusiasm served the more to interest our friend; nor did he think of questioning that now, at length, the mountain-visage had found its human counterpart. It is true, Ernest had imagined that this long-looked-for personage would appear in the character of a man of peace, uttering wisdom, and doing good, and making people happy. But, taking an habitual breadth of view, with all his simplicity, he contended that Providence should choose its own method of blessing mankind, and could conceive that this great end might be effected even by a warrior and a bloody sword, should inscrutable wisdom see fit to order matters so.

"The general! the general!" was now the cry. "Hush! silence! Old Blood-and-Thunder's going to make a speech."

Even so; for, the cloth being removed, the general's health had been drunk amid shouts of applause, and he now stood upon his feet to thank the company. Ernest saw him. There he was, over the shoulders of the crowd, from the two glittering epaulets and embroidered collar upward, beneath the arch of green boughs with interwined laurel, and the banner drooping as if to shade his brow! And there, too, visible in the same glance, through the vista of the forest, appeared the Great Stone Face! And was there, indeed, such a resemblance as the crowd had testified. Alas, Ernest could not recognize it! He beheld a war-worn and weather-beaten countenance, full of energy, and expressive of an iron will; but the gentle wisdom, the deep, broad, tender sympathies, were altogether wanting in Old Blood-and-Thunder's visage; and even if the Great Stone Face had assumed his look of stern command, the milder traits would still have tempered it.

"This is not the man of prophecy," sighed Ernest, to himself, as he made his way out of the throng. "And must the world wait longer yet?"

The mists had congregated about the distant mountain-side, and there were seen the grand and awful features of the Great Stone Face, awful but benignant, as if a mighty angel were sitting among the hills, and enrobing himself in a cloud-vesture of gold and purple. As he looked, Ernest could hardly believe but that a smile beamed over the whole visage, with a radiance still brightening, although without motion of the lips. It was probably the effect of the western sunshine, melting through the thinly diffused vapors that had swept between him and the object that he gazed at. But—as it always did—the aspect of his marvellous friend made Ernest as hopeful as if he had never hoped in vain.

"Fear not, Ernest," said his heart, even as if the Great Face were whispering him,—"fear not, Ernest; he will come."

More years sped swiftly and tranquilly away. Ernest still dwelt in his native valley, and was now a man of middle age. By imperceptible degrees, he had become known among the people. Now, as heretofore, he labored for his bread, and was the same simple-hearted man that he had always been. But he had thought and felt so much, he had given so many of the best hours of his life to unworldly hopes for some great good to mankind, that it seemed as though he had been talking with the angels, and had imbibed a portion of their wisdom unawares. It was visible in the calm and well-considered beneficence of his daily life, the quiet stream of which had made a wide green margin all along its course. Not a day passed by, that the world was not the better because this man, humble as he was, had lived. He never stepped aside from his own path, yet would always reach a blessing to his neighbor. Almost involuntarily, too, he had become a preacher. The pure and high simplicity of his thought, which, as one of its manifestations, took shape in the good deeds that dropped silently from his hand, flowed also forth in speech. He uttered truths that wrought upon and moulded the lives of those who heard him. His auditors, it may be, never suspected that Ernest, their own neighbor and familiar friend, was more than an ordinary man; least of all did Ernest himself suspect it; but, inevitably as the murmur of a rivulet, came thoughts out of his mouth that no other human lips had spoken.

When the people's minds had had a little time to cool, they were ready enough to acknowledge their mistake in imagining a similarity between General Blood-and-Thunder's truculent physiognomy and the benign visage on the mountain-side. But now, again, there were reports and many paragraphs in the newspapers, affirming that the likeness of the Great Stone Face had appeared upon the broad shoulders of a certain eminent statesman. He, like Mr. Gathergold and Old Blood-and-Thunder, was a native of the valley, but had left it in his early days, and taken up the trades of law and politics. Instead of the rich man's wealth and the warrior's sword, he had but a tongue, and it was mightier than both together. So wonderfully eloquent was he, that whatever he might choose to say, his auditors had no choice but to believe him; wrong looked like right, and right like wrong; for when it pleased him, he could make a kind of illuminated fog with his mere breath, and obscure the natural daylight with it. His tongue, indeed, was a magic instrument: sometimes it rumbled like the thunder; sometimes it warbled like the sweetest music. It was the blast of war,—the song of peace; and it seemed to have a heart in it, when there was no such matter. In good truth, he was a wondrous man; and when his tongue had acquired him all other imaginable success,—when it had been heard in halls of state, and in the courts of princes and potentates,—after it had made him known all over the world, even as a voice crying from shore to shore,—it finally persuaded his countrymen to select him for the Presidency. Before this time,—indeed, as soon as he began to grow celebrated,—his admirers had found out the resemblance between him and the Great Stone Face; and so much were they struck by it, that throughout the country this distinguished gentleman was known by the name of Old Stony Phiz. The phrase was considered as giving a highly favorable aspect to his political prospects; for, as is likewise the case with the Popedom, nobody ever becomes President without taking a name other than his own.

While his friends were doing their best to make him President, Old Stony Phiz, as he was called, set out on a visit to the valley where he was born. Of course, he had no other object than to shake hands with his fellow-citizens, and neither thought nor cared about any effect which his progress through the country might have upon the election. Magnificent preparations were made to receive the illustrious statesman; a cavalcade of horsemen set forth to meet him at the boundary line of the State, and all the people left their business and gathered along the wayside to see him pass. Among these was Ernest. Though more than once disappointed, as we have seen, he had such a hopeful and confiding nature, that he was always ready to believe in whatever seemed beautiful and good. He kept his heart continually open, and thus was sure to catch the blessing from on high, when it should come. So now again, as buoyantly as ever, he went forth to behold the likeness of the Great Stone Face.

The cavalcade came prancing along the road, with a great clattering of hoofs and a mighty cloud of dust, which rose up so dense and high that the visage of the mountain-side was completely hidden from Ernest's eyes. All the great men of the neighborhood were there on horseback: militia officers, in uniform; the member of Congress; the sheriff of the county; the editors of newspapers; and many a farmer, too, had mounted his patient steed, with his Sunday coat upon his back. It really was a very brilliant spectacle, especially as there were numerous banners flaunting over the cavalcade, on some of which were gorgeous portraits of the illustrious statesman and the Great Stone Face, smiling familiarly at one another, like two brothers. If the pictures were to be trusted, the mutual resemblance, it must be confessed, was marvellous. We must not forget to mention that there was a band of music, which made the echoes of the mountains ring and reverberate with the loud triumph of its strains; so that airy and soul-thrilling melodies broke out among all the heights and hollows, as if every nook of his native valley had found a voice, to welcome the distinguished guest. But the grandest effect was when the far-off mountain precipice flung back the music; for then the Great Stone Face itself seemed to be swelling the triumphant chorus, in acknowledgment that, at length, the man of prophecy was come.

All this while the people were throwing up their hats and shouting, with enthusiasm so contagious that the heart of Ernest kindled up, and he likewise threw up his hat, and shouted, as loudly as the loudest, "Huzza for the great man! Huzza, for Old Stony Phiz!" But as yet he had not seen him.

"Here he is, now!" cried those who stood near Ernest. "There! There! Look at Old Stony Phiz and then at the Old Man of the Mountain, and see if they are not as like as two twin-brothers!"

102

In the midst of all this gallant array, came an open barouche, drawn by four white horses; and in the barouche, with his massive head uncovered, sat the illustrious statesman, Old Stony Phiz himself.

"Confess it," said one of Ernest's neighbors to him; "the Great Stone Face has met its match at last!"

Now, it must be owned that, at his first glimpse of the countenance which was bowing and smiling from the barouche, Ernest did fancy that there was a resemblance between it and the old familiar face upon the mountain-side. The brow, with its massive depths and loftiness, and all the other features, indeed, were boldly and strongly hewn, as if in emulation of a more than heroic, of a Titanic model. But the sublimity and stateliness, the grand expression of a divine sympathy, that illuminated the mountain visage, and etherealized its ponderous granite substance into spirit, might here be sought in vain. Something had been originally left out, or had departed. And therefore the marvellously gifted statesman had always a weary gloom in the deep caverns of his eyes, as of a child that has outgrown its playthings, or a man of mighty faculties and little aims, whose life, with all its high performances, was vague and empty, because no high purpose had endowed it with reality.

Still, Ernest's neighbor was thrusting his elbow into his side, and pressing him for an answer.

"Confess! confess! Is not he the very picture of your Old Man of the Mountain?"

"No!" said Ernest, bluntly, "I see little or no likeness."

"Then so much the worse for the Great Stone Face!" answered his neighbor; and again he set up a shout for Old Stony Phiz.

But Ernest turned away, melancholy, and almost despondent; for this was the saddest of his disappointments, to behold a man who might have fulfilled the prophecy, and had not willed to do so. Meantime, the cavalcade, the banners, the music, and the barouches swept past him, with the vociferous crowd in the rear, leaving the dust to settle down, and the Great Stone Face to be revealed again, with the grandeur that it had worn for untold centuries.

"Lo, here I am, Ernest!" the benign lips seemed to say. "I have waited longer than thou, and am not yet weary. Fear not; the man will come."

The years hurried onward, treading in their haste on one another's heels. And now they began to bring white hairs, and scatter them over the head of Ernest; they made reverend wrinkles across his forehead, and furrows in his cheeks. He was an aged man. But not in vain had he grown old; more than the white hairs on his head were the sage thoughts in his mind; his wrinkles and furrows were inscriptions that Time had graved, and in which he had written legends of wisdom that had been tested by the tenor of a life. And Ernest had ceased to be obscure. Unsought for, undesired, had come the fame which so many seek, and made him known in the great world, beyond the limits of the valley in which he had dwelt so quietly. College professors, and even the active men of cities, came from far

103

to see and converse with Ernest; for the report had gone abroad that this simple husbandman had ideas unlike those of other men, not gained from books, but of a higher tone,—a tranquil and familiar majesty, as if he had been talking with the angels as his daily friends. Whether it were sage, statesman, or philanthropist, Ernest received these visitors with the gentle sincerity that had characterized him from boyhood, and spoke freely with them of whatever came uppermost, or lay deepest in his heart or their own. While they talked together, his face would kindle, unawares, and shine upon them, as with a mild evening light. Pensive with the fulness of such discourse, his guests took leave and went their way; and passing up the valley, paused to look at the Great Stone Face, imagining that they had seen its likeness in a human countenance, but could not remember where.

While Ernest had been growing up and growing old, a bountiful Providence had granted a new poet to this earth. He, likewise, was a native of the valley, but had spent the greater part of his life at a distance from that romantic region, pouring out his sweet music amid the bustle and din of cities. Often, however, did the mountains which had been familiar to him in his childhood lift their snowy peaks into the clear atmosphere of his poetry. Neither was the Great Stone Face forgotten, for the poet had celebrated it in an ode, which was grand enough to have been uttered by its own majestic lips. This man of genius, we may say, had come down from heaven with wonderful endowments. If he sang of a mountain, the eyes of all mankind beheld a mightier grandeur reposing on its breast, or soaring to its summit, than had before been seen there. If his theme were a lovely lake, a celestial smile had now been thrown over it, to gleam forever on its surface. If it were the vast old sea, even the deep immensity of its dread bosom seemed to swell the higher, as if moved by the emotions of the song. Thus the world assumed another and a better aspect from the hour that the poet blessed it with his happy eyes. The Creator had bestowed him, as the last best touch to his own handiwork. Creation was not finished till the poet came to interpret, and so complete it.

The effect was no less high and beautiful, when his human brethren were the subject of his verse. The man or woman, sordid with the common dust of life, who crossed his daily path, and the little child who played in it, were glorified if he beheld them in his mood of poetic faith. He showed the golden links of the great chain that intertwined them with an angelic kindred; he brought out the hidden traits of a celestial birth that made them worthy of such kin. Some, indeed, there were, who thought to show the soundness of their judgment by affirming that all the beauty and dignity of the natural world existed only in the poet's fancy. Let such men speak for themselves, who undoubtedly appear to have been spawned forth by Nature with a contemptuous bitterness; she having plastered them up out of her refuse stuff, after all the swine were made. As respects all things else, the poet's ideal was the truest truth.

The songs of this poet found their way to Ernest. He read them after his customary toil, seated on the bench before his cottage-door, where for such a length of time he had filled his repose with thought, by gazing at the

Great Stone Face. And now as he read stanzas that caused the soul to thrill within him, he lifted his eyes to the vast countenance beaming on him so benignantly.

"O majestic friend," he murmured, addressing the Great Stone Face, "is not this man worthy to resemble thee?"

The Face seemed to smile, but answered not a word.

Now it happened that the poet, though he dwelt so far away, had not only heard of Ernest, but had meditated much upon his character, until he deemed nothing so desirable as to meet this man, whose untaught wisdom walked hand in hand with the noble simplicity of his life. One summer morning, therefore, he took passage by the railroad, and, in the decline of the afternoon, alighted from the cars at no great distance from Ernest's cottage. The great hotel, which had formerly been the palace of Mr. Gathergold, was close at hand, but the poet, with his carpet-bag on his arm, inquired at once where Ernest dwelt, and was resolved to be accepted as his guest.

Approaching the door, he there found the good old man, holding a volume in his hand, which alternately he read, and then, with a finger between the leaves, looked lovingly at the Great Stone Face.

"Good evening," said the poet. "Can you give a traveller a night's lodging?"

"Willingly," answered Ernest; and then he added, smiling, "Methinks I never saw the Great Stone Face look so hospitably at a stranger."

The poet sat down on the bench beside him, and he and Ernest talked together. Often had the poet held intercourse with the wittiest and the wisest, but never before with a man like Ernest, whose thoughts and feelings gushed up with such a natural freedom, and who made great truths so familiar by his simple utterance of them. Angels, as had been so often said, seemed to have wrought with him at his labor in the fields; angels seemed to have sat with him by the fireside; and, dwelling with angels as friend with friends, he had imbibed the sublimity of their ideas, and imbued it with the sweet and lowly charm of household words. So thought the poet. And Ernest, on the other hand, was moved and agitated by the living images which the poet flung out of his mind, and which peopled all the air about the cottage-door with shapes of beauty, both gay and pensive. The sympathies of these two men instructed them with a profounder sense than either could have attained alone. Their minds accorded into one strain, and made delightful music which neither of them could have claimed as all his own, nor distinguished his own share from the other's. They led one another, as it were, into a high pavilion of their thoughts, so remote, and hitherto so dim, that they had never entered it before, and so beautiful that they desired to be there always.

As Ernest listened to the poet, he imagined that the Great Stone Face was bending forward to listen too. He gazed earnestly into the poet's glowing eyes.

"Who are you, my strangely gifted guest?" he said.

The poet laid his finger on the volume that Ernest had been reading.

"You have read these poems," said he. "You know me, then,—for I wrote them."

Again, and still more earnestly than before, Ernest examined the poet's features; then turned towards the Great Stone Face; then back, with an uncertain aspect, to his guest. But his countenance fell; he shook his head, and sighed.

"Wherefore are you sad?" inquired the poet.

"Because," replied Ernest, "all through life I have awaited the fulfilment of a prophecy; and, when I read these poems, I hoped that it might be fulfilled in you."

"You hoped," answered the poet, faintly smiling, "to find in me the likeness of the Great Stone Face. And you are disappointed, as formerly with Mr. Gathergold, and Old Blood-and-Thunder, and Old Stony Phiz. Yes, Ernest, it is my doom. You must add my name to the illustrious three, and record another failure of your hopes. For—in shame and sadness do I speak it, Ernest—I am not worthy to be typified by yonder benign and majestic image."

"And why?" asked Ernest. He pointed to the volume. "Are not those thoughts divine?"

"They have a strain of the Divinity," replied the poet. "You can hear in them the far-off echo of a heavenly song. But my life, dear Ernest, has not corresponded with my thought. I have had grand dreams, but they have been only dreams, because I have lived—and that, too, by my own choice—among poor and mean realities. Sometimes even—shall I dare to say it?—I lack faith in the grandeur, the beauty, and the goodness, which my own works are said to have made more evident in nature and in human life. Why, then, pure seeker of the good and true, shouldst thou hope to find me, in yonder image of the divine?"

The poet spoke sadly, and his eyes were dim with tears. So, likewise, were those of Ernest.

At the hour of sunset, as had long been his frequent custom, Ernest was to discourse to an assemblage of the neighboring inhabitants in the open air. He and the poet, arm in arm, still talking together as they went along, proceeded to the spot. It was a small nook among the hills, with a gray precipice behind, the stern front of which was relieved by the pleasant foliage of many creeping plants, that made a tapestry for the naked rock, by hanging their festoons from all its rugged angles. At a small elevation above the ground, set in a rich framework of verdure, there appeared a niche, spacious enough to admit a human figure, with freedom for such gestures as spontaneously accompany earnest thought and genuine emotion. Into this natural pulpit Ernest ascended, and threw a look of familiar kindness around upon his audience. They stood, or sat, or reclined upon the grass, as seemed good to each, with the departing sunshine falling obliquely over them, and mingling its subdued cheerfulness with the solemnity of a grove of ancient trees, beneath and amid the boughs of which the golden rays were constrained to pass. In another direction was seen the Great Stone Face, with the same cheer, combined with the same solemnity, in its benignant aspect.

Ernest began to speak, giving to the people of what was in his heart and mind. His words had power, because they accorded with his thoughts; and his thoughts had reality and depth, because they harmonized with the life which he had always lived. It was not mere breath that this preacher uttered; they were the words of life, because a life of good deeds and holy love was melted into them. Pearls, pure and rich, had been dissolved into this precious draught. The poet, as he listened, felt that the being and character of Ernest were a nobler strain of poetry than he had ever written. His eyes glistening with tears, he gazed reverentially at the venerable man, and said within himself that never was there an aspect so worthy of a prophet and a sage as that mild, sweet, thoughtful countenance, with the glory of white hair diffused about it. At a distance, but distinctly to be seen, high up in the golden light of the setting sun, appeared the Great Stone Face, with hoary mists around it, like the white hairs around the brow of Ernest. Its look of grand beneficence seemed to embrace the world.

At that moment, in sympathy with a thought which he was about to utter, the face of Ernest assumed a grandeur of expression, so imbued with benevolence, that the poet, by an irresistible impulse, threw his arms aloft, and shouted,—

"Behold! Behold! Ernest is himself the likeness of the Great Stone Face!"

Then all the people looked, and saw that what the deep-sighted poet said was true. The prophecy was fulfilled. But Ernest, having finished what he had to say, took the poet's arm, and walked slowly homeward, still hoping that some wiser and better man than himself would by and by appear, bearing a resemblance to the GREAT STONE FACE.

RAB AND HIS FRIENDS (1858) [11]

BY DR. JOHN BROWN (1810-1882)

[Setting. Dr. Brown was once driving with a friend through a crowded section of Edinburgh when he stopped in the middle of a sentence, seeming to be surprised at something behind the carriage. "Is it some one you know?" the friend asked. "No," was the reply, "it's a dog I don't know." Needless to say that "Rab and his Friends" is an Edinburgh story. The time is about 1824-1830. In the Scotch dialect "weel a weel" means "all right"; "till" means "to"; "I'se" means "I shall"; "he's" means "he shall"; "ower clean to beil" means "too clean to suppurate"; "fremyt" means "strange"; "a' the lave" means "all the rest"; "in the treviss wi' the mear" means "in the stall with the mare."

Plot. From Aesop's Fables to Kipling's Jungle Books literature is full of animal stories. But there is no dog story better told than this and none that appeals more to our deeper sympathies. It is more of a character sketch than a short story, the incidents and characters being bound together by a common relation to Rab. From his leisurely first appearance in the story, "a huge mastiff, sauntering down the middle of the causeway, as if with his hands in his pockets," to the unanswerable last question— "His teeth and his friends gone, why should he keep the peace, and be civil?"—we follow Rab's pathetic career with the growing conviction that "his like was na atween this and Thornhill," however distant Thornhill may have been. Character sketches are apt to be uninteresting because there is usually too little action and too much description. The adjectives tend to smother the verbs. "They have," said Hawthorne of his "Twice-Told Tales," "the pale tint of flowers that blossomed in too retired a shade,—the coolness of a meditative habit, which diffuses itself through the feeling and observation of every sketch." But no such charge can be laid at the door of "Rab and his Friends." The very dumbness of Rab, his mute yearning to help, his brave and loyal ministries in the hospital, doubly affecting because wordless and impotent, lend an appeal to this sketch that few sketches of men and women can be said to have.

Characters. In a later sketch called "Our Dogs" Dr. Brown tells how Rab became the property of James and Ailie. He had been terrifying everybody at Macbie Hill and his owner ordered him to be hanged. As Rab was getting the better of the contest, his owner commanded that he be shot. But Ailie, who happened to be near, noticed that he had a big splinter in his foreleg. "She gave him water," says Dr. Brown, "and by her woman's wit got his lame paw under a door, so that he couldn't suddenly get at her; then with a quick firm hand she plucked out the splinter, and put in an ample meal. She went in some time after, taking no notice of him, and he

---

[11] From "Rab and his Friends and Other Dogs and Men."

came limping up, and laid his great jaws in her lap." From that moment they became friends. A little later James was in a lonely part of the woods when a robber sprang at him and demanded his money. "Weel a weel, let me get it," said James, and stepping back he whispered to Rab, "Speak till him, my man." Rab had the robber down in an instant.

In "Rab and his Friends" the great mastiff shows just the qualities that we should expect from this account of his earlier career. But his sympathy and affection for Ailie, shown so tenderly in the hospital scenes, find an added pathos in the thought that he was serving his first and best friend, one who had healed his hurt as he would have healed hers if he could.]

Four-and-thirty years ago, Bob Ainslie and I were coming up Infirmary Street from the Edinburgh High School, our heads together, and our arms intertwisted, as only lovers and boys know how, or why.

When we got to the top of the street, and turned north, we espied a crowd at the Tron Church. "A dog-fight!" shouted Bob, and was off; and so was I, both of us all but praying that it might not be over before we got up! And is not this boy-nature? and human nature too? and don't we all wish a house on fire not to be out before we see it? Dogs like fighting; old Isaac says they "delight" in it, and for the best of all reasons; and boys are not cruel because they like to see the fight. They see three of the great cardinal virtues of dog or man—courage, endurance, and skill—in intense action. This is very different from a love of making dogs fight, and enjoying, and aggravating, and making gain by their pluck. A boy,—be he ever so fond himself of fighting,—if he be a good boy, hates and despises all this, but he would have run off with Bob and me fast enough: it is a natural, and a not wicked interest, that all boys and men have in witnessing intense energy in action.

Does any curious and finely-ignorant woman wish to know how Bob's eye at a glance announced a dog-fight to his brain? He did not, he could not see the dogs fighting; it was a flash of an inference, a rapid induction. The crowd round a couple of dogs fighting is a crowd masculine mainly, with an occasional active, compassionate woman, fluttering wildly round the outside, and using her tongue and her hands freely upon the men, as so many "brutes"; it is a crowd annular, compact, and mobile; a crowd centripetal, having its eyes and its heads all bent downwards and inwards, to one common focus.

Well, Bob and I are up, and find it is not over: a small thoroughbred, white Bull Terrier, is busy throttling a large shepherd's dog, unaccustomed to war, but not to be trifled with. They are hard at it; the scientific little fellow doing his work in great style, his pastoral enemy fighting wildly, but with the sharpest of teeth and a great courage. Science and breeding, however, soon had their own; the Game Chicken, as the premature Bob called him, working his way up, took his final grip of poor Yarrow's throat,—and he lay gasping and done for. His master, a brown, handsome, big young shepherd from Tweedsmuir, would have liked to have knocked down any man, would "drink up Esil, [12] or eat a crocodile," for that part, if he had a chance: it was no use kicking the little dog; that would only make him hold the closer. Many were the means shouted out in mouthfuls, of the best possible ways of ending it. "Water!" but there was none near, and many cried for it who might have got it from the well at Blackfriars Wynd. "Bite the tail!" and a large, vague, benevolent, middle-aged man, more desirous than wise, with some struggle got the bushy end of Yarrow's tail into his ample mouth, and bit it with all his might. This was more than enough for the much-enduring, much-perspiring shepherd, who, with a gleam of joy over his broad visage, delivered a terrific facer upon our large, vague, benevolent, middle-aged friend,—who went down like a shot.

Still the Chicken holds; death not far off. "Snuff! a pinch of snuff!" observed a calm, highly-dressed young buck, with an eye-glass in his eye. "Snuff, indeed!" growled the angry crowd, affronted and glaring. "Snuff! a pinch of snuff!" again observed the buck, but with more urgency; whereon were produced several open boxes, and from a mull which may have been at Culloden, he took a pinch, knelt down, and presented it to the nose of the Chicken. The laws of physiology and of snuff take their course; the Chicken sneezes, and Yarrow is free!

The young pastoral giant stalks off with Yarrow in his arms,—comforting him.

But the Bull Terrier's blood is up, and his soul unsatisfied; he grips the first dog he meets, and discovering she is not a dog, in Homeric phrase, he makes a brief sort of amende, and is off. The boys, with Bob and me at their head, are after him: down Niddry Street he goes, bent on mischief; up the Cowgate like an arrow—Bob and I, and our small men, panting behind.

There, under the single arch of the South Bridge, is a huge mastiff, sauntering down the middle of the causeway, as if with his hands in his pockets: he is old, gray, brindled, as big as a little Highland bull, and has the Shakesperian dewlaps shaking as he goes.

The Chicken makes straight at him, and fastens on his throat. To our astonishment, the great creature does nothing but stand still, hold himself up, and roar—yes, roar; a long, serious, remonstrative roar. How is this? Bob and I are up to them. He is muzzled! The bailies had proclaimed a general muzzling, and his master, studying strength and economy mainly, had encompassed his huge jaws in a home-made apparatus, constructed out of the leather of some ancient breechin. His mouth was open as far as it could; his lips curled up in rage—a sort of terrible grin; his teeth gleaming, ready, from out the darkness; the strap across his mouth tense as a bowstring; his whole frame stiff with indignation and surprise; his roar asking us all round, "Did you ever see the like of this?" He looked a statue of anger and astonishment, done in Aberdeen granite.

We soon had a crowd: the Chicken held on. "A knife!" cried Bob; and a cobbler gave him his knife: you know the kind of knife, worn away

---

[12] Esil, "vinegar" (Hamlet, V, I, 299).

obliquely to a point, and always keen. I put its edge to the tense leather; it ran before it; and then!—one sudden jerk of that enormous head, a sort of dirty mist about his mouth, no noise,—and the bright and fierce little fellow is dropped, limp, and dead. A solemn pause: this was more than any of us had bargained for. I turned the little fellow over, and saw he was quite dead; the mastiff had taken him by the small of the back like a rat, and broken it.

He looked down at his victim appeased, ashamed, and amazed; snuffed him all over, stared at him, and taking a sudden thought, turned round and trotted off. Bob took the dead dog up, and said, "John, we'll bury him after tea." "Yes," said I, and was off after the mastiff. He made up the Cowgate at a rapid swing; he had forgotten some engagement. He turned up the Candlemaker Row, and stopped at the Harrow Inn.

There was a carrier's cart ready to start, and a keen, thin, impatient, black-a-vised little man, his hand at his gray horse's head, looking about angrily for something. "Rab, ye thief!" said he, aiming a kick at my great friend, who drew cringing up, and avoiding the heavy shoe with more agility than dignity, and watching his master's eye, slunk dismayed under the cart,—his ears down, and as much as he had of tail down too.

What a man this must be—thought I—to whom my tremendous hero turns tail! The carrier saw the muzzle hanging, cut and useless, from his neck, and I eagerly told him the story, which Bob and I always thought, and still think, Homer, or King David, or Sir Walter alone were worthy to rehearse. The severe little man was mitigated, and condescended to say, "Rab, my man, puir Rabbie,"—whereupon the stump of a tail rose up, the ears were cocked, the eyes filled, and were comforted; the two friends were reconciled. "Hupp!" and a stroke of the whip were given to Jess; and off went the three.

* * * * *

Bob and I buried the Game Chicken that night (we had not much of a tea) in the back-green of his house in Melville Street, No. 17, with considerable gravity and silence; and being at the time in the Iliad, and, like all boys, Trojans, we called him Hector of course.

Six years have passed,—a long time for a boy and a dog: Bob Ainslie is off to the wars; I am a medical student, and clerk at Minto House Hospital.

Rab I saw almost every week, on the Wednesday, and we had much pleasant intimacy. I found the way to his heart by frequent scratching of his huge head, and an occasional bone. When I did not notice him he would plant himself straight before me, and stand wagging that bud of a tail, and looking up, with his head a little to the one side. His master I occasionally saw; he used to call me "Maister John," but was laconic as any Spartan.

One fine October afternoon, I was leaving the hospital, when I saw the large gate open, and in walked Rab, with that great and easy saunter of his. He looked as if taking general possession of the place; like the Duke of Wellington entering a subdued city, satiated with victory and peace. After him came Jess, now white from age, with her cart; and in it a woman, carefully wrapped up,—the carrier leading the horse anxiously, and looking back. When he saw me, James (for his name was James Noble) made a curt and grotesque "boo," and said, "Maister John, this is the mistress; she's got a trouble in her breest—some kind o' an income we're thinking."

By this time I saw the woman's face; she was sitting on a sack filled with straw, her husband's plaid round her, and his big-coat with its large white metal buttons, over her feet.

I never saw a more unforgettable face—pale, serious, lonely [13] delicate, sweet, without being at all what we call fine. She looked sixty, and had on a mutch, white as snow, with its black ribbon; her silvery, smooth hair setting off her dark-gray eyes—eyes such as one sees only twice or thrice in a lifetime, full of suffering, full also of the overcoming of it: her eyebrows black and delicate, and her mouth firm, patient, and contented, which few mouths ever are.

As I have said, I never saw a more beautiful countenance, or one more subdued to settled quiet. "Ailie," said James, "this is Maister John, the young doctor; Rab's freend, ye ken. We often speak aboot you, doctor." She smiled, and made a movement, but said nothing; and prepared to come down, putting her plaid aside and rising. Had Solomon, in all his glory, been handing down the Queen of Sheba at his palace gate he could not have done it more daintily, more tenderly, more like a gentleman, than did James the Howgate carrier, when he lifted down Ailie his wife. The contrast of his small, swarthy, weather-beaten, keen, worldly face to hers— pale, subdued, and beautiful—was something wonderful. Rab looked on concerned and puzzled, but ready for anything that might turn up,—were it to strangle the nurse, the porter, or even me. Ailie and he seemed great friends.

"As I was sayin' she's got a kind o' trouble in her breest, doctor; wull ye tak' a look at it?" We walked into the consulting-room, all four; Rab grim and comic, willing to be happy and confidential if cause could be shown, willing also to be the reverse, on the same terms. Ailie sat down, undid her open gown and her lawn handkerchief round her neck, and without a word, showed me her right breast. I looked at and examined it carefully,—she and James watching me, and Rab eying all three. What could I say? there it was, that had once been so soft, so shapely, so white, so gracious and bountiful, so "full of all blessed conditions,"—hard as a stone, a centre of horrid pain, making that pale face, with its gray, lucid, reasonable eyes, and its sweet resolved mouth, express the full measure of suffering overcome. Why was that gentle, modest, sweet woman, clean and lovable, condemned by God to bear such a burden?

I got her away to bed. "May Rab and me bide?" said James. "You may; and Rab, if he will behave himself." "I'se warrant he's do that, doctor;" and in slank the faithful beast. I wish you could have seen him.

---

[13] It is not easy giving this look by one word; it was expressive of her being so much of her life alone.

There are no such dogs now. He belonged to a lost tribe. As I have said, he was brindled and gray like Rubislaw granite; his hair short, hard, and close, like a lion's; his body thick set, like a little bull—a sort of compressed Hercules of a dog. He must have been ninety pounds' weight, at the least; he had a large blunt head; his muzzle black as night, his mouth blacker than any night, a tooth or two—being all he had—gleaming out of his jaws of darkness. His head was scarred with the records of old wounds, a sort of series of fields of battle all over it; one eye out, one ear cropped as close as was Archbishop Leighton's father's; the remaining eye had the power of two; and above it, and in constant communication with it, was a tattered rag of an ear, which was forever unfurling itself, like an old flag; and then that bud of a tail, about one inch long, if it could in any sense be said to be long, being as broad as long—the mobility, the instantaneousness of that bud were very funny and surprising, and its expressive twinklings and winkings, the intercommunications between the eye, the ear, and it, were of the oddest and swiftest.

Rab had the dignity and simplicity of great size; and having fought his way all along the road to absolute supremacy, he was as mighty in his own line as Julius Cæsar or the Duke of Wellington, and had the gravity [14] of all great fighters.

You must have often observed the likeness of certain men to certain animals, and of certain dogs to men. Now, I never looked at Rab without thinking of the great Baptist preacher, Andrew Fuller. [15] The same large, heavy, menacing, combative, sombre, honest countenance, the same deep inevitable eye, the same look,—as of thunder asleep, but ready,—neither a dog nor a man to be trifled with.

Next day, my master, the surgeon, examined Ailie. There was no doubt it must kill her, and soon. It could be removed—it might never return—it would give her speedy relief—she should have it done. She curtsied, looked at James, and said, "When?" "To-morrow," said the kind surgeon—a man of few words. She and James and Rab and I retired. I

---

[14] A Highland game-keeper, when asked why a certain terrier, of singular pluck, was so much more solemn than the other dogs, said, "Oh, Sir, life's full o' sairiousness to him—he just never can get enuff o' fechtin'."

[15] Fuller was, in early life, when a farmer lad at Soham, famous as a boxer; not quarrelsome, but not without "the stern delight" a man of strength and courage feels in their exercise. Dr. Charles Stewart, of Dunearn, whose rare gifts and graces as a physician, a divine, a scholar, and a gentleman, live only in the memory of those few who knew and survive him, liked to tell how Mr. Fuller used to say, that when he was in the pulpit, and saw a buirdly man come along the passage, he would instinctively draw himself up, measure his imaginary antagonist, and forecast how he would deal with him, his hands meanwhile condensing into fists, and tending to "square." He must have been a hard hitter if he boxed as he preached—what "The Fancy" would call "an ugly customer."

noticed that he and she spoke little, but seemed to anticipate everything in each other. The following day, at noon, the students came in, hurrying up the great stair. At the first landing-place, on a small well-known blackboard, was a bit of paper fastened by wafers and many remains of old wafers beside it. On the paper were the words,—"An operation to-day. J.B. Clerk."

Up ran the youths, eager to secure good places; in they crowded, full of interest and talk. "What's the case?" "Which side is it?"

Don't think them heartless; they are neither better nor worse than you or I; they get over their professional horrors, and into their proper work—and in them pity—as an emotion, ending in itself or at best in tears and a long-drawn breath—lessens, while pity as a motive is quickened, and gains power and purpose. It is well for poor human nature that it is so.

The operating theatre is crowded; much talk and fun, and all the cordiality and stir of youth. The surgeon with his staff of assistants is there. In comes Ailie: one look at her quiets and abates the eager students. That beautiful old woman is too much for them; they sit down, and are dumb, and gaze at her. These rough boys feel the power of her presence. She walks in quickly, but without haste; dressed in her mutch, her neckerchief, her white dimity short-gown, her black bombazine petticoat, showing her white worsted stockings and her carpet-shoes. Behind her was James with Rab. James sat down in the distance, and took that huge and noble head between his knees. Rab looked perplexed and dangerous; forever cocking his ear and dropping it as fast.

Ailie stepped up on a seat, and laid herself on the table, as her friend the surgeon told her; arranged herself, gave a rapid look at James, shut her eyes, rested herself on me, and took my hand. The operation was at once begun; it was necessarily slow; and chloroform—one of God's best gifts to his suffering children—was then unknown. The surgeon did his work. The pale face showed its pain, but was still and silent. Rab's soul was working within him; he saw that something strange was going on,—blood flowing from his mistress, and she suffering; his ragged ear was up, and importunate; he growled and gave now and then a sharp impatient yelp; he would have liked to have done something to that man. But James had him firm, and gave him a glower from time to time, and an intimation of a possible kick;—all the better for James, it kept his eye and his mind off Ailie.

It is over: she is dressed, steps gently and decently down from the table, looks for James; then, turning to the surgeon and the students, she curtsies,—and in a low, clear voice, begs their pardon if she has behaved ill. The students—all of us—wept like children; the surgeon happed her up carefully,—and, resting on James and me, Ailie went to her room, Rab following. We put her to bed. James took off his heavy shoes, crammed with tackets, heel-capt, and toe-capt and put them carefully under the table, saying, "Maister John, I'm for nane o' yer strynge nurse bodies for Ailie. I'll be her nurse, and I'll gang aboot on my stockin' soles as canny as pussy." And so he did; and handy and clever, and swift and tender as any woman, was that horny-handed, snell, peremptory little man. Everything she got he gave her: he seldom slept; and often I saw his small shrewd eyes out of the darkness, fixed on her. As before, they spoke little.

Rab behaved well, never moving, showing us how meek and gentle he could be, and occasionally, in his sleep, letting us know that he was demolishing some adversary. He took a walk with me every day, generally to the Candlemaker Row; but he was sombre and mild; declined doing battle, though some fit cases offered, and indeed submitted to sundry indignities; and was always very ready to turn, and came faster back, and trotted up the stair with much lightness, and went straight to that door.

Jess, the mare, had been sent, with her weather-worn cart, to Howgate, and had doubtless her own dim and placid meditations and confusions, on the absence of her master and Rab, and her unnatural freedom from the road and her cart.

For some days Ailie did well. The wound healed "by the first intention;" for as James said, "Our Ailie's skin's ower clean to beil." The students came in quiet and anxious, and surrounded her bed. She said she liked to see their young, honest faces. The surgeon dressed her, and spoke to her in his own short kind way, pitying her through his eyes, Rab and James outside the circle,—Rab being now reconciled, and even cordial, and having made up his mind that as yet nobody required worrying, but, as you may suppose, semper paratus.

So far well: but, four days after the operation, my patient had a sudden and long shivering, a "groosin'," as she called it. I saw her soon after; her eyes were too bright, her cheek colored; she was restless, and ashamed of being so; the balance was lost; mischief had begun. On looking at the wound, a blush of red told the secret: her pulse was rapid, her breathing anxious and quick, she wasn't herself, as she said, and was vexed at her restlessness. We tried what we could; James did everything, was everywhere; never in the way, never out of it; Rab subsided under the table into a dark place, and was motionless, all but his eye, which followed every one. Ailie got worse; began to wander in her mind, gently; was more demonstrative in her ways to James, rapid in her questions, and sharp at times. He was vexed, and said, "She was never that way afore; no, never." For a time she knew her head was wrong, and was always asking our pardon—the dear, gentle old woman: then delirium set in strong, without pause. Her brain gave way, and then came that terrible spectacle,—

    The intellectual power, through words and things,
    Went sounding on its dim and perilous way,

she sang bits of old songs and Psalms, stopping suddenly, mingling the Psalms of David and the diviner words of his Son and Lord, with homely odds and ends and scraps of ballads.

Nothing more touching, or in a sense more strangely beautiful, did I ever witness. Her tremulous, rapid, affectionate, eager, Scotch voice,—the swift, aimless, bewildered mind, the baffled utterance, the bright and perilous eye; some wild words, some household cares, something for James, the names of the dead, Rab called rapidly and in a "fremyt" voice, and he starting up surprised, and slinking off as if he were to blame somehow, or had been dreaming he heard; many eager questions and beseechings which James and I could make nothing of, and on which she seemed to set her all, and then sink back ununderstood. It was very sad, but better than many things that are not called sad. James hovered about, put out and miserable, but active and exact as ever; read to her, when there was a lull, short bits from the Psalms, prose and metre, chanting the latter in his own rude and serious way, showing great knowledge of the fit words, bearing up like a man, and doating over her as his "ain Ailie." "Ailie, ma woman!" "Ma ain bonnie wee dawtie!"

The end was drawing on: the golden bowl was breaking; the silver cord was fast being loosed—that animula blandula, vagula, hospes, comesque [16] was about to flee. The body and the soul—companions for sixty years—were being sundered, and taking leave. She was walking alone, through the valley of that shadow, into which one day we must all enter,—and yet she was not alone, for we know whose rod and staff were comforting her.

One night she had fallen quiet, and as we hoped, asleep; her eyes were shut. We put down the gas, and sat watching her. Suddenly she sat up in bed, and taking a bed-gown which was lying on it rolled up, she held it eagerly to her breast,—to the right side. We could see her eyes bright with a surprising tenderness and joy, bending over this bundle of clothes. She held it as a woman holds her sucking child; opening out her night-gown impatiently, and holding it close, and brooding over it, and murmuring foolish little words, as over one whom his mother comforteth, and who sucks and is satisfied. It was pitiful and strange to see her wasted dying look, keen and yet vague—her immense love.

"Preserve me!" groaned James, giving way. And then she rocked back and forward, as if to make it sleep, hushing it, and wasting on it her infinite fondness. "Wae's me, doctor; I declare she's thinkin' it's that bairn." "What bairn?" "The only bairn we ever had; our wee Mysie, and she's in the Kingdom, forty years and mair." It was plainly true: the pain in the breast, telling its urgent story to a bewildered, ruined brain, was misread and mistaken; it suggested to her the uneasiness of a breast full of milk, and then the child; and so again once more they were together, and she had her ain wee Mysie in her bosom.

This was the close. She sank rapidly: the delirium left her; but, as she whispered, she was "clean silly;" it was the lightening before the final darkness. After having for some time lain still—her eyes shut, she said "James!" He came close to her, and lifting up her calm, clear, beautiful eyes, she gave him a long look, turned to me kindly but shortly, looked for Rab but could not see him, then turned to her husband again, as if she would never leave off looking, shut her eyes, and composed herself. She lay for some time breathing quick, and passed away so gently that, when we

---

[16] "Little, gentle, wandering soul, guest and comrade."—Hadrian's "Address to his Soul"

thought she was gone, James, in his old-fashioned way, held the mirror to her face. After a long pause, one small spot of dimness was breathed out; it vanished away, and never returned, leaving the blank clear darkness of the mirror without a stain. "What is our life? it is even a vapor, which appeareth for a little time, and then vanisheth away."

Rab all this time had been full awake and motionless; he came forward beside us: Ailie's hand, which James had held, was hanging down; it was soaked with his tears; Rab licked it all over carefully, looked at her, and returned to his place under the table.

James and I sat, I don't know how long, but for some time,—saying nothing: he started up abruptly, and with some noise went to the table, and putting his right fore and middle fingers each into a shoe, pulled them out, and put them on, breaking one of the leather latchets, and muttering in anger, "I never did the like o' that afore!"

I believe he never did; nor after either. "Rab!" he said roughly, and pointing with his thumb to the bottom of the bed. Rab leapt up, and settled himself; his head and eye to the dead face. "Maister John, ye'll wait for me," said the carrier; and disappeared in the darkness, thundering downstairs in his heavy shoes. I ran to a front window; there he was, already round the house, and out at the gate, fleeing like a shadow.

I was afraid about him, and yet not afraid; so I sat down beside Rab, and being wearied, fell asleep. I awoke from a sudden noise outside. It was November, and there had been a heavy fall of snow. Rab was in statu quo; he heard the noise too, and plainly knew it, but never moved. I looked out; and there, at the gate, in the dim morning—for the sun was not up—was Jess and the cart,—a cloud of steam rising from the old mare. I did not see James; he was already at the door, and came up the stairs, and met me. It was less than three hours since he left, and he must have posted out—who knows how?—to Howgate, full nine miles off; yoked Jess, and driven her astonished into town. He had an armful of blankets, and was streaming with perspiration. He nodded to me, spread out on the floor two pairs of clean old blankets having at their corners, "A.G., 1794," in large letters in red worsted. These were the initials of Alison Græme, and James may have looked in at her from without—himself unseen but not unthought of—when he was "wat, wat, and weary," and after having walked many a mile over the hills, may have seen her sitting, while "a' the lave were sleepin':" and by the firelight working her name on the blankets, for her ain James's bed.

He motioned Rab down, and taking his wife in his arms, laid her in the blankets, and happed her carefully and firmly up, leaving the face uncovered; and then lifting her, he nodded again sharply to me, and with a resolved but utterly miserable face, strode along the passage, and downstairs, followed by Rab. I followed with a light; but he didn't need it. I went out, holding stupidly the candle in my hand in the calm frosty air; we were soon at the gate. I could have helped him, but I saw he was not to be meddled with, and he was strong, and did not need it. He laid her down as tenderly, as safely, as he had lifted her out ten days before—as tenderly as

117

when he had her first in his arms when she was only "A.G.,"—sorted her, leaving that beautiful sealed face open to the heavens; and then taking Jess by the head, he moved away. He did not notice me, neither did Rab, who presided behind the cart.

I stood till they passed through the long shadow of the College, and turned up Nicolson Street. I heard the solitary cart sound through the streets, and die away and come again; and I returned, thinking of that company going up Libberton Brae, then along Roslin Muir, the morning light touching the Pentlands and making them like on-looking ghosts, then down the hill through Auchindinny woods, past "haunted Woodhouselee;" and as daybreak came sweeping up the bleak Lammermuirs, and fell on his own door, the company would stop, and James would take the key, and lift Ailie up again, laying her on her own bed, and, having put Jess up, would return with Rab and shut the door.

James buried his wife, with his neighbors mourning, Rab inspecting the solemnity from a distance. It was snow, and that black ragged hole would look strange in the midst of the swelling spotless cushion of white. James looked after everything; then rather suddenly fell ill, and took to bed; was insensible when the doctor came, and soon died. A sort of low fever was prevailing in the village, and his want of sleep, his exhaustion, and his misery made him apt to take it. The grave was not difficult to reopen. A fresh fall of snow had again made all things white and smooth; Rab once more looked on, and slunk home to the stable.

* * * * *

And what of Rab? I asked for him next week of the new carrier who got the goodwill of James's business, and was now master of Jess and her cart. "How's Rab?" He put me off, and said rather rudely, "What's your business wi' the dowg?" I was not to be so put off. "Where's Rab?" He, getting confused and red, and intermeddling with his hair, said, "Deed, sir, Rab's deid." "Dead! what did he die of?" "Weel, sir," said he, getting redder, "he did na exactly dee; he was killed. I had to brain him wi' a rack-pin; there was nae doin' wi' him. He lay in the treviss wi' the mear, and wad na come oot. I tempit him wi' kail and meat, but he wad tak naething, and keepit me frae feedin' the beast, and he was aye gur gurrin', and grup gruppin' me by the legs. I was laith to make awa wi' the auld dowg, his like was na atween this and Thornhill,—but, 'deed, sir, I could do naething else." I believed him. Fit end for Rab, quick and complete. His teeth and his friends gone, why should he keep the peace, and be civil?

THE OUTCASTS OF POKER FLAT [17] (1869)

BY BRET HARTE (1836-1902)

[Setting. The group tragedy enacted in this story took place between November 23 and December 7, 1850, on the road from Poker Flat to Sandy Bar, in Sierra County, California. The time and place are those that Bret Harte has made peculiarly his own. The austerity and wildness of the scenery seem somehow to favor the intimate revelation of character that the story displays. There is no intervention of cities, crops, fashions, or conventions between the different members of the character group or between the group as a whole and the reader. All is bare like a white mountain peak. Notice also how the background of a common peril draws the characters together and brings out at last the best in each.

Plot. The story sets forth and interprets a dramatic situation. The plot is staged so as to answer the question, "Do not the people whom society regards as outcasts have yet some redeeming virtue?" Notice especially how a sense of common fellowship is developed in these outcasts. First, they are subjected to a common humiliation in being driven from Poker Flat by persons whom the outcasts consider no whit better than themselves. Next, they are exposed to a common danger, a danger that leads the stronger to care instinctively for the weaker, and the weaker to recognize that it is nobler to give than to receive. At last, in the unexpected entrance of the innocent Tom Simson and the guileless Piney Woods, the outcasts find a common challenge to the native goodness that had long lain dormant within them. Innocence and guilelessness may be laughed at, as they are here, but their appeal is often stronger than the appeal of disciplined virtue or of self-conscious superiority. When Bret Harte was charged with confusing the boundary lines of vice and virtue he replied that his plots "conformed to the rules laid down by a Great Poet who created the parable of the Prodigal Son and the Good Samaritan."

Characters. Oakhurst, who is always called "Mr." Oakhurst, is of course the dominant character. The story begins with him and ends with him. He is "the strongest and yet the weakest of the outcasts of Poker Flat,"—strong while there was anything to be done, weak even to suicide when he had only to wait for the inevitable end. He was a brave, desperate, solitary man, whose thought and speech and action, however, were always those of the professional gambler. Bret Harte, who has put him into several stories, says of him in another place: "Go where he would and with whom, he was always a notable man in ten thousand." The admiration that we yield to such a man, though it is only a qualified admiration, is doubtless

---

[17] Used by permission of, and by special arrangement with, Houghton Mifflin Company, publishers of Bret Harte's Works.

the admiration of power which, we cannot help thinking, might be used beneficently if it could only be harnessed to a noble cause.

But if Oakhurst is the dominant character, Piney Woods is, I think, the central character. She is central in this story just as little Aglaïa is central in Tennyson's "Princess," or Eppie in George Eliot's "Silas Marner," or the baby offspring of Cherokee Sal in "The Luck of Roaring Camp." Bret Harte had just written the last-named story when he began the composition of "The Outcasts of Poker Flat." The same great theme, the radiating and redeeming power of innocence and purity, was carried over from the first story to the second. The ministry of the baby and the ministry of the fifteen-year-old bride is the same in both. Like the Great Stone Face in Hawthorne's story or like little Pippa in Browning's poem, they awaken the better nature of those about them. They restore hopes that had become but memories and memories that had almost ceased to be hopes.]

As Mr. John Oakhurst, gambler, stepped into the main street of Poker Flat on the morning of the twenty-third of November, 1850, he was conscious of a change in its moral atmosphere since the preceding night. Two or three men, conversing earnestly together, ceased as he approached, and exchanged significant glances. There was a Sabbath lull in the air, which, in a settlement unused to Sabbath influences, looked ominous.

Mr. Oakhurst's calm, handsome face betrayed small concern in these indications. Whether he was conscious of any predisposing cause, was another question. "I reckon they're after somebody," he reflected; "likely it's me." He returned to his pocket the handkerchief with which he had been whipping away the red dust of Poker Flat from his neat boots, and quietly discharged his mind of any further conjecture.

In point of fact, Poker Flat was "after somebody." It had lately suffered the loss of several thousand dollars, two valuable horses, and a prominent citizen. It was experiencing a spasm of virtuous reaction, quite as lawless and ungovernable as any of the acts that had provoked it. A secret committee had determined to rid the town of all improper persons. This was done permanently in regard of two men who were then hanging from the boughs of a sycamore in the gulch, and temporarily in the banishment of certain other objectionable characters. I regret to say that some of these were ladies. It is but due to the sex, however, to state that their impropriety was professional, and it was only in such easily established standards of evil that Poker Flat ventured to sit in judgment.

Mr. Oakhurst was right in supposing that he was included in this category. A few of the committee had urged hanging him as a possible example, and a sure method of reimbursing themselves from his pockets of the sums he had won from them. "It's agin justice," said Jim Wheeler, "to let this yer young man from Roaring Camp—an entire stranger—carry away our money." But a crude sentiment of equity residing in the breasts of those who had been fortunate enough to win from Mr. Oakhurst overruled this narrower local prejudice.

Mr. Oakhurst received his sentence with philosophic calmness, none the less coolly that he was aware of the hesitation of his judges. He was too much of a gambler not to accept Fate. With him life was at best an uncertain game, and he recognized the usual percentage in favor of the dealer.

A body of armed men accompanied the deported wickedness of Poker Flat to the outskirts of the settlement. Besides Mr. Oakhurst, who was known to be a coolly desperate man, and for whose intimidation the armed escort was intended, the expatriated party consisted of a young woman familiarly known as "The Duchess"; another, who had won the title of "Mother Shipton"; and "Uncle Billy," a suspected sluice-robber and confirmed drunkard. The cavalcade provoked no comments from the spectators, nor was any word uttered by the escort. Only, when the gulch which marked the uttermost limit of Poker Flat was reached, the leader spoke briefly and to the point. The exiles were forbidden to return at the peril of their lives.

As the escort disappeared, their pent-up feelings found vent in a few hysterical tears from the Duchess, some bad language from Mother Shipton, and a Parthian volley of expletives from Uncle Billy. The philosophic Oakhurst alone remained silent. He listened calmly to Mother Shipton's desire to cut somebody's heart out, to the repeated statements of the Duchess that she would die in the road, and to the alarming oaths that seemed to be bumped out of Uncle Billy as he rode forward. With the easy good-humor characteristic of his class, he insisted upon exchanging his own riding-horse, "Five Spot," for the sorry mule which the Duchess rode. But even this act did not draw the party into any closer sympathy. The young woman readjusted her somewhat draggled plumes with a feeble, faded coquetry; Mother Shipton eyed the possessor of "Five Spot" with malevolence, and Uncle Billy included the whole party in one sweeping anathema.

The road to Sandy Bar—a camp that, not having as yet experienced the regenerating influences of Poker Flat, consequently seemed to offer some invitation to the emigrants—lay over a steep mountain range. It was distant a day's severe travel. In that advanced season, the party soon passed out of the moist, temperate regions of the foot-hills into the dry, cold, bracing air of the Sierras. The trail was narrow and difficult. At noon the Duchess, rolling out of her saddle upon the ground, declared her intention of going no farther, and the party halted.

The spot was singularly wild and impressive. A wooded amphitheatre, surrounded on three sides by precipitous cliffs of naked granite, sloped gently toward the crest of another precipice that overlooked the valley. It was, undoubtedly, the most suitable spot for a camp, had camping been advisable. But Mr. Oakhurst knew that scarcely half the journey to Sandy Bar was accomplished, and the party were not equipped or provisioned for delay. This fact he pointed out to his companions curtly,

121

with a philosophic commentary on the folly of "throwing up their hand before the game was played out." But they were furnished with liquor, which in this emergency stood them in place of food, fuel, rest, and prescience. In spite of his remonstrances, it was not long before they were more or less under its influence. Uncle Billy passed rapidly from a bellicose state into one of stupor, the Duchess became maudlin, and Mother Shipton snored. Mr. Oakhurst alone remained erect, leaning against a rock, calmly surveying them.

Mr. Oakhurst did not drink. It interfered with a profession which required coolness, impassiveness, and presence of mind, and, in his own language, he "couldn't afford it." As he gazed at his recumbent fellow-exiles, the loneliness begotten of his pariah-trade, his habits of life, his very vices, for the first time seriously oppressed him. He bestirred himself in dusting his black clothes, washing his hands and face, and other acts characteristic of his studiously neat habits, and for a moment forgot his annoyance. The thought of deserting his weaker and more pitiable companions never perhaps occurred to him. Yet he could not help feeling the want of that excitement which, singularly enough, was most conducive to that calm equanimity for which he was notorious. He looked at the gloomy walls that rose a thousand feet sheer above the circling pines around him; at the sky, ominously clouded; at the valley below, already deepening into shadow. And, doing so, suddenly he heard his own name called.

A horseman slowly ascended the trail. In the fresh, open face of the new-comer Mr. Oakhurst recognized Tom Simson, otherwise known as "The Innocent" of Sandy Bar. He had met him some months before over a "little game," and had, with perfect equanimity, won the entire fortune— amounting to some forty dollars—of that guileless youth. After the game was finished, Mr. Oakhurst drew the youthful speculator behind the door and thus addressed him: "Tommy, you're a good little man, but you can't gamble worth a cent. Don't try it over again." He then handed him his money back, pushed him gently from the room, and so made a devoted slave of Tom Simson.

There was a remembrance of this in his boyish and enthusiastic greeting of Mr. Oakhurst. He had started, he said, to go to Poker Flat to seek his fortune. "Alone?" No, not exactly alone; in fact (a giggle), he had run away with Piney Woods. Didn't Mr. Oakhurst remember Piney? She that used to wait on the table at the Temperance House? They had been engaged a long time, but old Jake Woods had objected, and so they had run away, and were going to Poker Flat to be married, and here they were. And they were tired out, and how lucky it was they had found a place to camp and company. All this the Innocent delivered rapidly, while Piney, a stout, comely damsel of fifteen, emerged from behind the pine-tree, where she had been blushing unseen, and rode to the side of her lover.

Mr. Oakhurst seldom troubled himself with sentiment, still less with propriety; but he had a vague idea that the situation was not fortunate. He retained, however, his presence of mind sufficiently to kick Uncle Billy, who was about to say something, and Uncle Billy was sober enough to recognize in Mr. Oakhurst's kick a superior power that would not bear trifling. He then endeavored to dissuade Tom Simson from delaying further, but in vain. He even pointed out the fact that there was no provision, nor means of making a camp. But, unluckily, the Innocent met this objection by assuring the party that he was provided with an extra mule loaded with provisions, and by the discovery of a rude attempt at a log-house near the trail. "Piney can stay with Mrs. Oakhurst," said the Innocent, pointing to the Duchess, "and I can shift for myself."

Nothing but Mr. Oakhurst's admonishing foot saved Uncle Billy from bursting into a roar of laughter. As it was, he felt compelled to retire up the cañon until he could recover his gravity. There he confided the joke to the tall pine-trees, with many slaps of his leg, contortions of his face, and the usual profanity. But when he returned to the party, he found them seated by a fire—for the air had grown strangely chill and the sky overcast—in apparently amicable conversation. Piney was actually talking in an impulsive, girlish fashion to the Duchess, who was listening with an interest and animation she had not shown for many days. The Innocent was holding forth, apparently with equal effect, to Mr. Oakhurst and Mother Shipton, who was actually relaxing into amiability. "Is this yer a d——d picnic?" said Uncle Billy, with inward scorn, as he surveyed the sylvan group, the glancing firelight, and the tethered animals in the foreground. Suddenly an idea mingled with the alcoholic fumes that disturbed his brain. It was apparently of a jocular nature, for he felt impelled to slap his leg again and cram his fist into his mouth.

As the shadows crept slowly up the mountain, a slight breeze rocked the tops of the pine-trees, and moaned through their long and gloomy aisles. The ruined cabin, patched and covered with pine-boughs, was set apart for the ladies. As the lovers parted, they unaffectedly exchanged a kiss, so honest and sincere that it might have been heard above the swaying pines. The frail Duchess and the malevolent Mother Shipton were probably too stunned to remark upon this last evidence of simplicity, and so turned without a word to the hut. The fire was replenished, the men lay down before the door, and in a few minutes were asleep.

Mr. Oakhurst was a light sleeper. Toward morning he awoke benumbed and cold. As he stirred the dying fire, the wind, which was now blowing strongly, brought to his cheek that which caused the blood to leave it,—snow!

He started to his feet with the intention of awakening the sleepers, for there was no time to lose. But turning to where Uncle Billy had been lying, he found him gone. A suspicion leaped to his brain and a curse to his lips. He ran to the spot where the mules had been tethered; they were no longer there. The tracks were already rapidly disappearing in the snow.

The momentary excitement brought Mr. Oakhurst back to the fire with his usual calm. He did not waken the sleepers. The Innocent slumbered peacefully, with a smile on his good-humored, freckled face; the virgin Piney slept beside her frailer sisters as sweetly as though attended by celestial guardians, and Mr. Oakhurst, drawing his blanket over his shoulders, stroked his mustaches and waited for the dawn. It came slowly in a whirling mist of snow-flakes, that dazzled and confused the eye. What could be seen of the landscape appeared magically changed. He looked over the valley, and summoned up the present and future in two words,— "snowed in!"

A careful inventory of the provisions, which, fortunately for the party, had been stored within the hut, and so escaped the felonious fingers of Uncle Billy, disclosed the fact that with care and prudence they might last ten days longer. "That is," said Mr. Oakhurst, sotto voce to the Innocent, "if you're willing to board us. If you ain't—and perhaps you'd better not—you can wait till Uncle Billy gets back with provisions." For some occult reason, Mr. Oakhurst could not bring himself to disclose Uncle Billy's rascality, and so offered the hypothesis that he had wandered from the camp and had accidentally stampeded the animals. He dropped a warning to the Duchess and Mother Shipton, who of course knew the facts of their associate's defection. "They'll find out the truth about us all when they find out anything," he added, significantly, "and there's no good frightening them now."

Tom Simson not only put all his worldly store at the disposal of Mr. Oakhurst, but seemed to enjoy the prospect of their enforced seclusion. "We'll have a good camp for a week, and then the snow'll melt, and we'll all go back together." The cheerful gayety of the young man, and Mr. Oakhurst's calm infected the others. The Innocent, with the aid of pine-boughs, extemporized a thatch for the roofless cabin, and the Duchess directed Piney in the rearrangement of the interior with a taste and tact that opened the blue eyes of that provincial maiden to their fullest extent. "I reckon now you're used to fine things at Poker Flat," said Piney. The Duchess turned away sharply to conceal something that reddened her cheeks through its professional tint, and Mother Shipton requested Piney not to "chatter." But when Mr. Oakhurst returned from a weary search for the trail, he heard the sound of happy laughter echoed from the rocks. He stopped in some alarm, and his thoughts first naturally reverted to the whiskey, which he had prudently cachéd. "And yet it don't somehow sound like whiskey," said the gambler. It was not until he caught sight of the blazing fire through the still blinding storm and the group around it that he settled to the conviction that it was "square fun."

Whether Mr. Oakhurst had cachéd his cards with the whiskey as something debarred the free access of the community, I cannot say. It was certain that, in Mother Shipton's words, he "didn't say cards once" during that evening. Haply the time was beguiled by an accordion, produced somewhat ostentatiously by Tom Simson from his pack. Notwithstanding some difficulties attending the manipulation of his instrument, Piney Woods managed to pluck several reluctant melodies from its keys, to an accompaniment by the Innocent on a pair of bone castanets. But the crowning festivity of the evening was reached in a rude camp-meeting hymn, which the lovers, joining hands, sang with great earnestness and vociferation. I fear that a certain defiant tone and Covenanter's swing to its chorus, rather than any devotional quality, caused it speedily to infect the others, who at last joined in the refrain:—

"I'm proud to live in the service of the Lord,
And I'm bound to die in His army."

The pines rocked, the storm eddied and whirled above the miserable group, and the flames of their altar leaped heavenward, as if in token of the vow.

At midnight the storm abated, the rolling clouds parted, and the stars glittered keenly above the sleeping camp. Mr. Oakhurst, whose professional habits had enabled him to live on the smallest possible amount of sleep, in dividing the watch with Tom Simson, somehow managed to take upon himself the greater part of that duty. He excused himself to the Innocent, by saying that he had "often been a week without sleep." "Doing what?" asked Tom. "Poker!" replied Oakhurst, sententiously; "when a man gets a streak of luck,—nigger-luck,—he don't get tired. The luck gives in first. Luck," continued the gambler, reflectively, "is a mighty queer thing. All you know about it for certain is that it's bound to change. And it's finding out when it's going to change that makes you. We've had a streak of bad luck since we left Poker Flat,—you come along, and slap you get into it, too. If you can hold your cards right along, you're all right. For," added the gambler, with cheerful irrelevance,—

"I'm proud to live in the service of the Lord,
And I'm bound to die in His army."

The third day came, and the sun, looking through the white-curtained valley, saw the outcasts divide their slowly decreasing store of provisions for the morning meal. It was one of the peculiarities of that mountain climate that its rays diffused a kindly warmth over the wintry landscape, as if in regretful commiseration of the past. But it revealed drift on drift of snow piled high around the hut,—a hopeless, uncharted, trackless sea of white lying below the rocky shores to which the castaways still clung. Through the marvellously clear air the smoke of the pastoral village of Poker Flat rose miles away. Mother Shipton saw it, and from a remote pinnacle of her rocky fastness, hurled in that direction a final malediction. It was her last vituperative attempt, and perhaps for that reason was invested with a certain degree of sublimity. It did her good, she privately informed the Duchess. "Just you go out there and cuss, and see." She then set herself to the task of amusing "the child," as she and the Duchess were pleased to call Piney. Piney was no chicken, but it was a soothing and original theory of the pair thus to account for the fact that she didn't swear and wasn't improper.

When night crept up again through the gorges, the reedy notes of the accordion rose and fell in fitful spasms and long-drawn gasps by the flickering camp-fire. But music failed to fill entirely the aching void left by insufficient food, and a new diversion was proposed by Piney,—story-telling. Neither Mr. Oakhurst nor his female companions caring to relate their personal experiences, this plan would have failed, too, but for the

Innocent. Some months before he had chanced upon a stray copy of Mr. Pope's ingenious translation of the Iliad. He now proposed to narrate the principal incidents of that poem—having thoroughly mastered the argument and fairly forgotten the words—in the current vernacular of Sandy Bar. And so for the rest of that night the Homeric demigods again walked the earth. Trojan bully and wily Greek wrestled in the winds, and the great pines in the cañon seemed to bow to the wrath of the son of Peleus. Mr. Oakhurst listened with quiet satisfaction. Most especially was he interested in the fate of "Ash-heels," as the Innocent persisted in denominating the "swift-footed Achilles."

So with small food and much of Homer and the accordion, a week passed over the heads of the outcasts. The sun again forsook them, and again from leaden skies the snow-flakes were sifted over the land. Day by day closer around them drew the snowy circle, until at last they looked from their prison over drifted walls of dazzling white, that towered twenty feet above their heads. It became more and more difficult to replenish their fires, even from the fallen trees beside them, now half hidden in the drifts. And yet no one complained. The lovers turned from the dreary prospect and looked into each other's eyes, and were happy. Mr. Oakhurst settled himself coolly to the losing game before him. The Duchess, more cheerful than she had been, assumed the care of Piney. Only Mother Shipton—once the strongest of the party—seemed to sicken and fade. At midnight on the tenth day she called Oakhurst to her side. "I'm going," she said, in a voice of querulous weakness, "but don't say anything about it. Don't waken the kids. Take the bundle from under my head and open it." Mr. Oakhurst did so. It contained Mother Shipton's rations for the last week, untouched. "Give 'em to the child," she said, pointing to the sleeping Piney. "You've starved yourself," said the gambler. "That's what they call it," said the woman, querulously, as she lay down again, and, turning her face to the wall, passed quietly away.

The accordion and the bones were put aside that day, and Homer was forgotten. When the body of Mother Shipton had been committed to the snow, Mr. Oakhurst took the Innocent aside, and showed him a pair of snow-shoes, which he had fashioned from the old pack-saddle. "There's one chance in a hundred to save her yet," he said, pointing to Piney; "but it's there," he added, pointing towards Poker Flat. "If you can reach there in two days she's safe." "And you?" asked Tom Simson. "I'll stay here," was the curt reply.

The lovers parted with a long embrace. "You are not going, too?" said the Duchess, as she saw Mr. Oakhurst apparently waiting to accompany him. "As far as the cañon," he replied. He turned suddenly, and kissed the Duchess, leaving her pallid face aflame, and her trembling lips rigid with amazement.

Night came, but not Mr. Oakhurst. It brought the storm again and the whirling snow. Then the Duchess, feeding the fire, found that some one had quietly piled beside the hut enough fuel to last a few days longer. The tears rose to her eyes, but she hid them from Piney.

The women slept but little. In the morning, looking into each other's faces, they read their fate. Neither spoke; but Piney, accepting the position of the stronger, drew near and placed her arm around the Duchess's waist. They kept this attitude for the rest of the day. That night the storm reached its greatest fury, and, rending asunder the protecting pines, invaded the very hut.

Toward morning they found themselves unable to feed the fire, which gradually died away. As the embers slowly blackened, the Duchess crept closer to Piney, and broke the silence of many hours: "Piney, can you pray?" "No, dear," said Piney, simply. The Duchess, without knowing exactly why, felt relieved, and, putting her head upon Piney's shoulder, spoke no more. And so reclining, the younger and purer pillowing the head of her soiled sister upon her virgin breast, they fell asleep.

The wind lulled as if it feared to waken them. Feathery drifts of snow, shaken from the long pine-boughs, flew like white-winged birds, and settled about them as they slept. The moon through the rifted clouds looked down upon what had been the camp. But all human stain, all trace of earthly travail, was hidden beneath the spotless mantle mercifully flung from above.

They slept all that day and the next, nor did they waken when voices and footsteps broke the silence of the camp. And when pitying fingers brushed the snow from their wan faces, you could scarcely have told from the equal peace that dwelt upon them, which was she that had sinned. Even the law of Poker Flat recognized this, and turned away, leaving them still locked in each other's arms.

But at the head of the gulch, on one of the largest pine-trees, they found the deuce of clubs pinned to the bark with a bowie-knife. It bore the following, written in pencil, in a firm hand:—

BENEATH THIS TREE LIES THE BODY OF JOHN OAKHURST, WHO STRUCK A STREAK OF BAD LUCK ON THE 23D OF NOVEMBER, 1850, AND HANDED IN HIS CHECKS ON THE 7TH DECEMBER, 1850.

And pulseless and cold, with a derringer by his side and a bullet in his heart, though still calm as in life, beneath the snow lay he who was at once the strongest and yet the weakest of the outcasts of Poker Flat.

MARKHEIM [18] (1884)

BY ROBERT LOUIS STEVENSON (1850-1894)

[Setting. There is no finer model for the study of setting than this story affords. It is three o'clock in the afternoon of a foggy Christmas Day in London. If Markheim's manner and the dimly lighted interior of the antique shop suggest murder, the garrulous clocks, the nodding shadows, and the reflecting mirrors seem almost to compel confession and surrender. "And still as he continued to fill his pockets, his mind accused him, with a sickening iteration, of the thousand faults of his design. He should have chosen a more quiet hour." So he should for the murder; but for the self-confession, which is Stevenson's ultimate design, no time or place could have been better.

Plot. There is little action in the plot. A man commits a dastardly murder and then, being alone and undetected, begins to think, think, think. It is the turning point in his life and he knows it. Instead of seizing the treasure and escaping, he submits his past career to a rigid scrutiny and review. This brooding over his past life and present outlook becomes so absorbing that what bade fair to be a soliloquy becomes a dialogue, a dialogue between the old self that committed the murder and the new self that begins to revolt at it. The old self bids him follow the line of least resistance and go on as he has begun; the newly awakened self bids him stop at once, check the momentum of other days, take this last chance, and be a man. His better nature wins. Markheim finds that though his deeds have been uniformly evil, he can still "conceive great deeds, renunciations, martyrdoms." Though the active love of good seems too weak to be reckoned as an asset, he still has a "hatred of evil"; and on this twin foundation, ability to think great thoughts and to hate evil deeds, he builds at last his culminating resolve.

The story is powerfully and yet subtly told. It sweeps the whole gamut of the moral law. Many stories develop the same theme but none just like this. Stevenson himself is drawn again to the same problem a little later in "Dr. Jekyll and Mr. Hyde." Hawthorne tried it in "Howe's Masquerade," in which the cloaked figure is the phantom or reduplication of Howe himself. In Poe's "William Wilson," to which Stevenson is plainly indebted, the evil nature triumphs over the good. But "Markheim," by touching more chords and by sounding lower depths, makes the triumph at the end seem like a permanent victory for universal human nature.

Characters. If the story is the study of a given situation, Markheim, who is another type of the developing character, is the central factor in the situation. We see and interpret the situation only through the personality

---

[18] From "The Merry Men." Used by permission of Charles Scribner's Sons, authorized American publishers of Stevenson's Works.

of Markheim himself. Another murderer might have acted differently, even with those clamorous clocks and accusing mirrors around him, but not this murderer. There is nothing abnormal about him, however, as a criminal. He is thirty-six years old and through sheer weakness has gone steadily downward, but he has never before done a deed approaching this in horror or in the power of sudden self-revelation. He sees himself now as he never saw himself before and begins to take stock of his moral assets. They are pitifully meager, though his opportunities for character building have been good. He has even had emotional revivals, which did not, however, issue in good deeds. But with it all, Markheim illustrates the nobility of human nature rather than its essential depravity. I do not doubt his complete and permanent conversion. When the terrible last question is put to him—or when he puts it to himself—whether he is better now in any one particular than he was, and when he is forced to say, "No, in none! I have gone down in all," the moral resources of human nature itself seem to be exhausted. But they are not. "I see clearly what remains for me," said Markheim, "by way of duty." This word, not used before, sounds a new challenge and marks the crisis of the story. Duty can fight without calling in reserves from the past and without the vision of victory in the future. I don't wonder that the features of the visitant "softened with a tender triumph." The visitant was neither "the devil" as Markheim first thought him nor "the Saviour of men" as a recent editor pronounces him. He is only Markheim's old self, the self that entered the antique shop, that with fear and trembling committed the deed, and that now, half-conscious all the time of inherent falseness, urges the old arguments and tries to energize the old purposes. It is this visitant that every man meets and overthrows when he comes to himself, when he breaks sharply with the old life and enters resolutely upon the new.]

"Yes," said the dealer, "our windfalls are of various kinds. Some customers are ignorant, and then I touch a dividend on my superior knowledge. Some are dishonest," and here he held up the candle, so that the light fell strongly on his visitor, "and in that case," he continued, "I profit by my virtue."

Markheim had but just entered from the daylight streets, and his eyes had not yet grown familiar with the mingled shine and darkness in the shop. At these pointed words, and before the near presence of the flame, he blinked painfully and looked aside.

The dealer chuckled. "You come to me on Christmas-day," he resumed, "when you know that I am alone in my house, put up my shutters, and make a point of refusing business. Well, you will have to pay for that; you will have to pay for my loss of time, when I should be balancing my books; you will have to pay, besides, for a kind of manner that I remark in you to-day very strongly. I am the essence of discretion, and ask no awkward questions; but when a customer can not look me in the eye, he has to pay for it." The dealer once more chuckled; and then, changing to his usual business voice, though still with a note of irony, "You can give, as usual, a clean account of how you came into the possession of the object?" he continued. "Still your uncle's cabinet? A remarkable collector, sir!"

And the little, pale, round-shouldered dealer stood almost on tip-toe, looking over the top of his gold spectacles, and nodding his head with every mark of disbelief. Markheim returned his gaze with one of infinite pity, and a touch of horror.

"This time," said he, "you are in error. I have not come to sell, but to buy. I have no curios to dispose of; my uncle's cabinet is bare to the wainscot; even were it still intact, I have done well on the Stock Exchange, and should more likely add to it than otherwise, and my errand to-day is simplicity itself. I seek a Christmas-present for a lady," he continued, waxing more fluent as he struck into the speech he had prepared; "and certainly I owe you every excuse for thus disturbing you upon so small a matter. But the thing was neglected yesterday; I must produce my little compliment at dinner; and, as you very well know, a rich marriage is not a thing to be neglected."

There followed a pause, during which the dealer seemed to weigh this statement incredulously. The ticking of many clocks among the curious lumber of the shop, and the faint rushing of the cabs in a near thoroughfare, filled up the interval of silence.

"Well, sir," said the dealer, "be it so. You are an old customer after all; and if, as you say, you have the chance of a good marriage, far be it from me to be an obstacle. Here is a nice thing for a lady now," he went on, "this hand-glass—fifteenth century, warranted; comes from a good collection, too; but I reserve the name, in the interests of my customer, who was just like yourself, my dear sir, the nephew and sole heir of a remarkable collector."

The dealer, while he thus ran on in his dry and biting voice, had stooped to take the object from its place; and, as he had done so, a shock had passed through Markheim, a start both of hand and foot, a sudden leap of many tumultuous passions to the face. It passed as swiftly as it came, and left no trace beyond a certain trembling of the hand that now received the glass.

"A glass," he said, hoarsely, and then paused, and repeated it more clearly. "A glass? For Christmas? Surely not?"

"And why not?" cried the dealer. "Why not a glass?"

Markheim was looking upon him with an indefinable expression. "You ask me why not?" he said. "Why, look here—look in it—look at yourself! Do you like to see it? No! nor I—nor any man."

The little man had jumped back when Markheim had so suddenly confronted him with the mirror; but now, perceiving there was nothing worse on hand, he chuckled. "Your future lady, sir, must be pretty hard favored," said he.

"I ask you," said Markheim, "for a Christmas-present, and you give me this—this damned reminder of years, and sins and follies—this hand-conscience! Did you mean it? Had you a thought in your mind? Tell me. It will be better for you if you do. Come, tell me about yourself. I hazard a guess now, that you are in secret a very charitable man?"

The dealer looked closely, at his companion. It was very odd, Markheim did not appear to be laughing; there was something in his face like an eager sparkle of hope, but nothing of mirth.

"What are you driving at?" the dealer asked.

"Not charitable?" returned the other, gloomily. "Not charitable; not pious; not scrupulous; unloving, unbeloved; a hand to get money, a safe to keep it. Is that all? Dear God, man, is that all?"

"I will tell you what it is," began the dealer, with some sharpness, and then broke off again into a chuckle. "But I see this is a love match of yours, and you have been drinking the lady's health."

"Ah!" cried Markheim, with a strange curiosity. "Ah, have you been in love? Tell me about that."

"I," cried the dealer. "I in love! I never had the time, nor have I the time to-day for all this nonsense. Will you take the glass?"

"Where is the hurry?" returned Markheim. "It is very pleasant to stand here talking; and life is so short and insecure that I would not hurry away from any pleasure—no, not even from so mild a one as this. We should rather cling, cling to what little we can get, like a man at a cliff's edge. Every second is a cliff, if you think upon it—a cliff a mile high—high enough, if we fall, to dash us out of every feature of humanity. Hence it is best to talk pleasantly. Let us talk of each other; why should we wear this mask? Let us be confidential. Who knows, we might become friends?"

"I have just one word to say to you," said the dealer. "Either make your purchase, or walk out of my shop."

"True, true," said Markheim. "Enough fooling. To business. Show me something else."

The dealer stooped once more, this time to replace the glass upon the shelf, his thin blonde hair falling over his eyes as he did so. Markheim moved a little nearer, with one hand in the pocket of his great-coat; he drew himself up and filled his lungs; at the same time many different emotions were depicted together on his face—terror, horror, and resolve, fascination and a physical repulsion; and through a haggard lift of his upper lip, his teeth looked out.

"This, perhaps, may suit," observed the dealer; and then, as he began to re-arise, Markheim bounded from behind upon his victim. The long, skewer-like dagger flashed and fell. The dealer struggled like a hen, striking his temple on the shelf, and then tumbled on the floor in a heap.

Time had some score of small voices in that shop, some stately and slow as was becoming to their great age; others garrulous and hurried. All these told out the seconds in an intricate chorus of tickings. Then the passage of a lad's feet, heavily running on the pavement, broke in upon these smaller voices and startled Markheim into the consciousness of his surroundings. He looked about him awfully. The candle stood on the counter, its flame solemnly wagging in a draught; and by that inconsiderable movement, the whole room was filled with noiseless bustle and kept heaving like a sea: the tall shadows nodding, the gross blots of darkness swelling and dwindling as with respiration, the faces of the portraits and the china gods changing and wavering like images in water. The inner door stood ajar, and peered into that leaguer of shadows with a long slit of daylight like a pointing finger.

From these fear-stricken rovings, Markheim's eyes returned to the body of his victim, where it lay both humped and sprawling, incredibly small and strangely meaner than in life. In these poor, miserly clothes, in that ungainly attitude, the dealer lay like so much sawdust. Markheim had feared to see it, and, lo! it was nothing. And yet, as he gazed, this bundle of old clothes and pool of blood began to find eloquent voices. There it must lie; there was none to work the cunning hinges or direct the miracle of locomotion—there it must lie till it was found. Found! ay, and then? Then would this dead flesh lift up a cry that would ring over England, and fill the world with the echoes of pursuit. Ay, dead or not, this was still the enemy. "Time was that when the brains were out," he thought; and the first word struck into his mind. Time, now that the deed was accomplished—time, which had closed for the victim, had become instant and momentous for the slayer.

The thought was yet in his mind, when, first one and then another, with every variety of pace and voice—one deep as the bell from a cathedral turret, another ringing on its treble notes the prelude of a waltz—the clocks began to strike the hour of three in the afternoon.

The sudden outbreak of so many tongues in that dumb chamber staggered him. He began to bestir himself, going to and fro with the candle, beleaguered by moving shadows, and startled to the soul by chance reflections. In many rich mirrors, some of home designs, some from Venice or Amsterdam, he saw his face repeated and repeated, as it were an army of spies; his own eyes met and detected him; and the sound of his own steps, lightly as they fell, vexed the surrounding quiet. And still as he continued to fill his pockets, his mind accused him, with a sickening iteration, of the thousand faults of his design. He should have chosen a more quiet hour; he should have prepared an alibi; he should not have used a knife; he should have been more cautious, and only bound and gagged the dealer, and not killed him; he should have been more bold, and killed the servant also; he should have done all things otherwise; poignant regrets, weary, incessant toiling of the mind to change what was unchangeable, to plan what was now useless, to be the architect of the irrevocable past. Meanwhile, and behind all this activity, brute terrors, like scurrying of rats in a deserted attic, filled the more remote chambers of his brain with riot; the hand of the constable would fall heavy on his shoulder, and his nerves would jerk like a hooked fish; or he beheld, in galloping defile, the dock, the prison, the gallows, and the black coffin.

Terror of the people in the street sat down before his mind like a besieging army. It was impossible, he thought, but that some rumor of the struggle must have reached their ears and set on edge their curiosity; and now, in all the neighboring houses, he divined them sitting motionless and with uplifted ear—solitary people, condemned to spend Christmas dwelling alone on memories of the past, and now startlingly recalled from that tender exercise; happy family parties, struck into silence round the table, the mother still with raised finger: every degree and age and humor, but all, by their own hearths, prying and hearkening and weaving the rope that was to hang him. Sometimes it seemed to him he could not move too softly; the clink of the tall Bohemian goblets rang out loudly like a bell; and alarmed by the bigness of the ticking, he was tempted to stop the clocks. And then, again, with a swift transition of his terrors, the very silence of the place appeared a source of peril, and a thing to strike and freeze the passer-by; and he would step more boldly, and bustle aloud among the contents of the shop, and imitate, with elaborate bravado, the movements of a busy man at ease in his own house.

But he was now so pulled about by different alarms that, while one portion of his mind was still alert and cunning, another trembled on the brink of lunacy. One hallucination in particular took a strong hold on his credulity. The neighbor hearkening with white face beside his window, the passer-by arrested by a horrible surmise on the pavement—these could at worst suspect, they could not know; through the brick walls and shuttered windows only sounds could penetrate. But here, within the house, was he alone? He knew he was; he had watched the servant set forth sweethearting, in her poor best, "out for the day" written in every ribbon and smile. Yes, he was alone, of course; and yet, in the bulk of empty house above him, he could surely hear a stir of delicate footing—he was surely conscious, inexplicably conscious of some presence. Ay, surely; to every room and corner of the house his imagination followed it; and now it was a faceless thing, and yet had eyes to see with; and again it was a shadow of himself; and yet again behold the image of the dead dealer, reinspired with cunning and hatred.

At times, with a strong effort, he would glance at the open door which still seemed to repel his eyes. The house was tall, the skylight small and dirty, the day blind with fog; and the light that filtered down to the ground story was exceedingly faint, and showed dimly on the threshold of the shop. And yet, in that strip of doubtful brightness, did there not hang wavering a shadow?

Suddenly, from the street outside, a very jovial gentleman began to beat with a staff on the shop-door, accompanying his blows with shouts and railleries in which the dealer was continually called upon by name. Markheim, smitten into ice, glanced at the dead man. But no! he lay quite still; he was fled away far beyond earshot of these blows and shoutings; he was sunk beneath seas of silence; and his name, which would once have caught his notice above the howling of a storm, had become an empty sound. And presently the jovial gentleman desisted from his knocking and departed.

Here was a broad hint to hurry what remained to be done, to get forth from this accusing neighborhood, to plunge into a bath of London multitudes, and to reach, on the other side of day, that haven of safety and apparent innocence—his bed. One visitor had come: at any moment another might follow and be more obstinate. To have done the deed, and yet not to reap the profit, would be too abhorrent a failure. The money, that was now Markheim's concern; and as a means to that, the keys.

He glanced over his shoulder at the open door, where the shadow was still lingering and shivering; and with no conscious repugnance of the mind, yet with a tremor of the belly, he drew near the body of his victim. The human character had quite departed. Like a suit half-stuffed with bran, the limbs lay scattered, the trunk doubled, on the floor; and yet the thing repelled him. Although so dingy and inconsiderable to the eye, he feared it might have more significance to the touch. He took the body by the shoulders, and turned it on its back. It was strangely light and supple, and the limbs, as if they had been broken, fell into the oddest postures. The face was robbed of all expression; but it was as pale as wax, and shockingly smeared with blood about one temple. That was, for Markheim, the one displeasing circumstance. It carried him back, upon the instant, to a certain fair day in a fisher's village: a gray day, a piping wind, a crowd upon the street, the blare of brasses, the booming of drums, the nasal voice of a ballad singer; and a boy going to and fro, buried over head in the crowd and divided between interest and fear, until, coming out upon the chief place of concourse, he beheld a booth and a great screen with pictures, dismally designed, garishly colored: Brownrigg with her apprentice; the Mannings with their murdered guest; Weare in the death-grip of Thurtell; and a score besides of famous crimes. The thing was as clear as an illusion; he was once again that little boy; he was looking once again, and with the same sense of physical revolt, at these vile pictures; he was still stunned by the thumping of the drums. A bar of that day's music returned upon his memory; and at that, for the first time, a qualm came over him, a breath of nausea, a sudden weakness of the joints, which he must instantly resist and conquer.

He judged it more prudent to confront than to flee from these considerations; looking the more hardily in the dead face, bending his mind to realize the nature and greatness of his crime. So little awhile ago that face had moved with every change of sentiment, that pale mouth had spoken, that body had been all on fire with governable energies; and now, and by his act, that piece of life had been arrested, as the horologist, with interjected finger, arrests the beating of the clock. So he reasoned in vain; he could rise to no more remorseful consciousness; the same heart which had shuddered before the painted effigies of crime, looked on its reality unmoved. At best, he felt a gleam of pity for one who had been endowed in vain with all those faculties that can make the world a garden of enchantment, one who had never lived and who was now dead. But of penitence, no, with a tremor.

With that, shaking himself clear of these considerations, he found the keys and advanced toward the open door of the shop. Outside, it had begun to rain smartly; and the sound of the shower upon the roof had banished silence. Like some dripping cavern, the chambers of the house were haunted by an incessant echoing, which filled the ear and mingled with the ticking of the clocks. And, as Markheim approached the door, he seemed to hear, in answer to his own cautious tread, the steps of another foot withdrawing up the stair. The shadow still palpitated loosely on the threshold. He threw a ton's weight of resolve upon his muscles, and drew back the door.

The faint, foggy daylight glimmered dimly on the bare floor and stairs; on the bright suit of armor posted, halbert in hand, upon the landing; and on the dark wood-carvings, and framed pictures that hung against the yellow panels of the wainscot. So loud was the beating of the rain through all the house that, in Markheim's ears, it began to be distinguished into many different sounds. Footsteps and sighs, the tread of regiments marching in the distance, the chink of money in the counting, and the creaking of doors held stealthily ajar, appeared to mingle with the patter of the drops upon the cupola and the gushing of the water in the pipes. The sense that he was not alone grew upon him to the verge of madness. On every side he was haunted and begirt by presences. He heard them moving in the upper chambers; from the shop, he heard the dead man getting to his legs; and as he began with a great effort to mount the stairs, feet fled quietly before him and followed stealthily behind. If he were but deaf, he thought, how tranquilly he would possess his soul. And then again, and hearkening with every fresh attention, he blessed himself for that unresisting sense which held the outposts and stood a trusty sentinel upon his life. His head turned continually on his neck; his eyes, which seemed starting from their orbits, scouted on every side, and on every side were half-rewarded as with the tail of something nameless vanishing. The four-and-twenty steps to the first floor were four-and-twenty agonies.

On that first story, the door stood ajar, three of them like three ambushes, shaking his nerves like the throats of cannon. He could never again, he felt, be sufficiently immured and fortified from men's observing eyes; he longed to be home, girt in by walls, buried among bedclothes, and invisible to all but God. And at that thought he wondered a little, recollecting tales of other murderers and the fear they were said to entertain of heavenly avengers. It was not so, at least, with him. He feared the laws of nature, lest, in their callous and immutable procedure, they should preserve some damning evidence of his crime. He feared tenfold more, with a slavish, superstitious terror, some scission in the continuity of man's experience, some willful illegality of nature. He played a game of skill, depending on the rules, calculating consequence from cause; and what if nature, as the defeated tyrant overthrew the chessboard, should break the mold of their succession? The like had befallen Napoleon (so writers said) when the winter changed the time of its appearance. The like might befall Markheim: the solid walls might become transparent and reveal his doings like those of bees in a glass hive; the stout planks might yield under his foot like quicksands and detain him in their clutch; ay, and there were soberer accidents that might destroy him: if, for instance, the house should fall and imprison him beside the body of his victim; the house next door should fly on fire, and the firemen invade him from all sides. These things he feared; and, in a sense, these things might be called the hands of God reached forth against sin. But about God himself he was at ease; his act was doubtless exceptional, but so were his excuses, which God knew; it was there, and not among men, that he felt sure of justice.

When he had got safe into the drawing-room, and shut the door behind him, he was aware of a respite from alarms. The room was quite dismantled, uncarpeted besides, and strewn with packing cases and incongruous furniture; several great pier-glasses, in which he beheld himself at various angles, like an actor on the stage; many pictures, framed and unframed, standing with their faces to the wall; a fine Sheraton sideboard, a cabinet of marquetry, and a great old bed, with tapestry hangings. The windows opened to the floor; but by great good fortune the lower part of the shutters had been closed, and this concealed him from the neighbors. Here, then, Markheim drew in a packing case before the cabinet, and began to search among the keys. It was a long business, for there were many; and it was irksome, besides; for, after all, there might be nothing in the cabinet, and time was on the wing. But the closeness of the occupation sobered him. With the tail of his eye he saw the door—even glanced at it from time to time directly, like a besieged commander pleased to verify the good estate of his defenses. But in truth he was at peace. The rain falling in the street sounded natural and pleasant. Presently, on the other side, the notes of a piano were wakened to the music of a hymn, and the voices of many children took up the air and words. How stately, how comfortable was the melody! How fresh the youthful voices! Markheim gave ear to it smilingly, as he sorted out the keys; and his mind was thronged with answerable ideas and images; church-going children and the pealing of the high organ; children afield, bathers by the brook-side, ramblers on the brambly common, kite-flyers in the windy and cloud-navigated sky; and then, at another cadence of the hymn, back again to church, and the somnolence of summer Sundays, and the high genteel voice of the parson (which he smiled a little to recall) and the painted Jacobean tombs, and the dim lettering of the Ten Commandments in the chancel.

And as he sat thus, at once busy and absent, he was startled to his feet. A flash of ice, a flash of fire, a bursting gush of blood, went over him, and then he stood transfixed and thrilling. A step mounted the stair slowly and steadily, and presently a hand was laid upon the knob, and the lock clicked, and the door opened.

Fear held Markheim in a vice. What to expect he knew not, whether the dead man walking, or the official ministers of human justice, or some chance witness blindly stumbling in to consign him to the gallows. But when a face was thrust into the aperture, glanced round the room, looked at him, nodded and smiled as if in friendly recognition, and then withdrew again, and the door closed behind it, his fear broke loose from his control in a hoarse cry. At the sound of this the visitant returned.

"Did you call me?" he asked, pleasantly, and with that he entered the room and closed the door behind him.

Markheim stood and gazed at him with all his eyes. Perhaps there was a film upon his sight, but the outlines of the newcomer seemed to change and waver like those of the idols in the wavering candle-light of the shop; and at times he thought he knew him; and at times he thought he bore a likeness to himself; and always, like a lump of living terror, there lay in his bosom the conviction that this thing was not of the earth and not of God.

And yet the creature had a strange air of the common-place, as he stood looking on Markheim with a smile; and when he added: "You are looking for the money, I believe?" it was in the tones of everyday politeness.

Markheim made no answer.

"I should warn you," resumed the other, "that the maid has left her sweetheart earlier than usual and will soon be here. If Mr. Markheim be found in this house, I need not describe to him the consequences."

"You know me?" cried the murderer.

The visitor smiled. "You have long been a favorite of mine," he said; "and I have long observed and often sought to help you."

"What are you?" cried Markheim: "the devil?"

"What I may be," returned the other, "can not affect the service I propose to render you."

"It can," cried Markheim; "it does! Be helped by you? No, never; not by you! You do not know me yet, thank God, you do not know me!"

"I know you," replied the visitant, with a sort of kind severity or rather firmness. "I know you to the soul."

"Know me!" cried Markheim. "Who can do so? My life is but a travesty and slander on myself. I have lived to belie my nature. All men do; all men are better than this disguise that grows about and stifles them. You see each dragged away by life, like one whom bravos have seized and muffled in a cloak. If they had their own control—if you could see their faces, they would be altogether different, they would shine out for heroes and saints! I am worse than most; my self is more overlaid; my excuse is known to me and God. But, had I the time, I could disclose myself."

"To me?" inquired the visitant.

"To you before all," returned the murderer. "I supposed you were intelligent. I thought—since you exist—you would prove a reader of the heart. And yet you would propose to judge me by my acts! Think of it; my acts! I was born and I have lived in a land of giants; giants have dragged me by the wrists since I was born out of my mother—the giants of circumstance. And you would judge me by my acts! But can you not look within? Can you not understand that evil is hateful to me? Can you not see within me the clear writing of conscience, never blurred by any willful sophistry, although too often disregarded? Can you not read me for a thing that surely must be common as humanity—the unwilling sinner?"

"All this is very feelingly expressed," was the reply, "but it regards me not. These points of consistency are beyond my province, and I care not in the least by what compulsion you may have been dragged away, so as you are but carried in the right direction. But time flies; the servant delays, looking in the faces of the crowd and at the pictures on the hoardings, but still she keeps moving nearer; and remember, it is as if the gallows itself was striding toward you through the Christmas streets! Shall I help you; I, who know all? Shall I tell you where to find the money?"

"For what price?" asked Markheim.

"I offer you the service for a Christmas gift," returned the other.

Markheim could not refrain from smiling with a kind of bitter triumph. "No," said he, "I will take nothing at your hands; if I were dying of thirst, and it was your hand that put the pitcher to my lips, I should find the courage to refuse. It may be credulous, but I will do nothing to commit myself to evil."

"I have no objection to a death-bed repentance," observed the visitant.

"Because you disbelieve their efficacy!" Markheim cried.

"I do not say so," returned the other; "but I look on these things from a different side, and when the life is done my interest falls. The man has lived to serve me, to spread black looks under color of religion, or to sow tares in the wheat-field, as you do, in a course of weak compliance with desire. Now that he draws so near to his deliverance, he can add but one act of service—to repent, to die smiling, and thus to build up in confidence and hope the more timorous of my surviving followers. I am not so hard a master. Try me. Accept my help. Please yourself in life as you have done hitherto; please yourself more amply, spread your elbows at the board; and when the night begins to fall and the curtains to be drawn, I tell you, for your greater comfort, that you will find it even easy to compound your quarrel with your conscience, and to make a truckling peace with God. I came but now from such a death-bed, and the room was full of sincere mourners, listening to the man's last words: and when I looked into that face, which had been set as a flint against mercy, I found it smiling with hope."

"And do you, then, suppose me such a creature?" asked Markheim. "Do you think I have no more generous aspirations than to sin, and sin, and sin, and, at last, sneak into heaven? My heart rises at the thought. Is this, then, your experience of mankind? or is it because you find me with red hands that you presume such baseness? and is this crime of murder indeed so impious as to dry up the very springs of good?"

"Murder is to me no special category," replied the other. "All sins are murder, even as all life is war. I behold your race, like starving mariners on a raft, plucking crusts out of the hands of famine and feeding on each other's lives. I follow sins beyond the moment of their acting; I find in all that the last consequence is death; and to my eyes, the pretty maid who thwarts her mother with such taking graces on a question of a ball, drips no less visibly with human gore than such a murderer as yourself. Do I say that I follow sins? I follow virtues also; they differ not by the thickness of a nail, they are both scythes for the reaping angel of Death. Evil, for which I live, consists not in action but in character. The bad man is dear to me; not the bad act, whose fruits, if we could follow them far enough down the hurtling cataract of the ages, might yet be found more blessed than those of the rarest virtues. And it is not because you have killed a dealer, but because you are Markheim, that I offered to forward your escape."

"I will lay my heart open to you," answered Markheim. "This crime on which you find me is my last. On my way to it I have learned many lessons; itself is a lesson, a momentous lesson. Hitherto I have been driven with revolt to what I would not; I was a bond-slave to poverty, driven and scourged. There are robust virtues that can stand in these temptations; mine was not so: I had a thirst of pleasure. But to-day, and out of this deed, I pluck both warning and riches—both the power and a fresh resolve to be myself. I become in all things a free actor in the world; I begin to see myself all changed, these hands the agents of good, this heart at peace. Something comes over me out of the past; something of what I have dreamed on Sabbath evenings to the sound of the church organ, of what I forecast when I shed tears over noble books, or talked, an innocent child, with my mother. There lies my life; I have wandered a few years, but now I see once more my city of destination."

"You are to use this money on the Stock Exchange, I think?" remarked the visitor; "and there, if I mistake not, you have already lost some thousands?"

"Ah," said Markheim, "but this time I have a sure thing."

"This time, again, you will lose," replied the visitor, quietly.

"Ah, but I keep back the half!" cried Markheim.

"That also you will lose," said the other.

The sweat started upon Markheim's brow. "Well, then, what matter?" he exclaimed. "Say it be lost, say I am plunged again in poverty, shall one part of me, and that the worse, continue until the end to override the better? Evil and good run strong in me, haling me both ways. I do not love the one thing, I love all. I can conceive great deeds, renunciations, martyrdoms; and though I be fallen to such a crime as murder, pity is no stranger to my thoughts. I pity the poor; who knows their trials better than myself? I pity and help them; I prize love, I love honest laughter; there is no good thing nor true thing on earth but I love it from my heart. And are my vices only to direct my life, and my virtues to lie without effect, like some passive lumber of the mind? Not so; good, also, is a spring of acts."

But the visitant raised his finger. "For six-and-thirty years that you have been in this world," said he, "through many changes of fortune and varieties of humor, I have watched you steadily fall. Fifteen years ago you would have started at a theft. Three years back you would have blenched at the name of murder. Is there any crime, is there any cruelty or meanness, from which you still recoil?—five years from now I shall detect you in the fact! Downward, downward, lies your way; nor can anything but death avail to stop you."

"It is true," Markheim said, huskily, "I have in some degree complied with evil. But it is so with all: the very saints, in the mere exercise of living, grow less dainty, and take on the tone of their surroundings."

"I will propound to you one simple question," said the other; "and as you answer, I shall read to you your moral horoscope. You have grown in many things more lax; possibly you do right to be so; and at any account, it is the same with all men. But granting that, are you in any one particular, however trifling, more difficult to please with your own conduct, or do you go in all things with a looser rein?"

"In any one?" repeated Markheim, with an anguish of consideration. "No," he added, with despair, "in none! I have gone down in all."

"Then," said the visitor, "content yourself with what you are, for you will never change; and the words of your part on this stage are irrevocably written down."

Markheim stood for a long while silent, and indeed it was the visitor who first broke the silence. "That being so," he said, "shall I show you the money?"

"And grace?" cried Markheim.

"Have you not tried it?" returned the other. "Two or three years ago, did I not see you on the platform of revival meetings, and was not your voice the loudest in the hymn?"

"It is true," said Markheim; "and I see clearly what remains for me by way of duty. I thank you for these lessons from my soul: my eyes are opened, and I behold myself at last for what I am."

At this moment, the sharp note of the door-bell rung through the house; and the visitant, as though this were some concerted signal for which he had been waiting, changed at once in his demeanor.

"The maid!" he cried. "She has returned, as I forewarned you, and there is now before you one more difficult passage. Her master, you must say, is ill; you must let her in, with an assured but rather serious countenance—no smiles, no overacting, and I promise you success! Once the girl within, and the door closed, the same dexterity that has already rid you of the dealer will relieve you of this last danger in your path. Thenceforward you have the whole evening—the whole night, if needful—to ransack the treasures of the house and to make good your safety. This is help that comes to you with the mask of danger. Up!" he cried: "up, friend; your life hangs trembling in the scales; up, and act!"

Markheim steadily regarded his counsellor. "If I be condemned to evil acts," he said, "there is still one door of freedom open—I can cease from action. If my life be an ill thing, I can lay it down. Though I be, as you say truly, at the beck of every small temptation, I can yet, by one decisive gesture, place myself beyond the reach of all. My love of good is damned to barrenness; it may, and let it be! But I have still my hatred of evil; and from that, to your galling disappointment, you shall see that I can draw both energy and courage."

The features of the visitor began to undergo a wonderful and lovely change; they brightened and softened with a tender triumph; and, even as they brightened, faded and dislimned. But Markheim did not pause to watch or understand the transformation. He opened the door and went down-stairs very slowly, thinking to himself. His past went soberly before him; he beheld it as it was, ugly and strenuous like a dream, random as chance-medley—a scene of defeat. Life, as he thus reviewed it, tempted him no longer; but on the further side he perceived a quiet haven for his bark. He paused in the passage, and looked into the shop, where the candle still burned by the dead body. It was strangely silent. Thoughts of the dealer swarmed into his mind, as he stood gazing. And then the bell once more broke out into impatient clamor.

He confronted the maid upon the threshold with something like a smile.

"You had better go for the police," said he: "I have killed your master."

THE NECKLACE [19] (1885)

BY GUY DE MAUPASSANT (1850-1893)

[Setting. The story is set in a Paris atmosphere of social aspiration and discontent. The background is one of studied contrasts, contrasts between the stolid contentment of a husband and the would-be luxuriousness of a wife, between what Madame Loisel had and what she wanted, between what she was and what she thought she could be, between her brief moment of triumph and the long years of her undoing, between the trivialness of what she did and the heaviness of her punishment. These contrasts are developed not by reasoning but by action, each action plunging Madame Loisel deeper and deeper into misery. The author's attitude toward his work forms also a part of the real background. Maupassant shows neither sympathy nor indignation. He writes as if he were the stenographer of impersonal and pitiless fate.

Plot. Madame Loisel, a poor but beautiful and ambitious woman, borrows and loses a diamond necklace valued at $7200. That, at least, is what Madame Loisel thought for ten terrible years, and that is what the reader thinks till he comes to the last words of the story. The plot belongs, therefore, to that large group known as hoax plots. In most of these stories one person plays a joke on another. In this story a grim fate is made to play the joke. In fact, the current phrase, "the irony of fate," finds here perfect illustration. We use the expression not so much of a great misfortune as of a misfortune that seems brought about by a peculiarly malignant train of circumstances. The injury in this case not only was irremediable but turned on an accident. Notice also how Maupassant has sharpened the poignancy and bitterness of Madame Loisel's misfortune by making it depend not only on an accident that might so easily not have happened but on a misunderstanding that might so easily have been explained. When Madame Loisel, just on the threshold of her life of drudgery, took the necklace bought on credit to Madame Forestier, the latter "did not open the case, to the relief of her friend." The irony of fate could hardly go further; but it does go further a little later, when Madame Forestier, still young and beautiful, fails to recognize Madame Loisel because the latter had lost youth, beauty, daintiness, her very self, in toiling to pay to Madame Forestier a debt that was not a debt. Just before the final revelation Madame Loisel is made to say, "I am very glad." There is a unique pathos in her use of this word: it lifted her a little from the ground that her fall might be all the harder.

There is no denying the art of this story, but it is art without heart. The author is a craftsman rather than a creator, a master of the loom rather than of the forge. Maupassant did perfectly what he wanted to do,

---

[19] "La parure" from "Contes et nouvelles."

but his greatness and his limitation are both revealed. "What would have happened," he says, "if she had not lost that necklace? Who knows, who knows? How strange life is, how changeful! How little a thing is needed for us to be lost or to be saved!" The greatest art may begin but not end this way.

Characters. The man is only a foil to his wife. He is introduced to bring into sharper relief her unhappiness and her powerlessness to better her condition. He is not a bad man, nor is she a bad woman. To say that the story turns entirely on his honor and on her false pride is to miss, I think, the author's purpose. There is nothing distinctive in these characters; he is better than she, but both are puppets in the grip of brute circumstance rather than everyday characters shaped by the ordinary pressures of life. They are not types as Rip is a type, or Scrooge, or Oakhurst. Maupassant shows in his stories that he is interested not so much in the free play or the full reaction of personality as in the enslavement of personality through passion or chance. He saw life without order because without center, without reward because without desert; and his characters are made to see it through the same lens and to experience it on the same level. They either do not react or do not react nobly. Had Madame Loisel and her husband been shaped to fit into a less mechanical scheme of things, they would have recognized in their ten years' trial the call to something higher. They could have used their testing as a means of understanding with keener sympathy the lifelong testing of others. They could have attained a self-development that would have brought a happiness undreamed of before the fateful January 18. But this is Browning's way, not Maupassant's. The latter prefers to make Madame Loisel and her husband chiefly of putty so that they may illustrate the blind thrusts of accident rather than the power of personality to turn stumbling-blocks into stepping-stones.]

She was one of those pretty and charming girls who, as if by a mistake of destiny, are born in a family of employees. She had no dowry, no expectations, no means of becoming known, understood, loved, wedded by any rich and distinguished man; and so she let herself be married to a petty clerk in the Bureau of Public Instruction.

She was simple in her dress because she could not be elaborate, but she was as unhappy as if she had fallen from a higher rank, for with women there is no inherited distinction of higher and lower. Their beauty, their grace, and their natural charm fill the place of birth and family. Natural delicacy, instinctive elegance, a lively wit, are the ruling forces in the social realm, and these make the daughters of the common people the equals of the finest ladies.

She suffered intensely, feeling herself born for all the refinements and luxuries of life. She suffered from the poverty of her home as she looked at the dirty walls, the worn-out chairs, the ugly curtains. All those things of which another woman of her station would have been quite unconscious tortured her and made her indignant. The sight of the country girl who was maid-of-all-work in her humble household filled her almost with desperation. She dreamed of echoing halls hung with Oriental draperies and lighted by tall bronze candelabra, while two tall footmen in knee-breeches drowsed in great armchairs by reason of the heating stove's oppressive warmth. She dreamed of splendid parlors furnished in rare old silks, of carved cabinets loaded with priceless bric-a-brac, and of entrancing little boudoirs just right for afternoon chats with bosom friends—men famous and sought after, the envy and the desire of all the other women.

When she sat down to dinner at a little table covered with a cloth three days old, and looked across at her husband as he uncovered the soup and exclaimed with an air of rapture, "Oh, the delicious stew! I know nothing better than that," she dreamed of dainty dinners, of shining silverware, of tapestries which peopled the walls with antique figures and strange birds in fairy forests; she dreamed of delicious viands served in wonderful dishes, of whispered gallantries heard with a sphinx-like smile as you eat the pink flesh of a trout or the wing of a quail.

She had no dresses, no jewels, nothing; and she loved nothing else. She felt made for that alone. She was filled with a desire to please, to be envied, to be bewitching and sought after. She had a rich friend, a former schoolmate at the convent, whom she no longer wished to visit because she suffered so much when she came home. For whole days at a time she wept without ceasing in bitterness and hopeless misery.

Now, one evening her husband came home with a triumphant air, holding in his hand a large envelope.

"There," said he, "there is something for you."

She quickly tore open the paper and drew out a printed card, bearing these words:—

"The Minister of Public Instruction and Mme. Georges Rampouneau request the honor of M. and Mme. Loisel's company at the palace of the Ministry, Monday evening, January 18th."

Instead of being overcome with delight, as her husband expected, she threw the invitation on the table with disdain, murmuring:

"What do you wish me to do with that?"

"Why, my dear, I thought you would be pleased. You never go out, and this is such a fine opportunity! I had awful trouble in getting it. Every one wants to go; it is very select, and they are not giving many invitations to clerks. You will see all the official world."

She looked at him with irritation, and said, impatiently:

"What do you expect me to put on my back if I go?"

He had not thought of that. He stammered:

"Why, the dress you go to the theatre in. It seems all right to me."

He stopped, stupefied, distracted, on seeing that his wife was crying. Two great tears descended slowly from the corners of her eyes toward the corners of her mouth. He stuttered:

"What's the matter? What's the matter?"

By a violent effort she subdued her feelings and replied in a calm voice, as she wiped her wet cheeks:

"Nothing. Only I have no dress and consequently I cannot go to this ball. Give your invitation to some friend whose wife has better clothes than I."

He was in despair, but began again:

"Let us see, Mathilde. How much would it cost, a suitable dress, which you could wear again on future occasions, something very simple?"

She reflected for some seconds, computing the cost, and also wondering what sum she could ask without bringing down upon herself an immediate refusal and an astonished exclamation from the economical clerk.

At last she answered hesitatingly:

"I don't know exactly, but it seems to me that with four hundred francs

I could manage."

He turned a trifle pale, for he had been saving just that sum to buy a gun and treat himself to a little hunting trip the following summer, in the country near Nanterre, with a few friends who went there to shoot larks on Sundays.

However, he said:

"Well, I think I can give you four hundred francs. But see that you have a pretty dress."

* * * * *

The day of the ball drew near, and Madame Loisel seemed sad, restless, anxious. Her dress was ready, however. Her husband said to her one evening:

"What is the matter? Come, now, you've been looking queer these last three days."

And she replied:

"It worries me that I have no jewels, not a single stone, nothing to put on. I shall look wretched enough. I would almost rather not go to this party."

He answered:

"You might wear natural flowers. They are very fashionable this season.

For ten francs you can get two or three magnificent roses."

She was not convinced.

"No; there is nothing more humiliating than to look poor among a lot of rich women."

But her husband cried:

"How stupid you are! Go and find your friend Madame Forestier and ask her to lend you some jewels. You are intimate enough with her for that."

She uttered a cry of joy.

"Of course. I had not thought of that."

The next day she went to her friend's house and told her distress.

145

Madame Forestier went to her handsome wardrobe, took out a large casket, brought it back, opened it, and said to Madame Loisel:

"Choose, my dear."

She saw first of all some bracelets, then a pearl necklace, then a Venetian cross of gold set with precious stones of wonderful workmanship. She tried on the ornaments before the glass, hesitated, could not make up her mind to part with them, to give them back. She kept asking:

"You have nothing else?"

"Why, yes. But I do not know what will please you."

All at once she discovered, in a black satin box, a splendid diamond necklace, and her heart began to beat with boundless desire. Her hands trembled as she took it. She fastened it around her throat, over her high-necked dress, and stood lost in ecstasy as she looked at herself.

Then she asked, hesitating, full of anxiety:

"Would you lend me that,—only that?"

"Why, yes, certainly."

She sprang upon the neck of her friend, embraced her rapturously, then fled with her treasure.

* * * * *

The day of the ball arrived. Madame Loisel was a success. She was prettier than all the others, elegant, gracious, smiling, and crazy with joy. All the men stared at her, asked her name, tried to be introduced. All the cabinet officials wished to waltz with her. The minister noticed her.

She danced with delight, with passion, intoxicated with pleasure, forgetting all in the triumph of her beauty, in the glory of her success, in a sort of mist of happiness, the result of all this homage, all this admiration, all these awakened desires, this victory so complete and so sweet to the heart of woman.

She left about four o'clock in the morning. Her husband had been dozing since midnight in a little deserted anteroom with three other gentlemen, whose wives were having a good time.

He threw about her shoulders the wraps which he had brought for her to go out in, the modest wraps of common life, whose poverty contrasted sharply with the elegance of the ball dress. She felt this and wished to escape, that she might not be noticed by the other women who were wrapping themselves in costly furs.

Loisel held her back.

"Wait here, you will catch cold outside. I will go and find a cab."

But she would not listen to him, and rapidly descended the stairs. When they were at last in the street, they could find no carriage, and began to look for one, hailing the cabmen they saw passing at a distance.

They walked down toward the Seine in despair, shivering with the cold. At last they found on the quay one of those ancient nocturnal cabs that one sees in Paris only after dark, as if they were ashamed to display their wretchedness during the day.

They were put down at their door in the Rue des Martyrs, and sadly mounted the steps to their apartments. It was all over, for her. And as for him, he reflected that he must be at his office at ten o'clock.

She took off the wraps which covered her shoulders, before the mirror, so as to take a final look at herself in all her glory. But suddenly she uttered a cry. She no longer had the necklace about her neck!

Her husband, already half undressed, inquired:

"What is the matter?"

She turned madly toward him.

"I have—I have—I no longer have Madame Forestier's necklace."

He stood up, distracted.

"What!—how!—it is impossible!"

They looked in the folds of her dress, in the folds of her cloak, in the pockets, everywhere. They could not find a trace of it.

He asked:

"You are sure you still had it when you left the ball?"

"Yes. I felt it on me in the vestibule at the palace."

"But if you had lost it in the street we should have heard it fall. It must be in the cab."

"Yes. That's probable. Did you take the number?"

"No. And you, you did not notice it?"

"No."

They looked at each other thunderstruck. At last Loisel put on his clothes again.

"I am going back," said he, "over every foot of the way we came, to see if I cannot find it."

So he started. She remained in her ball dress without strength to go to bed, sitting on a chair, with no fire, her mind a blank.

Her husband returned about seven o'clock. He had found nothing.

He went to police headquarters, to the newspapers to offer a reward, to the cab companies, everywhere, in short, where a trace of hope led him.

She watched all day, in the same state of blank despair before this frightful disaster.

Loisel returned in the evening with cheeks hollow and pale; he had found nothing.

"You must write to your friend," said he, "that you have broken the clasp of her necklace and that you are having it repaired. It will give us time to turn around."

She wrote as he dictated.

* * * * *

At the end of a week they had lost all hope.

And Loisel, looking five years older, declared:

"We must consider how to replace the necklace."

The next day they took the box which had contained it, and went to the place of the jeweller whose name they found inside. He consulted his books.

"It was not I, madame, who sold the necklace; I must simply have furnished the casket."

Then they went from jeweller to jeweller, looking for an ornament like the other, consulting their memories, both sick with grief and anguish.

They found, in a shop at the Palais Royal, a string of diamonds which seemed to them exactly what they were looking for. It was worth forty thousand francs. [20] They could have it for thirty-six thousand.

So they begged the jeweller not to sell it for three days. And they made an arrangement that he should take it back for thirty-four thousand francs if the other were found before the end of February.

Loisel had eighteen thousand francs which his father had left him. He would borrow the rest.

He did borrow, asking a thousand francs of one, five hundred of another, five louis here, three louis there. He gave notes, made ruinous engagements, dealt with usurers, with all the tribe of money-lenders. He compromised the rest of his life, risked his signature without knowing if he might not be involving his honor, and, terrified by the anguish yet to come, by the black misery about to fall upon him, by the prospect of every physical privation and every mental torture, he went to get the new necklace, and laid down on the dealer's counter thirty-six thousand francs.

When Madame Loisel took the necklace back to Madame Forestier, the latter said coldly:

"You should have returned it sooner, for I might have needed it."

She did not open the case, to the relief of her friend. If she had detected the substitution, what would she have thought? What would she have said? Would she have taken her friend for a thief?

* * * * *

Madame Loisel now knew the horrible life of the needy. But she took her part heroically. They must pay this frightful debt. She would pay it. They dismissed their maid; they gave up their room; they rented another, under the roof.

She came to know the drudgery of housework, the odious labors of the kitchen. She washed the dishes, staining her rosy nails on the greasy pots and the bottoms of the saucepans. She washed the dirty linen, the shirts and the dishcloths, which she hung to dry on a line; she carried the garbage down to the street every morning, and carried up the water, stopping at each landing to rest. And, dressed like a woman of the people, she went to the fruiterer's, the grocer's, the butcher's, her basket on her arm, bargaining, abusing, defending sou [21] by sou her miserable money.

Each month they had to pay some notes, renew others, obtain more time.

---

[20] A franc is equal to twenty cents of our money.

[21] A sou, or five-centime piece, is equal to one cent of our money.

The husband worked every evening, neatly footing up the account books of some tradesman, and often far into the night he sat copying manuscript at five sous a page.

And this life lasted ten years.

At the end of ten years they had paid everything,—everything, with the exactions of usury and the accumulations of compound interest.

Madame Loisel seemed aged now. She had become the woman of impoverished households,—strong and hard and rough. With hair half combed, with skirts awry, and reddened hands, she talked loud as she washed the floor with great swishes of water. But sometimes, when her husband was at the office, she sat down near the window and thought of that evening at the ball so long ago, when she had been so beautiful and so admired.

What would have happened if she had not lost that necklace? Who knows, who knows? How strange life is, how changeful! How little a thing is needed for us to be lost or to be saved!

* * * * *

But one Sunday, as she was going for a walk in the Champs Élysées to refresh herself after the labors of the week, all at once she saw a woman walking with a child. It was Madame Forestier, still young, still beautiful, still charming.

Madame Loisel was agitated. Should she speak to her? Why, of course. And now that she had paid, she would tell her all. Why not?

She drew near.

"Good morning, Jeanne."

The other, astonished to be addressed so familiarly by this woman of the people, did not recognize her. She stammered:

"But—madame—I do not know you. You must have made a mistake."

"No, I am Mathilde Loisel."

Her friend uttered a cry.

"Oh! my poor Mathilde, how changed you are!"

"Yes, I have had days hard enough since I saw you, days wretched enough—and all because of you!"

"Me? How so?"

"You remember that necklace of diamonds that you lent me to wear to the ministerial ball?"

"Yes. Well?"

"Well, I lost it."

"How can that be? You returned it to me."

"I returned to you another exactly like it. These ten years we've been paying for it. You know it was not easy for us, who had nothing. At last it is over, and I am very glad."

Madame Forestier was stunned.

"You say that you bought a diamond necklace to replace mine?"

"Yes; you did not notice it, then? They were just alike."

And she smiled with a proud and naïve pleasure.

Madame Forestier, deeply moved, took both her hands.

"Oh, my poor Mathilde! Why, my necklace was paste. It was worth five hundred francs at most."

THE MAN WHO WOULD BE KING [22] (1888)

BY RUDYARD KIPLING (1865-)

[Setting. "They call it Kafiristan," said Dravot, the unfortunate hero of the story. "By my reckoning it's the top right-hand corner of Afghanistan, not more than three hundred miles from Peshawar." Determined to be Kings of Kafiristan, Carnehan and Dravot started probably from the capital of the Punjab, Lahore, where the newspaper office seems to have been. Ten miles west of Peshawar they entered the famous Khaiber (or Khyber) Pass, a region which Kipling describes more at length in "The Man Who Was," "The Drums of the Fore and Aft," "The Lost Legion," "Love o' Women," "Wee Willie Winkie," and "With the Main Guard." No country in Asia is less known to civilization than Kafiristan. The Mohammedan traders say that it is the most attractive part of Afghanistan. The name means "country of unbelievers," the Kafirs having resisted all attempts to convert them to the Mohammedan faith. They are pure Aryans, being thus brothers to the Greeks, Romans, Germans, English, and ourselves. They are noted for their beauty and strength. India or rather Anglo-India has been almost re-discovered by Kipling, but this is his only story of Kafiristan. It too, as Carnehan and Dravot learn to their sorrow, is a land of impenetrable mystery.

Plot. The real plot does not begin to unfold itself until Carnehan, wrecked in body and mind, returns to the newspaper office and tries to report his experiences. Thus nearly one half of the story may be called introductory or preliminary. This is unusual with Kipling and with all other modern story writers. The introduction justifies itself, however, in this case because, since a half-crazed man with weakening memory is to tell the real tale, his narrative would have to be supplemented by explanations on nearly every page unless the introductory part could be taken for granted. Notice how often in reading Carnehan's broken story you supply what he omits and interpret what he only fragmentarily says by reference to what has gone before.

Kipling has done more in this story than to present a character of limitless audacity. He has impressed again one of his favorite teachings. There is, he holds, a barrier between East and West that can never be crossed. The West can go so far with the East but no farther. Brave men of the West may conquer the East and rule it, but to take liberties with it is to uncover a vast realm of the unknown and to invite disaster. In "The Return of Imray," a good-natured Englishman pats the head of Bahadur Khan's child and is killed for it. Another Englishman, in "Beyond the Pale," thought that he understood the heart of India, and here is his epitaph: "He took too deep an interest in native life, but he will never do so again."

---

[22] From "The Phantom 'Rickshaw."

Dravot could play king and even god in Kafiristan, but when he exposed himself ignorantly to an old racial superstition he met instant and inevitable destruction.

Characters. Carnehan tells the story, but Dravot is the energizing character. Captain James Cook, the discoverer of the Sandwich Islands, is plainly the original of Dravot. Read the thirtieth chapter of the second volume of Mark Twain's "Roughing It" (1872) and you will find Kipling's story clearly outlined. One cannot withhold a measure of admiration for this type of uncontrolled audacity. Dravot was not bad at heart, he was only boundless, a type of the adventurer that has given many a fascinating chapter to history as well as to literature. In "The Research Magnificent," by Mr. H.G. Wells, the hero, Benham, says: "I think what I want is to be king of the world.... It is the very core of me.... I mean to be a king in this earth. King. I'm not mad." His motive, however, is very different from Dravot's. "I see the world," he continues, "staggering from misery to misery, and there is little wisdom, less rule, folly, prejudice, limitation ... and it is my world and I am responsible.... As soon as your kingship is plain to you, there is no more rest, no peace, no delight, except in work, in service, in utmost effort." The three weaknesses to be overcome are Fear, Indulgence, and Jealousy. Both Dravot and Benham fail and the comment of each on his own failure is an autobiography. Benham: "I can feel that greater world I shall never see as one feels the dawn coming through the last darkness." Dravot: "We've had a dashed fine run for our money. What's coming next?"]

Brother to a Prince and fellow to a beggar if he be found worthy.

The Law, as quoted, lays down a fair conduct of life, and one not easy to follow. I have been fellow to a beggar again and again under circumstances which prevented either of us finding out whether the other was worthy. I have still to be brother to a Prince, though I once came near to kinship with what might have been a veritable King and was promised the reversion of a Kingdom—army, law-courts, revenue and policy all complete. But, to-day, I greatly fear that my King is dead, and if I want a crown I must go hunt it for myself.

The beginning of everything was in a railway train upon the road to Mhow from Ajmir. There had been a Deficit in the Budget, which necessitated travelling, not Second-class, which is only half as dear as First-class, but by Intermediate, which is very awful indeed. There are no cushions in the Intermediate class, and the population are either Intermediate, which is Eurasian, or native, which for a long night journey is nasty, or Loafer, which is amusing though intoxicated. Intermediates do not buy from refreshment-rooms. They carry their food in bundles and pots, and buy sweets from the native sweetmeat-sellers, and drink the roadside water. That is why in hot weather Intermediates are taken out of the carriages dead, and in all weathers are most properly looked down upon.

My particular Intermediate happened to be empty till I reached Nasirabad, when a big black-browed gentleman in shirt-sleeves entered, and, following the custom of Intermediates, passed the time of day. He was a wanderer and a vagabond like myself, but with an educated taste for whiskey. He told tales of things he had seen and done, of out-of-the-way corners of the Empire into which he had penetrated, and of adventures in which he risked his life for a few days' food.

"If India was filled with men like you and me, not knowing more than the crows where they'd get their next day's rations, it isn't seventy millions of revenue the land would be paying—it's seven hundred millions," said he; and as I looked at his mouth and chin I was disposed to agree with him.

We talked politics—the politics of Loaferdom that sees things from the underside where the lath and plaster is not smoothed off—and we talked postal arrangements because my friend wanted to send a telegram back from the next station to Ajmir, the turning-off place from the Bombay to the Mhow line as you travel westward. My friend had no money beyond eight annas which he wanted for dinner, and I had no money at all, owing to the hitch in the Budget before mentioned. Further, I was going into a wilderness where, though I should resume touch with the Treasury, there were no telegraph offices. I was, therefore, unable to help him in any way.

"We might threaten a Station-master, and make him send a wire on tick," said my friend, "but that'd mean enquiries for you and for me, and I've got my hands full these days. Did you say you were travelling back along this line within any days?"

"Within ten," I said.

"Can't you make it eight?" said he. "Mine is rather urgent business."

"I can send your telegram within ten days if that will serve you," I said.

"I couldn't trust the wire to fetch him now I think of it. It's this way. He leaves Delhi on the 23rd for Bombay. That means he'll be running through Ajmir about the night of the 23rd."

"But I'm going into the Indian Desert," I explained.

"Well and good," said he. "You'll be changing at Marwar Junction to get into Jodhpore territory—you must do that—and he'll be coming through Marwar Junction in the early morning of the 24th by the Bombay Mail. Can you be at Marwar Junction on that time? 'T won't be inconveniencing you because I know that there's precious few pickings to be got out of these Central India States—even though you pretend to be correspondent or the Backwoodsman."

"Have you ever tried that trick?" I asked.

"Again and again, but the Residents find you out, and then you get escorted to the Border before you've time to get your knife into them. But about my friend here. I must give him a word o' mouth to tell him what's come to me or else he won't know where to go. I would take it more than kind of you if you was to come out of Central India in time to catch him at Marwar Junction, and say to him: 'He has gone South for the week.' He'll know what that means. He's a big man with a red beard, and a great swell he is. You'll find him sleeping like a gentleman with all his luggage round him in a Second-class apartment. But don't you be afraid. Slip down the window and say: 'He has gone South for the week,' and he'll tumble. It's only cutting your time of stay in those parts by two days. I ask you as a stranger—going to the West," he said with emphasis.

"Where have you come from?" said I.

"From the East," said he, "and I am hoping that you will give him the message on the Square—for the sake of my Mother as well as your own."

Englishmen are not usually softened by appeals to the memory of their mothers; but for certain reasons, which will be fully apparent, I saw fit to agree.

"It's more than a little matter," said he, "and that's why I asked you to do it—and now I know that I can depend on you doing it. A Second-class carriage at Marwar Junction, and a red-haired man asleep in it. You'll be sure to remember. I get out at the next station, and I must hold on there till he comes or sends me what I want."

"I'll give the message if I catch him," I said, "and for the sake of your Mother as well as mine I'll give you a word of advice. Don't try to run the Central India States just now as the correspondent of the Backwoodsman. There's a real one knocking about here, and it might lead to trouble."

"Thank you," said he, simply, "and when will the swine be gone? I can't starve because he's ruining my work. I wanted to get hold of the Degumber Rajah down here about his father's widow, and give him a jump."

"What did he do to his father's widow, then?"

"Filled her up with red pepper and slippered her to death as she hung from a beam. I found that out myself and I'm the only man that would dare going into the State to get hush-money for it. They'll try to poison me, same as they did in Chortumna when I went on the loot there. But you'll give the man at Marwar Junction my message?"

He got out at a little roadside station, and I reflected. I had heard, more than once, of men personating correspondents of newspapers and bleeding small Native States with threats of exposure, but I had never met any of the caste before. They lead a hard life, and generally die with great suddenness. The Native States have a wholesome horror of English newspapers, which may throw light on their peculiar methods of government, and do their best to choke correspondents with champagne, or drive them out of their mind with four-in-hand barouches. They do not understand that nobody cares a straw for the internal administration of Native States so long as oppression and crime are kept within decent limits, and the ruler is not drugged, drunk, or diseased from one end of the year to the other. They are the dark places of the earth, full of unimaginable cruelty, touching the Railway and the Telegraph on one side, and, on the other, the days of Harun-al-Raschid. When I left the train I did business with divers Kings, and in eight days passed through many changes of life. Sometimes I wore dress-clothes and consorted with Princes and Politicals, drinking from crystal and eating from silver. Sometimes I lay out upon the ground and devoured what I could get, from a plate made of leaves, and drank the running water, and slept under the same rug as my servant. It was all in the day's work.

Then I headed for the Great Indian Desert upon the proper date, as I had promised, and the night Mail set me down at Marwar Junction, where a funny little, happy-go-lucky, native-managed railway runs to Jodhpore. The Bombay Mail from Delhi makes a short halt at Marwar. She arrived as I got in, and I had just time to hurry to her platform and go down the carriages. There was only one Second-class on the train. I slipped the window and looked down upon a flaming red beard, half covered by a railway rug. That was my man, fast asleep, and I dug him gently in the ribs. He woke with a grunt and I saw his face in the light of the lamps. It was a great and shining face.

"Tickets again?" said he.

"No," said I. "I am to tell you that he is gone South for the week. He has gone South for the week!"

The train had begun to move out. The red man rubbed his eyes. "He has gone South for the week," he repeated. "Now that's just like his impidence. Did he say that I was to give you anything? 'Cause I won't."

"He didn't," I said and dropped away, and watched the red lights die out in the dark. It was horribly cold because the wind was blowing off the sands. I climbed into my own train—not an Intermediate carriage this time—and went to sleep.

If the man with the beard had given me a rupee I should have kept it as a memento of a rather curious affair. But the consciousness of having done my duty was my only reward.

Later on I reflected that two gentlemen like my friends could not do any good if they forgathered and personated correspondents of newspapers, and might, if they blackmailed one of the little rat-trap states of Central India or Southern Rajputana, get themselves into serious difficulties. I therefore took some trouble to describe them as accurately as I could remember to people who would be interested in deporting them: and succeeded, so I was later informed, in having them headed back from the Degumber borders.

Then I became respectable, and returned to an Office where there were no Kings and no incidents outside the daily manufacture of a newspaper. A newspaper office seems to attract every conceivable sort of person, to the prejudice of discipline. Zenana-mission ladies arrive, and beg that the Editor will instantly abandon all his duties to describe a Christian prize-giving in a back-slum of a perfectly inaccessible village; Colonels who have been overpassed for command sit down and sketch the outline of a series of ten, twelve, or twenty-four leading articles on Seniority versus Selection; missionaries wish to know why they have not been permitted to escape from their regular vehicles of abuse and swear at a brother-missionary under special patronage of the editorial We; stranded

155

theatrical companies troop up to explain that they cannot pay for their advertisements, but on their return from New Zealand or Tahiti will do so with interest; inventors of patent punkah-pulling machines, carriage couplings and unbreakable swords and axle-trees call with specifications in their pockets and hours at their disposal; tea-companies enter and elaborate their prospectuses with the office pens; secretaries of ball-committees clamor to have the glories of their last dance more fully described; strange ladies rustle in and say: "I want a hundred lady's cards printed at once, please," which is manifestly part of an Editor's duty; and every dissolute ruffian that ever tramped the Grand Trunk Road makes it his business to ask for employment as a proof-reader. And, all the time, the telephone-bell is ringing madly, and Kings are being killed on the Continent, and Empires are saying—"You're another," and Mister Gladstone is calling down brimstone upon the British Dominions, and the little black copy-boys are whining "kaa-pi chay-ha-yeh" (copy wanted) like tired bees, and most of the paper is as blank as Modred's shield.

But that is the amusing part of the year. There are six other months when none ever come to call, and the thermometer walks inch by inch up to the top of the glass, and the office is darkened to just above reading-light, and the press-machines are red-hot of touch, and nobody writes anything but accounts of amusements in the Hill-stations or obituary notices. Then the telephone becomes a tinkling terror, because it tells you of the sudden deaths of men and women that you knew intimately, and the prickly-heat covers you with a garment, and you sit down and write: "A slight increase of sickness is reported from the Khuda Janta Khan District. The outbreak is purely sporadic in its nature, and, thanks to the energetic efforts of the District authorities, is now almost at an end. It is, however, with deep regret we record the death," etc.

Then the sickness really breaks out, and the less recording and reporting the better for the peace of the subscribers. But the Empires and the Kings continue to divert themselves as selfishly as before, and the Foreman thinks that a daily paper really ought to come out once in twenty-four hours, and all the people at the Hill-stations in the middle of their amusements say: "Good gracious! Why can't the paper be sparkling? I'm sure there's plenty going on up here."

That is the dark half of the moon, and, as the advertisements say, "must be experienced to be appreciated."

It was in that season, and a remarkably evil season, that the paper began running the last issue of the week on Saturday night, which is to say Sunday morning, after the custom of a London paper. This was a great convenience, for immediately after the paper was put to bed, the dawn would lower the thermometer from 96° to almost 84° for half an hour, and in that chill—you have no idea how cold is 84° on the grass until you begin to pray for it—a very tired man could get off to sleep ere the heat roused him.

One Saturday night it was my pleasant duty to put the paper to bed alone. A King or courtier or a courtesan or a Community was going to die or get a new Constitution, or do something that was important on the other side of the world, and the paper was to be held open till the latest possible minute in order to catch the telegram.

It was a pitchy black night, as stifling as a June night can be, and the loo, the red-hot wind from the westward, was booming among the tinder-dry trees and pretending that the rain was on its heels. Now and again a spot of almost boiling water would fall on the dust with the flop of a frog, but all our weary world knew that was only pretence. It was a shade cooler in the press-room than the office, so I sat there, while the type ticked and clicked, and the night-jars hooted at the windows, and the all but naked compositors wiped the sweat from their foreheads, and called for water. The thing that was keeping us back, whatever it was, would not come off, though the loo dropped and the last type was set, and the whole round earth stood still in the choking heat, with its finger on its lip, to wait the event. I drowsed, and wondered whether the telegraph was a blessing, and whether this dying man, or struggling people, might be aware of the inconvenience the delay was causing. There was no special reason beyond the heat and worry to make tension, but, as the clock-hands crept up to three o'clock and the machines spun their fly-wheels two and three times to see that all was in order, before I said the word that would set them off, I could have shrieked aloud.

Then the roar and rattle of the wheels shivered the quiet into little bits. I rose to go away, but two men in white clothes stood in front of me. The first one said: "It's him!" The second said: "So it is!" And they both laughed almost as loudly as the machinery roared, and mopped their foreheads. "We seed there was a light burning across the road and we were sleeping in that ditch there for coolness, and I said to my friend here, 'The office is open. Let's come along and speak to him as turned us back from the Degumber State,'" said the smaller of the two. He was the man I had met in the Mhow train, and his fellow was the red-bearded man of Marwar Junction. There was no mistaking the eyebrows of the one or the beard of the other.

I was not pleased, because I wished to go to sleep, not to squabble with loafers. "What do you want?" I asked.

"Half an hour's talk with you, cool and comfortable, in the office," said the red-bearded man. "We'd like some drink—the Contrack doesn't begin yet, Peachey, so you needn't look—but what we really want is advice. We don't want money. We ask you as a favor, because we found out you did us a bad turn about Degumber State."

I led from the press-room to the stifling office with the maps on the walls, and the red-haired man rubbed his hands. "That's something like," said he. "This was the proper shop to come to. Now, Sir, let me introduce to you Brother Peachey Carnehan, that's him, and Brother Daniel Dravot, that is me, and the less said about our professions the better, for we have been most things in our time. Soldier, sailor, compositor, photographer, proof-reader, street-preacher, and correspondents of the Backwoodsman when we thought the paper wanted one. Carnehan is sober, and so am I. Look at us first, and see that's sure. It will save you cutting into my talk. We'll take one of your cigars apiece, and you shall see us light up."

I watched the test. The men were absolutely sober, so I gave them each a tepid whiskey and soda.

"Well and good," said Carnehan of the eyebrows, wiping the froth from his moustache. "Let me talk now, Dan. We have been all over India, mostly on foot. We have been boiler-fitters, engine-drivers, petty contractors, and all that, and we have decided that India isn't big enough for such as us."

They certainly were too big for the office. Dravot's beard seemed to fill half the room and Carnehan's shoulders the other half, as they sat on the big table. Carnehan continued: "The country isn't half worked out because they that governs it won't let you touch it. They spend all their blessed time in governing it, and you can't lift a spade, nor chip a rock, nor look for oil, nor anything like that without all the Government saying—'Leave it alone, and let us govern.' Therefore, such as it is, we will let it alone, and go away to some other place where a man isn't crowded and can come to his own. We are not little men, and there is nothing that we are afraid of except Drink, and we have signed a Contrack on that. Therefore, we are going away to be Kings."

"Kings in our own right," muttered Dravot.

"Yes, of course," I said. "You've been tramping in the sun, and it's a very warm night, and hadn't you better sleep over the notion? Come to-morrow."

"Neither drunk nor sunstruck," said Dravot. "We have slept over the notion half a year, and require to see Books and Atlases, and we have decided that there is only one place now in the world that two strong men can sar-a-whack. They call it Kafiristan. By my reckoning it's the top right-hand corner of Afghanistan, not more than three hundred miles from Peshawar. They have two-and-thirty heathen idols there, and we'll be the thirty-third and fourth. It's a mountaineous country, and the women of those parts are very beautiful."

"But that is provided against in the Contrack," said Carnehan. "Neither

Woman nor Liqu-or, Daniel."

"And that's all we know, except that no one has gone there, and they fight, and in any place where they fight a man who knows how to drill men can always be a King. We shall go to those parts and say to any King we find—'D' you want to vanquish your foes?' and we will show him how to drill men; for that we know better than anything else. Then we will subvert that King and seize his Throne and establish a Dy-nasty."

"You'll be cut to pieces before you're fifty miles across the Border," I said. "You have to travel through Afghanistan to get to that country. It's one mass of mountains and peaks and glaciers, and no Englishman has been through it. The people are utter brutes, and even if you reached them you couldn't do anything."

"That's more like," said Carnehan. "If you could think us a little more mad we would be more pleased. We have come to you to know about this country, to read a book about it, and to be shown maps. We want you to tell us that we are fools and to show us your books." He turned to the book-cases.

"Are you at all in earnest?" I said.

"A little," said Dravot, sweetly. "As big a map as you have got, even if it's all blank where Kafiristan is, and any books you've got. We can read, though we aren't very educated."

I uncased the big thirty-two-miles-to-the-inch map of India, and two smaller Frontier maps, hauled down volume INF-KAN of the Encyclopædia Britannica, and the men consulted them.

"See here!" said Dravot, his thumb on the map. "Up to Jagdallak, Peachey and me know the road. We was there with Roberts's Army. We'll have to turn off to the right at Jagdallak through Laghmann territory. Then we get among the hills—fourteen thousand feet—fifteen thousand—it will be cold work there, but it don't look very far on the map."

I handed him Wood on the Sources of the Oxus. Carnehan was deep in the Encyclopædia.

"They're a mixed lot," said Dravot, reflectively; "and it won't help us to know the names of their tribes. The more tribes the more they'll fight, and the better for us. From Jagdallak to Ashang. H'mm!"

"But all the information about the country is as sketchy and inaccurate as can be," I protested. "No one knows anything about it really. Here's the file of the United Services' Institute. Read what Bellew says."

"Blow Bellew!" said Carnehan. "Dan, they're a stinkin' lot of heathens, but this book here says they think they're related to us English."

I smoked while the men pored over Raverty, Wood, the maps, and the Encyclopædia.

"There is no use your waiting," said Dravot, politely. "It's about four o'clock now. We'll go before six o'clock if you want to sleep, and we won't steal any of the papers. Don't you sit up. We're two harmless lunatics, and if you come to-morrow evening down to the Serai we'll say good-bye to you."

"You are two fools," I answered. "You'll be turned back at the Frontier or cut up the minute you set foot in Afghanistan. Do you want any money or a recommendation down-country? I can help you to the chance of work next week."

"Next week we shall be hard at work ourselves, thank you," said Dravot. "It isn't so easy being a King as it looks. When we've got our Kingdom in going order we'll let you know, and you can come up and help us to govern it."

"Would two lunatics make a Contrack like that?" said Carnehan, with subdued pride, showing me a greasy half-sheet of notepaper on which was written the following. I copied it, then and there, as a curiosity—

_This Contract between me and you persuing witnesseth in the name of God—Amen and so forth.

(One) That me and you will settle this matter together; i.e., to be Kings of Kafiristan.

(Two) That you and me will not, while this matter is being settled, look at any Liquor, nor any Woman black, white, or brown, so as to get mixed up with one or the other harmful.

(Three) That we conduct ourselves with Dignity and Discretion, and if one of us gets into trouble the other will stay by him.

Signed by you and me this day.

Peachey Taliaferro Carnehan.

Daniel Dravot.

Both Gentlemen at Large_.

"There was no need for the last article," said Carnehan, blushing modestly; "but it looks regular. Now you know the sort of men that loafers are—we are loafers, Dan, until we get out of India—and do you think that we would sign a Contrack like that unless we was in earnest? We have kept away from the two things that make life worth having."

"You won't enjoy your lives much longer if you are going to try this idiotic adventure. Don't set the office on fire," I said, "and go away before nine o'clock."

I left them still poring over the maps and making notes on the back of the "Contrack." "Be sure to come down to the Serai to-morrow," were their parting words.

The Kumharsen Serai is the great four-square sink of humanity where the strings of camels and horses from the North load and unload. All the nationalities of Central Asia may be found there, and most of the folk of India proper. Balkh and Bokhara there meet Bengal and Bombay, and try to draw eye-teeth. You can buy ponies, turquoises, Persian pussy-cats, saddle-bags, fat-tailed sheep, and musk in the Kumharsen Serai, and get many strange things for nothing. In the afternoon I went down to see whether my friends intended to keep their word or were lying there drunk.

A priest attired in fragments of ribbons and rags stalked up to me, gravely twisting a child's paper whirligig. Behind him was his servant bending under the load of a crate of mud toys. The two were loading up two camels, and the inhabitants of the Serai watched them with shrieks of laughter.

"The priest is mad," said a horse-dealer to me. "He is going up to Kabul to sell toys to the Amir. He will either be raised to honor or have his head cut off. He came in here this morning and has been behaving madly ever since."

"The witless are under the protection of God," stammered a flat-cheeked

Usbeg in broken Hindi. "They foretell future events."

"Would they could have foretold that my caravan would have been cut up by the Shinwaris almost within shadow of the Pass!" grunted the Eusufzai agent of a Rajputana trading-house whose goods had been diverted into the hands of other robbers just across the Border, and whose misfortunes were the laughing-stock of the bazar. "Ohé, priest, whence come you and whither do you go?"

"From Roum have I come," shouted the priest, waving his whirligig; "from Roum, blown by the breath of a hundred devils across the sea! O thieves, robbers, liars, the blessing of Pir Khan on pigs, dogs, and perjurers! Who will take the Protected of God to the North to sell charms that are never still to the Amir? The camels shall not gall, the sons shall not fall sick, and the wives shall remain faithful while they are away, of the men who give me place in their caravan. Who will assist me to slipper the King of the Roos with a golden slipper with a silver heel? The protection of Pir Khan be upon his labors!" He spread out the skirts of his gaberdine and pirouetted between the lines of tethered horses.

"There starts a caravan from Peshawar to Kabul in twenty days, Huzrut" said the Eusufzai trader. "My camels go therewith. Do thou also go and bring us good-luck."

"I will go even now!" shouted the priest. "I will depart upon my winged camels, and be at Peshawar in a day! Ho! Hazar Mir Khan," he yelled to his servant, "drive out the camels, but let me first mount my own."

He leaped on the back of his beast as it knelt, and, turning round to me, cried: "Come thou also, Sahib, a little along the road, and I will sell thee a charm—an amulet that shall make thee King of Kafiristan."

Then the light broke upon me, and I followed the two camels out of the Serai till we reached open road and the priest halted.

"What d'you think o' that?" said he in English. "Carnehan can't talk their patter, so I've made him my servant. He makes a handsome servant. 'T isn't for nothing that I've been knocking about the country for fourteen years. Didn't I do that talk neat? We'll hitch on to a caravan at Peshawar till we get to Jagdallak, and then we'll see if we can get donkeys for our camels, and strike into Kafiristan. Whirligigs for the Amir, O Lor! Put your hand under the camel-bags and tell me what you feel."

I felt the butt of a Martini, and another and another.

"Twenty of 'em," said Dravot, placidly. "Twenty of 'em and ammunition to correspond, under the whirligigs and the mud dolls."

"Heaven help you if you are caught with those things!" I said. "A Martini is worth her weight in silver among the Pathans."

"Fifteen hundred rupees of capital—every rupee we could beg, borrow, or steal—are invested on these two camels," said Dravot. "We won't get caught. We're going through the Khaiber with a regular caravan. Who'd touch a poor mad priest?"

"Have you got everything you want?" I asked, overcome with astonishment.

"Not yet, but we shall soon. Give us a memento of your kindness, Brother. You did me a service, yesterday, and that time in Marwar. Half my Kingdom shall you have, as the saying is." I slipped a small charm compass from my watch chain and handed it up to the priest.

"Good-bye," said Dravot, giving me hand cautiously. "It's the last time we'll shake hands with an Englishman these many days. Shake hands with him, Carnehan," he cried, as the second camel passed me.

Carnehan leaned down and shook hands. Then the camels passed away along the dusty road, and I was left alone to wonder. My eye could detect no failure in the disguises. The scene in the Serai proved that they were complete to the native mind. There was just the chance, therefore, that Carnehan and Dravot would be able to wander through Afghanistan without detection. But, beyond, they would find death—certain and awful death.

Ten days later a native correspondent giving me the news of the day from Peshawar, wound up his letter with: "There has been much laughter here on account of a certain mad priest who is going in his estimation to sell petty gauds and insignificant trinkets which he ascribes as great charms to H.H. the Amir of Bokhara. He passed through Peshawar and associated himself to the Second Summer caravan that goes to Kabul. The merchants are pleased because through superstition they imagine that such mad fellows bring good-fortune."

The two, then, were beyond the Border. I would have prayed for them, but, that night, a real King died in Europe, and demanded an obituary notice.

* * * * *

The wheel of the world swings through the same phases again and again. Summer passed and winter thereafter, and came and passed again. The daily paper continued and I with it, and upon the third summer there fell a hot night, a night-issue, and a strained waiting for something to be telegraphed from the other side of the world, exactly as had happened before. A few great men had died in the past two years, the machines worked with more clatter, and some of the trees in the Office garden were a few feet taller. But that was all the difference.

I passed over to the press-room, and went through just such a scene as I have already described. The nervous tension was stronger than it had been two years before, and I felt the heat more acutely. At three o'clock I cried, "Print off," and turned to go, when there crept to my chair what was left of a man. He was bent into a circle, his head was sunk between his shoulders, and he moved his feet one over the other like a bear. I could hardly see whether he walked or crawled—this rag-wrapped, whining cripple who addressed me by name, crying that he was come back. "Can you give me a drink?" he whimpered. "For the Lord's sake, give me a drink!"

I went back to the office, the man following with groans of pain, and I turned up the lamp.

"Don't you know me?" he gasped, dropping into a chair, and he turned his drawn face, surmounted by a shock of gray hair, to the light.

I looked at him intently. Once before had I seen eyebrows that met over the nose in an inch-broad black band, but for the life of me I could not tell where.

"I don't know you," I said, handing him the whiskey. "What can I do for you?"

He took a gulp of the spirit raw, and shivered in spite of the suffocating heat.

"I've come back," he repeated; "and I was the King of Kafiristan—me and

Dravot—crowned Kings we was! In this office we settled it—you setting

there and giving us the books. I am Peachey—Peachey Taliaferro Carnehan, and you've been setting here ever since—O Lord!"

I was more than a little astonished, and expressed my feelings accordingly.

"It's true," said Carnehan, with a dry cackle, nursing his feet, which were wrapped in rags. "True as gospel. Kings we were, with crowns upon our heads—me and Dravot—poor Dan—oh, poor, poor Dan, that would never take advice, not though I begged of him!"

"Take the whiskey," I said, "and take your own time. Tell me all you can recollect of everything from beginning to end. You got across the border on your camels, Dravot dressed as a mad priest and you his servant. Do you remember that?"

"I ain't mad—yet, but I shall be that way soon. Of course I remember. Keep looking at me, or maybe my words will go all to pieces. Keep looking at me in my eyes and don't say anything."

I leaned forward and looked into his face as steadily as I could. He dropped one hand upon the table and I grasped it by the wrist. It was twisted like a bird's claw, and upon the back was a ragged, red, diamond-shaped scar.

"No, don't look there. Look at me" said Carnehan. "That comes afterwards, but for the Lord's sake don't distrack me. We left with that caravan, me and Dravot playing all sorts of antics to amuse the people we were with. Dravot used to make us laugh in the evenings when all the people was cooking their dinners—cooking their dinners, and—what did they do then? They lit little fires with sparks that went into Dravot's beard, and we all laughed—fit to die. Little red fires they was, going into Dravot's big red beard—so funny." His eyes left mine and he smiled foolishly.

"You went as far as Jagdallak with that caravan," I said at a venture, "after you had lit those fires. To Jagdallak, where you turned off to try to get into Kafiristan."

"No, we didn't neither. What are you talking about? We turned off before Jagdallak, because we heard the roads was good. But they wasn't good enough for our two camels—mine and Dravot's. When we left the caravan, Dravot took off all his clothes and mine too, and said we would be heathen, because the Kafirs didn't allow Mohammedans to talk to them. So we dressed betwixt and between, and such a sight as Daniel Dravot I never saw yet nor expect to see again. He burned half his beard, and slung a sheep-skin over his shoulder, and shaved his head into patterns. He shaved mine, too, and made me wear outrageous things to look like a heathen.

163

That was in a most mountaineous country, and our camels couldn't go along any more because of the mountains. They were tall and black, and coming home I saw them fight like wild goats—there are lots of goats in Kafiristan. And these mountains, they never keep still, no more than the goats. Always fighting they are, and don't let you sleep at night."

"Take some more whiskey," I said, very slowly. "What did you and Daniel Dravot do when the camels could go no further because of the rough roads that led into Kafiristan?"

"What did which do? There was a party called Peachey Taliaferro Carnehan that was with Dravot. Shall I tell you about him? He died out there in the cold. Slap from the bridge fell old Peachey, turning and twisting in the air like a penny whirligig that you can sell to the Amir.—No; they was two for three ha'pence, those whirligigs, or I am much mistaken and woeful sore.—And then these camels were no use, and Peachey said to Dravot—'For the Lord's sake let's get out of this before our heads are chopped off,' and with that they killed the camels all among the mountains, not having anything in particular to eat, but first they took off the boxes with the guns and the ammunition, till two men came along driving four mules. Dravot up and dances in front of them, singing—'Sell me four mules.' Says the first man—'If you are rich enough to buy, you are rich enough to rob;' but before ever he could put his hand to his knife, Dravot breaks his neck over his knee, and the other party runs away. So Carnehan loaded the mules with the rifles that was taken off the camels, and together we starts forward into those bitter cold mountaineous parts, and never a road broader than the back of your hand."

He paused for a moment, while I asked him if he could remember the nature of the country through which he had journeyed.

"I am telling you as straight as I can, but my head isn't as good as it might be. They drove nails through it to make me hear better how Dravot died. The country was mountaineous and the mules were most contrary, and the inhabitants was dispersed and solitary. They went up and up, and down and down, and that other party, Carnehan, was imploring of Dravot not to sing and whistle so loud, for fear of bringing down the tremenjus avalanches. But Dravot says that if a King couldn't sing it wasn't worth being King, and whacked the mules over the rump, and never took no heed for ten cold days. We came to a big level valley all among the mountains, and the mules were near dead, so we killed them, not having anything in special for them or us to eat. We sat upon the boxes, and played odd and even with the cartridges that was jolted out.

"Then ten men with bows and arrows ran down that valley, chasing twenty men with bows and arrows, and the row was tremenjus. They was fair men—fairer than you or me—with yellow hair and remarkable well built. Says Dravot, unpacking the guns—'This is the beginning of the business. We'll fight for the ten men,' and with that he fires two rifles at the twenty men, and drops one of them at two hundred yards from the rock where he was sitting. The other men began to run, but Carnehan and Dravot sits on the boxes picking them off at all ranges, up and down the valley. Then we goes up to the ten men that had run across the snow too, and they fires a footy little arrow at us. Dravot he shoots above their heads and they all falls down flat. Then he walks over them and kicks them, and then he lifts them up and shakes hands all round to make them friendly like. He calls them and gives them the boxes to carry, and waves his hand for all the world as though he was King already. They takes the boxes and him across the valley and up the hill into a pine wood on the top, where there was half a dozen big stone idols. Dravot he goes to the biggest—a fellow they call Imbra—and lays a rifle and a cartridge at his feet, rubbing his nose respectful with his own nose, patting him on the head, and saluting in front of it. He turns round to the men and nods his head, and says—'That's all right. I'm in the know too, and all these old jim-jams are my friends.' Then he opens his mouth and points down it, and when the first man brings him food, he says—'No;' and when the second man brings him food, he says—'No;' but when one of the old priests and the boss of the village brings him food, he says—'Yes,' very haughty, and eats it slow. That was how we came to our first village, without any trouble, just as though we had tumbled from the skies. But we tumbled from one of those damned rope-bridges, you see, and—you couldn't expect a man to laugh much after that?"

"Take some more whiskey and go on," I said. "That was the first village you came into. How did you get to be King?"

"I wasn't King," said Carnehan. "Dravot, he was the King, and a handsome man he looked with the gold crown on his head and all. Him and the other party stayed in that village, and every morning Dravot sat by the side of old Imbra, and the people came and worshipped. That was Dravot's order. Then a lot of men came into the valley, and Carnehan and Dravot picks them off with the rifles before they knew where they was, and runs down into the valley and up again the other side and finds another village, same as the first one, and the people all falls down flat on their faces, and Dravot says—'Now what is the trouble between you two villages?' and the people points to a woman, as fair as you or me, that was carried off, and Dravot takes her back to the first village and counts up the dead—eight there was. For each dead man Dravot pours a little milk on the ground and waves his arms like a whirligig and 'That's all right,' says he. Then he and Carnehan takes the big boss of each village by the arm and walks them down into the valley, and shows them how to scratch a line with a spear right down the valley, and gives each a sod of turf from both sides of the line. Then all the people comes down and shouts like the devil and all, and Dravot says—'Go and dig the land, and be fruitful and multiply,' which they did, though they didn't understand. Then we asks the names of things in their lingo—bread and water and fire and idols and such, and Dravot leads the priest of each village up to the idol, and says he must sit there and judge the people, and if anything goes wrong he is to be shot.

"Next week they was all turning up the land in the valley as quiet as bees and much prettier, and the priests heard all the complaints and told

Dravot in dumb show what it was about. 'That's just the beginning,' says Dravot. 'They think we're Gods.' He and Carnehan picks out twenty good men and shows them how to click off a rifle, and form fours, and advance in line, and they was very pleased to do so, and clever to see the hang of it. Then he takes out his pipe and his baccy-pouch and leaves one at one village, and one at the other, and off we two goes to see what was to be done in the next valley. That was all rock, and there was a little village there, and Carnehan says—'Send 'em to the old valley to plant,' and takes 'em there and gives 'em some land that wasn't took before. They were a poor lot, and we blooded 'em with a kid before letting 'em into the new Kingdom. That was to impress the people, and then they settled down quiet, and Carnehan went back to Dravot who had got into another valley, all snow and ice and most mountaineous. There was no people there and the Army got afraid, so Dravot shoots one of them, and goes on till he finds some people in a village, and the Army explains that unless the people wants to be killed they had better not shoot their little matchlocks; for they had matchlocks. We makes friends with the priest and I stays there alone with two of the Army, teaching the men how to drill, and a thundering big Chief comes across the snow with kettle-drums and horns twanging, because he heard there was a new God kicking about. Carnehan sights for the brown of the men half a mile across the snow and wings one of them. Then he sends a message to the Chief that, unless he wished to be killed, he must come and shake hands with me and leave his arms behind. The Chief comes alone first, and Carnehan shakes hands with him and whirls his arms about, same as Dravot used, and very much surprised that Chief was, and strokes my eyebrows. Then Carnehan goes alone to the Chief, and asks him in dumb show if he had an enemy he hated. 'I have,' says the Chief. So Carnehan weeds out the pick of his men, and sets the two of the Army to show them drill and at the end of two weeks the men can manoeuvre about as well as Volunteers. So he marches with the Chief to a great big plain on the top of a mountain, and the Chief's men rushes into a village and takes it; we three Martinis firing into the brown of the enemy. So we took that village too, and I gives the Chief a rag from my coat and says, 'Occupy till I come;' which was scriptural. By way of a reminder, when me and the Army was eighteen hundred yards away, I drops a bullet near him standing on the snow, and all the people falls flat on their faces. Then I sends a letter to Dravot wherever he be by land or by sea."

At the risk of throwing the creature out of train I interrupted—"How could you write a letter up yonder?"

"The letter?—Oh!—The letter! Keep looking at me between the eyes, please. It was a string-talk letter, that we'd learned the way of it from a blind beggar in the Punjab."

I remember that there had once come to the office a blind man with a knotted twig and a piece of string which he wound round the twig according to some cipher of his own. He could, after the lapse of days or hours, repeat the sentence which he had reeled up. He had reduced the alphabet to eleven primitive sounds; and tried to teach me his method, but I could not understand.

"I sent that letter to Dravot," said Carnehan; "and told him to come back because this Kingdom was growing too big for me to handle, and then I struck for the first valley, to see how the priests were working. They called the village we took along with the Chief, Bashkai, and the first village we took, Er-Heb. The priests at Er-Heb was doing all right, but they had a lot of pending cases about land to show me, and some men from another village had been firing arrows at night. I went out and looked for that village, and fired four rounds at it from a thousand yards. That used all the cartridges I cared to spend, and I waited for Dravot, who had been away two or three months, and I kept my people quiet.

"One morning I heard the devil's own noise of drums and horns, and Dan Dravot marches down the hill with his Army and a tail of hundreds of men, and, which was the most amazing, a great gold crown on his head. 'My Gord, Carnehan,' says Daniel, 'this is a tremenjus business, and we've got the whole country as far as it's worth having. I am the son of Alexander by Queen Semiramis, and you're my younger brother and a God too! It's the biggest thing we've ever seen. I've been marching and fighting for six weeks with the Army, and every footy little village for fifty miles has come in rejoiceful; and more than that, I've got the key of the whole show, as you'll see, and I've got a crown for you! I told 'em to make two of 'em at a place called Shu, where the gold lies in the rock like suet in mutton. Gold I've seen, and turquoise I've kicked out of the cliffs, and there's garnets in the sands of the river, and here's a chunk of amber that a man brought me. Call up all the priests and, here, take your crown.'

"One of the men opens a black hair bag, and I slips the crown on. It was too small and too heavy, but I wore it for the glory. Hammered gold it was—five pound weight, like a hoop of a barrel.

"'Peachey,' says Dravot, 'we don't want to fight no more. The Craft's the trick, so help me!' and he brings forward that same Chief that I left at Bashkai—Billy Fish we called him afterwards, because he was so like Billy Fish that drove the big tank-engine at Mach on the Bolan in the old days. 'Shake hands with him,' says Dravot, and I shook hands and nearly dropped, for Billy Fish gave me the Grip. I said nothing, but tried him with the Fellow Craft Grip. He answers, all right, and I tried the Master's Grip, but that was a slip. 'A Fellow Craft he is!' I says to Dan. 'Does he know the word?'—'He does,' says Dan, 'and all the priests know. It's a miracle! The Chiefs and the priests can work a Fellow Craft Lodge in a way that's very like ours, and they've cut the marks on the rocks, but they don't know the Third Degree, and they've come to find out. It's Gord's Truth. I've known these long years that the Afghans knew up to the Fellow Craft Degree, but this is a miracle. A God and a Grand-Master of the Craft am I, and a Lodge in the Third Degree I will open, and we'll raise the head priests and the Chiefs of the villages.'

"'It's against all the law,' I says, 'holding a Lodge without warrant from any one; and you know we never held office in any Lodge.'

"'It's a master-stroke o' policy,' says Dravot. 'It means running the country as easy as a four-wheeled bogie on a down grade. We can't stop to inquire now, or they'll turn against us. I've forty Chiefs at my heel, and passed and raised according to their merit they shall be. Billet these men on the villages, and see that we run up a Lodge of some kind. The temple of Imbra will do for the Lodge-room. The women must make aprons as you show them. I'll hold a levee of Chiefs to-night and Lodge to-morrow.'

"I was fair run off my legs, but I wasn't such a fool as not to see what a pull this Craft business gave us. I showed the priests' families how to make aprons of the degrees, but for Dravot's apron the blue border and marks was made of turquoise lumps on white hide, not cloth. We took a great square stone in the temple for the Master's chair, and little stones for the officers' chairs, and painted the black pavement with white squares, and did what we could to make things regular.

"At the levee which was held that night on the hillside with big bonfires, Dravot gives out that him and me were Gods and sons of Alexander, and Past Grand-Masters in the Craft, and was come to make Kafiristan a country where every man should eat in peace and drink in quiet, and specially obey us. Then the Chiefs come round to shake hands, and they were so hairy and white and fair it was just shaking hands with old friends. We gave them names according as they was like men we had known in India—Billy Fish, Holly Dilworth, Pikky Kergan, that was Bazar-master when I was at Mhow, and so on, and so on.

"The most amazing miracles was at Lodge next night. One of the old priests was watching us continuous, and I felt uneasy, for I knew we'd have to fudge the Ritual, and I didn't know what the men knew. The old priest was a stranger come in from beyond the village of Bashkai. The minute Dravot puts on the Master's apron that the girls had made for him, the priest fetches a whoop and a howl, and tries to overturn the stone that Dravot was sitting on. 'It's all up now,' I says. 'That comes of meddling with the Craft without warrant!' Dravot never winked an eye, not when ten priests took and tilted over the Grand-Master's chair—which was to say the stone of Imbra. The priest begins rubbing the bottom end of it to clear away the black dirt, and presently he shows all the other priests the Master's Mark, same as was on Dravot's apron, cut into the stone. Not even the priests of the temple of Imbra knew it was there. The old chap falls flat on his face at Dravot's feet and kisses 'em. 'Luck again,' says Dravot, across the Lodge to me, 'they say it's the missing Mark that no one could understand the why of. We're more than safe now.' Then he bangs the butt of his gun for a gavel and says: 'By virtue of the authority vested in me by my own right hand and the help of Peachey, I declare myself Grand-Master of all Freemasonry in Kafiristan in this the Mother Lodge o' the country, and King of Kafiristan equally with Peachey!' At that he puts on his crown and I puts on mine—I was doing Senior Warden—and we opens the Lodge in most ample form. It was a amazing miracle! The priests moved in Lodge through the first two degrees almost without telling, as if the memory was coming back to them. After that, Peachey and Dravot raised such as was

168

worthy—high priests and Chiefs of far-off villages. Billy Fish was the first, and I can tell you we scared the soul out of him. It was not in any way according to Ritual, but it served our turn. We didn't raise more than ten of the biggest men, because we didn't want to make the Degree common. And they was clamoring to be raised.

"'In another six months,' says Dravot, 'we'll hold another Communication, and see how you are working.' Then he asks them about their villages, and learns that they was fighting one against the other, and were sick and tired of it. And when they wasn't doing that they was fighting with the Mohammedans. 'You can fight those when they come into our country,' says Dravot. 'Tell off every tenth man of your tribes for a Frontier guard, and send two hundred at a time to this valley to be drilled. Nobody is going to be shot or speared any more so long as he does well, and I know that you won't cheat me, because you're white people—sons of Alexander—and not like common, black Mohammedans. You are my people, and by God,' says he, running off into English at the end—'I'll make a damned fine Nation of you, or I'll die in the making!'

"I can't tell all we did for the next six months, because Dravot did a lot I couldn't see the hang of, and he learned their lingo in a way I never could. My work was to help the people plough, and now and again go out with some of the Army and see what the other villages were doing, and make 'em throw rope-bridges across the ravines which cut up the country horrid. Dravot was very kind to me, but when he walked up and down in the pine wood pulling that bloody red beard of his with both fists I knew he was thinking plans I could not advise about, and I just waited for orders.

"But Dravot never showed me disrespect before the people. They were afraid of me and the Army, but they loved Dan. He was the best of friends with the priests and the Chiefs; but any one could come across the hills with a complaint, and Dravot would hear him out fair, and call four priests together and say what was to be done. He used to call in Billy Fish from Bashkai, and Pikky Kergan from Shu, and an old Chief we call Kafuzelum—it was like enough to his real name—and hold councils with 'em when there was any fighting to be done in small villages. That was his Council of War, and the four priests of Bashkai, Shu, Khawak, and Madora was his Privy Council. Between the lot of 'em they sent me, with forty men and twenty rifles, and sixty men carrying turquoises, into the Ghorband country to buy those hand-made Martini rifles, that come out of the Amir's workshops at Kabul, from one of the Amir's Herati regiments that would have sold the very teeth out of their mouths for turquoises.

"I stayed in Ghorband a month, and gave the Governor there the pick of my baskets for hush-money, and bribed the Colonel of the regiment some more, and, between the two and the tribes-people, we got more than a hundred hand-made Martinis, a hundred good Kohat Jezails that'll throw to six hundred yards, and forty man-loads of very bad ammunition for the rifles. I came back with what I had, and distributed 'em among the men that the Chiefs sent in to me to drill. Dravot was too busy to attend to those things, but the old Army that we first made helped me, and we turned out five hundred men that could drill, and two hundred that knew how to hold arms pretty straight. Even those cork-screwed, hand-made guns was a miracle to them. Dravot talked big about powder-shops and factories, walking up and down in the pine wood when the winter was coming on.

"'I won't make a Nation,' says he. 'I'll make an Empire! These men aren't niggers; they're English! Look at their eyes—look at their mouths. Look at the way they stand up. They sit on chairs in their own houses. They're the Lost Tribes, or something like it, and they've grown to be English. I'll take a census in the spring if the priests don't get frightened. There must be a fair two million of 'em in these hills. The villages are full o' little children. Two million people—two hundred and fifty thousand fighting men—and all English! They only want the rifles and a little drilling. Two hundred and fifty thousand men, ready to cut in on Russia's right flank when she tries for India! Peachey, man,' he says, chewing his beard in great hunks, 'we shall be Emperors—Emperors of the Earth! Rajah Brooke will be a suckling to us. I'll treat with the Viceroy on equal terms. I'll ask him to send me twelve picked English—twelve that I know of—to help us govern a bit. There's Mackray, Sergeant-pensioner at Segowli—many's the good dinner he's given me, and his wife a pair of trousers. There's Donkin, the Warder of Tounghoo Jail; there's hundreds that I could lay my hand on if I was in India. The Viceroy shall do it for me, I'll send a man through in the spring for those men, and I'll write for a dispensation from the Grand Lodge for what I've done as Grand-Master. That—and all the Sniders that'll be thrown out when the native troops in India take up the Martini. They'll be worn smooth, but they'll do for fighting in these hills. Twelve English, a hundred thousand Sniders run through the Amir's country in dribblets—I'd be content with twenty thousand in one year—and we'd be an Empire. When everything was shipshape, I'd hand over the crown—this crown I'm wearing now—to Queen Victoria on my knees, and she'd say: "Rise up, Sir Daniel Dravot." Oh, it's big! It's big, I tell you! But there's so much to be done in every place—Bashkai, Khawak, Shu, and everywhere else.'

"'What is it?' I says. 'There are no more men coming in to be drilled this autumn. Look at those fat black clouds. They're bringing the snow.'

"'It isn't that,' says Daniel, putting his hand very hard on my shoulder; 'and I don't wish to say anything that's against you, for no other living man would have followed me and made me what I am as you have done. You're a first-class Commander-in-Chief, and the people know you; but—it's a big country, and somehow you can't help me, Peachey, in the way I want to be helped.'

"'Go to your blasted priests, then!' I said, and I was sorry when I made that remark, but it did hurt me sore to find Daniel talking so superior when I'd drilled all the men, and done all he told me.

"'Don't let's quarrel, Peachey,' says Daniel, without cursing. 'You're a King too, and the half of this Kingdom is yours; but can't you see, Peachey, we want cleverer men than us now—three or four of 'em, that we can scatter about for our Deputies. It's a hugeous great State, and I can't always tell the right thing to do, and I haven't time for all I want to do, and here's the winter coming on and all.' He put half his beard into his mouth, all red like the gold of his crown.

"'I'm sorry, Daniel,' says I. 'I've done all I could. I've drilled the men and shown the people how to stack their oats better; and I've brought in those tinware rifles from Ghorband—but I know what you're driving at. I take it Kings always feel oppressed that way.'

"'There's another thing too,' says Dravot, walking up and down. 'The winter's coming and these people won't be giving much trouble, and if they do we can't move about. I want a wife.'

"'For Gord's sake leave the women alone!' I says. 'We've both got all the work we can, though I am a fool. Remember the Contrack, and keep clear o' women.'

"'The Contrack only lasted till such time as we was Kings; and Kings we have been these months past,' says Dravot, weighing his crown in his hand. 'You go get a wife too, Peachey—a nice, strappin', plump girl that'll keep you warm in the winter. They're prettier than English girls, and we can take the pick of 'em. Boil 'em once or twice in hot water, and they'll come out like chicken and ham.'

"'Don't tempt me!' I says. 'I will not have any dealings with a woman not till we are a dam' side more settled than we are now. I've been doing the work o' two men, and you've been doing the work o' three. Let's lie off a bit, and see if we can get some better tobacco from Afghan country and run in some good liquor; but no women.'

"'Who's talking o' women?' says Dravot. 'I said wife—a Queen to breed a King's son for the King. A Queen out of the strongest tribe, that'll make them your blood-brothers, and that'll lie by your side and tell you all the people thinks about you and their own affairs. That's what I want.'

"'Do you remember that Bengali woman I kept at Mogul Serai when I was a plate-layer?' says I. 'A fat lot o' good she was to me. She taught me the lingo and one or two other things; but what happened? She ran away with the Station Master's servant and half my month's pay. Then she turned up at Dadur Junction in tow of a half-caste, and had the impidence to say I was her husband—all among the drivers in the running-shed too!'

"'We've done with that,' says Dravot, 'these women are whiter than you or me, and a Queen I will have for the winter months.'

"'For the last time o' asking, Dan, do not,' I says. 'It'll only bring us harm. The Bible says that Kings ain't to waste their strength on women, 'specially when they've got a new raw Kingdom to work over.'

"'For the last time of answering I will,' said Dravot, and he went away through the pine-trees looking like a big red devil, the sun being on his crown and beard and all.

"But getting a wife was not as easy as Dan thought. He put it before the Council, and there was no answer till Billy Fish said that he'd better ask the girls. Dravot damned them all round. 'What's wrong with me?' he shouts, standing by the idol Imbra. 'Am I a dog or am I not enough of a man for your wenches? Haven't I put the shadow of my hand over this country? Who stopped the last Afghan raid?' It was me really, but Dravot was too angry to remember. 'Who bought your guns? Who repaired the bridges? Who's the Grand-Master of the sign cut in the stone?' says he, and he thumped his hand on the block that he used to sit on in Lodge, and at Council, which opened like Lodge always. Billy Fish said nothing and no more did the others. 'Keep your hair on, Dan,' said I; 'and ask the girls. That's how it's done at Home, and these people are quite English.'

"'The marriage of the King is a matter of State,' says Dan, in a white-hot rage, for he could feel, I hope, that he was going against his better mind. He walked out of the Council-room, and the others sat still, looking at the ground.

"'Billy Fish,' says I to the Chief of Bashkai, 'what's the difficulty here? A straight answer to a true friend.'

"'You know,' says Billy Fish. 'How should a man tell you who knows everything? How can daughters of men marry Gods or Devils? It's not proper.'

"I remembered something like that in the Bible; but if, after seeing us as long as they had, they still believed we were Gods, it wasn't for me to undeceive them.

"'A God can do anything,' says I. 'If the King is fond of a girl he'll not let her die.'—'She'll have to,' said Billy Fish. 'There are all sorts of Gods and Devils in these mountains, and now and again a girl marries one of them and isn't seen any more. Besides, you two know the Mark cut in the stone. Only the Gods know that. We thought you were men till you showed the sign of the Master.'

"I wished then that we had explained about the loss of the genuine secrets of a Master-Mason at the first go-off; but I said nothing. All that night there was a blowing of horns in a little dark temple half-way down the hill, and I heard a girl crying fit to die. One of the priests told us that she was being prepared to marry the King.

"'I'll have no nonsense of that kind,' says Dan. 'I don't want to interfere with your customs, but I'll take my own wife.'—'The girl's a little bit afraid,' says the priest. 'She thinks she's going to die, and they are a-heartening of her up down in the temple.'

"'Hearten her very tender, then,' says Dravot, 'or I'll hearten you with the butt of a gun so you'll never want to be heartened again.' He licked his lips, did Dan, and stayed up walking about more than half the night, thinking of the wife that he was going to get in the morning. I wasn't by any means comfortable, for I knew that dealings with a woman in foreign parts, though you was a crowned King twenty times over, could not but be risky. I got up very early in the morning while Dravot was asleep, and I saw the priests talking together in whispers, and the Chiefs talking together too, and they looked at me out of the corners of their eyes.

"'What is up, Fish?' I say to the Bashkai man, who was wrapped up in his furs and looking splendid to behold.

"'I can't rightly say,' says he; 'but if you can make the King drop all

172

this nonsense about marriage, you'll be doing him and me and yourself a great service.'

"'That I do believe,' says I. 'But sure, you know, Billy, as well as me, having fought against and for us, that the King and me are nothing more than two of the finest men that God Almighty ever made. Nothing more, I do assure you.'

"'That may be,' says Billy Fish, 'and yet I should be sorry if it was.'

He sinks his head upon his great fur cloak for a minute and thinks.

'King,' says he, 'be you man or God or Devil, I'll stick by you to-day.

I have twenty of my men with me, and they will follow me. We'll go to Bashkai until the storm blows over.'

"A little snow had fallen in the night, and everything was white except the greasy fat clouds that blew down and down from the north. Dravot came out with his crown on his head, swinging his arms and stamping his feet, and looking more pleased than Punch.

"'For the last time, drop it, Dan,' says I in a whisper, 'Billy Fish here says that there will be a row.'

"'A row among my people!' says Dravot. 'Not much. Peachey, you're a fool not to get a wife too. Where's the girl?' says he with a voice as loud as the braying of a jackass. 'Call up all the Chiefs and priests, and let the Emperor see if his wife suits him.'

"There was no need to call any one. They were all there leaning on their guns and spears round the clearing in the centre of the pine wood. A lot of priests went down to the little temple to bring up the girl, and the horns blew fit to wake the dead. Billy Fish saunters round and gets as close to Daniel as he could, and behind him stood his twenty men with matchlocks. Not a man of them under six feet. I was next to Dravot, and behind me was twenty men of the regular Army. Up comes the girl, and a strapping wench she was, covered with silver and turquoises but white as death, and looking back every minute at the priests.

"'She'll do,' said Dan, looking her over. 'What's to be afraid of, lass? Come and kiss me.' He puts his arm round her. She shuts her eyes, gives a bit of a squeak, and down goes her face in the side of Dan's flaming red beard.

"'The slut's bitten me!' says he, clapping his hand to his neck, and, sure enough, his hand was red with blood. Billy Fish and two of his matchlock-men catches hold of Dan by the shoulders and drags him into the Bashkai lot, while the priests howls in their lingo,—'Neither God nor Devil but a man!' I was all taken aback, for a priest cut at me in front, and the Army behind began firing into the Bashkai men.

"'God A'mighty!' says Dan. 'What is the meaning o' this?'

"'Come back! Come away!' says Billy Fish. 'Ruin and Mutiny is the matter. We'll break for Bashkai if we can.'

"I tried to give some sort of orders to my men—the men o' the regular Army—but it was no use, so I fired into the brown of 'em with an English Martini and drilled three beggars in a line. The valley was full of shouting, howling creatures, and every soul was shrieking, 'Not a God nor

173

a Devil but only a man!' The Bashkai troops stuck to Billy Fish all they were worth, but their matchlocks wasn't half as good as the Kabul breech-loaders, and four of them dropped. Dan was bellowing like a bull, for he was very wrathy; and Billy Fish had a hard job to prevent him running out at the crowd.

"'We can't stand,' says Billy Fish. 'Make a run for it down the valley! The whole place is against us.' The matchlock-men ran, and we went down the valley in spite of Dravot. He was swearing horrible and crying out he was a King. The priests rolled great stones on us, and the regular Army fired hard, and there wasn't more than six men, not counting Dan, Billy Fish, and Me, that came down to the bottom of the valley alive.

"Then they stopped firing and the horns in the temple blew again. 'Come away—for Gord's sake come away!' says Billy Fish. 'They'll send runners out to all the villages before ever we get to Bashkai. I can protect you there, but I can't do anything now.'

"My own notion is that Dan began to go mad in his head from that hour. He stared up and down like a stuck pig. Then he was all for walking back alone and killing the priests with his bare hands; which he could have done. 'An Emperor am I,' says Daniel, 'and next year I shall be a Knight of the Queen.'

"'All right, Dan,' says I; 'but come along now while there's time.'

"'It's your fault,' says he, 'for not looking after your Army better. There was mutiny in the midst, and you didn't know—you damned engine-driving, plate-laying, missionary's-pass-hunting hound!' He sat upon a rock and called me every foul name he could lay tongue to. I was too heart-sick to care, though it was all his foolishness that brought the smash.

"'I'm sorry, Dan,' says I, 'but there's no accounting for natives. This business is our Fifty-Seven. Maybe we'll make something out of it yet, when we've got to Bashkai.'

"'Let's get to Bashkai, then,' says Dan, 'and, by God, when I come back here again I'll sweep the valley so there isn't a bug in a blanket left!'

"We walked all that day, and all that night Dan was stumping up and down on the snow, chewing his beard and muttering to himself.

"'There's no hope o' getting clear,' said Billy Fish. 'The priests will have sent runners to the villages to say that you are only men. Why didn't you stick on as Gods till things was more settled? I'm a dead man,' says Billy Fish, and he throws himself down on the snow and begins to pray to his Gods.

"Next morning we was in a cruel bad country—all up and down, no level ground at all, and no food either. The six Bashkai men looked at Billy Fish hungryway as if they wanted to ask something, but they said never a word. At noon we came to the top of a flat mountain all covered with snow, and when we climbed up into it, behold, there was an Army in position waiting in the middle!

"'The runners have been very quick,' says Billy Fish, with a little bit of a laugh. 'They are waiting for us.'

"Three or four men began to fire from the enemy's side, and a chance shot took Daniel in the calf of the leg. That brought him to his senses. He looks across the snow at the Army, and sees the rifles that we had brought into the country.

"'We're done for,' says he. 'They are Englishmen, these people,—and it's my blasted nonsense that has brought you to this. Get back, Billy Fish, and take your men away; you've done what you could, and now cut for it. Carnehan,' says he, 'shake hands with me and go along with Billy. Maybe they won't kill you. I'll go and meet 'em alone. It's me that did it. Me, the King!'

"'Go!' says I. 'Go to Hell, Dan. I am with you here. Billy Fish, you clear out, and we two will meet those folk.'

"'I'm a Chief,' says Billy Fish, quite quiet. 'I stay with you. My men can go.'

"The Bashkai fellows didn't wait for a second word but ran off, and Dan and Me and Billy Fish walked across to where the drums were drumming and the horns were horning. It was cold—awful cold. I've got that cold in the back of my head now. There's a lump of it there."

The punkah-coolies had gone to sleep. Two kerosene lamps were blazing in the office, and the perspiration poured down my face and splashed on the blotter as I leaned forward. Carnehan was shivering, and I feared that his mind might go. I wiped my face, took a fresh grip of the piteously mangled hands, and said: "What happened after that?"

The momentary shift of my eyes had broken the clear current.

"What was you pleased to say?" whined Carnehan. "They took them without any sound. Not a little whisper all along the snow, not though the King knocked down the first man that set hand on him—not though old Peachey fired his last cartridge into the brown of 'em. Not a single solitary sound did those swines make. They just closed up tight, and I tell you their furs stunk. There was a man called Billy Fish, a good friend of us all, and they cut his throat, Sir, then and there, like a pig; and the King kicks up the bloody snow and says: 'We've had a dashed fine run for our money. What's coming next?' But Peachey, Peachey Taliaferro, I tell you, Sir, in confidence as betwixt two friends, he lost his head, Sir. No, he didn't neither. The King lost his head, so he did, all along o' one of those cunning rope-bridges. Kindly let me have the paper-cutter, Sir. It tilted this way. They marched him a mile across that snow to a rope-bridge over a ravine with a river at the bottom. You may have seen such. They prodded him behind like an ox. 'Damn your eyes!' says the King. 'D' you suppose I can't die like a gentleman?' He turns to Peachey—Peachey that was crying like a child. 'I've brought you to this, Peachey,' says he. 'Brought you out of your happy life to be killed in Kafiristan, where you was late Commander-in-Chief of the Emperor's forces. Say you forgive me, Peachey.'—'I do,' says Peachey. 'Fully and freely do I forgive you, Dan.'—'Shake hands, Peachey,' says he. 'I'm going now.' Out he goes, looking neither right nor left, and when he was plumb in the middle of those dizzy dancing ropes,—'Cut, you beggars,' he shouts; and they cut, and old Dan fell, turning round and round and round, twenty thousand miles, for he took half an hour to fall till he struck the water, and I could see his body caught on a rock with the gold crown close beside.

"But do you know what they did to Peachey between two pine-trees? They crucified him, Sir, as Peachey's hand will show. They used wooden pegs for his hands and his feet; and he didn't die. He hung there and screamed, and they took him down next day, and said it was a miracle that he wasn't dead. They took him down—poor old Peachey that hadn't done them any harm—that hadn't done them any—"

He rocked to and fro and wept bitterly, wiping his eyes with the back of his scarred hands and moaning like a child for some ten minutes.

"They was cruel enough to feed him up in the temple, because they said he was more of a God than old Daniel that was a man. Then they turned him out on the snow, and told him to go home, and Peachey came home in about a year, begging along the roads quite safe; for Daniel Dravot he walked before and said: 'Come along, Peachey. It's a big thing we're doing.' The mountains they danced at night, and the mountains they tried to fall on Peachey's head, but Dan he held up his hand, and Peachey came along bent double. He never let go of Dan's hand, and he never let go of Dan's head. They gave it to him as a present in the temple, to remind him not to come again, and though the crown was pure gold, and Peachey was starving, never would Peachey sell the same. You knew Dravot, Sir! You knew Right Worshipful Brother Dravot! Look at him now!"

He fumbled in the mass of rags round his bent waist; brought out a black horsehair bag embroidered with silver thread; and shook therefrom on to my table—the dried, withered head of Daniel Dravot! The morning sun that had long been paling the lamps struck the red beard and blind sunken eyes; struck, too, a heavy circlet of gold studded with raw turquoises, that Carnehan placed tenderly on the battered temples.

"You be'old now," said Carnehan, "the Emperor in his 'abit as he lived—the King of Kafiristan with his crown upon his head. Poor old Daniel that was a monarch once!"

I shuddered, for, in spite of defacements manifold, I recognized the head of the man of Marwar Junction. Carnehan rose to go. I attempted to stop him. He was not fit to walk abroad. "Let me take away the whiskey, and give me a little money," he gasped. "I was a King once. I'll go to the Deputy Commissioner and ask to set in the Poorhouse till I get my health. No, thank you, I can't wait till you get a carriage for me. I've urgent private affairs—in the south—at Marwar."

He shambled out of the office and departed in the direction of the Deputy Commissioner's house. That day at noon I had occasion to go down the blinding hot Mall, and I saw a crooked man crawling along the white dust of the roadside, his hat in his hand, quavering dolorously after the fashion of street singers at Home. There was not a soul in sight, and he was out of all possible earshot of the houses. And he sang through his nose, turning his head from right to left:

176

The Son of Man goes forth to war,
  A golden crown to gain;
His blood-red banner streams afar—
  Who follows in his train?

I waited to hear no more, but put the poor wretch into my carriage and drove him off to the nearest missionary for eventual transfer to the Asylum. He repeated the hymn twice while he was with me whom he did not in the least recognize, and I left him singing it to the missionary.

Two days later I inquired after his welfare of the Superintendent of the Asylum.

"He was admitted suffering from sun-stroke. He died early yesterday morning," said the Superintendent. "Is it true that he was half an hour bare-headed in the sun at midday?"

"Yes," said I, "but do you happen to know if he had anything upon him by any chance when he died?"

"Not to my knowledge," said the Superintendent.

And there the matter rests.

THE GIFT OF THE MAGI [23] (1905)

BY O. HENRY [24] (1862-1910)

[Setting. Christmas Eve in New York and a furnished flat at $8 per week make the setting of this perfect little story. Della has only $1.87 with which to buy a present for Jim and outside is "a grey cat walking a grey fence in a grey backyard." But there is a spirit within that is to make the modest flat a place of glory and this Christmas Eve memorable in short-story annals. The flat is the stable with the manger, and New York widens into Bethlehem.

Plot. "And when they were come into the house, they saw the young child with Mary his mother, and fell down, and worshipped him; and when they had opened their treasures, they presented unto him gifts: gold, and frankincense, and myrrh." These were the gifts of the magi, but their gift was love. The infant Christ could make no use of gold or frankincense or myrrh, nor could Della and Jim make use of the combs and the chain; but the love that prompted the giving shines all the more resplendent because the gifts, humanly speaking, were egregious misfits. "That the gold at least," says a recent commentator, "would be highly serviceable to the parents in their unexpected journey to Egypt and during their stay there—thus much at least admits of no dispute." Perhaps so. But read the famous passage once more and turn again to O. Henry's story. Which interpretation goes deeper into the heart of the incident? Which leaves you more in love with love?

Characters. Della and Jim have been said to illustrate the "story of cross-purposes." But the phrase is not well used. Their purposes were one; only their methods crossed. O. Henry rarely comments on his characters, but he has here picked out one quality of these "two foolish children in a flat" for unreserved praise: "Of all who give gifts these two were the wisest. Of all who give and receive gifts, such as they are wisest. Everywhere they are wisest. They are the magi." If the magi, as O. Henry says, "invented the art of giving Christmas presents," Della and Jim re-discovered it. We have had no two characters in whose company it is better to leave our study of the short story.]

One dollar and eighty-seven cents. That was all. And sixty cents of it was in pennies. Pennies saved one and two at a time by bulldozing the grocer and the vegetable man and the butcher until one's cheeks burned

---

[23] From "The Four Million." Used by special arrangement with Doubleday, Page & Company, publishers of O. Henry's Works.

[24] The pen-name of William Sidney Porter.

with the silent imputation of parsimony that such close dealing implied. Three times Della counted it. One dollar and eighty-seven cents. And the next day would be Christmas.

There was clearly nothing to do but flop down on the shabby little couch and howl. So Della did it. Which instigates the moral reflection that life is made up of sobs, sniffles, and smiles, with sniffles predominating.

While the mistress of the home is gradually subsiding from the first stage to the second, take a look at the home. A furnished flat at $8 per week. It did not exactly beggar description, but it certainly had that word on the lookout for the mendicancy squad.

In the vestibule below was a letter-box into which no letter would go, and an electric button from which no mortal finger could coax a ring. Also appertaining thereunto was a card bearing the name "Mr. James Dillingham Young."

The "Dillingham" had been flung to the breeze during a former period of prosperity when its possessor was being paid $30 per week. Now, when the income was shrunk to $20, the letters of "Dillingham" looked blurred, as though they were thinking seriously of contracting to a modest and unassuming D. But whenever Mr. James Dillingham Young came home and reached his flat above he was called "Jim" and greatly hugged by Mrs. James Dillingham Young, already introduced to you as Della. Which is all very good.

Della finished her cry and attended to her cheeks with the powder rag. She stood by the window and looked out dully at a grey cat walking a grey fence in a grey backyard. To-morrow would be Christmas Day, and she had only $1.87 with which to buy Jim a present. She had been saving every penny she could for months, with this result. Twenty dollars a week doesn't go far. Expenses had been greater than she had calculated. They always are. Only $1.87 to buy a present for Jim. Her Jim. Many a happy hour she had spent planning for something nice for him. Something fine and rare and sterling—something just a little bit near to being worthy of the honour of being owned by Jim.

There was a pier-glass between the windows of the room. Perhaps you have seen a pier-glass in an $8 flat. A very thin and very agile person may, by observing his reflection in a rapid sequence of longitudinal strips, obtain a fairly accurate conception of his looks. Delia, being slender, had mastered the art.

Suddenly she whirled from the window and stood before the glass. Her eyes were shining brilliantly, but her face had lost its colour within twenty seconds. Rapidly she pulled down her hair and let it fall to its full length.

Now, there were two possessions of the James Dillingham Youngs in which they both took a mighty pride. One was Jim's gold watch that had been his father's and his grandfather's. The other was Della's hair. Had the Queen of Sheba lived in the flat across the airshaft, Della would have let her hair hang out the window some day to dry just to depreciate her Majesty's jewels and gifts. Had King Solomon been the janitor, with all his treasures piled up in the basement, Jim would have pulled out his watch every time he passed, just to see him pluck at his beard from envy.

So now Della's beautiful hair fell about her, rippling and shining like a cascade of brown waters. It reached below her knee and made itself almost a garment for her. And then she did it up again nervously and quickly. Once she faltered for a minute and stood still while a tear or two splashed on the worn red carpet.

On went her old brown jacket; on went her old brown hat. With a whirl of skirts and with the brilliant sparkle still in her eyes, she fluttered out the door and down the stairs to the street.

Where she stopped the sign read: "Mme. Sofronie. Hair Goods of all Kinds." One flight up Della ran, and collected herself, panting. Madame, large, too white, chilly, hardly looked the "Sofronie."

"Will you buy my hair?" asked Della.

"I buy hair," said Madame. "Take yer hat off and let's have a sight at the looks of it."

Down rippled the brown cascade.

"Twenty dollars," said Madame, lifting the mass with a practised hand.

"Give it to me quick," said Della.

Oh, and the next two hours tripped by on rosy wings. Forget the hashed metaphor. She was ransacking the stores for Jim's present.

She found it at last. It surely had been made for Jim and no one else. There was no other like it in any of the stores, and she had turned all of them inside out. It was a platinum fob chain simple and chaste in design, properly proclaiming its value by substance alone and not by meretricious ornamentation—as all good things should do. It was even worthy of The Watch. As soon as she saw it she knew that it must be Jim's. It was like him. Quietness and value—the description applied to both. Twenty-one dollars they took from her for it, and she hurried home with the 87 cents. With that chain on his watch Jim might be properly anxious about the time in any company. Grand as the watch was, he sometimes looked at it on the sly on account of the old leather strap that he used in place of a chain.

When Delia reached home her intoxication gave way a little to prudence and reason. She got out her curling irons and lighted the gas and went to work repairing the ravages made by generosity added to love. Which is always a tremendous task, dear friends—a mammoth task.

Within forty minutes her head was covered with tiny, close-lying curls that made her look wonderfully like a truant schoolboy. She looked at her reflection in the mirror long, carefully, and critically.

"If Jim doesn't kill me," she said to herself, "before he takes a second look at me, he'll say I look like a Coney Island chorus girl. But what could I do—oh! what could I do with a dollar and eighty-seven cents?"

At 7 o'clock the coffee was made and the frying-pan was on the back of the stove hot and ready to cook the chops.

Jim was never late. Delia doubled the fob chain in her hand and sat on the corner of the table near the door that he always entered. Then she heard his step on the stair away down on the first flight, and she turned white for just a moment. She had a habit of saying little silent prayers about the simplest everyday things, and now she whispered: "Please God, make him think I am still pretty."

The door opened and Jim stepped in and closed it. He looked thin and very serious. Poor fellow, he was only twenty-two—and to be burdened with a family! He needed a new overcoat and he was without gloves.

Jim stopped inside the door, as immovable as a setter at the scent of quail. His eyes were fixed upon Della, and there was an expression in them that she could not read, and it terrified her. It was not anger, nor surprise, nor disapproval, nor horror, nor any of the sentiments that she had been prepared for. He simply stared at her fixedly with that peculiar expression on his face.

Della wriggled off the table and went for him.

"Jim, darling," she cried, "don't look at me that way. I had my hair cut off and sold it because I couldn't have lived through Christmas without giving you a present. It'll grow out again—you won't mind, will you? I just had to do it. My hair grows awfully fast. Say 'Merry Christmas!' Jim, and let's be happy. You don't know what a nice—what a beautiful, nice gift I've got for you."

"You've cut off your hair?" asked Jim, laboriously, as if he had not arrived at that patent fact yet even after the hardest mental labour.

"Cut it off and sold it," said Delia. "Don't you like me just as well, anyhow? I'm me without my hair, ain't I?"

Jim looked about the room curiously.

"You say your hair is gone?" he said, with an air almost of idiocy.

"You needn't look for it," said Delia. "It's sold, I tell you—sold and gone, too. It's Christmas Eve, boy. Be good to me, for it went for you. Maybe the hairs of my head were numbered," she went on with a sudden serious sweetness, "but nobody could ever count my love for you. Shall I put the chops on, Jim?"

Out of his trance Jim seemed quickly to wake. He enfolded his Della. For ten seconds let us regard with discreet scrutiny some inconsequential object in the other direction. Eight dollars a week or a million a year—what is the difference? A mathematician or a wit would give you the wrong answer. The magi brought valuable gifts, but that was not among them. This dark assertion will be illuminated later on.

Jim drew a package from his overcoat pocket and threw it upon the table.

"Don't make any mistake, Dell," he said, "about me. I don't think there's anything in the way of a haircut or a shave or a shampoo that could make me like my girl any less. But if you'll unwrap that package you may see why you had me going a while at first."

White fingers and nimble tore at the string and paper. And then an ecstatic scream of joy; and then, alas! a quick feminine change to hysterical tears and wails, necessitating the immediate employment of all the comforting powers of the lord of the flat.

For there lay The Combs—the set of combs, side and back, that Della had worshipped for long in a Broadway window. Beautiful combs, pure tortoise shell, with jewelled rims—just the shade to wear in the beautiful vanished hair. They were expensive combs, she knew, and her heart had simply craved and yearned over them without the least hope of possession. And now, they were hers, but the tresses that should have adorned the coveted adornments were gone.

But she hugged them to her bosom, and at length she was able to look up with dim eyes and a smile and say: "My hair grows so fast, Jim!"

And then Della leaped up like a little singed cat and cried, "Oh, oh!"

Jim had not yet seen his beautiful present. She held it out to him eagerly upon her open palm. The dull precious metal seemed to flash with a reflection of her bright and ardent spirit.

"Isn't it a dandy, Jim? I hunted all over town to find it. You'll have to look at the time a hundred times a day now. Give me your watch. I want to see how it looks on it."

Instead of obeying, Jim tumbled down on the couch and put his hands under the back of his head and smiled. "Dell," said he, "let's put our Christmas presents away and keep 'em a while. They're too nice to use just at present. I sold the watch to get the money to buy your combs. And now suppose you put the chops on."

The magi, as you know, were wise men—wonderfully wise men—who brought gifts to the Babe in the manger. They invented the art of giving Christmas presents. Being wise, their gifts were no doubt wise ones, possibly bearing the privilege of exchange in case of duplication. And here I have lamely related to you the uneventful chronicle of two foolish children in a flat who most unwisely sacrificed for each other the greatest treasures of their house. But in a last word to the wise of these days let it be said that of all who give gifts these two were the wisest. Of all who give and receive gifts, such as they are wisest. Everywhere they are wisest. They are the magi.